VOID KING
A ROGUE TRADERS NOVEL

VOID KING
A ROGUE TRADERS NOVEL

MARC COLLINS

BLACK LIBRARY

A BLACK LIBRARY PUBLICATION

First published in 2022.
This edition published in Great Britain in 2023 by
Black Library, Games Workshop Ltd., Willow Road,
Nottingham, NG7 2WS, UK.

Represented by: Games Workshop Limited – Irish branch,
Unit 3, Lower Liffey Street, Dublin 1,
D01 K199, Ireland.

10 9 8 7 6 5 4 3 2 1

Produced by Games Workshop in Nottingham.
Cover illustration by Jodie Muir.

A CIP record for this book is available from the British Library.

ISBN 13: 978-1-80407-298-1

See Black Library on the internet at

blacklibrary.com

Find out more about Games Workshop
and the worlds of Warhammer at

games-workshop.com

Printed and bound in the UK.

---

*To my parents, who always read to me,
and for my wife – who now reads with me.
And for Whiskey, our own new little Void King.*

For more than a hundred centuries the Emperor has sat immobile on the Golden Throne of Earth. He is the Master of Mankind. By the might of His inexhaustible armies a million worlds stand against the dark.

Yet, He is a rotting carcass, the Carrion Lord of the Imperium held in life by marvels from the Dark Age of Technology and the thousand souls sacrificed each day so that His may continue to burn.

To be a man in such times is to be one amongst untold billions. It is to live in the cruellest and most bloody regime imaginable. It is to suffer an eternity of carnage and slaughter. It is to have cries of anguish and sorrow drowned by the thirsting laughter of dark gods.

This is a dark and terrible era where you will find little comfort or hope. Forget the power of technology and science. Forget the promise of progress and advancement. Forget any notion of common humanity or compassion.

There is no peace amongst the stars, for in the grim darkness of the far future,
there is only war.

ACT I

THROUGH THE FIRE

'We are sworn to Him.

By bond of blood.

By Letter of Marque,

And Warrant of Trade.

To claim the all-encompassing void,

For sacred Mankind, in all her terrible wonder.

To push further.

To fight harder.

To strive, not for glory alone.

Not for empty plunder, nor hollow profit.

We are the vanguard, a light in the black.

Oath-sworn, solemn.

We are the Davamir Compact.'

– The Words of the First King

Chapter One

The Summons Home

Erastus Lamertine lived his days beneath the eyes of the long dead.

There was almost no part of the upper reaches of the Cradle that were not adorned with the sombre ouslite busts and death masks of the kings and queens who had gone before. The eyes seemed to follow him, sometimes sparkling with precious gems or gold embellishment. Servo-skulls, cherubs and stranger constructs drifted past the higher plinths from which the statues glowered, and so there seemed an unnatural motion to them.

He did not glance up as he passed beneath the sharp features of a Helvintr death mask, the scars carved into the plaster with almost savage relish, or the captured preening of a Radrexxus bust. He had lived within the great station for so many years now that he could recite their names and titles all in turn. He could keep his way by them as he navigated the ancient, winding halls. The weight of the place's history had been etched into him, soul-deep lines that even rejuvenat could not fully hide.

His meandering path had carried him from the core of the station, the Bladespire, through the Arches of Victory and the Halls of the Lost, till he arrived here, at the Starlit Marches. The great viewports looked out across the gnarled docking spurs and their relentless activity. Ships of the line crowded in, jostling for space like pugilists. The crimson light of the Davamir star caught on the bladed prows of the ships and the outermost spires of the station, casting it as bloody as the ambition that had forged them all.

And before it, silhouetted in the light cast by the flurry of movement beyond, stood his father. Davos Lamertine gazed out, his expression fixed. His entire weight was hunched forward, balanced on the cane that was less and less an affectation. The silvered tip of it rocked back and forth in the marble, and Erastus wondered if it might wear some impossible groove there.

'Father?' he said. His voice felt insufficient in the vast silence of the space. Once again he was reduced to little more than a cadet in his father's sanctum, his words weak and wavering. The older man turned, regarding him with his cold grey eyes. He did not smile. His dark skin did not crinkle with any form of paternal recognition, the pale scars on his cheeks were not lessened by joy. His frown remained, his disappointment as pointed as it had always been.

'Erastus.'

He felt his father's scrutiny pass from him, and return to the bustle of the docks.

'They have come,' Davos whispered, almost as though he thought Erastus could not hear him. 'But so few.' He shook his head. 'It is to be expected. Whether kept from us by a wall of fire, or bound up in their own ambitions. So many of our fellows prove themselves lacking. How long since the Draiks walked amongst us, eh? They spurned us again – committed to the west, they say. As though there were anything of worth.'

'Who has actually answered the summons?' Erastus spoke carefully, measuring his every word. His father's scrutiny did not settle upon him again; the old man's gaze swept back and forth, in time with the tapping of his cane.

'Look there.' Davos pointed. 'The *Wyrmslayer Queen*.' He laughed. 'Of all those who come to us, it is the savages who rush to the fore.' His gaze drifted. 'Radrexxus comes, though likely only to gloat of his latest trade endeavour, or what new alchemical concoction graces his veins. The Astraneus? None trust them, or their bastard faith, but they have power. Influence.' He paused, considering.

'Surely there are more than three?' Erastus asked.

'Oh yes,' his father said. 'The shepherds of men come.'

'The Torvanders?'

'The very same. A son and a daughter, both of their lesser stock.' He scoffed as he spoke, gesturing to a heaving mass conveyer as it disgorged a tide of grey-robed multitudes. The edges of the immense vessel still sparkled with old gilding, though it seemed tarnished and bronzed in the harsh starlight. 'All pilgrim piety and recrimination. Useful enough if you want to move men, but ultimately? An empty gesture.'

'Is there anyone you actually approve of?' Erastus said. 'Anyone whose support doesn't come with caveats, or concerns?'

'You cannot *approve* of any of them,' Davos said. There was a sudden edge of iron in his voice. 'They may be peers, they may be useful, but they are not our allies. Not in truth. Point them at a target, and they may play the tame hunting pack, but their teeth are ever aimed at our throats.' He paused. 'Your sister knew that well enough.'

Another hand-me-down lesson, Erastus thought, *ill-fitting and worn through.*

He ignored it. 'Your choice of metaphor is telling, though. I didn't think you were afraid of anything, let alone the huntresses of Helvintr.'

That brought a dry chuckle from his father. His mirth had curdled of late, grown as dark as the broken galaxy beyond their fief. 'I do not fear.'

Erastus could see his fingers grow white around the eagle's head of the cane. Tightening and loosening, as though he sought to convince himself as much as his ersatz son.

'They are almost beasts themselves, running the stars the way their ancestors rode the ice seas. The chill of the winter world is in them, and the fire of the Wolf's Eye. We forget that at our peril.'

Erastus nodded. 'I know, Father–'

'Do you?' Davos snapped. 'Do you truly understand, when you have slunk around the corners of our family? When you have no honour save that tarnished by your grasping attempts at advancement?'

Erastus flinched back as though struck.

'We have lost so much, and our rivals gather. Called by my hand, yes, but with their knives ready for my back. And you tell me you know? The stakes have never been higher.'

'Forgive me, Father,' Erastus said. He held back from abasing himself. He looked at his father as though seeing him for the first time, in the light he had cast across Erastus' entire life. The starched, pale blue military uniforms, never ostentatious or ever truly wielding the grandeur of his position. He was a man and a warrior before he was a king. Or a father.

Davos turned, striding past his son without a backward glance. The confrontation seemed to have enlivened him, his cane barely touching the floor as he moved away from the crystal-flex panels and into the corridors of power.

'How did you do it, Ev?' Erastus wondered aloud. Evelyne, his sister, had been the heir, and so had borne the brunt of their father's favour. The storms of wrath and disappointment seemed never to faze her. She did not merely weather them, or survive them, she thrived under the stern eye of their patriarch. Yet she had never let his attitude taint her, not truly.

He watched a while longer, as the ships crowded in, like supplicants. Locked to the bloated structure of the Cradle by docking gantries and arterial lines of fuel, they haemorrhaged men and took on materiel in the fitful osmosis that ensued whenever a vessel berthed. He could see knots of colour as crews gathered, congealing around leaders as they awaited the true permission to come aboard.

To be received into the court of the Void King of the Davamir Compact.

Chapter Two

Wolves and Other Predators

The old dynasties gathered, and if they felt any exasperation at being summoned they did not show it. The docks teemed with rival houses and their sworn kinsmen as they ducked beneath the shadows cast by the cranes and clearance towers. Alarums and tocsins blared as workers tried to push through the thronging masses of armsmen and crew, while servitors trundled forwards laden with supply crates. A few of the crewmen were almost crushed beneath the lobotomised advance of the cyborgs, who chirruped emptily as they plodded across the rockcrete.

'Compliance.' 'Compliance.' 'Compliance.'

The huntress watched their progress and held back a smile. Homecoming, such as it was, was ever bittersweet. Every time she bestrode the great station and its storied halls, she was reminded of the legacy of the Compact. She had borne its weight upon her shoulders and passed it on, yet every time she returned the burden was renewed.

Katla Helvintr stood upon a gantry extruding from the side of her vessel, the *Wyrmslayer Queen*, and watched as each of the dynasty's ships emptied.

Officers barged through the crowds, barking orders and waving their symbols of command. Some, of her own dynasty, bore runes woven into the leather of their uniforms, while others brandished golden batons as tokens of rule. A gaggle of black-robed figures held their hands aloft in the shape of the holy aquila, drawing others of their kind to them by dint of faith alone. As one, the clutch of worshippers went on their knees and bowed in worship before the mighty edifice that now carried them.

The Cradle was truly as ancient as it was massive. The station had grown as organically as it had been able to in the millennia since the Great Crusade, slowly drawing other vessels into its fabric with a near-parasitic relish. Not with the crawling chaos of a space hulk, but with a measured and considered *hunger* to be complete. At the core of the station, so tradition held, the great flagship of the First King waited. Time had rendered it massive and mighty, transforming it gradually into the majesty of the Bladespire. Even now it exuded strength and domination, whether it was aweing the human swarm disembarking upon it or the Davamir System itself.

It was, above all else, a seat of power, a throne in mimicry of greater thrones. Some might have thought that blasphemy in a system so close to Holy Terra, but the Compact had no such shame. As the pilgrims raised themselves up and advanced, they passed beneath a gilded archway inscribed with the words: *By my hand are they cast into the stars, and thus the stars reclaimed.*

Standard bearers lurched forward as they steadied their banners in the artificial breeze of immense air-recyc engines, the ironweave fabric snapping. There was the sombre grey of the Helvintrs, crimson spears crossed beneath the snarling visage of a wolf. Those who bore it wore leather masks twisted into the features of beasts. They strutted almost arrogantly, the ferrules of their banner-poles slamming into the decking in an incessant tattoo. As they asserted themselves, the other crewmen fell in behind them. They formed ranks of grey, purple, black, bronze and brown. There was a ritual to it; an order.

One by one, they marched under the golden arch and the great doors of the docking bays slid open. Iron and silver glimmered, as golden light flooded from beyond. Like a welcome.

The Hall of Equals was vast, like an immense senate chamber. Row upon row of seating had been prepared around long tables of cool, black marble. Attendants were making the final touches, ensuring that every seat had its place, with glasses and platters at each stance.

All of them were within sight of the dais, where Davos sat. His posture was straight against the gilded back of the throne, and his cane lay against one of its arms. He reached up and adjusted the glossy black circlet of the Umbral Crown. It caught the light in odd ways, distorting it to strange angles. The starlight was directed through the glassaic windows in the upper galleries, illuminating the dais with the crimson radiance of the Davamir star. Light was sacred here. Under the light of this star, the Compact had been forged; in its sight, the Emperor had empowered them. Murals around the chamber displayed Him as the gathered dynasts knelt before Him, alongside the stylised images of the fleets as they cast out amidst the Great Crusade.

To one side of the throne there sat another chair: less ornate, like an echo of the seat of power. In better days, before the Rift, Evelyne would have sat there, the better to learn at her father's right hand.

Erastus stood off to one side, watching the proceedings. His father raised a hand and men rushed to attend his every whim. He did not envy his father his power. Frankly, the idea of wielding it terrified him. He crossed his arms across his chest and leant back against the cool stone of a column. If his father saw him, he gave no sign.

Erastus had grown accustomed to this peculiar form of stealth. For so long he had languished low in the hierarchy, barely considered as an officer, let alone an asset. He had slowly made himself useful, though, even if his father could not appreciate it. He had *compromised*.

He had reached out to his opposite numbers in other dynasties, or in trade concerns. Fixers. Men of charm and confidence – the kind of assets his father despised having to use. His father relied on his own personal charisma, born of might and fear, to cow and direct those he made use of. He had no sense of compromise, no understanding of what was required to truly forge lasting bonds. For his father, respect was something to be taken, not truly earned.

Erastus was about to cross the room when bells began to toll somewhere in the vaulted ceiling. He turned, looking to the door. Horns sounded, not in onerous mourning or discordant skirl. Their roar was a howl, near bestial, a primal rhythm coaxed up by musicians whose craft lay in goading the Helvintr troops to battle-readiness. Mechanisms clattered, adding to the surreal chorus, as the doors to the chamber began to open. They folded inwards, gilt surfaces shimmering in the light of the hall's braziers. Erastus looked back in time to see his father's features sharpen and fix into a smile.

The wolves were amongst them.

At the head of the pack, for there was no better word for the rabble of crew, came Katla Helvintr. She stalked into the hall with a grace and confidence which belied her wounds. Like a conquering hero, she advanced, raising her fists in greeting. Her retainers slammed their own fists against their breasts or pounded at leathern drums in response. They cheered their chieftain, their jarl, their queen. The air turned electric and urgent, almost tribal, yet riven through with hints of the void's cold.

Her eyes sparkled, the blue of storm-tossed seas, set in a face rendered magnificent through ruin. Its left half was pitted and scarred with the touch of bio-acid. Whatever beast had done this to her, whatever mighty slaying had remade her, was lost to legend. Far from diminishing her, it had made her seem mightier. Artfully inked tattoos had been woven across the scar tissue, depicting the skeletal visage of a wolf. The half-death-mask leered at them with its human eye, passing from Erastus to settle upon his father. She smirked, and her hands dropped to run through the shock of auburn hair which remained on the unscarred side of her head.

'My king!' she declared, deigning to bow. 'The Helvintr Dynasty returns to the Cradle at your summons. We bear fealty in our hearts, and gifts from the Wild Hunt amidst the Emperor's realm. Do you welcome us to your hearth?'

'You are welcome, Jarl Helvintr, to my hall and hearth.' Davos inclined his head. There was no truth in his smile as he leant forward. 'How fare the edges of the Imperium? How goes the hunt?'

'The hunt is stranger now than ever before.' She laughed. 'The galaxy burns, and all is cast to the wind. Beasts grow bolder. Wilder.' She flashed her teeth in a furious grin. 'And we relish it. Our forebears would be proud. The Season of Fire has made its way to the stars, and stirred even the mightiest of kraken from their lairs. I say, let them come.'

'As you say.' His features had tightened, set into a smile that did not reach his eyes. Likewise there was no true joy in her grin, only the echo of the void.

21

Even here, Erastus realised, she was still hunting.

Katla raised her hand and one of her throng broke ranks, moving to stand at her side. The newcomer had a warrior's bearing as she swaggered to primacy, her blonde braids shaking with the motion. She looked up at Davos without fear, wearing her resolve as proudly as she displayed her bloodline.

'You remember my daughter, Astrid? My second spear.' The other woman bowed as Katla spoke, and Erastus turned to watch his father's reaction. The forced smile was gone, replaced by one that bordered upon the indulgent.

'I remember. You have raised a fine warrior.' He paused. 'A noble heir.'

'Ah,' Katla said, as though realising for the first time. 'Of course. You have my sympathies on the loss of your daughter. She was a credit to your line.' She gestured to where Erastus stood. 'As, I am sure, is your son.'

Davos did not follow her glance. He did not acknowledge Erastus or dignify her remarks with a response.

'Be seated,' he said. 'Enter this hall as peers, for though we stand mighty in the Imperium, we are as equals in this place. Bound by blood and oath to the Compact.'

'Bound by blood and oath,' the crew repeated. They filed into the first row of seats, as the standard bearers stowed their banners at one end of the great tables.

'Who comes next?' Davos asked. Erastus could hear the weariness breaking the façade. 'Who will honour us?'

Erastus moved round the edges of the chamber as the parade of rogue traders continued. Where the Lamertines and the Helvintrs were unmistakably martial, others had taken more diverse routes to power. The Lord Technologist, Absalom Noras-tye, clattered into the hall on a small plinth carried on dozens of ceaseless mechanical feet. He regarded Davos with his gleaming augmetic eyes, turning every glance into a crimson glare. Even so, he bowed low, lacing his steel fingers into the sign of the cog, before flourishing them into the aquila. Like many of the rogue trader dynasties which spanned the galaxy, Absalom Norastye had not been born into such privilege. Where the Helvintrs, Lamertines or the Radrexxus were familial organisations, others such as the modern iteration of the Norastye had ascended through service. Absalom had been a humble explorator once – before his long years of service had culminated in his ascension to rank.

'Our oaths are iron, my king. Norastye answers the summons.'

When they had passed to their allotted place, there came the moribund procession of the Astraneus. Erastus shuddered to look at them. They were a strange breed, lank and pale in the manner of many voidborn, but it was their faith that truly set them apart. Erastus knew little of the Church of the Shrouded Emperor, save that they honoured Him as being in the dark of the void as much as the light of the stars.

'We come to you, in fidelity and revelation. We bear His light, and His shadow.' Delvetar Astraneus spoke in a low whisper, mercifully amplified by the vox-grid woven into their black hood. In them the pallor of the bloodline was more pronounced, almost luminous around blackened lips. The Arch-Lecter closed their heavily lidded eyes, tilted back their head, and a low chorus built behind them as the entire congregation began their hymn.

Oh blade of light, oh shield of night…

They carried it back to their tables, even as Davos reached up and cradled the side of his head as though in pain, or exasperation. Erastus could empathise. He slunk beneath the gemstone-lined fabric of a tapestry, still skirting the edges of the chamber.

There was another rustling of robes, as another group glided into the room.

If the Astraneus were a dark reflection of conventional Imperial faith, then the Torvanders were the crystallisation of it. Mara and Barisan Torvander affected the look of humble, simple souls. Their robes were white, though as rough-spun as any penitent's, and they wore gold bracelets in place of a supplicant's chains. Each wore an ornate aquila necklace at their throat, and they bowed low in greeting to their king. They did not waste time with song, or idle threats. They simply walked to their places, and were silent.

They were a newer addition to the Compact; their father had once served as a worthy seneschal, and had been granted a Warrant for his service. Now he spent his heirs and hangers-on with the eagerness of a merchant prince, as though he could merely buy position with hoarded gold and curdled piety. They kept their heads low, and their expressions sombre, barely even looking at the finery which practically dripped from the walls.

You'll enjoy that, Father, Erastus thought. *Finally, someone here knows the place you expect them to occupy.*

A sudden fanfare broke him from his thoughts. Where the Helvintr horns had been the baying of wolves, these were more the bugles of the parade ground. The clamour of drums went up, orderly and well drilled. A voice cut across the vastness of the hall, vox-amplified and ecstatic.

'All hail the lord admiral, Lord Radrexxus, Lord Gunther of that most noble house! Bearing the glory of ages, and the blood of kings! He who walks in the Emperor's true sight! Hail! Radrexxus! Hail!'

The ranks of armsmen that paraded through the central aisle were joyous as they played their instruments. Pipes skirled and wailed alongside the relentless percussion. They stopped ahead of the dais and parted as a figure swaggered forward. He was a storm of motion, of fluttering purple silks and a haze of perfumed air. He bowed low, ostentatiously flailing his arms as he did so. When he looked up again, his pale green eyes sparkled – one orbed with a gleaming gold monocle. Runtish attendants hurried up behind him, holding the long tails of his frock coat up off the ground, as though the vaunted lord admiral was too good for the sacred decking of the Cradle. At his side came Maximillian, his major-domo – black-clad and sombre as a headsman. Where Gunther was a constant, riotous blur, Maximillian was stolid. Stable. Focused.

'Davos!' Gunther Radrexxus beamed as he raised a hand sinfully adorned with rings to adjust the folds of his powdered periwig. 'It has been far too long, an eternity!' He flounced melodramatically, and Erastus could practically hear his father's eyes roll.

'Indeed, Lord Radrexxus. Be welcome.'

'Most gracious,' Gunther said. His eyes were wild with amusement.

And who knows how many narcotics, thought Erastus, as the lord admiral nodded with new enthusiasm and led his crews to their places.

CHAPTER THREE

A FEAST OF REVELATIONS

When all had gathered and taken their places, Davos signalled for the servants to bring forth the feast.

Hungry crews were presented with heaped platters of food from every corner of the Imperium. There was butchered grox, the steaks glazed with exotic fruits. Rivulets of sauce ran down the meat like blood as eager hands tore at it. Strange tentacled sea-life was laid out upon beds of ice, or coiled around the lips of steaming bowls, drawing less attention from the diners save a feeling of unease. Whether it was the sheer strangeness of it, or a diet too rich for mere crewmen, Erastus could not tell. He plucked something which looked altogether like an eyeball from one plate, and popped it into his mouth. The orb, some form of fruit, burst on his tongue with a sour tang.

He swallowed, and reached for a glass. Where some availed themselves of fine vintages of amasec or wine, he settled for water. If his father saw him partaking, there would be consequences.

You cannot allow yourself to be addled, Erastus. You are ruled by your vices. Your sister would never–

He scoffed. Erastus knew it was pointless to try and fight his father's disapproval, especially here in the heart of his power.

He distracted himself by looking to the other dynasties, gathered in their own knots of influence. The Helvintrs moved among their people with easy camaraderie, the kind of fellowship Erastus had only ever seen born of protracted combat tours. He had never experienced it himself. He thought of the trade delegations and missions of low import his father had deigned to throw to him. Tame crews, for meagre earnings.

'Admirable, isn't it?' The voice came from beside him, vaguely slurred, and when he turned it was to look into the sparkling eyes of Gunther Radrexxus. 'Your father's table. His largesse. All this power, all this bounty, and such an even hand.'

He grinned, but all Erastus could see was the predatory cunning there. The Helvintrs were wolfish, but Gunther had a lean, almost vulpine cast to him.

'It must be quite a thing, to sit at his table, rather than wait for scraps from it.'

Erastus laughed. 'Well, as you can see, I'm not at his table.'

'A poor choice of words, perhaps,' Gunther said. 'You sit amongst trusted retainers, not rabble. That may be as close as the man veers to honour–'

'The man,' Erastus allowed carefully, 'is still my father, Lord Radrexxus.' He reached for his glass and took a long sip of the cool water. 'I may not be my sister, but the bond is still one of blood. Loyalty. Perhaps your most noble line has forgotten that, in their fugues and vapours.'

'Oh you are a delight, Erastus,' Gunther tittered. 'Not at all the starch and seriousness of our dear king. No, you are a little songbird, biting at the bars of its cage.'

'You'll forgive me, Lord Radrexxus, for not taking that as a compliment.'

'You are a vibrant thing, Erastus. He has never seen that, but others have taken note. Your father, Throne bless him, does not and cannot understand one such as you.' His heavily powdered face creased with a smile. 'Others think me idle, I know. Foppish, useless, self-aggrandising. But I *see*, Erastus. Others do not take the time to truly watch their fellows.' He clapped his hands together suddenly, drawing stares even as it recentred Erastus' focus. 'Your father wants results on his own terms. The huntresses are only ever alive in the moment, their focus on their prey absolute. Norastye? Lost to the wiles of logic and the mysteries of iron. And the other two are so deep in their own mania that they cannot understand anything beyond their dogma. I have no shortage of faith, my friend, but I do not let it curdle. It lives in me.'

'I think you and my father have more in common than you think,' Erastus said. He looked at his glass. He had not realised that he had emptied it, and was toying with it nervously. 'Your paranoia does you both credit, at your rank.'

'This isn't merely a matter of paranoia, Erastus. I warn you, as a friend. None here is what they seem.'

Erastus was about to respond when a sudden fanfare filled the chamber. Everyone quieted, save for the pounding of palms against tables and the thunderous banging of feet. Gunther grinned, and folded himself into yet another extravagant bow.

'You'll excuse me, of course.' He breathed through his smile. 'I have a king to honour.'

As was customary of the great gatherings of the Compact, gifts had been offered.

Katla and Astrid strode before an immense stasis plinth dragged by a group of bare-chested retainers. They strained, sweat glistening upon their pale skin and over the tribal tattoos which graced it. The undertaking paled before what the plinth carried.

It was a head. Huge and tusked, its maw hung loose. Comingled fluids had been caught, forever suspended in bloody exhalation, when the field had been engaged. It stared with too many eyes, slitted and reptilian yet in a more typically insectoid pattern.

Gasps went up as the conquering huntresses led the bestial trophy before Davos. He hunched forward on his throne, eyes narrowed till they seemed the very mirror of the dead beast.

'My king,' Katla said, with all the sincerity she could muster. 'Behold, a gift from the Wild Hunt at the galaxy's edge. A beast slain by my own hand and brought in tribute, as the Compact demands.'

'A fine prize, Jarl Helvintr,' Davos said carefully. 'Yet it seems perhaps the runt of the brood, if it can fit within these halls?'

Her laughter was bitter, a bark of cold joy. 'I thought that you might declare it so, my king. The beast you see before you was a brood parasite, roaming the carapace plains of its host. As the mighty horror died, our lances piercing its flanks, so these rained down upon us.'

'The ship crawled with them, in their numbers and their bulk.' Astrid spoke now, taking up her mother's saga. 'And the crew rejoiced, to see such sport. A challenge.'

'We met them. Spear to claw. Till the blood of man and monster stained the decks. And this was the greatest of them.' Her hands worked urgently, remembering the haft of her spear. Katla's eyes glimmered, and her ruined visage seemed more feral than ever. 'This is our offering. Blood, and glory.'

'And it is most welcome.' Davos nodded. 'Who brings the next offering?'

Absalom Norastye prostrated himself, as though his fealty could be demonstrated through the contortions of his body alone. His eye-lenses clicked as they focused, and he held up a trinket in his iron fingers.

'Let it be known,' he said using the voice he had been born with, 'that the Norastye Dynasty has ever been friend and ally to the Void King. We have scoured the galaxy for lost secrets, and held to the pacts laid down with hallowed Mars by our ancestors. I bring to you this token, an example of our dedication.'

When he turned the device in the light, it became clear that it was wrought in the shape of an ornate brooch. Gemstones glittered in the lights of the hall, and the lustre of the gold was made star-bright.

'Beneath this aegis, even the greatest of wounds can be turned away,' Absalom said, and bowed his head.

'A fine offering from the void, Absalom. Be at peace.'

Almost before Absalom could slink from the centre of the chamber, Radrexxus was in motion, flourishing a phial from his sleeve like some deluded conjurer.

'The native pollinators of Faranti V utilise only the most potent of the world's toxic flowers to form their honey. From that rich nectar, a variety of compounds can be derived, most notably' – Gunther looked from side to side, the very caricature of a black market dealer proposing a trade – 'renowned for their mind-opening potential. Beyond which I am told this has quite the invigorating effect upon...'

His speech was drowned out as the crowd bayed their distaste or approval. The Radrexxus ranks were near riotous in their enthusiasm, as Davos sighed and shook his head.

'Yes, quite the wonder, Gunther. You may sit. Should others wish to… partake, then they may do so with my blessing. A gift, to our fellows.' The crowd whooped and hollered at the generosity, and Gunther practically cackled as he threw himself back into the revels of the feast.

There was much fussing as the Torvander siblings hurried forward. Mara clutched a gilded reliquary to her chest, looking around furtively as her brother began to speak.

'Ah, my lord, great and noble king, we bring a relic from the pilgrim paths amidst the stars. We have served our own lord father, and been rewarded with the opportunity to pass on this sign of grace.'

Barisan turned and opened the jewel-hinged doors of the reliquary, revealing a simple scrap of fabric under glass. The pale, rippling blue light of a stasis field shone out between the doors. Many craned their necks to get a better view. Davos merely gestured.

'And what is it I am looking at?'

'Honoured, most esteemed king,' Mara said, her inflection breathy. 'This is a fragment of cloak taken from a member of His own Custodian Guard. This fabric wiped the blood and tears from the very face of the God-Emperor, whose light shines eternal from Terra.' Her eyes had grown wide and frantic. 'Praise be unto this most holy relic that we bequeath unto your care. In fidelity and trust.'

Erastus snorted as he watched. He reached for a thin glass of ruddy wine and downed it in one swift motion. Void take his father's judgement. He could not put up with this farce sober. His father, for once, seemed in agreement. He nodded simply, as though unwilling to endure their delusions any further, and the zealots shuffled off meekly.

'We bring you a gift beyond compare, a thing that cannot be

bought or bargained for, that cannot be carved out in blood or drowned in shallow vice.' A new voice rose, sure despite its reedy tone.

A group of Astraneus had clumped together, like an Ecclesiarchal procession, and advanced towards the dais. Erastus could see some of them swinging small censers, clouding the air with pungent clouds of incense. They had formed a rough diamond shape, with Delvetar at its head. They stepped to one side and revealed a figure in pale robes, like a beacon in the sea of dark cloth.

'Oh blade of light, that brings the night eternal,' Delvetar hissed, and the prayer was taken up by their compatriots. The Arch-Lecter reached into their robes and there was the sudden flash of a blade. The pale-robed figure did not flinch at the weapon's appearance. Their pale features were placid in their androgyny. Beatific.

The first cut caught them across the throat, and the calm broke like the disturbance of still waters. The other faithful took hold of their fellow, restraining them as Delvetar calmly drew the blade across their eyes. There was a low gurgled scream, as the sacrifice – for it could be nothing else – drowned in their own blood.

When Delvetar turned back to the dais, their eyes were wild. Blood had spattered upon their terribly pale skin, leaving incongruously ruddy streaks upon the pallor. Their chest heaved with the effort. As they stepped forward, so the others fell upon the victim. Their faint hymnal rose and fell with the blades.

'A sacrifice, my king, to sanctify the proceedings. Let others bring you trinkets, baubles' – they shot a glare at the cowering Torvanders – 'and lies, all they wish. We bring purity of purpose and sanctity.'

'This is… ' Davos shook himself as though from a stupor. 'This is unworthy of our halls.' Erastus had moved back towards the dais, around the stunned ranks of onlookers. He felt the sudden need to be near his father, the mortal weight of the place coiling about them. The Astraneus were ill-liked and poorly trusted by most. Rumours abounded of their rites and strange ceremonies. Some whispered that they practised the abominable Custom of the Void, *cannibalism*, even when there was no dire privation to justify it, beyond the necessary evil of corpse starch. Some spoke of the act as an enshrined inhumanity. To most others this was simply another sign, amidst many, of their strange voidborn mindset, their shrouded faith.

'Nevertheless,' Delvetar said carefully, 'it is our offering.' With that the congregation moved as one, back into their seats, drawing a bloody smear along the ground as they went.

Davos rose, shaking his head. He raised his cane and cracked its silver tip against the dais. The sound carried, and all fell silent.

'Enough! We have tarried enough with feasts and gifts and folly,' he said, coughing as he cleared his throat. 'I have called you here for a singular purpose, one we have not seen in our lifetimes, and likely shall not again.'

All eyes were upon him. Every mouth was stilled. Davos looked up and caught his son's gaze, poised on the edge of the platform.

'I have received a communication.' He held out a hand and a servant hurried to his side, carrying a golden tray. Upon it was a leather-wrapped scroll, banded with silver. Davos took it in one ringed hand, weighing it before them. 'This is no mere astropathic missive,' he said, unwrapping it. 'This is an Edict.'

His eyes lowered, scanning the first line. He drew in his breath, bracing himself for a plunge.

'From the hand of Roboute Guilliman. The Primarch Reborn.
Lord Regent of the Imperium–'

And at that, the room erupted in uproar.

Chapter Four

The various factions were either on their feet, bellowing in out-rage, or sitting in stunned silence. The Torvanders were amongst the most vocal, both of them howling and tearing at their vest-ments. The Astraneus, by contrast, sat and smiled their hollow smiles. It was as though this was no great surprise to them, simply another unfolding of the Emperor's designs.

There were savage whoops and jeers from the Helvintr contin-gent; the fact that myths walked anew seemed not to faze them, but to invigorate them. Katla was grinning savagely, punching the air, as ale-filled horns clattered together. Absalom Norastye seemed to have shrunk in on himself, lost in some logical rev-erie as he tried to process the new and revelatory information. Even Gunther had fallen silent, whatever narco-pipe he had been snuffing slipping from his slack mouth.

None of this mattered to Erastus. He saw and understood it all, he took in their reactions as the chamber was rocked by jubilation and shock. But he was lost in his own sudden burst of betrayal.

He never told me. How long could he have known? Carried such a secret? And never told me. The galaxy changed, fundamentally, and he never told me. She would have known, of course. Wouldn't she, Father?

His hands clenched into fists, and he bit his tongue. He looked up at his father; the older man's face was locked in a determined grimace, as though he might outlast the tumult. As he surely intended to outlast all things.

'Be silent!' The king's words rang out as he stood, Edict in hand. 'This is the word of the primarch. Carried to us through the ether by those who wear the gold. Delivered to my hand, that our enterprise be directed. By his will. For the sake of all humanity.'

The hush that followed was absolute, and Erastus could see that his father took it as a tacit sign that he could continue.

'The galaxy is changed, my friends. It burns from end to end. The Great Rift has split the heavens. We have all lost, in this. I do not speak of mercantile concerns, or favoured hunting grounds.' He paused, and Erastus was surprised that his father might actually be *collecting himself*. 'We have not only lost kin, as my own heir has been taken from me. Humanity has lost. Been wounded. Half the Imperium is silent, and suffers beyond a barrier of spite.'

He put the Edict down, and spread his hands.

'But it need not be so. The primarch proposes a grand crusade, of the kind that once forged our galactic domain. It shall split the darkness, and bring succour to those who languish beneath the lash of heretics and the predations of the xenos.'

His father had them, Erastus knew. In the palm of his hand. A rapt audience. Even as Erastus trembled with barely suppressed rage at how removed he was from his family's plans, he could not look away. He would not stop listening.

'We will be outriders, seeking advantage ahead of the main advance. We shall seek, fortify, and hold the mostly likely points of egress across the Rift, and wait for the crusade fleets to begin their translation. In return for this service and the joining of our strength with the Imperium's military might, we shall be rewarded. Not merely in Throne gelt, but with Throne-sanctioned undertakings. As the Emperor once gave unto us, so too shall His son, with the primarch's seal upon your Warrants of Trade and *new* Letters of Marque. The galaxy is changed, and we shall change with it. We shall have advantage undreamed of. The rights and responsibilities of our houses renewed! As they were in the earliest days, when the first of us could sail the void unchallenged and seize anything in His name.' He tapped his cane against the dais as he paced. 'Can you imagine? The God-Emperor's own son promises us access, power and authority undreamed of. We will not merely be the void's princes. We shall stand exalted by the favour of a demigod, and the gratitude of the Imperium.'

'Why us?' a voice called from the crowd, dwarfed beneath the carved marble of the columns that ridged the chamber. The acoustics carried it up, and soon it was joined by others. 'What brings this favour to our door?'

'The Compact is old. Laid down in first principles when the first fleets left Terra. When so many were lords militant, by design or circumstance. Our oaths are ancient. Perhaps he remembers.'

Laughter echoed that pronouncement, loud and bitter. Erastus was almost surprised when eyes turned towards him; it had been his laughter. His father ignored it.

'Tomorrow I will lay out my plans for determining the optimal points of crossing. I will present my astrocartographic observations and seek insight from my noble fellows. This is a grand opportunity for all of us.' His wizened features curdled into a smile. 'This–'

'This is blasphemy!' Mara Torvander screamed. Her eyes were red with tears, and she had torn at her own hair. Her retainers were likewise dishevelled, her brother silent and drawn. 'You claim to speak with the will of the primarch, a being of legend, a very fragment of the divine gracing the galaxy anew with their presence! And we have only your word? Where is the Primarch Reborn?'

Mara swept her arm round, and the pilgrim throng of the Torvander dynasty fell to their knees, prostrating themselves before her ebbing outrage.

'How can you say that this is so, and expect us to follow meekly? The Great Rift has birthed lies and abomination! Deceit that walks! I shall not believe that His son has risen from death unless I see it with my own eyes. My father, and the concerns of faith which he follows, would think me a fool or worse, to hurl our family headlong into this... this heresy!'

She turned her back upon Davos, and stormed from the chamber. A trail of shell-shocked, confused and babbling zealots followed after her. Barisan sheepishly brought up the rear, withered beneath the enormity of the situation.

'If there are no further interruptions?' Davos said simply.

None challenged him. The chill quiet that descended was like a shroud. Perhaps, Erastus mused, that was why the Astraneus remained so calm. Bloodstained and utterly content, as though the galaxy had not changed at its core.

His father stood, waving away the support of attendants as he left the dais, parading out beneath the marbled arches of the hall and towards his own private chambers. Erastus waited a moment, for the voices to rise and the clamour of the feast to resume. He caught the eye of others as he moved to follow his father's path. Astrid Helvintr nodded to him, as stern as the first frosts. Gunther Radrexxus offered him a tired wink.

Erastus shook his head.

I fear whatever course you set, Father, with this ship of fools.

Chapter Five

The corridors of the Cradle weaved and coiled through the superstructure like veins through flesh, tissue tortured and scarred by millennia of growth and crude surgery.

It had changed so much that it was hard to remember that so many portions of it were in fact repurposed. Walls and floors had been altered down the centuries, changed to accommodate the integration. The cold steel and adamantine of ship's corridors had long since given way to lacquered wood and ornamental gilt.

The closer one came to the heart of the Bladespire, the more room was given over to the display of relics and artefacts, prised from the galaxy by generation after generation of adventurous and avaricious kings. Erastus did not look at the crossed aeldari blades as they hovered in their stasis field, but he remembered the tale of how Liss Helvintr had bested one of their blade-dancers to earn them. The Cradle was built upon the stories and legends of those who had gone before. Greater treasures might be hoarded, but the kings of the Davamir Compact had a legacy to uphold. At the end of each century of rule, new displays would be wrought – the better to show the nature of the king, the character of his rule.

Erastus' father was a blade. Erastus was still not certain what he was, himself.

He stopped before the door, raising his hand to knock even as the armsmen straightened. He was the king's son, but he was held to the same standard as any other visitor. He knew that any abuse of protocol would trigger the hidden murder-servitors in their nooks, concealed behind the pale blue velvet of the corridor's curtains. There were hidden explosives. Gas vents. Flamer exhausts. An entire repertoire of lethal paranoia merely waited for its chance to unfurl, and taste blood.

'Come!'

Erastus stepped forward and pushed the doors open, standing at last in his father's sanctum. The King's Retreat was a squat, drum-like room. Its ribbed walls were hung with tapestries: great starscapes that spoke to the storied past of Compacts and kings. His eyes danced across ancient vistas, battlefields long gone. There was a portrait of his father, lordly and refined. Oil paint had stolen nothing from his presence; instead it had enshrined it. Behind the shining black shadowwood of the desk, there hung the Lamertine Warrant of Trade, alongside the original Oath of Compact.

Beneath it sat his father. He held an electro-quill in his fingers. They were twisted but still radiated strength. He did not look up as Erastus entered. Cyborgised things moved in the shadows above, cooing avariciously. Their lenses clattered in the quiet, in time with the scratching of the quill. As with so many other aspects of the Cradle, they were little more than extensions of its monarch. The archaic spires of the place had become synonymous with Erastus' father, looming like expectations. As pressing as doubt. Or distrust.

'Is there something I can help you with?' Davos' reading optics caught the light like the eyes of a prowling felid, but he did not look up.

'Were you ever going to tell me?' Erastus asked simply. 'If you had not deigned to sit me amongst your trusted *servants*, would I have known?'

Davos placed the quill down with weary resignation, and finally looked up at his son. Erastus hated that look. The judgement. The disappointment. It had haunted his steps, from almost the moment he could walk.

'Would it have made a difference, had you known? Would my trust have buoyed you up, Erastus? Would you have felt like a man, hmm?' The old man chuckled dryly. 'This is beneath even you. The sheer pettiness. The entitlement.'

'Entitlement?' Erastus slammed his fist against the desk. Stacks of data-slates shuddered, threatening to topple. 'I am your son! Your heir, now.'

Davos' eyes flared with a sudden burst of poison wrath.

'That's right.' Erastus bared his teeth, not in a grin but in a savage snarl of triumph. 'That. Is. Right. She is gone, Father. Evelyne is gone. You have to accept that.'

'And what? Trust you? Teach you? My wastrel son? The man of compromise!' He stood, walking around the desk until they were face to face. 'You could only ever be trusted to act as instructed, to work with what I gave you. With what little you could be allowed.' His father glared down at him, and all Erastus could do was try to stand tall in the strength of that gale. 'Would that you were half, even a quarter of what was taken from me!'

'And haven't I lost, too? She was my sister!'

'She was our future!' Davos lashed out, bringing his ring-adorned hand across his son's face. Erastus flinched back, felt the burst of blood against his skin, and then bodily pushed his father away.

'Your future, perhaps. The dynasty's future. But when have I ever been trusted with a place in that? Why should I care?'

They both stood, chests heaving, panting like maddened beasts.

'Get out,' Davos hissed. 'You think yourself mighty, to come here and stand against me, but I tell you this, you are nothing. Not because I stand as king, not because I am your father. It is because of the calibre of man that you are. The kind I could not raise you up from. I invested in your sister, but with you? It is a mere waste of my time and effort. I gave so much to you and you squandered it! Every lesson and advantage! You will not accompany us on this endeavour.' His eyes were wild, and he trembled as though palsied. His body seemed barely enough to contain his rage. 'You will stay here and hold the Cradle – a castellan in name, an exile in truth. When I return we shall discuss your future here.'

'As you will, my king,' Erastus said, his jaw set. He turned on his heel and strode from the chamber, throwing open the doors as he stormed out into the hallway. To their credit the guards did not flinch. They acted as though they had seen and heard nothing.

Unlike Erastus, they were nothing if not good soldiers.

Chapter Six

Oh Blade of Night

Davos sat alone, still brooding over the confrontation. His child, his irascible and impulsive now-heir, was a source of near-limitless frustration. He had never lavished his attention upon Erastus as he had with Evelyne, content to watch them develop in their divergent pathways, to better serve the legacy of their family. Generations long since dead had struggled to forge their dynasty, and it had endured ten thousand years. More sure and steady than any number of the Imperium's crumbling institutions.

It is a curse, to live long enough to see times such as these. The thought drifted through his mind, even as his quill worked, scratching away at the vellum as he recorded old pilgrim's paths across the stars, measuring them against recent astrocartography. Wherever he looked, there was the seeping horror of the Rift. Infecting the galaxy, staining everything with its dire and fluctuating tides. To plot a course through it verged upon madness, but to find those points; those places where metaphysics waned and human ambition might prevail... That was the mark of true glory.

'Perhaps,' he mused aloud, and the vox-thief built into his desk clicked avariciously at the sound, 'if Egeria could look at these records? Maybe her Navigator's sight might see what I cannot.'

He rubbed his eyes, and stood to stretch. When doubt plagued him, he found comfort in pacing the great chamber. He had vague memories of his own father doing the same, while Davos sat at his studies, an occasional question being cast across the room at him.

The current stability of the last promethium intake?

The gunnery complement numbers for the starboard gun decks?

The dominant trade paradigms of Galleti?

Every day of his youth had been a challenge. Everything had been a test. He had taken those lessons to heart, imparted them in turn to Evelyne. Erastus...

He sighed, and quickened his pacing. He walked the edges of the chamber, letting his hand drift across the stellar maps rendered in gold thread upon the tapestries. He toyed with crystalline sculptures as his mind raced.

It was the duty of a father to prepare his children for the wider universe; to prime them for their roles in life. This was as true of the lowest hive-scum as it was for the mightiest of Imperial nobility. He had done as he had thought best. The galaxy was not a kind cradle, and so he had armoured them as they ought to be: with a father's determination and the terse guidance his own patriarch had handed down to him. Evelyne had risen to the challenge, as befitted the heir, but Erastus... The boy had never truly understood the necessity of what Davos had done. To force him to walk the path of the warrior. To see the Emperor's dominions as they were, not simply a larder for Erastus' baser mercantile appetites.

If Davos had been too stringent and unyielding – if he was considered cruel – then let it be so.

There was, of course, the other matter.

He did not look back at the desk, where the missive lay, its presence almost looming up from the wooden surface. When Haran, chief of his astropathic choir, had brought it to him the old psyker had seemed ashen, even by the standards of his stunted complexion. He had left it, and slunk away trembling. To be rid of it was to have discharged a burden. Davos had tried to read it, but it made less sense than the pilgrim's maps. It was a warped thing. Twisted by the tides of the Rift and a near-impossible transit. A communication from Imperium Nihilus, as impossible as that seemed.

There are few who would attempt such a communion. Could it be–?

He had turned back towards the desk, distractedly reading the text of the Warrant, when he heard a noise behind him. Faint, like the barest hint of movement. He did not look back. He had an idea of who he would find there.

'Erastus, if you have come to grovel, then–'

The first fall of the blade stopped his words in his throat.

He gasped at the sudden rush of pain and violation, feeling the metal scrape against his spine. A gloved hand, musty leather, forced itself against his mouth as the blade was dragged up. He could feel the spreading wetness of blood, the hot burst of agony. He struggled like a pinned beast, thrashing in the iron-hard grip of his assassin. Davos braced his foot against the desk and pushed back hard, knocking over data-slates and letting the desk-lumen crash to the floor.

Still his assailant did not relent. Instead the hand clenched tighter. Davos tried to spin free, to find some way to put distance between them. To put him in reach of a weapon, or to be one. His hand lashed out, seeking his foe. As he moved round, the assassin shifted, allowing him to wriggle out of his grasp so he could almost escape, could feel the faintest, hopeful desperation.

Davos' fist found its mark, impacting against the solidity of flesh. It made no difference. The blade came up and across his eyes; there was a flash of white-hot pain, red-stained, before the darkness came. He stumbled backwards, sprawling onto the desk. His blood was soaking into the dark wood of it, seeping into the maps that remained upon its now tarnished surface. He could not see it. It ran under his fingers in a mortal tide. He could feel his life haemorrhaging away, out across the dominions of Man that he had sworn to serve. Only in death would such duty end.

He tried to push himself up, suddenly aware of how weak he was. His limbs flailed, like some grounded oceanic beast. He gawped and gasped for air, alone in the darkness. Isolated in his blind suffering. He felt a hand take hold of his hair, yanking his head up with brutal efficiency. He could feel the blade, cold against his skin and yet warm with his own vitae. He tried to speak. To ask why, to understand. Instead, the blade slid across his throat with a wet rush of release.

He was still alive long enough to feel the assassin's fingers as they probed the wound in his back.

The assassin turned away from the body, raised its fingers to one of the paler tapestries upon the wall, and began to write.

Chapter Seven

The Body

It was not the pounding that woke him, the urgent hammering of fists against the door to his room. It was the alarms. The sudden ringing of them. At first he thought they were alerts: attack, proximity. But there was something else beneath that. Something sombre, mournful. As though they were wailing.

Erastus rose unsteadily and reached for a robe, hurrying to the door. When he opened it he found himself face to face with Tomas, his family's High Retainer. The man's face was drawn, pale where it was not red around the eyes. Erastus had never seen any man of his household so distraught, so broken. Not even in battle.

'What's going on?' Erastus asked. 'What's happened?'

'My lord, most noble Erastus. It… Oh, I can hardly bear it,' Tomas whimpered. One clasping, clammy hand came out to tug at the shoulder of Erastus' robes, and he shrugged free of the grip. 'It is your father. He… I…' Tomas shook his head. 'He is dead, sir. Murdered. A savage and terrible end for our most beloved king.'

Erastus barely heard as the man collapsed again into wracking, desperate sobs. He could not move. His every muscle was locked, incapacitated by shock. His mouth worked, emptily. He could feel a tremor building in his hand, and clenched it shut in a vain attempt to head it off.

Dead? The thought was so alien, so inimical that he considered the universe must be playing some cruel joke. *And to think how we parted! Were our last words to each other nothing but spite and recrimination?* He shook himself, trying to regain composure. There was only one answer to this; only one path through the fire. He had to see for himself.

'Show me,' he said simply. 'Bring me to my father.'

The exterior of his father's chambers bustled with activity, as security forces pressed in. The guards from the night previous had been detained, and were standing in shackles as the process of investigation ticked ever closer to interrogation. They were silent and shame-faced, and tried to slink lower as Erastus passed them. His eyes flicked across them in a flash of anger, and then the cordon parted and he entered the scene of the crime.

He was surprised at just how much blood there was.

The entire room seemed tainted with it. Saturated on some primal level. He thought that it had covered a light source, to so comprehensively twist the perception of the room. It took Erastus a moment to realise that much of it was not the natural fall of blood after violence. It had taken a deliberate effort. By design. Gory patterns had been smeared across the walls and tapestries like the finger-paintings of an infant. Where it had spattered naturally, it had been smudged to join into the greater desecration. The whorls and coils of drying blood made no sense. He looked around the room, across the floor, until he saw his father.

Davos Lamertine had not died easy. His hands were gnarled

into claws, and his mouth was fixed open in a grim rictus of defiance. There were countless wounds in his abdomen, snaking up his body in a vicious ascent. His chest was almost carved open, but paled beneath the ruin of his throat. Slitting it once had not been enough – the old man's head had been almost sawn off in the depravity. His eyes were gone. Obliterated. Only gaping, bloody sockets remained.

Would there have been fear in those eyes? Or hate?

Erastus looked up, to the Warrant that still hung behind his father's corpse. He felt transfixed in the shadow of its legacy, pinned by the weight of it. But the Warrant itself was not what caught his eye.

There the patterns resolved, and ceased their flow. There, they became words. Familiar, and yet hideously foreign. Recognisable, and hateful in their implications.

Oh blade of night, read the scrawl, and Erastus could practically hear the dry whisper of Delvetar Astraneus at his ear.

He advanced slowly, cautiously. He feared his father's corpse might suddenly jerk up, hissing yet more of his final spite and scorn. He remained still and quiet, truly dead. Erastus leant closer. Davos looked smaller than he remembered. Death had, perhaps, diminished him – stripped away the power and the grandeur. He was no longer a king, simply a man.

'Father.' He spoke the word almost before he realised it. He shook his head, and looked away. It was too much to bear; something no man should have to endure. 'You deserved so much better.'

'He did,' Tomas said with a whimper.

Erastus turned in surprise. He had been so focused on getting to his father's body that he had almost forgotten that Tomas was there. He had not expected the little man's sense of duty to be so absolute.

'What do we do now?' Tomas looked to Erastus with his wet eyes. 'Who could have done such a thing?'

'At a grand gathering such as this?' Erastus breathed the question. 'We are surrounded by suspects, rivals and assassins.' He looked at the message again, the taunt written in his father's blood. *Would they have been so bold? Inflamed by the madness of their faith?*

'I want everyone in the audience chamber,' Erastus said. The hissed anger in his own voice surprised him. His heart was racing, his hands clenched into such tight fists that blood would surely seep between his fingers. He could bleed his rage from him, exorcise his loss in pain.

Or in the absence of pain, vengeance.

CHAPTER EIGHT

THE BURDEN OF THE CROWN

When they gathered anew, it was not with joy or in celebration. Suspicion reigned, and what had before seemed gatherings of loyalty and blood were now reduced to little more than armed camps.

No one had yet brandished a weapon, but that they carried them at all was a sign. Spears, swords and axes were strapped across the backs of Helvintr warriors. Katla's and Astrid's own ornate spears sat idle across their backs: bronze and gold, masterworked exemplars of the weaponsmith's craft. Lamertine armsmen tried to hem in the savage crews, but the leather-brown ranks contracted and pushed against them. It was like watching the tide war with the land on a habitable world.

Gunther Radrexxus sat upon the edge of one of the tables, a booted foot perched against a chair. He rocked it back and forth dreamily, lost in his own world. As his coat shifted, it became clear that he had pistols at his belt, alongside an ornate sabre. Occasionally his hand would stray, lovingly caressing the pommel before he resumed his idle motions.

All across the hall they filed into their rows, jostling for space, pushing at each other as kindred were rendered unkind.

Erastus watched, pressing a hand to his temple as he sat in the throne. Watching every one of them, considering each in their turn, from the bombast of the more aggressive and cocksure dynasties, to the reserved spiritualists of the Astraneus – each head bowed solemnly, murmuring under their breaths.

Praying, he thought. *Even now, they have the audacity to pray.*

He had dressed in a crisp uniform, very much his father's style. The high collar was lined with gold, shining against his dark skin. His father's plasma pistol sat in its holster, ready to be unleashed – to burn his enemies to ashes. A power sabre sat at his hip, its hilt carved with rampant lions and flaming eagle wings.

He needed no cane, and so he brought the flat of his hand down against the arm of the throne. Around the chamber his guards clattered weapons against their breastplates or pounded them against the floor. When the din finally broke and silence returned, only then did he begin to speak.

'You are summoned here,' he said, 'in answer to a crime. My father, Davos Lamertine, is dead. Your king is dead.'

There were murmurs of discontent rippling through the crowd. Even upon the dais, Erastus could hear someone beginning to wail. His father would have quashed such a display.

He slammed his fist against the throne again. 'Be silent!'

All looked to him. Some with fear and surprise, others with simple sadness; the pity for a son robbed of his father. A dynasty whose future had been stolen. Even Gunther managed to rally, swaying to his feet. He had plucked a flask of something from his voluminous coat, and raised it to his lips.

'In honour of the valiant dead, eh?'

'This was no valiant death,' Erastus snarled. There was vigour in him that he had never known, a fire within his soul. Incandescent rage pulsed through every fibre of his being, and he glared down upon the assembly like the wrath of the God-Emperor Himself. This, he realised, was what it meant to be king. What had animated his father through the long centuries of his life, and carried the generations long since passed forward. From the maelstrom of lightless Strife, and the dream of the Great Crusade, through millennia of ruin and loss. The Compact had endured, annealing together the ambitions of mortal men; making them components of something greater than themselves, just as the Imperium did.

Had I sat at your side, would I have known this sooner?

Erastus bit back the sudden rush of pride and understanding. 'My father died in his sanctum, butchered like an animal. There was no glory in this. Ours was the honour of service, and the joy of unity. That has ended, in betrayal.'

'Betrayal?' Katla Helvintr's eyes went wide, not with shock or surprise, but with a predator's enthusiasm. 'You think one of us has done this thing? Slaughtered a man, like an ailing grox?'

'I do,' Erastus said, his disdain writ across his tight features. 'The ritual of the scene has much in common with the rites observed by the disciples of the Astraneus Dynasty and their adherence to their Cult of the Shrouded Emperor.' Erastus stood, and pointed across the open floor of the chamber. 'I name them as suspects in my father's death, as usurpers who would take from us all that we have striven to build. Who crave in cowardice what others would gain when my father stepped aside as king.' He gestured broadly with his free hand. 'What say you to the charges?'

'We reject these accusations,' Delvetar said in their quiet whisper, amplified as it was by vox-emitter. 'As we reject you. You, the least of the House of Lamertine. You are not your sister, Erastus, to threaten us, or cajole us by feat of arms. All here know you, as your father knew you.' They smiled their cold smile, dripping with insincerity and zealot's poison. 'Too long have your kind ruled by fear and threat. No longer. By the rights of the Compact, and the bond of blood oath, I renounce the Lamertine Kingship. I invoke the First King's Charter, and I declare that we have no confidence in our lord – who comes to us not in formal ascension, but as a lesser son handed a boon of which he is unworthy.'

'Unworthy?' Erastus could not help himself as he rushed down off of the dais, across the floor to face Delvetar. 'You dare! In this place, with my father barely even cold.'

'It is not a matter of daring, Erastus.' Delvetar smiled, cruelty in place of the usual angelic bliss. Their pale, androgynous features had barely the hint of ruddy choler as they leant forward. 'The Emperor is with us, in every thought and deed. He has blessed our lineage for generations. When we act, it is by His will. So do not think to threaten us, while you strut and fuss in your father's borrowed raiment.'

They sniffed haughtily, as though the entire affair were beneath their concern.

'We state again,' they said. 'We call for a vote. The dynasties must choose whether we languish with this boy king, or gift the throne to a firmer hand. One that will set this matter to rest, and find the truth amidst these dark deeds.'

Erastus looked around the chamber. Already the lords of the dynasties were stepping forward. Katla, Gunther and Absalom closed in about them. Delvetar took a step back, smiling simply.

'The masters of the great houses here represented shall vote, and determine the fate of the Lamertine Dynasty's rule upon this Compact. In the Emperor's light, and in His shadow. What say you, cousins?'

Chapter Nine

They gathered on the dais, with Erastus at their centre, pacing about him in circles too precise to be anything but ritual. The room had grown quiet of murmurs and whispers, and was instead filled with the steady rhythmic pounding of boots. Of fists against breastplates and steel against steel.

Slowly, the leaders of the dynasties began to speak. Each taking up their place in the almost dance-like flow of the movements, each lending their voice to the emergent chorus.

'By the many, may the few be judged,' Katla whispered.

'By our kin is power checked,' Gunther hissed.

'By His will are we guided,' Absalom intoned.

'And by His grace, kept free.'

'We submit to His judgement, through the judgement of our peers.'

'And in that judgement, are we bound and sanctified.' Delvetar finished the words, like the culmination of a prayer or an invocation. They smiled thinly. 'Who stands in judgement?'

'Helvintr, Radrexxus and Norastye.' The answer came as one from the three gathered.

'And Torvander?'

'Fled,' Gunther tittered. 'Demigods walking anew seems to have terrified them. A pity. I do so enjoy sport with the shepherds.'

'Be silent,' Delvetar hissed.

Gunther shrugged, grinned and stepped back.

'And whom do we judge?'

'Erastus, second-born of Davos Lamertine,' intoned Katla. 'Heir apparent only through the malice of chance.'

'And what is his declaration? What is his oath?'

All eyes turned to Erastus as Delvetar spoke. Erastus felt like a specimen under glass, pinned by the attention of so many. Yet it was the ring of eyes and voices that cut the deepest. He was unprepared for this battleground, in a way his father or sister never would have been. His mouth was dry, his forehead sheened with sweat. He took a long moment, swallowing before he spoke.

'I have much to learn, but I have watched my father work.' He stepped forward, head held high. 'I am not my sister, and I am not my father.' He went down on one knee, head bowed. 'I will strive to honour the legacy of my house and the spirit of the Compact. My father taught me many things.' He bit back bile, keeping his voice measured. 'He taught me the worth of this institution. That we are the pathfinders in the darkness, an example for others to look to. We are nobility stripped of pretence. We are honest implements, in an unkind galaxy. He never lost sight of that, and neither shall I.'

There was a long moment of silence. Even the drumming of hands and feet had fallen quiet. All eyes were locked upon him, knelt in obeisance, in shame and in desperation.

There was a tapping at the edge of his awareness, silver against the gold and stone of the dais. He looked up. A shadow seemed to drift behind the circle of figures. All that marked its passing was the tapping of its cane against the floor. *Tap. Tap. Tap.* The same sound that had coloured his adult life.

'*Pitiful,*' the shade said, and shook the indistinct umbra that formed its head. '*No son of the Lamertine name should grovel in the dust. You ought, my son, to have killed them all. Evelyne would have had their heads, and let others rise, to serve in fear.*'

Erastus bit his tongue, and closed his eyes. When he opened them again, it was gone. As though it had never been. Perhaps it had not. Perhaps he had simply imagined it; the racing of a stressed and suffering mind.

'The Astraneus say no,' Delvetar stated simply. 'We hold no faith in Erastus Lamertine or his ability to command the Davamir Compact.'

Erastus almost smiled. This was the most obvious of the detractors, of course, but all of them had reason to hate his family. To envy and fear his father's reputation, and the threat of vengeance. The Astraneus, rightly or wrongly, had been slighted. Or at least, felt as such.

The others, though...

Erastus cast his mind back across the years of service under his father's eye. The rivalries he had stoked, the febrile alliances he had struggled to maintain. His father had ruled by right, and by fear, and the edge of the blade. Not all had enjoyed such a dichotomy of service and rule. Though they had thrived and prospered, and the name of the Davamir Compact had carried its weight across the stars, there were still some who would have named his father *tyrant*.

'We have wracked our minds for the most logical of paths.' Absalom Norastye was a blunt creature. This close his inhumanity seemed utterly plain. His augmetic eyes whirred and clicked with avarice, emotionless save for those beaten into their construction. He was a grasping thing, Erastus realised suddenly. The long centuries of service to Mars had changed him into a being as fundamentally yoked to the hunt as any of the Helvintrs, or the most dedicated of Martian explorators. 'What is clear to us is that the current state of affairs is an unsustainable one. We support the Astraneus call for no confidence in Erastus Lamertine.'

Two against him. Erastus sighed, and rose from his prone position. He looked at them both, eyes fixed, jaw set. He did not display any weakness, he simply nodded. There was a titter off to one side, and Erastus turned to face Gunther Radrexxus. The man's eyes danced with amusement, as he reached up with his heavy, glittering hand to adjust his wig again.

'I am a simple soul,' he offered politely. There was a ripple of laughter even amidst the solemnity at that. 'I knew Davos Lamertine of old – our covenants and clashes went back a long way. I did not necessarily like the man, but I respected him. He may have judged me for my vices, and who amongst you would not?' Even Erastus smiled at that. 'Nevertheless, he respected my abilities, and the trade which ran through my enterprises into the veins of this station and the heart of our Compact.'

He turned to the others and threw his arms wide, stepping inside the circle till he was face to face with Erastus.

'Now, I do not know the worth of this young pup. I cannot claim that I have some secret insight into his heart or soul.' He waved a hand idly, twirling it in the air as though stirring it through water. 'What I will say is this. I care nothing for whosoever sits on this throne. My place is amongst the stars, in the void. Seeking the next horizon. That is what we were made and bred for, is it not? Those are the core of the words we hold to, in the First King's oath.' He turned from Erastus and regarded his kindred. 'I hold my confidence in Erastus and his family. I want to see the caged bird fly.'

Erastus breathed a sigh of relief as Gunther moved back to his place, then felt it curdle in his throat as Katla Helvintr stalked forward. Never before had he felt so much like prey. She smiled without warmth, a wolf's smile. She did not reach for her spear but that did not render her any less lethal. He had not been this close to her for some time. The scents drifted from her: old leather, void-chill, and the spice of whatever caustic ichor had remade so much of her. When her smile vanished, the tattoos creased and flexed, and the beast returned to the fore.

'You all know me. I am Katla Helvintr, and my line stretches back to the ice of Fenris. Even that cage of sea and fire could not hold us, nor did its storms tame us. It was to the stars that we looked, and to the stars that the Allfather of Man called us.' She drew the spear from its sheath upon her back. Low, muted gasps filled the chamber, though no one moved to stop her. The dissenting voices smiled, imagining that his defeat and disgrace were now complete. Gunther hunched forward with eager glee, desperate to see what would happen.

Erastus braced himself for a killing blow, to join his father and sister in death. Perhaps the Helvintrs had been the architects of this ruin, all along. He had left himself exposed, and would pay the price. He looked down, closed his eyes, for the last time.

And felt the cold metal of the blade touch beneath his chin, and tilt it upwards.

'Our families have never been… friendly,' Katla allowed, with a tilt of her head. 'But the lessons of loyalty have long since been carved into us. The seasons change, from peace to war. Profit becomes ruin. Davos Lamertine, for all his failings, for all he did not respect us… He was king. Jarl of jarls.' She rounded on the others, spear up. The blade passed mere inches from their faces. Absalom held firm, barely even blinking, but Delvetar flinched back.

'You dare–'

'I dare nothing. It is you who dares. To pile sanctimony upon calamity. Our king is *dead*,' she snarled. 'Murdered in the heart of his power, by one who may yet walk these halls! Who wheedles for power and influence! Who tries to seize the chains of command!'

Gunther chuckled dryly as she spoke, and clucked his tongue. He moved round to stand beside Erastus and Katla. 'Friends from the oddest of quarters, little bird,' he said. 'It seems you command more respect than you know.'

'There would be no honour,' Katla continued, as much to them as to their opposition, 'in tearing down the boy in this way. I would happily see my family's fortunes eclipse his, but I would do it honestly.' She turned to Erastus, her gaze languid. 'If I come for you, boy, it will be clear for all to see. Not a blade in the dark, but eye to eye on the open plain.'

'Thank you,' he said, and finally began to breathe again. 'You do me a great honour, Jarl Helvintr, as does Lord Admiral Radrexxus. I will make sure your faith is not misplaced.' Erastus looked to Delvetar, and smiled coldly. 'A tie, I'm afraid, is not your victory.'

Their face clouded into an ugly sneer, pale skin rippling as they turned away in a flutter of black robes. Absalom looked after them, and then shrugged gently, deigning not to follow.

'Hold,' Erastus said. His voice was clear and focused.

Delvetar stopped, spun on their heel and glared back at Erastus.

'Arch-Lecter,' Erastus said. His voice boomed in the still of the hall. 'Whether or not you killed my father, you have wronged me.' His hands clenched, and he stalked forward. The other lords parted before his wrath, like avians before the onslaught of a storm.

'You have borne discontent into the heart of this gathering, and tried to break us at our lowest ebb. Had there been men or women such as you, of low character and lower cunning, at its inception, then this Compact would never have risen from the muck to claim the stars. We would have been forsaken, and forgotten by the march of history. We would have proven unworthy of the trust He put in us. I banish you, Delvetar Astraneus, and all your brood and all your works. I cleave you from the Compact, and cast you into the Outer Dark. If His light finds you there, may it lead you to forgiveness. May you find redemption.'

Delvetar looked back for a long moment. Not a single soul spoke. He imagined that the Arch-Lecter might hurl themselves at him, shrieking of vengeance and reprisal. That a digi-weapon-bedecked hand might rise and strike him down.

Instead, the Arch-Lecter merely muttered a prayer, or perhaps a curse, and stormed from the hall, followed by their retainers.

CHAPTER TEN

IN THE CRUCIBLE OF COMBAT

He had dismissed the others almost immediately afterwards, daring no advice or reproach.

The crews had filed sullenly from the chamber, till the ringing of boots against marble shifted to the clatter of pounding against metal. The Cradle sang with movement, joyous to be inhabited by the myriad wayfarers of humanity.

It was a hollow joy. One Erastus could not share.

He stood alone in the Hall of Equals, let the quiet settle in around him, before exiting via a small servant's antechamber. The station had many secrets beneath the observations of its masters, and in his years there Erastus had exploited many of them. The glamour of the high halls faded into the reassuring wreck of maintenance tunnels, their lume-strips flickering weakly. In places the light changed from the muted sodium yellow to the sharp red of emergency lumens. He had to duck into alcoves to avoid the mindless trudging of servitors, before he finally re-emerged into the common areas of the station.

The doors to the training halls were unlocked, and he stepped inside with the surety of purpose he had carried from the chambers above. It was a clean economical space; the walls bare stone girded with iron, with servitors lined before them. Each mechanical limb ended in a blade: hooked, curved, straight and long. He looked at them, judging each of the implements of death.

Erastus reached down and unhooked the plasma pistol from his belt, placing it gently upon a nearby ledge. He drew the power sabre, turning it in his hand. He felt its weight, unfamiliar and yet reassuring. The weapon glimmered as the light caught its edge, the blade of cold, pure metal; silvered, where its hilt was gilded. A weapon fit for a king. Handed down from one generation of Lamertines to the next.

'You were never supposed to be my burden,' he said softly. 'I should never have had to carry you. But I do, so we might as well get acquainted with one another.'

The sword was called Bloodsong, and it was a relic of a bygone age. It had been his father's. He hefted it, and stepped forward. The lights of the chamber shifted as it detected his presence. He took a deep breath, and centred himself.

'Training cycle, pattern Sigma Omega.'

The servitors clattered, eye-lenses gleaming as they ratcheted up to combat readiness. Adrenal-jacks pushed their burning contents into the atrophied bloodstreams of the combat units, and they lurched forward. Blades scraped against the floor before suddenly snapping up, with the thunder of steel against steel. Erastus kept his sabre raised, watching their marionette movements as they jerked and shuddered towards him.

He moved before the first blade rotated round, primed to strike. He whirled left, bringing the sabre around to clatter against the first cyborg's guard. There was a sudden alarm, and the machine's jaw flapped with a spasmodic burbling of binary as it registered damage. He let himself grin as he spun between their strikes, ducking under the swipes of the swords. He pivoted, scoring Bloodsong down the chest armour of the next servitor. It reeled back with its own sirens of shock.

His father had taught him rudimentary combat, lessons of blade and shot in pale imitation of his sister. He remembered watching them from the edges of a chamber such as this: her effortless grace, her hair tied back in a dark bundle as she weaved and flowed through the melee. Their father's eyes burning with something approaching pride, something so alien to Erastus as to be utterly unfamiliar.

He hesitated in the dance of swords and the blade-limb of a servitor clipped him, eliciting a cry of pain. He could feel the hot blood streaking his arm, soaking into his uniform. Erastus cursed, bringing the blade round in a vengeful arc. The servitor flinched back, joining the background radiation of wailing alarms. He gritted his teeth and stepped back. The clunking, plodding mechanical steps followed him, and he raised his guard. He caught one blade, turned it aside. The next slammed against his sabre, near the hilt. He almost dropped it.

'Throne of...' he muttered, pushing back against the servitor's augmented strength. He could feel the sweat tracing its hot rivulets down his brow, along his spine, joining the blood in soiling his uniform. He held back from igniting the blade, content to let the stringent training protocols run their course.

'If you die, then you die,' his father had always said before training. 'Better I lose you here, in practice, than you shame me on the field. After all...'

Erastus shook his head at the memory, before finishing his father's long ago admonition.

'After all,' he grunted, and brought the sword round and across the side of the servitor's head. Its joints snarled with feedback, but he turned the blade and let it slam back into the thing's iron skull. 'After all, your sister would never shame me so.' He brought the sword back up, and then drove it down directly into its face. It sputtered erratically, then toppled backwards.

'One way to exorcise your daemons,' he heard someone say.

He turned to look at the speaker, as he wiped a hand across his brow. The servitors began to power down, and he sighed as he looked at them. Astrid Helvintr was smiling wryly, pale skin creased with paler scars. She did not move. She remained poised, echoing her mother's animal grace. He had no doubt that she was aware of every vulnerability in this chamber, every crack she could exploit. He noted that her spear was absent, and was very aware of the unpowered blade still held in his hands. Still ready to do violence. He turned the sabre, and slid it back into the scabbard at his hip.

'You shouldn't be here,' he said.

'No.' Astrid bared her teeth. 'I probably shouldn't, but here we are.' She gestured around the chamber. 'A fine place to hone your craft, or to begin to at the very least?' She was taunting him, but he would not allow himself to rise to it.

'I am no stranger to places such as these,' he said. 'I am my father's son, if nothing else.'

'Oh, indeed,' she laughed. 'Every inch the warrior prince! A Lamertine poet-king – no bluster, only blades. The stories you will write across the stars in blood and fire.'

'You mock me,' he stated dryly, and she beamed at that.

'I do, but it is the way of things. The king is mocked by the wolves, no matter how well he rules, for they will always be at the edges, awaiting advantage.'

'Is that what you're doing? You and your mother? Prowling around the borders, like reavers in the old tales?' He leant towards her, his hand back to resting on Bloodsong's pommel.

'You do yourself no favours, if you mean to set my mind at ease. You have supported me, and I appreciate that…' He trailed off, and looked away from her. 'But now I have to ask what you want, and what you intend.'

'What we have always wanted,' she said. 'Men like you and your father may be the ones who sell the meat at market, but it is we who run the beasts down.' She nodded to his sword. 'It is good that you practise, though. The assassins who claimed your father may linger.'

'Even when banished?'

'Especially when banished!' Her voice hitched as she spoke, as if scolding a child. 'You think they will stop merely because you send them from your hearth?' She grew quiet, and tense. 'Assuming you have sent the right ones away.'

'You doubt that it was the Astraneus?'

'My mother and I, both,' she said, smiling. 'They are a strange breed, yes, the void soaked into their very marrow. Probably very easy to break.' She tilted her head as though musing over that point, playing out how each of them could be taken apart. 'But they are not idle killers, and they are not fools. Perhaps exile was a foolish choice, but it is done now.'

'Perhaps,' he allowed. 'If not them, then who?'

'I could not tell you, Lord Lamertine.' She smiled again, a wicked flash of teeth. 'As my mother has told you already, we would not lower ourselves to such treachery. We kill in the old way – red snow beneath you, and the foe before you. We would lay out a circle of spears, that you might know the challenge has been made.' She pushed off the wall and paced to the centre of the sparring hall. She knelt, examining the servitors with a critical eye. 'Not bad, for a pup.'

That made him laugh. He leant back against an iron column, cast his eyes to the tasteful murals upon the ceiling, and then looked back to her. 'Perhaps one day I'll see what you're capable of.'

'Oh, Erastus,' she said with a sigh. She walked over to him, leaning in as she passed by him. 'Let us hope we're on the same side when you do.' She walked on and out of the chamber, leaving him staring in her wake.

He let a smile flicker across his features. 'Throne, save me from unreliable allies.'

Erastus finally allowed himself to return to his father's chambers, *his* chambers now. The reflection gave him pause as he surveyed the room. The blood had been cleaned away, meticulously scrubbed by serfs and servitors. He would almost never know a murder had taken place here. Yet he saw the stains in his mind, a blemish he could not help but be aware of.

He moved around the desk, seating himself in his father's chair. His hands felt locked on the arms as he looked at the desk's cold expanse, broken only by the piled charts and papers. Some of them were stained, soaked through with the crimson of his father's life. He took a deep breath, and reached for the first of them.

Erastus Lamertine began to read.

CHAPTER ELEVEN

ROADS LESS TRAVELLED

Once he had changed, and tended to his wound, he had called a summons to one of the many meeting chambers that ringed the upper circle of the Cradle. Erastus stood at one of the great banks of observation platforms, much as his father had done to watch the arrivals. He kept his back to the door, fingers interlaced behind him, as he watched the exodus.

The Astraneus had not lingered to face their judgement, and had instead taken his banishment to heart. He watched the ships, their gilded silhouettes eerie in the waning light of the Davamir star. Their hulls were void-black, crawling with spider-like script. The shadowed night-city of the *Remembrance of the Throne*, their flagship, seemed to glower petulantly as it began to draw away from the docks.

The ships had been broadcasting mournful orisons of loss and betrayal as they left, till the vox-calls, binharic-communions and astropathic wails had melded together into a background static of wounded pride. Erastus had used his authority to block what

he could, and paid no heed to the rest. He would wear his indifference plainly, the better to wound them with his disdain. He
turned from the window as the last of the great pilgrim ships disengaged from the docking spurs. Mooring cables and materiel
transfer pipes fell away in a flurry of disconnections, sirens wailed
and bells tolled as the fleet pulled out into the open void.

Somewhere across that gulf of space, Erastus knew that Delvetar was looking back. In judgement? With spite? Frustrated at
their own failure? He reached up with one hand and laid it
against the glass.

'It should never have come to this,' he whispered.

The doors behind him slid open with a hydraulic hiss, and he
finally allowed his eyes to move from the fleet as it readied to
set sail. Three lords of the Imperium stood before him, repre-
senting their dynasties.

'Be welcome,' Erastus began, 'and let all animosity that has
existed between us be forgotten.' They each nodded and took a
seat around the marble table which dominated the room. Above
them the panelling creaked with the movement of hidden servitors, the low whirr of servo-skulls as they flitted from one wing
to another. The structure groaned as though haunted, as though
alive, before it finally settled.

'Have the preparations for a funeral been made?' Gunther
Radrexxus leant back, eyebrows raised as he looked to Erastus.
'I only ask so I might prepare the correct apparel. One would
so hate to be found wanting at such an occasion.'

'You are as caring as ever,' Katla said with a shake of her head.
'Allfather preserve us, Radrexxus, this is a matter of death. Not
another social gala for some planetary governor.'

Gunther tittered. 'I'm amazed you know of such things. I
didn't think that they had beasts at the ball.'

'Enough,' Absalom intoned. 'I too would like to know the

details of any funerary arrangements, my lord. If only so that I may be present to give your father my regards, before eternity.'

'Thank you all. There will be a service to remember my father, and inter our king, in good time,' Erastus said as he took his seat. 'Until then, our objective.' He toyed with a keypad at the head of the table, and there was a shuddering of servos as mechanisms realigned. The light of a hololith filled the chamber, centred over the table. The galaxy itself was laid bare in a crackle of energy. He reached up, tapping a small, glowing region of space. 'Here is the Cradle...' He looked up across the hololith, where hateful crimson stained the purity of humanity's empire. 'And there is the expanse of the Great Rift. The obstacle which the coming crusade will have to overcome.'

Katla peered at it, raising one hand to trace its way through the stars. Absalom stared at it impassively, making a slow and logical assessment of the map. Gunther looked at it fleetingly, as though already bored, before returning his attention to his well-manicured nails.

'The oldest hunt-routes may not be of use to us,' Katla allowed. She sighed and shook her head. 'The skin of the galaxy is cracked, and the muscles beneath have shifted. They once coiled out from Fenris, and followed lines of migration. Beyond that, now, they are the trails of the Devourer's tendrils.' She drummed her fingers against the table anxiously. 'Forgive us this failure.'

'That is not your failing, nor your fault,' Erastus said softly. 'Absalom?'

The Lord Technologist leant back in his chair, clicking like a cogitator as it processed data-inloads. 'There are many points that display properties inconsistent with the mass material-empyrean overlap of the Great Rift.' He stood, gesturing to the map. A variety of areas flared red in response to his movements. 'Investigation and consolidation of these points would, I believe, prove to be the optimal starting points for any endeavours to cross. I shall collate the relevant data, and provide it for your perusal.'

'Thank you, Absalom.' Erastus bowed his head, and then added his own points of emphasis to the map. 'My father had tentatively identified a number of potential points of egress. These lay, primarily, along the old pilgrim routes of the Via Satrosi. It was his belief, at least as far as I can glean from his researches, that these stellar routes – so suffused with the faith of generations – would be more proof against the effects of the Rift.' He chuckled. 'Sadly, those who once proclaimed to be the most faithful of us are no longer here to offer judgement or opinion on the matter.'

The others added their own polite laughter, but Erastus could not help but notice that not all of them did. He looked up, and found Gunther Radrexxus staring intently at the hololith. It was as though a mask had slipped, or a shadow had passed momentarily across the sun. He looked at it with a set, almost reptilian focus. A fascination that far outstripped any of his gaudy showmanship. Erastus was about to call out to him, when the lord admiral spoke a single word.

'Endymica.'

'Endymica?' Erastus asked.

'Endymica,' Gunther repeated. 'A fortress-world – previously of little note, save for its obvious exuberant commitment to martial prowess.' He pinched at the map and it responded reactively. The light of the image flickered and twisted as it realigned, casting fractal patterns across the skull-faced, trumpet-bearing angels from which the picture was being projected. The world was a flashing orb, poised between two burning prongs of fluctuating Rift-light. 'Now it straddles one end of what the defenders term the Draedes Gap, forming a strategic bulwark against whatever might tumble through to threaten our dear Imperium. It used to be rather lovely. A fine posting, despite its martial bearing. The Draedes Nebula, now gone rotten and burning cold.'

'You are certain of this?' Katla asked.

'Oh, quite. We have a trading arrangement with the men of Endymica. Garrison duty can be such a chore – the same routine, day after hollow day. We simply provide a little fire for their bellies. Not quite wine, women and song...' He laughed bleakly. 'But close enough.' He spread his hands, and looked to his fellows. 'We meld our strength with theirs, hold the line until the primarch's forces arrive, and then we profit. They might need pathfinders, for those brave enough to risk it...' He eyed Katla at that. 'They might bring back treasures of reclaimed technology.' Absalom leant forward, scratching at his chin. 'The sky is the limit, my friends. All achieved through simple diplomatic sleight of hand.'

'An interesting proposal, certainly.'

'And one without any strings, Erastus. I know you fear being in my debt, so soon into your reign, but I assure you I want for nothing. Merely my share of the spoils, when they are divided.' He leant his rouged cheek upon his hand, and grinned. 'The Compact exists, after all, so that the gifts of one might become the boon of all.'

'The Compact exists to serve the Imperium,' Erastus said, and Gunther's laughter met his statement.

'Of course, of course,' the lord admiral said with a smile. 'We all serve the Emperor before anything else. We are all good servants.'

'And yet,' said Katla, 'we find ourselves doubting you. A funny thing, that.'

'Hilarious,' Gunther said, as he reached for a glass of wine. 'I bear no ill will to our humble little gathering.' He folded his hands, like a contrite child. 'I haven't raised a knife against any of you.' He turned his languid gaze to Absalom. 'Nor have I supported attempts to usurp authority, unlike some.'

The Lord Technologist bristled, bracing one spread hand against the table as he glared at Gunther with his crimson eyes. 'You would do well to hold your tongue, lord admiral. We are here under ancient pact and truce. Such things can be forgotten, beyond the station. The void is a harsh mistress.'

'Ah, she and I are old lovers. The void is in the blood of the Radrexxus, as much as it is any of you. More, even!' Gunther hunched forward, and Erastus could see the man's own predatory joy writ across his face, as fierce as the snarling wolf's visage that adorned Katla. She watched, impassive, her adornment prone and poised. The tattoos were distracting, constantly drawing the eye in with their tribal whorls. There was a contrast there, between the patterns she had chosen, and the savage lines that fate had forced upon her.

'Do not bicker like pups,' she said softly. 'Infighting shames the Allfather, and the memory of our king. This was his dream, this undertaking, but more than that it is the will of a primarch. A son of the Emperor walks the galaxy again, as they say the Great Wolf shall stalk the stars come the end of all things.' She bowed her head, almost in reverence. 'It is a time of tragedy, yes, but also an age of miracles.'

Erastus was still staring at the map, at the glowing areas of interest. He reached out, plucked up his own silver goblet of wine, and swirled it thoughtfully in his hand. His father's proposition had the ring of superstition to it, of leaning into matters of faith. Davos Lamertine had never struck his son as a man overburdened with faith. He had loved the Emperor, certainly. He had used the Cradle's sizeable chapel often enough. Their travels had taken them to shrine worlds and pilgrim way stations across the decades, and their placement within Imperial society had meant that his father had frequently rubbed shoulders with senior clergy: arch-cardinals and ecclesiarchs had played for his favour, for the material advantages that a rogue trader could bring to them.

Erastus knew that this was not the same thing as faith. His father had been a warrior, but never a crusader. He had used power as a weapon; had known the manifold edges of it, the barbs and blades of it. He had known how to wield it to avoid damaging himself. He had lacked the appreciation of the less-direct approach, the subtler knives of power. Those weapons which Erastus deployed with skill; which men like Gunther Radrexxus had mastered.

'We will vote on it,' Erastus said suddenly. All eyes turned to him. Gunther laughed.

'Another vote. Well, the first one did go rather well for you, didn't it? Why not another?'

'This is a shared burden,' Erastus said. 'A joint undertaking. I will not yoke us to a vision that we lack unity on.' He stood and reached out to touch the map. 'You've convinced me, Lord Radrexxus. I would have us sail for Endymica.'

'There is logic in this,' Absalom said, chest puffed out with false pride. 'This Draedes Gap is one of the areas I had mentioned previously.' His eyes clicked and reset as he regarded the precise area of the map. The light caught the crimson lenses, making him seem almost diabolic; swathed in red and black, his metallic fingers clattering against the table's hard surface. 'The interplay of the materium and immaterium are optimal here, a fine choice. We of the Norastye support the Endymica motion.'

'As fine a choice as any other,' Katla said with a shrug. 'In truth I do not care who wishes to hold this side of the Rift. I shall do my part, and hold to my oaths...' She trailed off, her eyes sparkling as she stared up at the horror of the Rift and the darkness that smouldered beyond it.

They called it Imperium Nihilus. The Dark Imperium. Lost, broken, screaming. Erastus could understand the fascination it would hold for a huntress such as Katla. A bloodline such as the Helvintrs did not play guard dog when they could run and hunt.

'We shall petition to accompany the crusade host when it comes to Endymica. Until then, we are at your service.'

'Excellent!' Gunther said. He stood and looked around the table, before bowing with a flourish towards Erastus. 'Agreement, true consensus. Wonders will never cease.' He chortled and turned to leave the chamber. After a long moment, and no shortage of shared glances, the other lords did the same.

Erastus stood and watched them go, before depressing the rune-key again. The light of the map died at last, the taint of the Rift banished back into the darkness.

He was left alone, with only the light of the stars to fill the chamber.

Chapter Twelve

The Rest of Ages

When he awoke it was to the disorientation of being elsewhere; the realisation that he had not actually made it to his bed. His head was lolled back in the high-backed chair, his hands gripping the arms until they were white with lack of blood. He blinked awake, and saw that he was in his father's office. It seemed alien from this side of the desk, the dulled lights rendering it dreamlike and strange. There was a sterility to it that had not existed during his father's reign. A sense that it was a room merely occupied, rather than inhabited.

Erastus looked at the desk, at the unmarked and unmarred surface where his father had expired. It seemed wrong, somehow, that it should be so free of tarnish. As though the blood of a king should have no hold, no influence, beyond death. He examined the items which still lay upon it: the revised astrocartographs which spoke of the Draedes Gap and the fortress-world of Endymica. The text of the great Edict itself, which had precipitated the calamitous events.

There was another document he had not yet examined. Erastus traced his hand along the filigreed exterior of the missive, slowly unfurling it. It was, he realised, an astropathic transmission. Sealed and sanctified by the Cradle's choir. There was no legible text within, only a garbled and warped communication. No details had survived whatever circuitous and tumultuous passage the message had weaved through the tides of the warp.

He rubbed his eyes with the back of one hand. He had been here for days, he was sure. Slowly working through the detritus of his father's reign and life. Sorting through documents and communications. Pacing the floor till he thought he might wear a groove into it. Sometimes he felt he was lost in memories of the past, as his perceptions of the room seemed to settle into familiar patterns. It had not begun to feel normal. Not yet.

He waved the astropathic communication in the air, as though weighing its worth. It could be nothing. The last gasp of a dying ship; a mortis cry from some distant, burning world. He held it, and thought of a hundred reasons why his father might have had this close to hand before the end.

'Another secret, was it?' he asked the empty air. 'Something else you might have told me? Had there been time, or trust.' He let it fall, and turned away from the desk. The dim light of the chamber caught on the brass buttons of the black suit which hung from the back of the office door. He looked at it, as though scrutiny would render it less real. The dark, sombre garment sat, still, accepting his judgement.

His jaw tightened as he stepped towards it, brushing a hand down the silken fabric. It was, in the end, a thing fit for one purpose. The garb of mourning. He turned away from it and padded back towards the desk. He scooped up a nearly empty glass and threw back the bitter dregs of amasec.

'Nothing else for it,' he whispered to himself. He took a

moment to steel himself, and then turned to face the mourning suit, like a man facing battle or the gallows.

The procession was monumental.

Even in the massive halls of the Cradle, wide as boarding causeways, the crowd was notable. Every serf and servant of their house had gathered – all in black, with sashes or some other splash of the dynasty's pale blue about their person – flooding the ways that led to the Halls of the Lost. As they progressed, the corridors became narrower and ship-steel gave way to old, hand-wrought stone. They passed by ancient biers of pale marble, and great sepulchres of yellowed bone. Sarcophagi of tarnished gold shimmered faintly beneath the low firelight of braziers.

They emerged from the shadowed arches and the inconstant flame of the low lights into a vast space – immense like the grandest of planetary cathedrals. It had been built into the heart of the great edifice, to process the endless dead of the station. So like a world unto itself, so mighty in purpose and design, and yet its various populations all inevitably flowed through the Halls of the Lost. Kings as well as serfs, from heroes to helots. Death claimed each and every soul that walked the Cradle, in time. All were equal before the Throne.

They passed beneath rearing columns, under the fires of the hab-block-sized ovens. Gouts of flame reached skyward periodically, coating the gargoyle-encrusted upper reaches with a fine layer of soot and vaporised human fat. The macro-crematory furnaces that ringed the chamber were being stoked to furious purpose, in honour of the glorious dead. As the Lamertine procession drew in, pale faces lit by the flare of the furnaces, so the other dynasties began to appear. The clattering red-grey tide of the Norastye came, swinging censers and fingering prayer beads that broadcast in subtle binharic. By contrast the Helvintr assembly whooped and cheered like participants in a heathen revel, singing and chanting of the life lost, and the deeds of the glorious fallen. The skirl of horns accompanied the Radrexxus as they crept forward, each of their front ranks bearing an instrument so that the corridors rang with bells and the lilting tunes of stringed instruments.

At the head of each converging column came the leaders of the dynasties. Each wore restrained, dark clothing; even Gunther had settled for a reserved suit not unlike Erastus' own. He bowed his periwigged head low, and Erastus nodded gravely.

The central chamber of the halls was a rectangle of white marble amidst the smoke and bleak stone of the surrounding districts. It gleamed with the pure light of lumens, and runnels of burning oil ran along the edges of it. The fragrant oils were sweet as they burned, surrounding everything in an almost floral aroma. Like soft meadows, or the Alessian Fields of ancient myth. At its heart, shrouded in white atop the bier, lay his father. Mortuary acolytes had prepared him, their blade- and needle-tipped fingers incising and re-forming. Even hidden, he seemed sculpted. Complete. A statue of a man, rendered flawless, hidden in preparation for viewing.

Dead, his father had become far more of a symbol than he had been in life. A colossus, casting his own deep shadow across lives and decades.

The leaders of each dynasty stepped forward, going down on one knee before the body. Erastus was at the head of their small gathering, head bowed. A grey-robed priest had stepped forward, beginning to pontificate about the worth of a human soul in the Emperor's service. The man swung a silver mace up, gesticulating wildly into the crowd. There were tears in his rheumy eyes, and his white beard was flecked with spittle as he raved.

'Here there lies a great man, a king of men! And yet, as nothing in the sight of the Emperor! His service has been mighty, yes! His deeds were worthy of song, but he was yet a man.'

Around the edges of the sanctum, a choir of mournful voices began to sing. Black-robed mourners pushed in from the fringe, through the knots of muted colour, wailing and tearing at their hair. The priest held out his hand.

'Behold the grief, that a champion no longer strides forth in the Emperor's name!'

Erastus kept his head low as the sermon continued, biting back his retorts. A great man? Certainly. One of deed and note. And yet a distant, cruel, excoriating father. A ruin, coiled inexorably around Erastus' life, hemming in his own ambitions while nurturing the spires of Evelyne's. He closed his eyes, blocking out the assault of the morbid spectacle. The priest's words were ringing in his ears, each word as percussive as a gunshot.

He let himself sink into his emotions. Let his sorrow and his rage and his disillusion drown him.

He knelt, silent and contemplative, until the others had begun to disperse. Erastus felt cold metal tap the side of his head, and looked up, opening his eyes. The priest's mace was pressed to his temple, gently drawing his gaze up.

'This cannot be easy for you, Lord Lamertine,' Confessor Silas Cartus said solemnly. 'It pains me to see you so, and to have to commend your lord father so soon to the Emperor's care.'

'He would appreciate that,' Erastus said. He looked down again. 'He was ever the good and faithful servant.'

'As you must be,' Silas said as he smiled. 'The Emperor is with you, even in this time of darkness. Your life collapses around you, you feel? The galaxy burns, end to end. But He is with us! In every action we undertake.' His eyes were wide, burning with zeal. 'You have much ahead of you, but I can see that you have doubt.'

'I do,' Erastus said, and he was surprised to find himself admitting it. 'This was never what I was prepared for. It was never my destiny.'

'It was not the destiny that men would shape for you.' Silas spoke the words softly, in stark contrast to his martial religiosity. He drew back the silver mace, and Erastus stood to look the older man in the eye. This was a man who had marched to war and been the inspiration to millions, before ever he had found his way to the Cradle and the service of the Compact. 'It is His will. The wish of the God-Emperor is that you serve through leadership.'

In an undertaking as massive as the Imperium, there were tides and eddies. Sumps and sinkholes where the myriad detritus of man inevitably settled. Individuals were tithed from astropathic conclaves and Navigator houses, or they came by the vagaries of war. From the Astra Militarum, from void clans and mercenary combines, they all inevitably found their way into the hands of opportunists such as rogue traders. Silas had been a soldier, one amongst thousands that constituted the private armies with which men such as Erastus' father – and now Erastus himself – waged war and sought profit in the Emperor's name. Beyond that, he was a man of the Compact. Not a well-drilled Lamertine, or a war-chanting Helvintr, or one of the Radrexxus dandies. He served the Cradle, which had become his world. In faith. In war. It would make little difference. He would serve whomever his king was, with iron determination and advice.

'I understand,' Erastus said. He was surprised to find that he did. 'It is not a matter of my father's failing, or my lack. What has happened… It has been ordained? Made ready by the hand of the Emperor Himself?'

'Does His son not bestride the stars, as a colossus?' Silas asked. 'All sons are echoes of their fathers, reflections, be they true or distorted.' His voice had fallen to a whisper. 'Simply because you are not the same man as your father, does not mean that you have failed. Great things may yet spring forth from divergence.'

'You truly believe that?'

'Nine were the Great Primarchs, set amongst the firmament to hold against damnation. As one returns, so might others.' Silas allowed himself a smile. 'Had the Emperor wished for all things to be of one character, then would His sons not have been the same?'

'I'll admit,' Erastus said with a faint laugh, 'that I never considered it that way.'

'Few who live in the moment do.' Silas chuckled. 'You have ever been the edge of the blade, as surely as your father. You merely cut in a different manner.'

He gestured with his mace again, and Erastus' eyes followed it. The intricate, almost biological carving of it, the flowing lines of silver, and the faint stub of the displacement field activation rune along its haft. It was beautiful in the way only a weapon could be.

'We are all implements in the armoury of the divine. You ought to remember that, as you carry your own varied tools into the void.'

'Thank you, confessor,' Erastus said. 'Your words were ever a comfort to my father, I did not doubt that they would be a salve for me.'

'It is the duty of the Ecclesiarchy to speak truth to power,' Silas said with a grin. 'For all temporal power and authority is fleeting, next to His power. It is the Emperor's glory that turns the galaxy. Even broken, it is by His will that the stars yet burn amidst the firmament.'

'And all I do,' Erastus breathed, 'shall be to serve His will, and the designs of His son.' He looked past Silas at the shrouded form, and walked to it. He laid his hand upon the cold marble, unable to look away from the pure white of the covered body. This would be the last time he would look upon his father, before he was interred. Replaced by some gleaming, sculpted simulacrum, Davos Lamertine would join the honoured royalty of generations past; of his own line and all those who had served and led the Compact. And for Erastus, as his father had died, so too had the past he represented, and any choice in Erastus' own future. There was only one course left to him.

'There is one more thing,' Silas said softly. Hooded acolytes came to his side, one of them holding a shrouded bundle. Erastus looked from it to Silas, and the man nodded. They drew back the covering, and Erastus found himself staring into the pale marble eyes of his father's death mask. It bore a neutral expression, an almost placid look that Erastus had rarely seen his father wear in life.

He looked back up at Silas, and sighed. He turned to the acolytes. 'Have it brought to my chambers, upon the *Soul*.'

They wound the cloth back around the bust, and then left the chamber without a word.

Erastus turned, and nodded to Silas. The man clapped his hands, and the bier began to slowly grind its way into its waiting alcove. From somewhere above, a choir began to sing again. That mournful elegy of loss, until death and the Emperor's light brought them together again.

'Goodbye, Father,' Erastus said. 'Perhaps in this, in completing your last act, I will bring some honour that you would approve of.'

Chapter Thirteen

At the Edge of Eternity

It seemed as though every available hand had flooded the great docking spurs of the Cradle. Everything was in motion, relentless with the enthusiasm of a bursting dam, the ceaseless urgency of an insect hive. Servitor-controlled cranes swung low across the massive gantries, dropping their heaving pallets of materiel before arcing back across the gulf. Sparks flew from hasty repairs, staining the air with harsh electric flares that lingered behind the eyelids.

Erastus watched it all with a bemused detachment. He had seen it all before, but rarely on this scale. His own forays out amidst the stars had involved monumental movements of men and resources, but to see the dynasties pulling in one direction, for the same purpose... It was impressive, certainly, but he could not truly immerse himself in it.

Embarking and disembarking are their own form of warfare. A flood of spies, a sea of hidden enemies. Be on your guard.

The sting of his father's wisdom still had the power to colour everything, to render every interaction as a military engagement. Lessons beaten into him, as though his skin had been parchment. From oceans of acrimony and disrespect, there had been pearls of knowledge dredged up into the light.

He had been right, too. It was that thought which kept Erastus on edge, poised and waiting for the next blow to strike. He turned from the docks and their incessant industry, focusing instead on the data-slate clutched in his hand. As facts and figures, the mobilisation took a keener shape. Order, compared to the chaos that raged beyond.

'Reports from the other dynasties suggest that we are proceeding on schedule, Lord Lamertine.' Tomas' voice was chipper, one of many who seemed exorcised of their grief following the funeral. Whether it was a professional courtesy or he had moved on already, Erastus could not tell. He returned the man's smile as he placed the slate down on the nearby table.

'So it would appear, Tomas,' he said – not quite as brightly. 'I'm sure my father would be proud that standards haven't slipped.'

Tomas' smile became fixed, and he simply nodded. 'Will that be all, lord?'

'It will, thank you,' Erastus said. Tomas bowed, and then scuttled off to attend to one of the countless other matters the preparations required. Erastus let him go, and began the long walk down towards the docks proper.

The spurs were threaded with passageways, warrens through which the crew could move freely from the body of the station down to the ships – and from there, from ship to ship. The ramp was solid beneath his feet, but the movement of so many sent great convulsions through it. The entire station seemed to vibrate with every step. The footfalls of giants.

Ship and station life had its own routine, the enforced

necessity that separated day cycle into night cycle. Everything in such a life was artificial: recycled, processed, generated and ordered in ways to preserve human life – if not human sanity. It was not an easy life, and many faltered at the first obstacles. Rogue traders, though, had a duty to thrive. For some, that meant regular sojourns to true-worlds, and for others it had meant changing. Slowly, down through the generations, becoming truly voidborn. Adaptation, generating aversion from some and acceptance from others. Bloodlines becoming almost speciation, till they were fundamentally distinct. Something human, yet other, in the way Erastus sometimes thought of Navigators.

'All that we are and all that we have,' he mused, 'began as something else.'

He walked on, along the great support berth which extended beside the immense vessel he was expected to captain. The *Indomitable Soul* was mighty: three miles of pale blue adamantine, its keel laid down by the Jovian Void Clans at the Imperium's birth. It had served Davos Lamertine as flagship since the opening of the Great Rift, and the loss of his daughter amidst the roiling stars. Others might have thought the grief his father had carried had been for their true treasure, the vast warship that had once been the heart of their power – the *Untempered Wrath*, the vessel which Evelyne had been abroad upon – but Erastus could not believe it.

His father had loved Evelyne, with the entirety of his rare mortal passion. She was to be the hope and the glory of their house in the decades ahead, when age and death finally caught up with the lord militant.

'Not quite how you expected it, I imagine,' Erastus said. His voice was low as he spoke to himself and reached out his hand, as though he could close the distance and touch the caged fury of the ship. Never before had he commanded a vessel such as this. No vessel had borne within its heart such history of will and rage. No matter if he lived for a thousand years, he would never again know a power as terrifyingly vast as the spirit of one of his family's two bound vessels.

Gangways and boarding platforms swarmed the hull, finding whatever fitful berths they could manage in order to take on or disgorge their cargo. They swung wide and away from the *Indomitable Soul*, or drew back with something approaching reverence. Erastus' guards pushed past the braying armsmen and the urgent press of dockers, until he finally came to the silver-edged crossing that served the bridge crew and senior staff. He paused, taking hold of the railing, gazing up at the looming power of the vessel. Lesser men would wither in its shadow, cowed for a lifetime like the milling supplicants who tended to its needs. For men forged for greater things, there was only one course. One possibility. One inevitability.

Erastus Lamertine stepped forward onto the ship.

The corridors of the *Soul* were not the winding veins of the Cradle. They were straight and orderly and clean. The walls were unadorned, ungilded, as though the pretence of wealth and status was offensive to the reality of it. Plain wood, steel and stone vied with arches of vitrified glass, black and near volcanic. It glimmered darkly in the lume-light, casting strange shadows and refractions. To walk and work the ship was to proceed as through a dream, or a story. A reflection of past glory, and future promise.

As Erastus progressed into the higher reaches of the ship, the number of crew he passed dwindled. They were squirrelled away in alcoves, working with the fierce diligence common to their caste. Tech-priests seemed to ooze from the shadows, their mechadendrites frantic as they communed with the ship's ancient systems. Tiny aspergil appendages flicked, anointing the panels with sacred unguents. They bowed low, like grounds-keepers suddenly confronted by the lord of their fief. He passed them with a nod. Here even the affectations of terrestrial habitation, the wood and stone of a spartan temple or barracks, were reduced to clean utilitarian metal.

He passed under an archway of embedded skulls, their eyes glinting with surveillance optics, and into the tranquil storm at the heart of the ship.

The bridge was ovoid, tiers of cogitator banks and control consoles winding downwards towards the command throne. Information streamed across screens in oily lines of burning green text, or hovered in hololithic projections. In the higher tiers were crewmen forever wired into the systems of the ship, parsing massed data-inloads and noospheric communions as though it were an act of devotion, or penance. There was a constant charge in the air, the electricity and the industry as the ship readied; a pulse in the metal as the engines wound up, the thrum of engaging reactors. Even here, in the armoured command bridge, he could feel it: a power so all-encompassing that even the most well defended of sanctums was rendered exposed.

Where other ships would brazenly show their bridges to the enemy, with massive viewports to better glare their defiance at the universe, the *Soul* was of a different humour. It was bellicose and furious, of that there could be no doubt, but it was immune to what his father had termed *the bold folly of others*. Erastus paced through the centre of the space, and no eyes followed him. They were focused on their tasks, professional in such a driven and single-minded fashion that his father had undoubtedly punished any laxity. Perhaps one of the servitors edging their way around the command deck had been an early example of the price of mediocrity.

Erastus traced a hand along the back of the throne, fingers teasing over the graven scrollwork and lions rampant. Down along the arms, the metal carved and folded till it resembled the great wings of an eagle, rows of buttons and dials set into the feathers like glittering jewels. He walked around it, examining every aspect of it, letting his eyes drift across what he had never thought to possess. A command his father would never have relinquished to him.

'My lord?'

He turned at the voice, and came face to face with the pallid features of Egeria Vas Kastebor, Navigator Primus of the Lamertine Dynasty. She was swathed in pale blue robes, the voluminous hood and cerebral bindings making her seem shrunken, paler, though there was no doubting her strength. She stood tall, straight-backed, radiating defiance. She was no stranger to the trappings of power, or the necessities bred by a place such as this. Even so, the words were strange on her lips. She had not thought to address anyone but Davos in such a way for many years.

'I have examined the charts provided by yourself and the Radrexxus Navigators,' she said with a slight curl of her lip. 'They are satisfactory. The course to Endymica should, Throne-willing, be free of aberrant astropsykana.'

'Thank you, Egeria. Once you are safely ensconced, we can begin.' He tilted his head as he contemplated her reactions. 'You do not approve of their Navigators?'

She shook her head. 'My lord, I have communed with Lady Euryale, of the...' Egeria paused, as though struggling to voice the word. 'The *noble* House Tarescos.' She shuddered. 'The curs sworn to Radrexxus... They are a house of low birth and ill repute, rumour-shrouded beggars. Their strength is without question, and the lord admiral's patronage has done them well... but they cleave to the rites and rituals of their destitution. Such privation breeds low cunning in men, and in our houses... it invites the judgement of our kith and kin.' She bowed, and shuffled backwards, turning to head to her hallowed observation bubble. Her sanctum.

He nodded and sat, almost without considering the import of his actions. There was a clatter of metal as a crew serf began to toll a ponderous bell.

'Captain at the helm!' The serf, a mere boy, cried out into the storm of activity and all fell silent. They bowed their heads or went to their knees, offering fealty as their ancestors had once sworn. 'May they who sit the thrones be as Him upon the Golden Throne of Terra.' Some drew weapons, ringing them against their breastplates or hammering the hafts of halberds against the decking. Erastus watched, momentarily awestruck, before he raised his hand.

'You, all of you, have my thanks.' He lowered his hand and let his gaze drift through their ranks. He was untested, he knew. Few of them would have had the opportunity or the inclination to ride out with him on minor trade disputes. Now he led them out into the fire and madness of the broken void. They would have followed Davos. He knew that. None would have raised a voice against him. Not from fear, but from respect. Out of love, perhaps.

Erastus did not see fear in their eyes. He saw distrust, and that cut deeper.

'We are bound upon a grand expedition. Not merely us, but all who have come to pledge themselves anew to the Compact.' His fingers tightened on the arms of his throne, white against steel. 'We will honour the primarch's call, and in turn shall reap rewards such as we have never known. The power and prestige of my office pales before this.'

He raised his hands, spreading them to encompass the entire bridge.

'We go forth from here, into legend.'

The combat bridge of the *Wyrmslayer Queen* could not have been more different from that of the *Indomitable Soul*. Everything was hewn from cold iron and driftwood, in imitation of a jarl's long-house or great hall. Firelight caught on the rough surfaces and harsh edges, flames trapped in reflection like bottled lightning. Runes glowed, even this far from the heat. Dull muted red, harsh electric blue. They ran with witch-light, snagging on the shields which lay across the ceiling, and the spears which braced them.

Katla Helvintr let the signs burn as she lounged in the throne, her eyes following them as they smouldered. She looked out of the great viewports, her twisted visage utterly at peace while a small army of her men readied the ship for sail. Her bridge crew, and her bodyguard – her huscarls, all trusted men and women – filtered into the chamber piecemeal.

All stopped to honour the *gothi*, Bodil, before taking their places. She was old – ancient in a way that the Idunni rejuve-nat had spared Katla. The old woman drew marks of aversion across the cheeks of some, smearing them there with soot and spit. For others she cast bone runes from a leather bag tied at her bird-like wrist. She dispensed fortunes and fates with a flash of crooked teeth, sending crew off to their posts with smiles or frowns locked upon their faces. Such was the way of fate; the weft of men's *wyrd* could only be borne – rarely changed.

Some of the crew made oaths on their arm rings, or cast them before the throne as a token of fidelity. Others laid down weapons, fine swords and spears and axes, as tribute. They were offerings and promises, and she savoured each one, thanking those who offered gifts with a simple nod. She would remember, though. She always remembered those who were owed.

'Almost ready, Mother,' Astrid called from somewhere behind her. She was eager, as they all were. Katla regarded her daughter with a fierce pride. She had risen to every challenge set before her, and proven worthy of the trust Katla had placed in her.

'Excellent. All is well?'

'All is as it should be,' Astrid said, nodding. 'The boy king will soon give the signal. The Radrexxus are keeping to themselves, and the Norastye have completed their fleet maintenance. Their iron priests have roamed far and wide, and given their blessings.'

'Not on the *Queen* they haven't,' Katla growled. 'Nor on any of the other ships of quality, I'll warrant. False aid is a blade at every back, even with oaths of safe harbour and shared hearth. The boy king's oaths will only hold the worst angels of men's nature for so long.' She shook her head and leaned forward, hunched over. The furs draping the throne shifted as she moved, rings clattering against its arms. Tokens were strung to it, haphazardly. Coins on silvered chains, etched with the images of wolves, oaths to the hearthworld and remembrances of the slain. Her hand slipped through the furs to close around the reassuring weight of a hand-axe. The jarl of the Helvintrs, the Huntress Queen, was never far from a weapon.

She smiled her split grin, and the wolf smiled with her. It seemed sometimes to be less a decoration or affectation, and more an aspect of her true self, gazing out from its cage of flesh and circumstance. To hunt the stars was to embrace that, and to accept that the beast within was as much a part of her as the art on her skin which glorified it.

'We are ever the hunter,' she whispered to herself. 'Never the prey. That is our creed.' Astrid gave her a strange look, but Katla ignored it. She was looking out, past the growing din of her crew – the war cries and the prayers for safe passage and stable harbour – and back out into the abyss.

The hunt awaited. Even within such a seemingly routine duty as this. She could taste it. The void was waiting, hungry and expectant, in all its wonder and horror.

Faint mists drifted through the wards of the bridge, meandering like the soft floral perfume of a well-cultivated garden. It was not a soporific infusion, nothing to dull or mislead the mind. Instead it was a focus enhancer, a delectable neuro-stimulant known as *Prime*. It had a way of coiling into the forebrain, sliding through the questing mammalian mind, until it reached the base echelons of the human animal. Reptilian drives rose and fell, like the parade of empires through mortal history.

Gunther Radrexxus leant into it, embraced it like a lover or an old friend, and let it flood him. He knew many thought him an addict, a broken thing, and he let them maintain their illusions. Better to play the innocent or the incompetent, than to show your teeth too early. That was what the Lamertines and their adventurism betrayed, and what the huntresses could never understand. There was a power in patience.

'Beautiful, isn't it, Maximillian?' Gunther breathed the question, pacing through the chemical haze with crystal clarity. 'To stand on the edge of greatness, at the very precipice of the abyss. There is, I hold, nothing finer in all creation. It has been made so, ordained, one might say.'

'Quite, my lord,' Maximillian offered. Compared to his master, he was sullen and reserved. The black synthleather bodyglove was free of the extravagance which typified high-ranking Radrexxus representatives. Everything superfluous had been pared away till only the essence remained. Lethal and polished, like an antique blade. Another weapon in his master's arsenal – for that was all his life had been shaped for. Duty. Service. Death.

'Sometimes,' Gunther said, 'it seems to me as though you have no soul. No enjoyment!'

'That may be so, my lord,' Maximillian replied. He drew his blade, a heavy serrated weapon, turning it in the air, assessing it. 'I am not entirely sure that your more visceral passions were included in my make-up.'

'We each have our roles to play,' Gunther said with a grin. 'You were ever the blade, and I have the honour of being the noble face of our enterprise.' He drummed his fingers along the gold-filigreed back of the throne, tracing the images of writhing serpents, intricate masks and rearing flames. 'You lack even the most basic diplomacy, my friend.'

'That is indeed so,' Maximillian said and shrugged gently. 'I can only apologise, my lord. Though, if you would allow, I might say that my martial capabilities more than accommodate for the lack.'

'They most assuredly do.' Gunther turned about and sat in the throne with a sigh of responding systems. The bridge crew worked in perfect silence, perfect unity. Hands clattered over keys or adjusted the correct levers. The low hum of machinery rose, peaked, and then fell back again like the rhythm of a heart. 'We are in the belly of the beast now, my fellows. Greatness lies ahead of us, make no mistake.' He depressed a button on the arm of his throne. 'Euryale?'

'*The light comes, the whispering song. It shines, it sings. Oh, my lord, I can see it.*' Her voice was a sudden rasp as the vox-conduit to her Navigator's sanctum went live.

'The path is charted? The omens are clear?'

'*Voidsong and voidlight, most noble lord. It calls across the abyss.*

I see, I see, I–' Her breathing shifted, a thready, drawn-out rattle. *'The* Lustful Paradox *shall sail true, and we shall be embraced. Held close to the divine.'*

'Excellent.' He nodded as though her babble were the most sensible utterance he had ever heard. 'You bear the sight, my dear. You are whom I trust most to guide us safely to journey's end, and the glories that await.' He steepled his fingers under his chin and leaned back. All the mirth bled from him as he closed his eyes, meditating on what lay before them. The path which stretched from Davamir to Endymica. The potential inherent in every step.

When he opened his eyes again, his smile was cold. Utterly without warmth or joy.

'Ours shall be the glory.'

The Lord Technologist entertained no throne. He stood in the centre of the bridge-space. The cogitator-orrery turned about him, filling the space with heat, light and the ratcheting sound of servos and gears. Great spheres of metal spun, each one broadcasting its own noospheric cadence.

Absalom Norastye raised his hands, drinking in the information. Rings and bracelets glimmered with binharic uplink, and the collar about his neck chimed as it whispered in translation. He was not truly of the Adeptus Mechanicus, but their patronage had afforded him much in the way of understanding. Adepts flocked around the bridge, tending to essential systems – trailed by flocks of servo-skulls and frolicking cherubs. They clung to the spheres as they rotated, as they cast forth their song, and joined their chittering chorus with it.

'Is all prepared?' he asked, and one of the adepts bowed low, mechadendrites sniffing the air like questing serpents.

<All is well, Lord Technologist,> the adept, Roteus-Gamma

canted. <The preparations throughout the fleet have reached optimum levels.>

'Most satisfactory,' Absalom allowed. He drew his steel hands up, like a sorcerer invoking the unnatural. The spheres halted, data pulsing with momentary urgency, before they continued on. 'At last, we are ready.'

Every bay and berth of the station shuddered, trembling with captive thunder as reactors were kindled and engines ignited. Great plumes of plasma cut through the blackness, picking out the rearing gothic details of the Cradle. At the height of a fleet's arrival or sojourn, the entire structure was set aglow, burning with the import and weight of history. It glittered like a castle of old marble in the first light of a rising sun – a frozen droplet of blood caught in the airless void.

At Erastus' command, and as was his right, the *Indomitable Soul* took the lead, with its train of attendant vessels following closely in its wake. Supply ships, barrack-vessels and war-haulers trailed like camp followers behind an army. They bristled with weaponry, openly and subtly, as befitted warships of the Imperium of Man. At the head of these support vessels, blustering like bodyguards, came two cruisers. The *Vindication of Terra* and the *Throne's Justice* were killers, though they paled before the murderer's grace of the *Soul*. Erastus watched their delicate dance upon the auspex and in the weave of hololithic light that shone through the heart of the bridge.

The *Wyrmslayer Queen* cut her hunter's arc across the system, peeling away from the Cradle with a pack of hunting ships at her side. Self-contained armouries teemed across the vessels of the Helvintr fleet. Anvils rang in song, and the tanneries were given over to the crafting of arms and armour. The warriors of Katla's dynasty gave their voices to the industry, as they raised their own song of Fenris: of the ice and fire eternal, and the rise and fall of tribes. They sang of the Emperor's halls, where the brave might live forever at the side of Russ, and of the halls their ancestors had been called to generations before. The Halls of Helvintr, and the service of the long hunt.

The Radrexxus and the Norastye fleets, true to their dynasties' natures, were leisurely and logical in equal measure. Victualler ships and supply hulks followed the sleek progress of the *Lustful Paradox*, a gaudy blade next to the intricate weapons of the Lamertines or Helvintrs. Radrexxus had even thought to bring a menagerie ship, a glass-and-gilt bauble called the *Fickle Vault*. The Norastye ships, slab-sided forge vessels and munitions barges, kept their distance from the Radrexxus – as though fearing moral contamination. They deployed in orderly formation, precise and mathematical. There was a beauty to it, a calculated grace. The *Steel Amidst Infirmity* was a hulking shadow of lost technology, yet it danced amidst the permutations of its fleet with a composer's whimsy.

The vessels wound their own way out from the station, their slow thrust gradually accelerating as they drew out and into the system. Their paths were set to collide again in the outer system, at the Mandeville point, where warp travel was possible – free from the gravitational influence of Davamir's bloated star.

The ships did not look back and neither did Erastus. Every augury and auspex was locked ahead in preparation for eventual transit. Past the outer planets, the lone gas giant and its small icy attendants, signals stopped passing between the Cradle and the fleet elements, becoming instead a coiled nest of internal communion, centred around the *Indomitable Soul*.

On the crenellated backs of long-dead ships, along the vast battlements that formed the Cradle, the first horns began to ring out as the lords and masters of Davamir readied themselves to

leave the system and begin their long journey into the treacherous void.

ACT II

INTO THAT SILENT SEA

ACT II

'The rights and responsibilities of the entities who would eventually become known by the sobriquet of rogue traders were established in the fires and martial excesses of the Great Crusade. In that era they were as pathfinders and loyal allies to the established expeditionary fleets. Members of that complex fellowship were peers to lords-general of the Imperial Army, admirals of the Fleet, and were counted amongst the confidants of the primarchs themselves.

Cast, by design or circumstance, before the advance of the crusade fleets, they were expected – and indeed, empowered – to act and survive beyond their means. By force of arms, will and the power entrusted to them by the Warrants of Trade, they were deemed able to commandeer whichever support was required. It was by His will that they were sent forth so. Illuminators to the loyal, and stormcrows of ill omen for those who stood in opposition.

Thus, in circumstances considered in extremis, those who bore the sacred Warrants of Trade were permitted to take what they desired, as though it were by the Emperor's own hand. Terrible were the sanctions they could deliver against those who would oppose them.'

– Histories and Considerations Regarding the
Duties of the Bodies Politick of the Imperium,
attributed to Senior Scribe
Principus Yrkalla Homadryn

Chapter Fourteen

The Soul's Voyage

It did not do to think of the warp as an old friend, and yet it was a necessity that starfarers became accustomed to it. This was the great contradiction which had haunted mankind in every questing journey from its birthworld. That the reliable method of traversing the stars was to dive into a sea of poison. Of damnation. No matter how familiar it became, it was always *other*. One did not break bread in hell.

Erastus had tried not to think of it, but the thought haunted him. He had made many previous warp transits, all without incident. He had never been victim to a Geller field collapse, or any form of lesser reality desynchronisation. Throne willing he never would be. Days had passed into weeks, and weeks into months. Still without incident. He had watched from the bridge as his crew fell into well-drilled routines beneath the ever-shifting lumens, the simulated day and night cycle which continued to underpin their lives. Often, as now, he had taken to running laps of the ship's corridors. First it had been in the company of the dynasty's troops, and now it was frequently alone.

The corridors rang with his footfalls, the sound carrying through the vast body of the *Soul*, to sing throughout its hallways. He was alone. As alone as he could be in a construct as immense as a starship. His fatigues clung to him, damp with sweat. He reached out and braced himself on the cold wall of the passageway, trying to catch his breath. He closed his eyes. Waited. Braced.

The first of the attacks swung from around a corner with a sudden scream, lashing out with a clenched fist.

Erastus parried, batting the punch to one side as he moved into the assailant's guard. He drove his own fist into the attacker's side, feeling the resistance of tensed muscle and armour padding. He gritted his teeth, turning and slamming his elbow into their stomach even as another set of arms wrapped around his neck.

He swivelled and kicked out, bracing his leg against the wall as he smashed his second attacker into the wall behind. He brought his foot down, braced, and hunched forward. He grabbed his assailant's arm as he did, and heaved their weight over his body. They tumbled, hitting the ground with a yelp muffled by their combat helm. Two more of their number bled into the corridor, a sudden presence that he turned to confront.

Erastus saw the silver flash of the blade as it arced for his stomach. He felt pain spiral through him as it clipped his side. He snarled, aiming his next blow squarely for the knifeman's throat. There was a crunch, and a wet choking sound as they doubled over. Erastus drew back his knee and thrust it into the assassin's faceplate. The lenses shattered in a flood of crimson glass tears. He allowed himself a grin, as he spun round to face the last attacker–

And found himself face to face with the snub barrel of a stubber.

'Epsilon?' the faceless helm asked, tilting slightly as it advanced. The gun did not move, or waver.

'Epsilon,' Erastus allowed. The assassin pressed a button on their vambrace, and the distant sound of an alarm went out. Erastus let himself sag. 'That was better, though,' he said. 'Wasn't it?'

'It sufficed,' they said as they reached up and unhooked their helm. Captain Zofia Taravel smiled coldly. Her features were pinched and pale, in contrast with her clipped dark hair. She, as captain of the Lamertine Shipguard, had taken a personal hand in Erastus' training – ensuring both that he was protected throughout the transit, and that he was able to defend himself should they be absent. The rudiments of sabre and shot had gradually evolved into these surprise ambushes during his physical training.

Erastus knelt, scooping up the fallen knife and examining its keen edge. He could still see where the blood lay along its blade, putting him in mind of his father's transfixed corpse.

'You're getting bolder,' he said. 'Not that I'm complaining, of course.'

'Of course,' Zofia said with a smirk, as she reached out and grabbed the hilt of the blade. She tugged it from his grasp, like a parent disarming a child – an indulgent gesture that brought a raised eyebrow from Erastus.

'You still don't trust me? As a king and as a warrior?'

'I prefer to err on the side of caution, my lord,' she said simply. 'Evelyne, I could trust – but even then, only after the passage of years. Old familiarity. You would have the same rapport, the same synchronicity, with any of your tutors. You ran with diplomatic envoys and trade moguls. She ran with former generals and storm troops.' She shrugged. 'Different tools for different jobs. Sometimes you need a blade, sometimes you need a melta.'

Erastus furrowed his brow. 'And… which am I?'

She laughed and shook her head as she watched him. 'I'm not quite sure what you are yet, Erastus. What matters is that we make sure you can do some sort of damage.'

He leant back against the wall. 'I'm not an idiot, Zofia,' he sighed. 'I know that the odds are against us. My father was murdered, in our own place of power. In his guarded sanctum. That bodes ill. At best it is a vendetta against the Compact, and at worst it's a personal attack on our family. Take out my father, and they think we'll be easy pickings. Especially with Ev dead and gone.' He shook his head. 'No heir, no leadership, and then they take us apart piecemeal. But who stands to gain?'

'Any one of your rivals within the Compact,' she said bluntly.

'I was thinking in broader terms,' he said. 'It could be anyone. Another dynasty who didn't answer the summons. One of my father's many rivals. System warlords, or trade cartels? The Church, perhaps, if the involvement of the Astraneus is anything to go by.'

Zofia scoffed, and Erastus looked at her questioningly.

'Those hidebound fanatics? You can't honestly consider them as your prime suspects?' she asked, shaking her head. 'They're capable voidsmen, but theirs isn't the way of the hidden blade. I can't see it being them.'

'I have my doubts, I admit,' he said with a sigh. 'But until we know more, we have to maintain an open mind. If nothing else comes to light then I plan to send missives of summons once the journey is over. Have them attend me at Endymica, and plead their case. Perhaps I will be lenient, but in time, I pray, it will deliver the truth to us.'

'As you will,' she said and bowed her head. 'I take it we're doing this again tomorrow?'

Erastus nodded. 'Same routine as before.'

'Until then, my lord.' She turned on her heel and walked off into the corridors, her fellow guards following close behind. He touched his fingers to his wound, wincing as he did so. It was shallow, and had mostly stopped bleeding.

He gingerly stretched, and then began his steady progress through the ship again.

It was ill luck and foolishness to gaze, unshielded, into the warp. Mortal minds were not equipped for such sights, and the risks it carried could scar the very soul. Vast shutters were lowered at immaterial transit, to protect the crew from the roiling seas of madness.

Egeria had no such luxury.

The Navigator mutation existed for this purpose alone, to parse the tides of insanity and find the paths through the fire. She had been bred for this, and trained to the exacting standards of House Vas Kastebor.

'It is one thing to see with the eye, child. You must train yourself to see with your very being.' Her father, Gaius Remus Vas Kastebor, had been an exacting instructor. She remembered every lesson – delivered in his monotonous rattle, and reinforced by sharp raps from an instructive cudgel. Their spire upon Vandium had been a cruel and sterile cradle, where they lived and served at his increasingly erratic whim.

Egeria rarely thought of home. Only in the moment, in the worst of warp eddies, did her thoughts guide her back to the warren-world of her inception. The dark and winding tunnels and atmos-cages which had linked each spire to its kindred – all the way to the heights of her house's ocularum. There had been beauty there, and happiness for a time. She had enjoyed the company of her siblings, and the attentions of the house serfs. She had been kind, then.

Life, as ever, had had other plans. Her father's spiral into madness had intensified, till all that remained was to lock him away like a filthy secret. She had been far down the line of succession: the sixth child, and second daughter besides. It was to men such as her brother Maximus, or even Petrus, to rule. She would serve, as was her duty, and one day contribute to the genetic tapestry of some other house.

She sighed despite herself, and the chamber shifted in sympathy as though anticipating her needs. She would have fluttered a hand at it, had they not been locked to the arms of her throne, white-knuckled with the interpretation of the ship's passage.

She felt it, and she cursed that her father had been right. She felt it with her entire being. Every moment within the sea of souls was a low burr of agony, crawling along her spine as the immaterium tested the Geller fields, again and again. The relentless attempts at erosion, the way that the ocean ate away at the shore... It might take a thousand years, but inevitably it would creep in.

And a thousand years was the most optimistic of estimates.

Their course was a reasonably stable one. Endymica had been a fortress-world for a reason, set at a confluence of active warp routes whose use extended all the way back to pre-Strife epochs. The journey should, Throne-willing, only become perilous as they drew nearer to the new boundary which had infected the Imperium. The wall of fire and death and screaming which the mind-blinded called the Great Rift.

She shook her head, and the chamber shuddered again. Her eyes were fixed forward, as chaos resolved into patterns, and the ways ahead became clear.

The Great Rift. How short the term fell. As though it were a mere chasm to be leapt in a single bound, and not a devourer of the very spirit.

She looked away, her eyes seeking the golden light of the Astronomican and the calm it cut through the squalls. Even now, forty years into her service aboard ships, it never failed to bring a tear to her eye. It had been gone, not too long ago. The Days of Blindness had been a physical pain for her, for all who bore the warp-sight. It was like losing the sun. The thought of drawing too near to what had facilitated it made her worry.

'I will not fail you,' she whispered to herself in the gently shaking silence of her sanctum. 'I shall see us through the storms.'

Chapter Fifteen

The Treachery of Steel

The passage had been uneventful thus far, and there was debate as to whether this was a good sign or an ill omen. Erastus considered it as he sat in the command throne, bolt upright with his back firmly against it. He knew there were many amongst the crew who expected the worst of him – that the entire Lamertine enterprise might crumble around his ears, while he did little more than squander his advantage and impugn his family name. They thought him some hedonist, like one of Gunther's acolytes. A man of charm who weaselled and cajoled where Davos would have taken by might. He had, in his time, shared fine amasec and finer meals with those he sought accords with, but he was no sybarite.

The thought would have made him laugh in better times, but now only brought a cold certainty of purpose. He would not sprawl, or slouch, or prove their slander true.

He would not be found wanting.

'Status?' he asked, turning to regard his bridge crew with what he hoped was a withering gaze. His Master of Auspex, a younger man named Kaddas, looked up, drew a deep breath, and began to speak – eyes now resolutely fixed upon the floor.

'All proceeds apace, my lord. We have reports that we are advancing at speed, with the rest of the fleet easily maintaining parity of transit. It is hard to keep track of them through the immaterium, and harder still to communicate, but we believe that the other dynastic forces are also experiencing no issues.' He brought his fist up to his chest in a swift salute. 'Is there anything else, sir?'

'No, that will be all. Thank you.' Erastus drummed his fingers against the throne's arm and then pushed himself up. 'At current speed and heading we should arrive within two weeks. Better than our most hopeful estimates.' He grinned, extending a hand around the bridge. 'The Emperor favours our undertaking, wouldn't you agree?'

A weak chorus of affirmative responses rippled around the chamber.

'When we are able, commune with the other vessels and ensure that all is well. I don't want there to be any surprises when we break warp at Endymica.'

During active warp translation the *Wyrmslayer Queen* took on the vibrant odour of burning. Braziers leapt and crackled along the hallways, casting the corridors of iron and steel in the dull pall of woodsmoke. Servitors trundled from place to place, periodically refuelling the fires, like shambling fire giants from a child's hearth stories.

As much as it was a ship, as much as they were a fleet and a dynasty, they were also a jarl's hall. They were their culture, cast to the stellar winds.

Katla did not remember who amongst her ancestors had first

raised them up from the ice of Fenris, and carried their kinsmen to the stars. She had been back many times through her life. She and Astrid had stood beneath the storm-riddled skies, and watched the tumult of the seas. A calm had taken her, a peace she had only otherwise felt when the *Queen* sailed the void. In the service of the hunt.

She smiled as she paced the bridge.

Her father, Stian, had led the first hunt she had been permitted to take part in. He had been an able jarl, leading them out into the black with joy in his heart. She remembered the *Queen* shaking, rocked by the blows of some vast void-beast. Whipping tendrils, the great questing beak scraping against the hull. She had heard it, the monster's impossible scream ringing through the bones of the ship. The thrum of the macrocannon broadsides had cut through the machine's agony, and replaced it with the animal roar of wounded prey.

'They bite deep, and you must bite deeper.'

That had been their way. That was still her way.

She turned the haft of her spear over and over again in her grip as she stalked from point to point. Occasionally she stopped, to thrust or cut the air experimentally. Serfs and huscarls knew well enough to keep their distance. Her guards watched impassively from beneath the heavy brims of their helms.

'Where is the glory in this?' Astrid asked, from her gunnery station. Katla did not allow idleness upon her bridge, not even from kin. 'This is a listless undertaking. We advance merely to hold and reinforce a world? Even if it is a commandment from the hand of one of His own sons… it is beneath us, Mother.'

'Perhaps,' Katla said as she stabbed forward again. 'Perhaps we waste our time, chase tarnished glory. Or maybe I simply wish to stand before the Rift, that I might laugh in its face, hmm?' She chuckled.

'I...' Astrid sighed. 'Mother, I do not think you could go all that way and merely look, or laugh.' She watched her mother's swift, decisive motions. There was no doubting her warrior bearing, or her determination. 'You would stand at the edge of hell, only to throw yourself through the fire. Is that not right?'

'Let it never be said that you do not know me.'

'I spoke with Lord Lamertine, before we left the Cradle. I told you that, didn't I?'

'You have mentioned the boy king, yes,' Katla said with a savage smile. She brought the spear down to her side. 'Was it of use?'

'I think so. Perhaps it is too early in our hunt, and his reign, to know for sure.' Astrid toyed with a braid, a nervous habit. A child's comfort. 'He is ignorant of the games he has found himself caught within.'

'Oh, my child,' Katla laughed. 'Aren't we all?'

Absalom Norastye stood in the centre of the chamber, his arms in constant motion, caught in composition. He moved to music that others within his sphere of power did not hear, to steps of which they were unaware. Above him the spheres of the orrery moved in great sweeping arcs, trailing their gravitational wake of data. The surfaces crawled with information, like writhing lightning storms of knowledge. Noospheric bleed-off saturated the local datasphere, bruising it with ugly questing pulses. The cogitator orbs rotated, aligned, found conjunction. They swung from apogee to perigee, locked in their ascribed patterns.

<The optimal point of system saturation has passed, Lord Technologist.> Roteus-Gamma knelt before Absalom, head bowed, features lost in the shadows of his hood. <The techno-auguries advise that the immaterial vectors approach their peak. If you would act, if you would do this thing, then it should be now.>

'I am well aware of the operational parameters, adept.' His flesh-voice was steady. Untroubled. 'How many, I wonder, will consider this an act of treachery?' He paused. 'Our fellows and our rivals have all done much worse in the service of their ambition. There is no evil in business.' Absalom allowed himself a chuckle. 'Whatever else happens, we cannot turn our back on what has been set in motion.'

<My lord?>

'Do it,' Absalom said. Roteus-Gamma nodded, shuffled over to a console and pressed a number of buttons in quick succession.

Beyond, in the tides of the warp, something was born in fire and treachery.

Chapter Sixteen

Fury and Silence

A ship died in the first moments – rent apart by the impossible collision of the material and the immaterial. There was an explosion along its starboard flank, at the enginarium decks. For a second, the Geller fields blinked, and the tide of the warp finally attained its long-denied access. The ship had been called the *Wanton Embrace*, a lesser pleasure barque of the Radrexxus. Its amethyst hull peeled away beneath the fiery mouths of a million questing daemons, laughing as they gnawed the metal into strange and newborn shapes.

The crew might have screamed, in those impossible moments as instant became eternity. There may have been a chance for them to fight the tide of madness that boiled through every airlock, that flowed through the walls, that took flesh at its leisure. The intruders had waited and been denied for aeons of mortal understanding, and now relished their release.

The fragile bubble of reality burst. The floodgates of the

warp opened, swamping the ship in a boiling ocean of piti-less, yearning hate.

Others fared better, but only barely.

The death of the *Embrace* rippled through the non-void of the sea of souls. Its mortal crew's mayfly existences bled out into the abyss, sending shockwaves through the empyrean near-space. Screams, death rattles, the inchoate agonies of an entire vessel. Thousands upon thousands of lives and deaths and ends slammed against the Geller fields of the accompany-ing ships, even as the first explosions tore from their hulls. Crippled their engines. The *Lustful Paradox* quivered in some-thing like fear, like a living beast suddenly terrified. A grox facing down the armatures of the slaughterhouse. A tech-priest somewhere invoked a rite, and the ship slid from the warp in a rush of relief and adulation, even as others were forced from it by myriad equipment failures, power fluctuations and detonations.

The twinned hunting ships *Spear of Ice* and *Shield of Wolves* spun out of control, hurtling through clouds of conjured malice. Their fields burned against the tides of spite with a sound like the laughter of children, echoing through the corridors as they struggled to resist the daemonic. Both ships forced their break from the warp in the same moment, even as their escape sent the *Wyrmslayer Queen* into its own savage death spiral. The ship's superstructure screamed, it howled at the pressures placed upon it. Cracks broke out along its spinal battlements, venting men and air into the infinite.

The sleek huntress, wounded, undertook its own return to the materium.

A cascade of failures echoed across the fleet. Radrexxus. Helvintr. Both suffered and bled, as the warp took its price. Even this far from the Rift, there were aspects and intelligences which hungered. Which remembered uncounted slights at the hands of the human race, of rogue traders who had defied them, and the prices they expected to be paid. Some of them babbled these things as they sought to hew ships apart, or as they slammed themselves to fiery debris against the ailing Geller fields. They remembered, and they hated, and they hungered.

And that hunger rattled on. Against the shields of the *Vindication of Terra* and the *Throne's Justice* as their engines were rocked by explosions.

Till at last, with something approaching reverence, the calamity reached the pale blue hull and silvered bastions of the *Indomitable Soul*.

Chapter Seventeen

Exit Wounds

The ship shuddered, quaking with sudden savage jolts. Erastus pitched forward from his throne, palms out to catch himself as he hit the floor. Rivets dug into his skin and he cried out, rolling as he did. Everything pitched, suddenly. Unsecured data-slates spilled across the floor. Alarm klaxons rang out, shrill and harsh, but dwarfed by the low scream that bled from the vox-speakers.

Egeria, the Navigator, was screaming. Screaming. Screaming, her voice drawn out into one long protracted cry of agony. Erastus pushed himself to his feet, reaching for the nearby vox-horn. Before he could take hold of it, Egeria's scream died in a wash of static feedback. The dull monotonous drone of a servitor replaced her.

<Mass immaterial transit failure. Mass immaterial transit failure.>

The signal jumped and skipped, like a recording on a wax cylinder, before a secondary message kicked in.

<Engaging Navigator-mediated emergency translation. Ave Omnissi–>

A console exploded, hurling the officer manning it back in a shower of sparks and blood. The lumens flickered and then died, the tubes cracking with the sudden strain. Red emergency lighting engaged, smearing everything into a crimson scrawl of motion. Men and women moved as though underwater, as reality seemed to stretch and dilate. The shaking grew, from the normal pangs of translation to a ceaseless spasm. Everything was in motion, as the crew clung to cogitator banks, chairs, anything that would keep them from tumbling across the pitching deck.

Erastus held on to the arm of the throne, his grip locked around the cold metal. The ship's juddering passage shifted, and then yawed wide. Every person on the *Soul* felt the tremendous forces being unleashed upon them, as they were hurled across rooms or face first into corridor walls.

'Hold us steady!' Erastus bellowed over the rush of air and the shrilling of sirens. Those still at their stations frantically tried to make adjustments, sprawled across their consoles and jabbing vainly at switches. Finally, the ship's insane course seemed to steady. The tremble dissipated into the skeleton of the ship until all that remained was the dull thrum of engine and reactor.

Erastus let out a shaky breath and forced himself up off the side of the throne. He bit back pain as he moved.

'Someone get me a status report.' He slammed his hand down onto the communications panel of the armrest. 'Egeria! Throne-damn-and-blast! What happened? Do you live? Tell me what is going on out there!'

'The fleet,' she whispered, her voice hoarse and strained. '*The fleet fell. Gone from out of the warp in a single moment. Their psychic shockwaves…*' Her voice trailed off, before returning, weak and shaking. '*It was all I could do to maintain cohesion as they dropped out of the warp. There was no time. Only pain. I fear, my lord. I fear for the other ships. Their exit was not as… controlled as ours was.*'

'Keep me posted,' he said as he cut off the signal. He whirled about, turning his wrath back upon Kaddas at the auspex station. 'Show me what's going on out there!'

The auspex painted a grim picture.

The fleet, such as it remained, idled at the edge of a star system, cast adrift amidst rocks and ice, ancient leavings of planetary formation that baffled the sensors, returning ghost readings even as Kaddas tried to resolve them. Every ship save the flagships was ailing, and even the great leviathans of the void were not without their wounds. Debris choked the space around each of the damaged vessels, crowded about their stilled engines. Each of them, from the lowest transport to the mightiest warship, had prioritised power to their shields in place of propulsion or other systems. Every last one of them had primed what weapons they possessed. The *Indomitable Soul* had stumbled into the middle of a stand-off.

'Do we have comms?' Erastus asked, looking at the hololithic representation of the system's edge, and the pale green streams of data which coursed down it like rain. 'As soon as we are able I want communion with the *Wyrmslayer Queen*, the *Lustful Paradox* or the *Steel Amidst*–'

'My lord, the Norastye flagship is not there.'

'What?' Erastus snapped.

'The *Steel Amidst Infirmity*, my lord. It isn't there.' Kaddas checked the auspex again for good measure. 'None of their ships are.'

He stared blankly for a long moment. The lumens were stabilising, playing over the chromed stations, interplaying with the hololith and turning the light weak and fragile. The ships caught in its patterns juddered and refracted. 'Could they have come out somewhere else? Or been swallowed by the warp? Throne of Terra, the *Steel*? The whole of their fleet and house?'

'Incoming communications from the *Lustful Paradox*, lord,' said Atreus, his Master of Communications. The man bowed his shaven head at the interruption, and his headset jabbered with half-heard whispers from the ether.

'Put it through,' Erastus said with a sigh. He stroked the bridge of his nose, trying to head off the migraine building behind his eyes. 'And get someone to check the enginariums! I want status reports on every inch of our ships. Find out what made this happen!'

'Well, well, well,' oozed Gunther's voice from the speakers in the back of the throne. *'The men of steel prove their weight false, eh?'*

'What?' Erastus asked with a scowl.

'Is it not obvious? The Norastye are not here. The ships they tended with such false zeal have been sabotaged.'

'The bastards,' Erastus hissed. 'They spit upon all honour. They cannot presume to–'

'They can, my lord, and they would, and they have. We have lingered here longer than you have. We have checked our ships, and found their base sabotage. Entire engine districts crippled. Geller fields compromised. Plasma conduits oversaturated. They were comprehensive in their ruin. I would expect nothing less from the cold-blooded sons of the machine.'

'They planned this,' Erastus said finally. 'They ingratiated themselves, said they would tend to our ships, and they repay us with this treason? The bastards.' He sighed. 'What are your losses?'

'Minimal. My ships are crippled, holed through. Whatever they've done to the engines may very well be irreversible. I have my own adepts scrambling over it.' There was a pause, a flicker of near-static that Erastus realised was laughter. *'All but the flagship. I think Absalom either could not or would not harm them.'*

'He doesn't have to,' Erastus sighed. 'All he has to do is leave us scrambling in the void, trying to save our ships, move our materiel, or otherwise catch up to them. He wanted us dead in the water – choosing between catching him with minimal force, or turning up far too late with a wounded fleet. He has all but guaranteed advantage. To profit, alone and without rival. To return to the Cradle as a conqueror king, with the primarch's blessing.'

And to think I cast aside the Astraneus for the company of serpents. Erastus scowled. *Would the Arch-Lecter have defied me so? Would they have wounded me? I will make peace with them. When this is over I will place my faith in those who can be trusted.*

'Oh do not despair, little bird,' Gunther tittered, and Erastus' mind refocused at his words. *'There is more than one way to skin a cur, when it has turned and bitten you. These matters, though, would be best discussed in person I think. I shall send word to the huntress, and you shall join me upon my humble barque. Yes?'*

Erastus closed his eyes, weighing his options as his mind raced. *Would you have suffered these indignities, Ev?* he wondered. *Would Father have let it come to this?*

'I will come to you, lord admiral. Together we shall set our course through this.' He broke the communion, though he could still hear Gunther's wry chuckle, even as he rose from the silent throne and walked from the bridge.

Chapter Eighteen

The Folly of Men

The *Lustful Paradox* was a strange beast. Sleek like a blockade runner, yet with the bite of a larger yield of ship. Oddly austere halls led from place to place, winding through its belly and only stopping at gleaming chambers of gold and jewels. They passed through rooms encrusted with amber, hung with intricate tapestries, and close by bubbling alembics and macro-distillation units. Erastus had to bow his head as he passed under an arch of intricately carved marble, or perhaps, he realised, some strange form of ivory. The bone glimmered as the light caught it, reflecting as though oiled. Like the ribs of some vast beast, freshly cleaned and presented for inspection.

Katla will feel at home, at least, Erastus thought, and then smothered the idea. It was unfair, after all. Each of them bore savagery in their lineage. Even the bloodless Norastye had shown themselves capable. Had it been them, perhaps? Had some cybernetic horror scuttled through the vents and sinews of the Cradle, to lay his father low? Was it any more likely that the Astraneus had found their spine?

He wondered again where they were now, what course their errant wanderings had carried them on. The Astraneus were a reclusive and strange breed. Their ways were barely the ways of the Imperium, let alone the other dynasties.

Perhaps he had been too reckless, in calling so immediately for exile, now that other, more vital treacheries had come to light. He would redouble his efforts to bring them back into the fold, he resolved. He would not spurn their gifts.

And what does that make me, to have acted so recklessly? What gift was left in my lineage, Father? Your doubt?

The crew of the *Paradox* entertained the unnerving practice of wearing masks. Full-face, covering everything save their eyes. They were all of fine make, wrought from precious metals and encrusted with jewels. They seemed to symbolise rank. Two men in silver masks bowed low, and pushed open the doors to the main hall.

The smell hit the group in a wave. Something vaguely narcotic tickled their senses, the hint of spice. It coiled in the faint mist, and mingled with the smoke of roasting meat. Spits turned, heavy with grox and braised birds. The meat steamed, dripping with juices and glazed with sauces and marinades. Attendants in bronze masks sliced great slivers of the meat off, presenting it on porcelain plates and carrying it to the waiting multitudes. A discordant shrilling cut across the chamber, before it resolved itself and an orchestra began to play. The low drumbeat began to build, like a heart beginning to race.

At the centre of proceedings, at the head of a long table, sat Gunther Radrexxus. He held out one long-fingered hand as a servant filled his glass with rich red liquor. He raised it to his lips and swallowed deeply. His eyes sparkled as they settled on

Erastus and Zofia. Among the oldest traditions amongst their fraternity was that each lord would be accompanied by a single attendant, a second if matters ever had to be resolved through duelling.

Erastus' hand lay on the hilt of Bloodsong, half-hidden by his coat's blue folds. He inclined his head, not willing to bow. 'Lord Radrexxus.'

'Gunther, please!' He laughed as he rose, clapping his hands together. 'Welcome to my ship, such as she is!' As he passed down the table, Katla and Astrid rose from their places, maintaining a comfortable distance, poised as they watched Gunther.

The way a predator would.

Erastus smiled, even as Gunther slapped the side of his arms, then dusted down his shoulders. Beneath the powders and rouge and wig, Gunther was a much older man than Erastus. He put him in mind of Davos, had the years been crueller and his nature more barbed. His tongue drifted along his teeth, as a grin split his features. Erastus shook his head and smiled back. 'What is it you wanted to show me, Gunther?'

'Salvation,' Gunther said. 'I have an answer to our prayers.'

'Oh?' Erastus couldn't help but raise his eyebrow. 'And what is this miracle you present to us?'

'Our sensors are keen, and we are…' He gestured idly into the air. 'We are at the edge of the fleet's new displacement area.' He tittered lightly. 'Best placed to see all and act accordingly, thus to pluck advantage from the jaws of defeat.'

'And this leaves us where?'

'I was getting to that,' Gunther grumbled. 'Euryale!' he called, and he spun around in a bustle of silks. Katla and Astrid backed away and parted, as another figure detached itself from the shadows.

She was hooded, and where it peeled back from her skull

it revealed sallow skin and lank black hair. Gill-like apertures pulsed in her throat, flexing as they tasted the air. She stalked forward on unsteady feet, and grinned with yellowed teeth.

'My lord,' she trilled. 'You have need of me?'

'Euryale,' he said, beaming with pride. He turned to the other lords. 'Euryale is my chief Navigator. A most valued and trusted asset of our house.' He chuckled gently. 'She is my Mistress of Signals. All things pass through her. Tell them what you saw, my sweet.'

'Ship spoor,' she said with her jaundiced grin. 'The warp is well worn, here. I have gazed upon the tides, and I have overlaid it with our auspex inloads. This system was a way station, once. It has fallen upon... shall we say, hard times?'

'And what does this have to do with our current predicament?' Katla asked, looking from the hunched figure of the Navigator back to Gunther. To his credit, Gunther held his resolve, smiling placidly as he waited for Euryale to continue.

They cleave to the rites and rituals of their destitution, Egeria had said. Erastus' grip upon his sword tightened, but his face betrayed nothing of his conflict. He held it steady, unsmiling. Watchful, and waiting.

'This is Ghrent,' she said. The Navigator gestured and the information unspooled into the air from a holographic projector. Fleet dispositions unfurled like flowers, astronavigational ciphers ran like nectar. Slowly, from out of the confluence of data, their current location began to crystalise. 'A minor port of call in ages past. A way station, as I have said. It is sparsely populated, save for a bastion station.'

She gestured and serfs dragged a vast ream of parchment to the table. They unfurled it, and she flicked her finger across the inked marks upon it. It was an astrocartograph, the ink only just dried. The dark spirals of it traced out the arc of planets, and the tumbling scree of asteroid fields. Red smears of pigment marked out the current disposition of their fleet, traced with a swift yet loving hand.

Towards the centre of the web of patterns, nestled like a spider, was a more ornate design. The curves and coils of it suggested spires and curtain walls and all the panoply of a fortress amidst the stars.

'It is… not as daunting as it might first appear,' Euryale said with a chuckle. 'Our auspex scrying suggests that for all its bluster, it will be easy prey.'

'Prey?' Erastus asked. He could not hide the question or the trepidation in his voice, no more than Katla could hide the sudden fire of interest in her eyes. 'You think we should attack?'

'I think, my good and noble lord,' Euryale crooned, 'that you should take what you require and damn the consequences.'

'My friend,' Gunther broached gently. 'We stand on the brink. Annihilation is very much a possibility.'

'I am well aware of that.'

'Excellent!' Gunther said, clapping his hands together again. 'We cannot hover in the void, hand outstretched for scraps. We must be decisive, Erastus.' He flashed his grin. 'What would your most noble father have done?'

Set upon them with wrath and ruin. Burned their holdings and taken whatever he thought might be his due. He would have ruled with iron. He would have been as iron.

Erastus sighed. 'He would have been decisive. He would have done all you ask, and more besides.'

'It is always easier, little bird, to ask for forgiveness than permission.'

'That may be so,' Erastus said, and turned to eye Katla. Her tattooed face bore her own subtle smile. 'What do you think, Jarl Helvintr?'

'You would ask me?' Katla raised an eyebrow. 'Your father would never have extended that honour. I doubt it would ever have crossed his mind.'

'I am not my father,' Erastus said.

'Clearly,' Katla said. She scratched at her chin, pacing while she pondered. 'Gunther's plan has certain merits. The element of surprise chief amongst them.'

'Of course.'

'Do we have any notion of their disposition, their capabilities, or their intent?' Katla asked. 'If we do go to war here, I wish to make sure that we are not overstepping.'

'We have parsed their signals, and they have been found wanting,' Euryale hissed, a line of drool dribbling down her chin. Erastus looked away, unable to stomach the degenerate Navigator's displays. He met Astrid's gaze, pale blue like a reflection of her mother's. The warrior nodded to him, and he smiled lightly.

'Wanting how?' Katla asked.

'Our auspex has drunk deep. Our cipher-breakers have been at work. This place is wreathed in lies. They are Imperial only as much as they are indulged by their master, when he hides them behind falsehoods and counterfeit logs,' Euryale said. 'Signals intelligence puts nominal control of the station in the hands of one Nikolai Vaskin. Governor in name only. A lord of privateers and brigands, who considers himself most slighted in not possessing a Warrant of his own.'

'You gleaned all this? Just by listening?' Katla looked unconvinced.

'We are very good at what we do, oh mighty king,' Euryale drawled. 'We listen, and we watch. We see with more than mortal eyes.'

'I can only take your word for that,' Erastus said.

'Euryale, blessed and beautiful, fulfils many functions upon my vessel, my friend. She has a mind, such a mind, and it has been sworn to me. The things she could tell you, simply by sniffing the skin of the world.' Gunther tittered dryly. 'Do not doubt her information. You can determine it for yourself once you move the *Soul* within range, Erastus,' he said with a shrug. 'Feel free to confirm all that we present to you, but I assure you it is the truth.'

'So you propose, what?'

'Is it not obvious, Erastus? We will take what we want from them, at the point of the sword.'

CHAPTER NINETEEN

MATTERS OF WAR

The two children watched the flotilla burn.

They stood before the viewport and stared, impassive, as the cannons and lances of the Untempered Wrath *tore apart the alien ships. They had been beautiful, in a way. The way a knife was beautiful, or the caged denizen of some bestiary. Both knew better than to speak aloud the idea of there being any beauty in them, though.*

Spires like deep-sea coral melted to slag beneath the focused attention of lances. The material sloughed apart, like meat from bone. They stared impassively. The older child, a girl, swallowed hard. She had only recently reached her twelfth Terran standard year. The boy, only seven, chewed his lip nervously, and fidgeted. He wrung his hands, as his eyes darted from scene to scene. The ancient coral ships began to come apart, shedding a rain of tiny detritus. On some level the boy knew they were bodies. Little lives, dearly sold.

'Such is the ruin of the enemy,' said a voice from behind them.

Their father advanced, though neither child turned to greet him.

The girl stiffened as his hand touched her shoulder, and then relaxed with an exhalation of breath.

'Beautiful, is it not?' he asked.

'Yes, Father,' Evelyne said. She did not turn, or look back. Her eyes were riveted upon the unfolding battle. Their father smelt of weapon oils, smoke, and the spice of strange blood. Bloodsong was scabbarded at his hip, its blade still faintly warm and steaming with the powdered flesh of the enemy.

'The aeldari,' Davos said simply. 'A pernicious and recurrent threat – both to our undertakings, and to the wider Imperium. Do you know why?'

'Hubris,' Evelyne said. 'They cannot accept that their time has come and passed. They cling to memories of a galaxy that no longer exists. To a dominion they no longer command. The dream of empire is a cycle, and as the aeldari once ruled so mankind rules now. By His grace, and our own will. Thus in the hands of the true servants of the Emperor, the cycle is broken. For the Throne is forever.'

'Very good, Evelyne,' he said. He looked to his younger child and shook his head. 'And you, Erastus? Do you have anything you wish to contribute?' The unspoken was clear. He considered that Erastus had nothing to add. No mind, nor soul, for rule.

It was not because he was yet a child, it was because he was unworthy of attention or time.

'In previous times there have been opportunities where the aeldari have worked with the Imperium,' Erastus began, as he chewed his lip.

He heard the rush of air, the sound of sudden movement, before the back of his father's hand clattered against his cheek. He felt the pain as one of his father's many rings snagged in his flesh. He yelped, and then felt a flood of shame at showing such weakness.

'Father…' Evelyne said softly, but he ignored her as he rounded upon his son.

'Let us pray, Erastus, that you are never faced with battle as I have

been. I do not think you would have the stomach for even a moment of it, if your first thought is how it might be avoided.'

He drew Bloodsong and forced it into the boy's trembling hands. It slipped from his wet palms, and clattered upon the ground. Davos laughed. A cruel bark that would dog Erastus' steps his entire life. The sound of utter disappointment.

'You cannot even hold the blade,' he snarled. 'How will you ever hold your nerve?'

Erastus shook himself free of the shroud of memory, and gazed at the hololithic representation of the Ghrent System. The outer planets, small icy orbs and vast gas giants, were rendered in dull reds and browns – their lack of any real interest demonstrated in the choice of colour, and the absence of any scrolling amendments. Towards the centre of the rotating image, the worlds were crisp and green. Information streamed around them, coiling through the gaps in the picture to wind its way around the golden beacon which represented the station.

Its name, so far as they could determine, was Noatun Station – an informal designation for Ghrent Primary Fleet Engagement Facility. Gunther's masked serfs transcribed information about the station, and the comings and goings of its ships, onto parchment. Quills scratched constantly as they noted and annotated.

Gunther himself hunched over the table, gesturing from the hololith to the renderings. His hands moved swiftly and efficiently, and his servants transcribed his explanations faithfully. Katla and Erastus had joined him, watching with wary detachment. There was a light cough, and Maximillian entered from a side chamber – taking his place at Gunther's side. The bodyguard nodded at the other lords, and as he did his belt rattled with a preponderance of fine blades. His sword, imposing as it was, was buckled at his hip, opposite an ivory-chased needle pistol.

'My lord,' he said graciously to Gunther, and then turned to face the others, correcting himself. 'My lords.'

'Ah, Maximillian!' Gunther enthused. 'You all remember Maximillian, I trust?' he asked, grinning broadly. 'My most trusted servant shall lead our portion of any assault.'

Katla laughed. 'Are you afraid, lord admiral? Is this what your indolent life has left you? A coward? A fool?'

'You know I am neither, Katla,' he said with a snort. 'A good leader knows when to delegate.' He leant forward, and the green light of the hololith gave his powdered skin a ghoulish cast. 'And I am nothing if not a good leader. My responsibility, and my surest skill, lies with the fleet this time.'

'We shall see whether or not you are up to the task,' Katla said with a shrug.

'I have led men into war many times, Katla,' Gunther said. 'As have you, on your great hunts. The only untried blade amongst us is our new-fledged king here.'

'I've served my family,' Erastus said. 'I've proven myself.'

'Oh I have no doubt... but others will not be quite as convinced.' Gunther tittered lightly, and gestured back to the display. 'Regardless, we have to focus.'

'Very well,' Erastus said.

He stepped forward and gestured at the map. As he traced his fingers along the projection, a red line of progress began to etch itself across the image. Like a smear of blood. The promise of ruination.

'We will divide our forces.'

'We will?' Katla asked, leaning forward to rest her chin on her hands. 'Why?'

'We will utilise the flagships in order to lay down covering and suppressing fire. Our combined arms will be enough to draw their attention, and also to weaken their defences.'

'An admirable first blow,' Gunther said. 'But that is not dividing our forces. All our military might rests in these ships. The *Paradox*, the *Soul* and the *Queen*.'

'It does, yes, but before that we will deploy our ground troops in transports. We will slow burn towards the target deployment area, and we will take them by surprise while the ships draw their fire and attention.'

'I look forward to testing my skill against theirs. And once that is done?'

'We're going to take whatever ships we can – force their compliance, and bring them into the fold. Once we have these ships we can transfer our materiel, our men, and we can use them to continue the pursuit. If we cannot put them to use then we can strip them for parts and supplies. It's the best, most direct path to what we need.'

'It is,' Gunther practically purred. 'Your father would be proud.'

Involuntarily, Erastus' hand went to his cheek. He could feel the memory pain, intruding on the present like the prickling of a phantom limb. He balled it into a fist, and then lowered it to his side.

'Thank you, lord admiral. I'm sure he would be.'

'We will have to be swift,' Katla interjected. 'Speed will be key to overcoming the enemy's defences, penetrating their shipyards and taking what we need.' She bared her teeth. 'Once that is done we can chase down the Norastye, and bring them properly to heel. I look forward to catching their treacherous throats between my teeth.'

'A fine sentiment,' Gunther breathed. 'Something I very much look forward to seeing.'

She shot him a withering look, but said nothing more.

'We are in agreement, then?' Erastus asked. 'A swift, surgical strike to take control of the vessels, and then link up with the fleet proper – combining our strengths and rejoining the pursuit.'

'Indeed,' Gunther said with a nod.

'Yes,' Katla affirmed.

'The only issue I foresee is ensuring that the crews remain compliant, and actively aid us.'

'That is often a problem which resolves itself,' Gunther said with a smile; the sort of smile that spoke of reliving pleasant memories. 'When a ship is taken, in a decisive blow, then even the most dedicated and driven of crews become wonderfully pragmatic.' He sighed dreamily, lost in thought. 'Besides which, I have some delightful soporifics that quite wonderfully loosen the mind. They make individuals most suggestible. I would highly recommend them.'

'I will... keep that under advisement, Lord Radrexxus,' Erastus said, his tones clipped.

'You will keep your poisons away from me and mine,' Katla snarled, banging her fist against the table. 'We do not need the aid of one who withers minds to get what he wants.'

'It's quite the opposite, I assure you. It is a most illuminating experience for all involved.'

'Enough,' Erastus said.

Everyone turned to look at him. He read their expressions. Doubt, amusement, wary admiration. Their faces showed an echo, a shadow, of what his father had once commanded from them.

'You are not him, little brother,' Evelyne whispered with the past's voice, sighing as she tilted his head, checking his wound. 'And you do not have to be.'

'There is much to prepare,' Erastus said. His words were the falling of a hammer. An end to debate. 'To your vessels, and your duties. When we meet again it will be in the open void.

Katla, Astrid, myself and Maximillian. Gunther will command the fleet engagement from the *Paradox*.'

He looked at each of them, meeting each gaze in turn, be they equal or servant.

'And then, we shall have our true prize.'

Chapter Twenty

The Void's Price

It was dark within the boarding craft, the cabin lit only by low-burning red lumens. Every occupant was cast in blood and shadow, rendered stark and strange. Erastus leant back into his harness and tried to control his breathing. Zofia sat opposite him, smiling contentedly. She had made a show of checking and double-checking her weapons, her restraints, and the general layout of the craft. Now she sat, her breathing perfectly measured, pulse steady. Just like the other members of Squad Primus.

Primus had been his father's bodyguard corps, not that he would have admitted to needing them. The most senior martial members of the crew had been drafted into it, combining their talents into what Davos had considered a flawless network of support, advisors and defenders. They were, he had insisted, far more of a shield for his mind and soul than they ever had been for his body.

'Nervous?' Zofia asked, her voice a crackle in the vox-amplifier within his helmet. He couldn't see her eyes, only the red-tinted lenses. It made her seem alien, unnatural. Like an automaton. The others were quiet in their cradles, and he guessed at their identities through their general size and shape. The hulking muscle of Soradrin Vax, his melta stowed away. The wiry presence of Fasilli Nurt, constantly in motion until the moment his sniper's eye was needed. They, along with the others, were clad in the grey and blue of the Shipguard – trimmed with subtle gold as a sign of their status. He looked from them back to Zofia.

'I'll be fine,' Erastus said. The ship shuddered gently as it adjusted its course, venting minute amounts of air as it sought the maximum alteration with the least expenditure of energy. 'Any word?' he asked over the vox. There was a negative from the pilot, and the ship shook once again.

'Lord Radrexxus will be in touch soon, I'm sure,' Zofia said. She sounded more confident than he felt. It was a rough plan; a quick and dirty raid that spoke more of base piracy than it did of any noble pretences of the Compact.

Is this what we truly are, beneath all the finery? No better than the beasts of Katla's home world?

Zofia fell silent. They both did. They leant into it, instead of trying to break it. Let the sounds carry around the boarding craft. The dull lung-hiss of atmosphere venting and saturating, his own breathing close and harsh in his ears. The dull clang of metal on metal as a hardwired servitor banged its head back against the wall, over and over. The light held steady, leaving them suspended in their bubble of blood.

There was a crackle as the vox went live again, and a familiar chuckle burst forth into their ears.

'*Assault commences,*' Gunther Radrexxus said. '*In His name.*'

The three ships cut across the outer system in a loose arrowhead formation, with the *Paradox* at its tip. Signals passed between the three in a constant stream, as they aligned their approach and coordinated their undertaking. Plasma reactors strained, and the engines burned hot to bring them out in their arc towards Noatun.

The station was a standard Castagarax pattern. The central mass of spires flickered with active void shields, extending around the great docking torus which surrounded it. Defensive guns turned along armour plates, like the segmented exoskeleton of an immense arthropod. It was solidly built, and undoubtedly ancient – as so many of mankind's stellar dominions were. Those sworn to the Compact, gazing from their viewports, would think it a poor reflection of the Cradle. A weak imitation, as pale and flawed as a candle trying to mimic a star.

It was still capable, though. Still a bastion, set amongst the stars with the imperative to rule. It would not go idly into ruin.

'Bring us about,' Gunther said, and his bridge crew moved with perfect efficiency at his words. Each station was occupied, the masked crewmen working feverishly to ensure his orders were followed. They did not speak, for it was not their place to speak.

Gunther missed Maximillian. His counsel in these moments was often invaluable; the lord admiral's bellicose aspects, distilled and shaped into a man. He grinned at the thought. In many ways he had been fortunate, to be gifted with such a crew. To be surrounded and touched by greatness. Others could never understand the true power of their dynasty. It was not shaped by will alone. It was the gift of flesh. The commitment, body and soul, to something *more*.

'How many others,' Gunther wondered aloud, 'would understand what has carried us to the stars and sustained us in the void?' The ship rumbled around him, and he watched through the gilt-edged viewports as the station loomed closer.

Somewhere far below, in near-perfect synchronicity, the gun-crews were running out their charges. Shells as large as hab-buildings were painstakingly levered into place, moved through the effort of thousands of muscles – all straining in common purpose. Sweat-sheened in the darkness, they worked on even as their bodies ached and cried out for food, water, rest. They ignored their mortal foibles and failings. They pushed on, knowing that on some level their lord understood their sacrifices.

The shells slid home with thunderous bangs, echoing through the gun decks one after another as the weapons were primed. Macrocannons sat alongside the carefully aligning lance batteries, crackling with lambent static as they charged.

'Now.'

Fire crossed the gulf between the ships and the station as their weapons committed. Immense shells hurtled through the void even as lance strikes snapped home in a flash of energy. Active void shields crackled and danced, alive with feedback as energy and matter were annihilated into the warp.

Return fire lashed out, haphazard and seeking its range. The ships kept moving, maintaining their advance as they weathered the assault. Their own voids blazed, wreathing the flagships in light and fire. The bridge shook, and Gunther simply grinned. He rocked back and forth in his throne, threw back his head and laughed.

'Return fire! Target their defences. I want them occupied, I want them blood-drunk and blind. Bring their eyes upon us, and us alone!'

The *Paradox* was singing. Her iron bones juddered, her engines burned hot and urgent. Plasma and caged lightning saturated her being; they were her blood. The *Soul* and the *Queen* were mighty ships in their own right, committing their own fury to the fight... but they lacked the true poetry of the *Paradox* and her warlike soul.

She was beautiful.

Gunther let her sing. He let her rage and spit her fire against the enemy. His words and will guided the three ships as they closed the distance. As their shields burned brighter, and the impacts escalated on either side. He grinned as the first shells broke through and the first spires began to burn.

'This should be enough,' he whispered.

The boarding craft engaged their engines, coasting low beneath the fire of burning shields and clouds of venting atmosphere. Defence lasers and flak cannons seared across the void, detonating around them with bursts of smoke and shrapnel. A lucky blast tore one of the craft apart, rending it open like a ripened seed pod. Human detritus spilled into the abyss, bodies flash-frozen while others burned.

It was the void's price. All those who sailed it knew that. At any moment, it could reach out and seize you. End a life. Cut a thread, as the Helvintrs held it. As the first of them died, the others counted their blessings. They clung to talismans, chanted orisons.

The ships tore into the hangar, trailing fire, leaving scorch marks along the metal decking. They touched down even as small-arms fire pattered against their hulls. The ramps slammed down, the harnesses lifted, and the warriors rushed out into the firestorm.

Erastus lifted his hand and raised Bloodsong, leading the way for his men. He looked across the hangar, where Katla and Maximillian were disembarking from their own ships. Alarms bellowed and screamed as the air filled with the chaos of battle.

CHAPTER TWENTY-ONE

The sirens were ringing out across Noatun, filling every crevice of it with sound. The thunder of guns and the clash of metal against metal melded with the alarums and tocsins, becoming the background refrain of the unfolding strife.

Erastus hurled himself from the boarding craft, sword in one hand and plasma pistol in the other. He fired and an enemy soldier exploded, reduced to a cloud of bloodsmoke and ashes. Las and stubber fire scythed around him, hammering into the sides of the craft. He ducked and fired again, throwing himself behind a support beam. Zofia leapt into cover beside him, cursing under her breath as she slammed another magazine into her bolt pistol.

'They're not tough,' she snapped with a scowl, 'but there's a lot of them.'

'I noticed that!' Erastus shouted over the din.

The hangar was a long indent in the station's hull, ringed with docking gantries and support platforms. Their landing pattern had brought them down across the outer edges of the gantries, behind the giant columns which supported the distant ceiling. Cavern-vast, cathedral-huge. The station's crew and guards were holding a rough line of defence, laying down suppressing fire from behind crane control booths or hastily improvised barricades. Barrels and metal sheeting were forced together, where they could be used to shelter from the invaders' relentless fire.

Erastus leant out, firing blind. The caged sunburst of the plasma pistol reduced a control console to slag, erupting in a rain of sparks and white-hot components. He drew back, waiting for the weapon to cool, before he engaged Bloodsong's power field. He sprinted from cover, moving up to the next pillar as the enemy's las-fire scorched the air around them. One of the Lamertine soldiers to his left jerked backwards, caught through the chest by a burst of fire. They tumbled to the deck, visor fogging with the sudden heat of urgent, dying breaths. Erastus cursed, holding his body tight to cover. 'Throne damn them all,' he snarled, and fired again.

Something flammable cooked off, a barrel detonated in the wake of his plasma shot – an eruption of crimson flame amidst the harsh blue of the plasma. Men staggered from the smoke, flailing and screaming as they burned. Precise fire found them, and they fell one last time beneath the onslaught. Zofia was the very picture of focus, each shot economical and considered. From behind them there came percussive booms as Fasilli found targets. Only the sound of his shots told Erastus that he was there. By contrast Soradrin was impossible to miss. Fusion blasts screamed through the fray, atomising those unfortunate enough to be caught in their killing light. The melta steamed in his hands, though he seemed not to notice. Erastus could not hear him over the vox, but he had no doubt that Soradrin was laughing.

'Maintain fire,' Erastus called over the vox. 'We need to take this primary dock, before we can get access to the ship berths. Let's just hope our allies are doing well.'

She lived for this.

Katla ducked under the fusillade and weaved through the ranks of her huscarls. They closed the gap between themselves and the enemy, teeth bared in feral challenge. The enemy were dull creatures in their plain grey void-suits. So cautious. So vulnerable. They did not have it in them to fight as the ice-kissed of her crew fought.

Her spear flashed up in all its powered glory, cleaving through armsmen as she closed the distance. Her face was a savage grin behind her clear faceplate. They could all see it. The animal visage staring out, wild and unrestrained. Eirik, one of her best, moved from her side, already anticipating her needs. She could see his bearded face behind his own helmet's glass, the eagerness of his smile. She pushed onwards, laughing.

Blades clattered against the spear as she spun through their line, whirling in a rush of attack and parry. They deflected off the blade and scraped along the metal haft, unable to gain purchase. She roared, a bark of static through the vox-emitters, and then hurled the spear. It transfixed an enemy sergeant, pinning them to a pillar in a rush of blood. She drew twin axes from her belt, turning aside another sword, before burying one in her assailant's chest.

In the void, a single cut is death.

Blood and air vented from her enemy's suit, and she hurled them to one side. They tumbled off the gantry, joining the other bodies and debris as they fell into nothingness.

The station shook with explosions, and the decking trembled underfoot. Astrid stumbled to her side, panting. Other huscarls clung to railings or threw themselves against the monolithic surety of the pillars. Katla plunged forward, holstered one of her axes, and took hold of the haft of her spear again. In that moment she felt once more complete.

'Careful!' she snarled over the vox. The others looked at her, as though they were being scolded, but the true object of her ire understood. He responded.

'I am the very picture of restraint!' Gunther crowed. 'It's still in one piece, isn't it? I'm just ensuring that they're aware of the stakes. If you don't set something on fire then they won't think you're serious!'

She cut him off with a growl of frustration.

'Fire from above and without. Throne preserve us from the arrogance of lesser men.' She shook her head and looked to Astrid. Her daughter was leaning out of cover, firing at the enemy positions with her lasgun. She turned to Katla, and smiled behind her faceplate.

'Stronger resistance than you were expecting?'

Katla scowled. 'Between them and Radrexxus, the ceiling will give way like the softest of land.' As if acknowledging her words, the station shook again. 'Who knows what damage the reckless fool is doing?'

'He knows–' Astrid began to say, and then leant out to fire again. She braced the lasgun against her shoulder and took precise aim, searing a hole into the skull of one of the enemy soldiers. 'He knows what he is doing, Mother. Radrexxus is a capable voidsman. He is a captain of note and rank, and has the trust of the Compact.'

'Even so.' Katla shook her head. She looked across the vast space that separated them from their allies – the great empty void berth, slowly becoming congealed with burning wreckage and bodies. They turned in the darkness, thin trails of blood sluicing from them. She gritted her teeth, forced her eyes up, seeking Erastus' men. There were flashes across the gulf, the flared detonations of plasma weapons and the steady streams of las and stubber fire. She felt the reassuring weight of her pistol at her belt, but did not reach for it.

'Send word,' she said quietly to Astrid. 'We have to coordinate our advance, break them here. Where the hell are the Radrexxus forces?'

They danced through the tunnels, with a languid grace that quite belied their utterly lethal intent. They were focused, placid and sharply efficient. The firing of their weapons cast flickering lights, and everything was wreathed in smoke. The warriors who served the Radrexxus Dynasty did not whoop or holler like savages or conquerors. They fought with a chill detachment that others would shudder to look upon. They were not the foppish courtesans and degenerates that others laughed about behind cupped palms. When they moved, it was as a tide. An army with a single grim determination.

Maximillian led from the front, as was his custom. The lord admiral himself had taught him as much. To be a symbol. To be a shining fragment of something greater.

'Even as you do your work in the shadows, you should endeavour ever to bear His light.' His master had laughed, once. Rare was it that he saw the truth of his lord's mirth.

For all the feast and fires they put on for those not of their covenant, the House of Radrexxus was a cold place. Service, though, brought some warmth to Maximillian. It was enough, he had long ago decided.

He pivoted, leaping up and driving his blade into the throat of one of the defenders. He felt the crunch as it impacted against a vertebrae, and drew it up, shattering the man's helm. Blood and bone sprayed across his immaculate armour. Pale white, with violet trim. Maximillian wore a full-helm, eschewing the brazen displays of others. His face was not for these reprobates.

'Onward,' he said, and the house guard moved with him. They fell into lockstep, advancing in ranks three men across. They were like phantoms in the low light, moving swiftly in their silence. Their craft, coasting in on similar vectors to the others, had ignored the docking berth and instead swarmed along a series of air-gates. From there they had poured into the station like a contagion, advancing in discrete units to fight their way towards their target ships.

In the confined quarters, the battles were more pitched than upon the sprawling gantries, and Radrexxus armsmen found themselves resorting more and more to blades. They bore cruel, jagged weapons, barbed and serrated. Some of them were marked with poisons. The defenders died harder here. Each inch of ground obtained was won through brutal, gruelling slog. The corridors were pressurised, and so cuts and shots that would have murdered a man outright were lacking here. Maximillian found himself cutting and gouging through armoured void-suits and dispatching foes with shots straight through the faceplates. His needle gun grew hot in his hand, warm and eager from use. He sighed resignedly.

'There is no pleasure in this,' he said, almost to himself. His vox had gone quiet, and the words filled the cavernous silence within his helm. 'It is most regrettable.' He turned his blade in his hand and drove the pommel into the side of another skull. The helm cracked like an egg, and blood spilled down the side of it. He noticed, with some distaste, that some had spattered onto the pale plates of his own encompassing suit. He brushed at it with his gauntleted fingers, and then continued on.

'*Do matters proceed as planned, my dear Maximillian?*' Gunther purred. Maximillian bowed his head involuntarily.

'As well as can be expected, my lord,' he replied as he turned aside another blade. It scraped along the plates at his side, and he flinched back from it. Maximillian raised his pistol and fired, three times. The first needle broke against his foe's chestplate, and the warrior stumbled. The second and third caught them in the throat.

Maximillian smiled, though no one could see it. 'As well as can be expected.'

Chapter Twenty-Two

Into the Bellies of Beasts

Bolter fire scythed at them from the outer edges of the gantries, where the entrenched positions were more comprehensive. Shells burst around them, tearing through the fragile grating and ripping men apart. They advanced under fire, darting from cover to cover and shooting as they went. Erastus' plasma pistol unleashed and then cooled, even as sniper fire and protracted melta blasts drove the enemy back. When he glanced across, he could see the haphazard advance of the Helvintrs.

'We're gaining ground!' Erastus called, and a cheer rose over the vox. He grinned to hear it. He understood, in that moment, a fraction of his father's love of battle, his respect for the arts of war. He had seen it at a remove, and never truly known what it felt like. Evelyne had been the one groomed for that honour; shaped and sharpened into an instrument of cruelty. He had watched the light in her die by degrees, like a fire reduced to its last embers. By contrast, to be in the moment of battle stoked his own passion. Others had spoken of conflict being in his blood, being a part of him. Now, in so small a conflagration, he understood.

'Doing well,' Zofia said. Her breathing was laboured, as was his, as they crouched together behind a barricade. They leant out, firing. Return volleys slammed against their shelter, and one of their own was cut down to their left. The man fell to one knee, firing as he did, before finally succumbing. Runnels of blood flowed past them. Erastus looked at her.

'Throne, I thought we were doing well,' he said. 'We can't afford to lose too many. We need men and materiel to carry the day once we reach our destination!'

'Well within parameters,' she said, and fired.

At their example, the rest of the Lamertine troops opened up. Defenders fell back through the smoke and shadow, or tumbled to the floor venting blood and air.

'Enough of this,' Erastus growled. He holstered his pistol again and held Bloodsong in both hands. He embraced his nature, and let it guide his hand. He remembered the combat drills upon the *Soul* and the sparring chambers of the Cradle. They seemed so far away compared to the moment, the immediacy of this combat.

He felt every shudder of the deck beneath his feet. He felt the pulse of the walls as the station's reactor heart thrummed, and the void shields crackled and burned. He could feel, intimately, the flow of the battle.

He forced himself up and into the throng of combat. Bullets grazed just past his ear, a las-bolt clipped his side. He spun out and round, swinging his sword. A man parted in the middle, bisected by his stroke. Blood gouted with the sudden pressure, splashing the blue of his armour. It coated his faceplate, and half of Erastus' vision turned red. He ducked, and aimed low. Another enemy came apart, screaming as her shins splintered. He drove his knee into her helmet as she fell, and there was another crunch and a rush of air. Everywhere was a madness of shot and blade. Armsmen wrestled with defenders. Zofia drove a long, thin knife under an exposed chin, wrenching it to one side with a sickening hiss.

The gantry-mounted heavy bolter positions pivoted and fired. Shells burst around Erastus as he spun out of their arc and into the shadow of another cyclopean pillar.

'I want those positions gone,' Erastus said. He gestured with his blade, the power field shimmering like a beacon.

'*On it,*' came Soradrin's reply over the vox. There was a flash of energy, and the first of the heavy weapons stations exploded. Soradrin laughed, but Erastus couldn't find it in himself to share his joy. The enemy fell, burning. Sniper fire lashed out, culling the survivors as they scrambled from the burning ruin of their defences. Other weapons added their voices, till their entire line was firing with something approaching unity.

There was respite in the storm – the enemy were under such a pressure of fire that they were unable to return any without putting themselves at mortal risk.

Erastus sprinted across the open decking to the next of the pillars; they were almost the whole way across now. The push along the docking gantries had felt like hours of gruelling progress. The give and take of battle had slowly abated, and their advance had become reassuringly steady.

The enemy's rate of fire had fallen off, and they had turned and fled into the side tunnels which led deeper into the station, and towards the other docking areas. One trooper looked back fearfully as Erastus strode at the head of his men – his army, the thought still sat strangely – and didn't notice as he slammed into a figure coming from the opposite direction. The trooper sprawled to the floor and gawped up at the pale-armoured form as it raised its pistol and fired near point-blank. The trooper jerked back, and the figure holstered their weapon in a gesture ripe with contempt.

Erastus' lip curled. 'Maximillian,' he said coldly.

'Lord Lamertine,' Maximillian replied as he bowed at the waist. 'A success then?'

'Within reason,' Erastus said. He looked back down the long avenue of grief that they had traversed, the Lamertine bodies lying amidst the enemy dead. He shook his head. 'And you? The outer tunnels?'

'Within our control, all within acceptable parameters. Losses as expected.'

'Excellent,' Erastus said, and turned away from him. There was something unnerving about Maximillian, a feeling brought to the fore that merely lingered in the background when personalities like Gunther asserted themselves. A lack. A hollowness. A detachment. Behind the smiles and japes, there was something cold and reptilian. Where the fire of battle filled Erastus, and likely the Helvintrs as well, conflict seemed to drain some innate humanity from men such as Maximillian.

Katla and Astrid strode up to the gathering, cocky and self-assured. There was a swagger about them, even dampened by the heavy void-suits. The brass panelling was hand-etched with runic script, amidst the images of pouncing wolves. Erastus nodded to them.

'No trouble?'

Katla smiled. 'A fine blooding to begin with.'

'Do we have any sense of their disposition? Numbers?' Erastus asked.

She looked to Astrid and shook her head.

'We need to keep pushing them. Get into a position where we can take and hold the docking stations. I want to know the progress of the other units, as soon as possible.'

'We are working on getting the lie of the land. We should soon be able to get precise maps from local systems. You know how it is with these structures. They may have begun as standard constructs, but that could have been millennia ago. Time changes them. The will of men changes them.'

'I know. In the same way as ships are beasts of their own making and nature.'

Katla laughed dryly, fogging her faceplate. The beast's grimace vanished. 'We will make a poet of you yet, my young king.'

Erastus shook his head and chuckled. 'Perhaps we will, Jarl Helvintr.' He looked to Maximillian and the gathering crowd of Radrexxus soldiers. Even compared to the savage brawlers of Katla's dynasty, they were daubed in smears and rivulets of blood. There was a bloody handprint dragging its way down Maximillian's chest. Erastus couldn't look away, fixated on the totemic display.

'They're an odd breed, aren't they?' Katla tilted her head as she joined him in watching Maximillian. 'You think them a joke until you come to know them. Their mask is that of the indolent, the bored and the languid. There are serpents such as this, do you know that? They seem placid, lost amongst the roots of the great trees. They gnaw, and wait, and then when you least expect it they strike for the throat. All sinew and venom.'

'I take your point.'

'Do you really, Lord Lamertine?' Katla replied. 'One day, mark my words, they will have a knife at all our backs. Even their words can be poison.'

'Then why are we with them?' Erastus asked.

'Because they are necessary,' she said, completely seriously. 'And because we are watchful. You should learn that lesson swiftly, my king. Hold it close to your heart, like armour. Remember to be wary, to learn from them and to understand them.' She smiled. 'When you have mastered that, you will be ready.'

'If I'm not ready, then why do you follow me?'

'Because we have honour, as we did amidst the ice and fire of Fenris.' She flashed her predator's grin again, and Erastus echoed it. A faint, pale mimicry.

'And I thank you for it.'

She reached up, her hand gnarled into a claw – locked around the back of his neck – and pulled him forward. 'Do not prove unworthy of it,' she hissed at his ear.

There was a politely broadcast cough as Maximillian drew up to them again. He nodded to Katla, and then folded his hands behind his back, waiting.

'Do we have systems access?' Erastus asked.

A blurt of binharic answered him, as one of the adepts raised a metal hand. Their body was coiled, sinuously, about a data conduit. Mechadendrites wound their way into access ports, and the adept's head lolled back in digital ecstasy.

<Systems access achieved, Lord Lamertine. Diagrammatic representations of the station interior are being processed. Processing. Accessing. Access granted. Glory be to the Omnissiah, who walks in flesh and data. Praise, praise...>

The translated rush of information faded as Erastus tuned it out. Green lines traced their way down his faceplate, forming images before his eyes. Slowly the map of the station interior began to resolve. He looked to the others, seeing the same image replicating across their helm interiors. A flicker of emerald light in Maximillian's eye-lens showed that he was also inloading the information.

'Much better,' Erastus said as he parsed the map's data. The map shifted as his eye drifted across it, and he was able to blink-click a number of areas of interest. 'From here we can advance along the outer docking rings and gain control of the ships there. Once we have them, we burn hard for the fleet, transfer the materiel and men, and then depart. Anything we can't use, we'll strip for parts and get as much of the fleet primed as we can. Some of these ships...' He blinked again and the ships in question pulsed an icy blue. 'Some of these ships will be useful as focal tugs for our vessels. We can use them to shepherd our wounded in their Geller field bubbles, and should be able to effect transit with minimal repairs to their motive systems.'

'Bold, if it works,' Astrid offered.

'It will work,' Erastus said. His hand was on his sword's hilt again, eager to return to the fray.

'You doubt him,' Katla laughed, and turned to her daughter, before gesturing to Erastus with the flat of her axe. 'You will go with him. Ensure his vision comes to pass.'

'Mother...' Astrid began, but then stopped. She sighed deeply. 'As you will, Mother.'

'I do.' Katla smiled, less at her daughter and more at the two Helvintr serfs who had joined them. Each carried a case.

They went to their knees in one motion and opened the cases. There was a click, and a hiss of venting atmosphere. Somewhere a low buzzing began, and two tapered shapes hovered into the air. They were servo-skulls, but not of human origin. They were the long skulls of wolves, bolter barrels gleaming between their sharp white teeth. The buzzing of their suspensor units became a low, feral growl.

'Now,' Katla said, 'let us hunt.'

In the true air of the station, in the darkness beyond the airlocks, Katla finally allowed herself to let go. To commit to the thrill and flow of it. She had taken her helmet off, her short hair shivering in the vague zephyrs cast up by the recyc units. She felt it on her skin, as liberating as the salt of sea spray. She felt alive again.

Killing became a gift once more. Not a chore, not a simple thing of single cuts or shots. It became a challenge.

Her slaved skulls moved ahead, echoing her own eagerness. They fired into the dark. Rough barks filled the space with thunderous noise and the muzzle flare lit the faces of their victims. Pale, staring faces, too long and thin. Voidborn faces, for whom this station was the world; her air, her recycled water – these were the mother's milk of the spacefaring.

Katla grinned, and dived under the return fire, rolling under the arc of their guns before her axes came up. The skulls continued their supporting fusillade. Bolt-shells burst around them, gouging holes in the ancient pitted metal of the walls, or detonating within bodies. Thick, wet explosions echoed in her ears, even as her powered blades cleaved through armour and skin with barely a whisper.

Huscarls advanced behind her, drumming swords and axes against their weathered bucklers. Las-bolts seared against them, etching dark lines into the already marred wood. The warriors never stopped, advancing relentlessly as they slammed their weapons against their shields. Ululating war cries rose from their throats, in the primal cant of Fenris. They had thrown back the hoods and helmets of their void-suits, and displayed their pale and grinning faces. Some were marked with tattoos or pierced with bone, others wore grimacing leather masks. They wore helms and scrimshawed masks, and were every inch the savages that men feared.

Behind the wall of shields, other soldiers advanced, and as the first line of shieldbearers dropped to their knees the second rank opened fire. Laslock-fire filled the confined space with light and smoke. The station's defenders reeled, their line breaking as men fell to the ground, holed through with glowing wounds. The stink of burning flesh was everywhere.

The huscarls bellowed, hurling themselves forward into the fray. Axes split skulls, swords cleaved faces in twain. One back-handed their enemy with the flat of their shield, smearing it with blood. Katla caught an officer's sword between her axe blades, and flipped it from his hands. She grinned, and slammed the axes into his sternum, bearing him to the ground.

'Forward!' she screamed, and her huscarls punched the air. A chorus of agreements and chants of progress made. Knives clattered against armour and shield, or carved marks into the walls to show how far they had gouged into the enemy's realm.

They surged forward, a flood of brawn and muscle. They swung hap-hazardly, like drunken brawlers, as they fell in with their leader. She fought shoulder to shoulder with them, hea-ving alongside them as they drove the enemy back.

A lucky shot took one of her men in the eye, and his head snapped back in a spray of blood. He fell to the floor, spasming as he did, and she stepped over him. She holstered one axe, and took up his shield. She pressed forward, replacing him in the wall. Small-arms fire pattered against it like rain, and she braced herself as they moved forward as one.

They closed the distance in great strides, bringing their weap-ons to bear again. Blades rose and fell, guns snapped and fizzed and spat death. They had mastered many of the arts of killing amidst the stars. The warrior fire of Fenris was in their veins, but they had known many teachers upon many worlds. You did not fight in the retinue of a rogue trader, let alone one such as Katla Helvintr, without acquiring new talents and advantages.

She holstered her other axe, taking shelter behind her shield as she did, and reached for her pistol. The weapon was ancient, heavy and utterly lethal. It engaged with a click and a whine, before she raised it and fired. Crimson energy blossomed around its barrels in rings of thermal discharge as the volkite serpenta roared. It bored a hole through the defenders' line, annihilating flesh in a burst of ashes. There were cries of alarm as the men broke in fear, turning on their heels and running down the corridor. They left weapons and equipment in their wake, trampled underfoot as Katla and her pack gave chase.

Above, the wolf skulls howled and fired – on and on.

They were going the right way, closing in on their targets. The vessels were nearby. The mounting resistance could only be confirmation.

Erastus threw himself to one side, hugging the wall as fire and fury filled the corridor. Bolt-rounds exploded by his head, filling the air with shrapnel. He almost bit his tongue, cursing under his breath as he held out his arm and fired blind. There was a flash of blue light, as the plasma blast blew out a wall to the left of their assailants. Thick, acrid smoke billowed out, blocking their line of sight. The ceaseless fire relented, though only marginally: a skipped beat in the aria of battle.

Despite the well-drilled shots of the Lamertine Shipguard, they had begun to fall. Men burst, and the reduced gravity spread their gore further than seemed natural. They were all smeared in it, with blood and bone dust, ash and smoke. Erastus wiped the back of his hand along his forehead, leaving a greasy smear across his gauntlet.

Astrid and Zofia were at his side, constant shadows. Astrid laughed as she fought. Beneath her concentration there was a savage joy, eager to be let loose. When she caught his eye, her gaze was hungry. Almost mad.

'Good sport, is it not?'

'Hardly the time!' Erastus hissed. She laughed again, full of the Fenrisian joy at war.

'She has a point,' Zofia interjected.

He looked around at her in disbelief, even as las-bolts impacted about their heads.

'I've fought much better, but I've also faced down worse.' Her suited shoulders moved in a shrug.

They fired, then hunched back into cover. The enemy fired, and then they fired. It set a strange and baleful rhythm, like the swinging of a pendulum. The beating of a heart.

And our hearts still beat. He almost laughed too, now. They had survived. Endured. They could win.

He fired again, and then spun out from cover. Zofia and Astrid's shots echoed behind him, and he drove Bloodsong into a soldier's chest. The man's breastplate, scarred and worn as it was, cracked and bled weeping metal as Erastus bore him to the ground. He pushed up again, dragging the sword with him through the shadowed corridor.

He passed under low arches of worn and pitted steel. Like so much of mankind's stellar realm, the place had once been proud and martial. Now it was reduced to squalor by the idleness of its caretakers. Smooth lines and refined facades had long since faded, barnacled under encrustations of obsolete technology. The patina of age had been reinforced with needless bulwarks, creeping gothic ornamentation that spoke more of humanity's ruin than its ascendancy.

Erastus had crossed the galaxy many times. He had strode forth in service of his family name. He had beheld wonders, miracles and horrors in equal measure. Noatun was none of these things. It was a banal shard of withered might, cast to the solar winds.

We were meant for so much more than this, he thought. His

father had always tried to impart that lesson to him. They were the edge of the Emperor's blade, as surely as Bloodsong held its sharpness. They had been sent forth in an age long dead, in a time of rediscovery. Of strength.

They passed under the last of the arches, and emerged into a vast crystalflex-panelled umbilical. It glimmered glossily in the starlight, the illumination shifting as ship-fire lit it from beyond. The light of Gunther's attacks, of the burning void shields and the station's flame-wracked spires, caught and danced in the air. When they opened fire, the light grew stronger and stranger. The entire space lit up, as though sanctified in the heat of the fighting. He wondered if it had ever seen the like before. If raids such as theirs were common, if these defenders were battle-hardened privateers, or simply fighting in defence of their homes.

He obliterated one of them with an almost idle firing of his plasma pistol, disintegrating them at the waist. He looked at the gawping body, mouth working bloodlessly and silent. The armour lacked the uniformity of his own forces'. It was ragtag. Slapdash. Mismatched plates barely fitted together. It was a scraped-back steel grey, each portion baring traces of previous coats. Mottled, like reptile scales. Dappled with the memory of old lives and past mistakes. Militia, then. Forced into service by cruel masters or circumstance.

Further ahead, before the massive doors that barred access to the ship, the troops were better equipped. Their armour was pale green, marked with blue-and-purple sigils. He couldn't read them at this distance, but their sharp and elegant movements were clear. They hoisted their guns, and began to fire. Entrenched positions opened up, tearing up the rockcrete and decking in front of the Lamertine advance.

Erastus hurled himself to one side, even as a squad exploded beside him. Limbs and viscera tumbled through the air as he hit the ground hard. He could feel blood seeping from his leg, even inside the armour. A bullet, shrapnel – something had gouged him. He winced, forcing himself up onto his knees.

The docking umbilical causeway was broad enough for four tanks to parade across, side by side. The entire passageway shook, trembling with the station's pain and its wrath. Return fire streaked across the void, in a bleak mirror of the defenders' defiance. Within and without they were learning, rallying, and retaliating.

'They're opening up with their main guns,' Erastus hissed into his suit's vox. There was a crackle, a muffled signal realignment, and Gunther Radrexxus responded taciturnly.

I am well aware, little bird. You don't have to worry about me. Worry more about yourselves. Take those ships. Get us what we need, and I won't have to tear that station to scrap.'

Erastus cut off the vox-link with a snarl of frustration. More shells detonated around him. Las-fire scored the air, and he could hear the distant whine of other weapons charging. The boom of sniper shots cut through the din, as Fasilli picked targets and dispatched them. Heavy weapons crews lost their gunners, heads blown apart with detached precision. Erastus could hear the vox-clicks that accompanied each shot, as Fasilli kept his count. He was a diligent warrior, though never without a flair for the dramatic.

'We need to get into that ship!' Erastus called. Astrid and Zofia looked to him, not nodding or acknowledging, simply staring at him as he stated the obvious. 'We're too evenly matched here. We need to press whatever advantage we have.'

'And how do you suggest we do that?' Astrid called over the din, head low and braids shaking. She growled low in her throat, threw herself up and fired into the opposing line.

175

'What would your mother do?' Erastus asked, and then turned to Zofia. 'What would my father do?'

Astrid laughed despite herself, despite the situation pressing down upon them. 'My mother would stride across this bridge and cleave them all to ribbons. She would leave them sleeping on red snow, with none to mourn their passing.'

'Your father, on the other hand…' Zofia said, shaking her head. 'He would wear them down with fire, and drown them in blood. He knew the value of his men, as you ought to.'

Erastus closed his eyes. He exhaled sharply. He could feel the flow of battle as it ebbed and shifted. The air was burning around them, thick with shot and the lurid slashes of light and heat. Above them an angel of granite and glass burst apart, raining shards down upon their heads. Voices cried out, in the flesh and over the vox. Demanding orders. Clarity. Something. *Anything.*

He opened his eyes and gripped the hilt of Bloodsong. He knew what he had to do.

'Gunther,' he called over the vox. 'I'm going to need some support.'

CHAPTER TWENTY-THREE

COME NOW THE WRATH OF HEAVEN

Noatun Control was a storm of activity as attendants rushed from station to station. It was nestled in the heart of the ancient way station, the focal point of every last node and function which tended the inconstant flow of ships through their harbours.

Noatun had been many things down the years. A breaking yard for the ever-hungry industries of the Calperan Belt polities. A muster post for the minor spasms of the Intarian Crusade. Such times of plenty had become distant memories, though. Their fortunes, much like the structure of the station, had corroded. In the cracks and shadows, lesser vices had crept in. They had been embraced, so that the people of Noatun could survive – even prosper. The population had not cared, even as they slipped further and further from the Imperial ideal.

In systems such as Ghrent, the Emperor's light was a fine notion, but a distant reality compared to the necessity born of privation. Whatever they had once been, now there was only exploitation and privateering.

The serfs and attendants desperately intoned the rites, that the station's ancient systems might be roused to full readiness. They were trained for moments such as these, but the sudden intensity of the assault had disrupted even the most well-practised of routines.

No plan ever survived its first brush with the enemy. What mattered was being able to adapt to your foes.

'Outermost docking rings have been compromised, my lord,' Sasha, one of the attendants, called from the tumult. 'There are attack vectors recognised as threatening numerous fleet elements, including the *Forsworn Blade*, the *Bounty of Patience*, *Sinner's Lament* and the *Gracious Light*. No invasion forces have yet breached coreward.'

A hydraulic hiss filled the great cylindrical chamber that formed the central control node. Crimson warning lights flashed, and sirens cut through the babble of voices. A section of the ceiling parted, and a platform began its steady descent into the station's heart. It was like an idol carved from black iron, a great gnarled and twisted approximation of a ship's command throne. It seemed to have grown over the years, as additional systems were wired into it, becoming less of a throne and more a cancerous approximation of a sickbed. Some of the additions were cogitator relays, processing data from the control node's systems, while others had the grim bearing of medicae pumps, vitae-engines and dialysis webs. The hydraulics of the platform's descent gave way to the laboured artificial hiss of the occupant's breathing.

Nikolai Vaskin was not a well man. Some whispered he was not even truly a man any longer. Too enmeshed with the mechanisms of the station. The lumens pulsed lazily in time with the master's respiration. His eyes flicked open and closed, and his hands were clawed with rheumatism. He drew himself up as best as he was able, with a barely perceptible shifting of what could be seen of his body. His skin was pallid, grey and drawn – like parchment wrapped around the approximation of a skeleton. His hair, once blond and lustrous, had grown thin and pale, flecked here and there with machine oils and unguents.

'Good,' he rasped. 'We have weathered greater storms than these vagabonds can cast down upon us. We are the masters here. I am the master here. They will not endanger all I have built. They will be driven back, air-starved and screaming, into the void.'

The platform rotated and pivoted, letting him lean forward from his place of power. Coiled cabling wrapped about his limbs, giving him the appearance of a marionette. A puppet at the station's whim and whimsy. Those who merely tended to consoles or maintained the sanctity of the systems wondered what the ancient edifice's machine-spirit whispered to Nikolai when he was secluded in his eyrie, away from prying eyes.

Some things were not worth dwelling upon.

'Have we considered that their objectives are not to sack the station, as previous raiders might have done?' Sasha bowed her head. 'They could take our ships, leave us bereft. With no influence upon the surrounding systems, no power of our own. We would wither upon the vine, my lord, and we would die here.'

'Peace, Sasha,' Nikolai breathed. His eyes had closed again, but the lids were in constant motion. A dreamer as they dwelt in their own silent worlds, or someone hearing faint and distant music that escaped all other ears. 'The lines hold, for the moment. Their weapons are terrible, their ships mighty, but they are interlopers. Nothing more. The station is life, and life is the station.'

'And life is the station,' Sasha echoed nervously. She glanced down at her screen again, and her eyes widened. 'My lord, the ships are coming around again.'

'Still beyond our range?'

'No, my lord. They're veering right into our firing range.'

His eyes flew open, wide with rage and triumph. 'Plot all firing solutions.' There was a diffuse murmur of prayers and calculations from the rows of cogitators and weapons stations. 'I want them rent apart. Reduced to atoms. I want them burning, and cast into the sun.'

'My lord–'

'Do as you are told!' Nikolai snapped. The lumens flickered with his rage, and then the chamber began to shake.

The entire station was trembling, convulsing. The lumens blew in a shower of sparks and glass, and emergency lighting replaced them with a crimson glow. The whine of the shields sang through the station, burning, screaming, near ready to burst. He groaned in sympathetic pain, and blood bubbled and thrummed in the vitae-engines. His fingers tensed, dancing a spidery staccato against the iron of the prison that sustained him.

'By the void, what are they doing?' he whispered finally.

The ships swept in, under the arcs of the station's guns. They had a lock on Erastus' location, and came around upon it, drawing nearer through the tangle of station near-space. Debris and wreckage annihilated itself against the shields, and return fire from Noatun hammered into them in their wake.

Their engines strained, burning hard. Gunther was forcing every last iota of momentum out of the three great flagships. Each one was the match of droves of lesser ships, any of them could have laid waste to systems. Brought civilisations to their knees.

And they had.

Across the cold expanse of space, each had done the Emperor's will in their own way. Their guns had tasted the blood of ship and station, or carved immense void-beasts from out of the abyss. They had been hunters and warriors, diplomats and merchantmen, each bearing their own unique authority and personal zeal. There was a power in the Warrant, beyond ships and fleets, or armies of men. It was a power that spoke of His will, and His plans for the universe.

That power bore down upon Noatun, called by the will of a king, and wielded at the hand of a lord admiral.

The ships rushed by, and their guns committed, staining the void with fire, trailing their own fluctuating shields in a wake of ethereal light. The station vibrated under their barrage, the entire structure quivering the way a body shakes with fever.

The main causeway upon which Erastus fought was trans-fixed, lit up by the tirade of fire as though caught in the glare of a stab-lumen. The gantry flexed under the onslaught, the light prisming into a smear of tortured energy.

The structure trembled and shook, and screamed with the architectural agony of it.

The defenders screamed with it.

Chapter Twenty-Four

The Light of Wrathful Angels

The light was absolute. Everything. All-consuming. For a moment Erastus was convinced that the entire structure would come apart, melting the way old pict-film did when too near a flame. He had seen hives die by orbital fire, and once under the onslaught of simple atomics. He had worried that the causeway would corrode in the same way, a mountain sloughing away under the unleashed fury of a sun.

It held, though every part of the structure was in motion. A tremor coloured everything, and the rockcrete was unsteady under their feet as they advanced. The enemy was disorientated, and their shots went wide in the storm of light and sound. Men tumbled, clutching at their eyes, or with blood running from their ears. Others lost their footing. The constant pressure of Lamertine fire found them, and then they began to fall wounded or in death. The Lamertines were helmed now, and their lenses and faceplates cut the glare to manageable levels. They had been prepared, and had advanced as Gunther's attack run had begun.

Erastus fired his plasma pistol and a squad of green-armoured figures vanished in a flash of blue light. Ashen debris caught in the air for a moment, before Erastus and the others charged through it. He swung Bloodsong through one warrior, and turned to swing at another.

A blade caught his sword in mid-swing. A woman, an officer by the ornamentation of her armour, grimaced with the effort of meeting his attack. She spun away from him, ducking under his follow-up swipe as she angled her blade for his torso. He felt it kiss plate with a hiss, and kicked out at her, driving her back.

'Invader!' she snarled, teeth bared.

There was a desperation in her eyes, coloured through with hatred. He was fighting for an objective, but she was fighting for a home. For survival. He cursed the circumstances that had brought them to this end. He cursed Absalom for his treachery, and Gunther for his wanton encouragement. Above all, he cursed himself.

Father, Ev. Forgive me. All I have done has been as I learned from you.

He parried again. His blade came down, and the active power fields collided with a crackle of energy. He could hear the whine even through his helmet, setting his teeth on edge. He pushed forward, and she gave ground.

Around them everything was still in motion. Parts of the station were burning. The air was thick with black smoke and the ozone stink of weapons discharge. They were close enough that they could see the details in the great looming doors that led to the ship itself, the *Forsworn Blade*. Ancient murals glared from them with the dour faces of heroes and founding fathers. He could feel their judgement, weighing down upon him. He was a stranger here. An outsider. An invader. He had come from out of the night, and brought ruin with him.

The officer struck at his guard, savagely seeking to break it. There was a snarl on her lips now, a feral grimace of pending triumph. She loathed him, and that hatred made her strong. Erastus couldn't bring his pistol to bear, there was only the frantic desperate melee they found themselves caught in.

He braced his feet on the steel and rockcrete, slick with blood and condensation. He felt himself losing ground, falling back as she struck again. He took each blow, savouring the shocks of pain along his arm. It felt like penance. The price that had to be paid, for victory. For honour.

Their blades met, and he pushed back. Sparks flared, blindingly bright. He felt the sharp tang of burning, the sudden pain making him jerk away. He slashed again, a brutal hacking motion, and she was on the defensive now. He channelled his own rage and frustration into every strike, exorcising them in a flurry of cut and thrust. Her guard broke, and she swung for him in a panic. He stepped aside, and brought the sword down across her arm. It spun away, the stump neatly cauterised. She tumbled back, hitting the deck with a heavy thud and a shallow scream. She did not move again.

The others followed him as the enemy broke and ran, moving up towards the great doors. Fasilli's rifle boomed, and Erastus fancied he could hear the whisper of realignment, even before the next click echoed across the vox. Soradrin fired without subtlety, cutting fusion-bright smears through the fray. Men exploded, annihilated in his sweeping bursts of energy. Zofia fired, precise and focused as always. That only left...

Erastus glanced around, and smiled thinly. Astrid stalked forward, her mother's echo, smeared with blood and smoke. She carried an axe in each hand, turning them eagerly. She grinned at him, and bowed her head.

He looked away as the din of battle shifted and changed,

fading beneath the roar of immense mechanisms coming to life. The world began to alter once again. Someone, he realised, must have found a way to force the door. To compromise the systems by arms or artifice; the method had ceased to matter.

Before them, ponderous as a Titan's footfalls, the door began to open.

Chapter Twenty-Five

Two Wolves

The ship was oddly silent as Katla moved through the darkness. Occasionally tremors would seize it, and all would be motion and the creaking of its vast iron skeleton, but between the storm silence reigned. Emergency lumens and sirens had triggered, and then died. Even the groaning background ague of an ageing hull seemed muted. A system had failed somewhere, or damage had found its way into the vessel. Either way, it was dark, and it was still.

Katla owned the darkness, as surely as the ship was becoming hers. Her huscarls, true and trusted souls, all. *Sworn* swords. They bore the marks of crossed spears and rearing wolves. They wore inked hunting masks, in imitation of her own flesh-brands. And now they swarmed through the ship in their hunting packs, to take it piece by piece. To tear out the throat. To pierce the heart. To bind the limbs. It was a hunt – perhaps not a worthy one, but a hunt.

'All things are hunts,' she breathed. She drove herself on, down through the recesses of a generatorium trench. She was in the bowels of the ship, below the waterline. She should be the tip of a spear, primed and ready to transfix the bridge. Instead, she hunted.

Katla tapped the unpowered blade of her spear against the engine-shells of the generators. They idled, lacking even a grumble of activation. They loomed, judgemental as menhirs, with ritual disdain.

To walk in the underholds of the great vessels was to walk the cavernous cathedrals of slumbering gods. The understanding of such hollow sanctity was something she had carried with her from Fenris. The iron god-spirits of starships were not the world-spirits of sea and sky and storm. Such caged and directed lightning was where her passion lay. Those quirks and magicks of the enginarium had ever been the domain of cold-blooded savants such as the Norastye, but she was a quick student.

The Norastye. She spat to one side at even the thought of the name. When this was done, she would see Absalom's head upon a spike. Whatever fellowship there had once been between them, he had sullied it.

'That my only allies should be the Radrexxus and the Lamertines,' she muttered aloud. The thought itself was alien. It echoed strangely in the vaulted chamber, dancing under the ribbed ceiling, to return mangled and unfamiliar. She was alone, save for her own reverberated voice. It brought with it a calmness, a peace and a comfort that enveloped her even in the heart of an enemy's domain.

She was used to the primal electricity of such places. Fighting across chitin plates that were practically tectonic, watching blood erupt into the void as magma bursts from worlds. She had brought ruin to greenskin scrap-hulks, hewing them apart with graceful fury. Close or at a distance, she had taken lives. She had won battles, and been lauded for it.

She drew the blade of the spear along the next generator with a squeal. Machines were, so the Iron Priests said, beyond pain. Not beyond insult, of course, but that was another matter. This was not battle. Not any more. Not truly. Not with victory so near, and the soul of the ship within her talons.

It was not insult, or defilement. She had not clawed her way to the stars to be a puling heretek.

'You are proud,' she whispered. She reached out and traced her hand along the sides of the trench, fingers dancing across barely understood machinery. It remained silent, and she laughed. 'I know pride. I have borne it out a hundred times. Jarl, I call myself! Some have called me the Winter's Queen, or the Mother of Hunters. Fine titles, aye, for those who enjoy collecting such things.'

The ship rumbled again, gently. The shudder of a ship on a choppy sea, not that of a starfarer under fire. Around her the systems began to wake, almost as though roused by her admissions.

'Ah, yes. There you are,' she purred. 'There is fire in your soul. I have that same fire. We are very different, you and I, but we have both done our duty. Come what may.'

'My jarl, we are advancing on the bridge. Skitja! They are fierce in defiance, but we have the measu–'

'Gunnery decks breached, O Queen of Winter! We fight and die for the honour of Helvintr! Commend us to the halls of our ancestors, should we–'

'In the name of Russ, and the Allfather of Man!'

She ignored them, one after another. Her men knew their craft, just as she did. They had fought and bled together across so many battlefields. Too many. She clenched her hand into a fist, and rapped it against the generator. It thrummed, started, and there was light and heat about her now.

If there were any helots, serfs or adepts, then they kept to the shadows.

'You are the *Gracious Light*,' she said with a soft smile. 'A fine name. Not a warrior's name, but you have a warrior's heart. All ships, in their way, are ships of war. Cast to the void by His hand, to serve, and to fight.' Katla nodded. 'That is why you were made, just as it is why I was made. To fight and endure, with all that we have to hand.'

She could feel the metal straining, pulsing as more of its systems engaged. It built into a roar, a scream of activation. A howl.

'You have been ill used. I know that. Slaved to blind and blinkered masters who care only for profit, and their own advancement.' She stalked along the trench and up into the ship proper. The lights followed her, winking on in a sea of captive stars. 'I will give you a new life. A new purpose. You will be sleek, and swift, and glorious.' Her divided visage split into a savage grin. She drew up her spear, like a light to guide her way. Up, towards the ship's bridge, and the victory that awaited.

'I will make you a huntress, and you shall shine.'

Astrid fought her way through the *Forsworn Blade*, mercifully alone now. She chafed at being set as a watchdog for Erastus. He did not trust her, not truly, and her mother clearly did not trust him. She was a token. A shield, and a sword in equal measure.

Now, though, she ran free. She was fighting along one of the ship's main arterials. It was not a sprawling colonnade as might be found upon a true ship of war such as the *Queen* or the *Soul*; instead it was a cramped and overgrown approximation of those greater vessels. It had narrowed over the decades and centuries, crowded with additional layers of machinery and repair work. Scar tissue, bracing a wound.

She smiled grimly at the thought, as she swung her axe

through another of the ineffectual armsmen. The ship teemed with would-be defenders, yet there had been none to pose a threat. She wondered if her mother was finding it any more of a challenge, or if Maximillian and his men were struggling. Astrid hooked the blade of her axe behind the head of another armsman and then slammed their helmeted skull into a bulkhead.

Such sport. If this was all the joy to be taken from the place then so be it, she would take it.

'Astrid?' whispered a voice in her ear. Erastus, calling for her as a master summons a hound. She scoffed aloud, gritted her teeth, and lazily ducked another swipe of an enemy's blade. She went under their guard, and cut a swift pattern of wounds across their chest. She kicked them back, and they tumbled to the ground – rolling end over end, through the grime and oil of the corridor.

She laughed. It was the laughter of her mother as she laid low another beast of the void, the laughter of everyone who had ever spat into the face of the storm and made their enemies sleep upon red snow. The mirth of Fenris was boisterous and brash, and it lingered long upon the tongue as it did within the soul.

'Astrid, what is your status? We're advancing on the bridge.' The signal broke up, before she heard Erastus speak again. This time it was not to her. 'Does anyone have eyes on Helvintr? Throne of Terra – bring that weapons station down!'

She contemplated whether or not to respond. She was not shirking her duty. She was serving. Simply not at his side, or at his whim. Control of this arterial would allow swift movement from the gunnery decks to the bridge, and complete command of the underdecks and holds.

Las-fire impacted around them, and she staggered back. She looked down at the burn mark seared into her armour, and let loose a feral growl.

'Do you know who I am?' she snarled. 'Do you know who you threaten and toy with? I am a daughter of Helvintr. I am the spear of the Huntress Queen!'

The shots fell away, as though cowed by her words. She stalked forward, brandishing her axes. She passed by two shadowed alcoves, and did not see the figures move until it was too late. They hurled themselves from the darkness, armour smudged with oil and muck. Heavy hands took hold of her, wrapping around and trying to restrain her arms. She threw her body back, slamming one of them into the wall, but the other cracked the side of a rifle into her head. Once. Twice. She spat blood, struggling all the while. The final blow sent her head snapping back, and she fell to the deck. Darkness took her, and she felt the first bonds close around her limbs before unconsciousness followed.

CHAPTER TWENTY-SIX

GAIN AND LOSS

The door to the bridge caved in with a burst of blue light and a shower of ruined, smoking metal. Erastus strode through the flames and debris, but he did not fire. The soldiers who came with him held their fire as well. Zofia was at his side, panning from crewman to crewman.

When a ship was taken, when the blade was pressed to the throat, then that was the time for surrender. For negotiation. There would be use for men of quality in such transitions. The crew were silent, their eyes downcast. Some had already fallen to their knees.

'Where is your captain?' Erastus asked. None answered, and he gestured with his smoking plasma pistol. 'A shipmaster? Shipmistress? Who is in command here?' He looked to Zofia. 'Ensure nothing is damaged. Spread out, secure each station.' He turned back to look at the ashen-faced crew. 'I ask again – where is the master of this vessel?'

'Fled, lord,' said a plaintive voice. The Officer of the Watch looked up from her kneeling pose. 'Shipmaster Yurat has fled for the safety of Noatun Control. There is no command here now.'

'Excellent.' Erastus laughed as he strode forward, bracing himself against a cogitator bank. 'I am Erastus Lamertine, of that dynasty. I am a rogue trader, his Warrant of Trade sanctified in the Emperor's own sight.'

Gasps arose from around the bridge at his proclamation, somehow louder than those that had accompanied the influx of armsmen and the threat of martial violence.

'By the power of that Warrant,' he continued, 'I am pressing this vessel into service – that she, and all who sail within her, shall serve the will of the Lamertine name, and the power invested in it by the Davamir Compact.'

Whispers followed his words as they turned to each other at their stations, or leant close in their kneeling submission. Erastus could barely suppress his smile. This was the power his father had always wielded, and yet it was through Erastus' own words that it took root. His place had always been amongst the mercantile expeditions, the trade disputes and delegations. He had been trusted with minor skirmishes, while his father and Evelyne had waged their wars of commerce. It had been Erastus who had honoured the family name with words: stories, songs, praise at the right moment... He laughed quietly, and a few of the crew looked up, surprised at the conqueror's joy.

'Be at peace,' he said. 'If you serve, then you will be rewarded. Stand with me, and the Davamir Compact. Stand with me in the Emperor's light, and you shall reap the benefits that flow from such undertakings. We sail to Endymica, into the very jaws of the Great Rift, to fortify and to secure passage.' He paused, weighing his words. 'A crusade comes. Only the Emperor's own Great Crusade is its superior in scale and ambition. The Primarch...' he began, and fresh gasps rose from the chamber. Prayers were muttered under breaths, even as the crew made the sign of the aquila. One man fell to his knees, weeping.

'The Primarch Reborn, Roboute Guilliman,' he continued, 'has beseeched me, and others like me, to do this in the name of the Emperor. If you stand with us, then you shall stand in his light and favour. You shall enjoy rank and privilege as few have known down the millennia. Where I stand before you, a rogue trader – accredited and sanctified – so you shall be as princes amongst men. On this you have my solemn vow. As a Lamertine. As a rogue trader. As a true and faithful servant of the God-Emperor, beloved saviour of all mankind.'

A hush fell. Erastus looked out across the bridge, at the masses of servile humanity. Wide eyes looked back at him, hollowed out by time and suffering. They were silent for a long moment, and the hush that fell deadened the sound of combat from without. Throughout the ship the last spasms of defiance were fading, and the distant guns were stilled or too far away to make any difference.

The Officer of the Watch stood, brushing her dark hair from her face. Her lip trembled, but she drew a deep breath, and began to speak. 'I will serve, Lord Lamertine. For your glory, and the glory of the Emperor upon Terra.'

'I will serve.' 'We will serve.' 'Let us serve.' The voices rose and fell, with the tempo of human desperation. Erastus closed his eyes for a moment, and finally allowed himself to sheathe his weapon.

'Now,' he said. 'We shall serve Him and His will. Together.'

Erastus stood at the communications station, resting his hand upon it as the attendant worked over its clattering keys. He sighed gently, clenching his hand into a fist. He was anxious to proceed. The ship's systems were being roused, bit by bit.

Chief amongst his priorities were weapons and shields, but he was also eager to re-establish communications with his fellow boarding parties.

The attendant looked up at him nervously, not used to the close proximity of a ship's lord. He strained against the cabling which bound him to the station, feeling it tighten along his neck. It was slick with sweat, and pungent with sacred oils.

'Communications established,' he said breathily. 'I have a link to the *Gracious Light*.'

'Thank you.' Erastus smiled as he spoke. He turned towards the comms unit, and nodded to himself. 'Katla? Do you hear me? How goes the hunt?'

There was a whisper of static and then the signal resolved itself into the rough laughter of Katla Helvintr. *'As well as can be expected, Erastus. No real challenge. That lies ahead for us, does it not? What of you? How went the fight? Did my daughter distinguish herself in your service? Were you awed, as you ought to be?'*

Astrid… The thought gave him pause, and he took a moment before responding. 'She performed well,' he said. 'She is, at this time, securing other sections of the ship. We hold the bridge now, the crew are being compliant.'

'We have cowed them here, too,' she replied. *'Nothing to fear. As I said, no great challenge. Have you checked in with Gunther's proxy? I would like to hear what he has to say in his master's stead.'*

'I'll do my best to check,' Erastus said, as he shot the attendant a meaningful look. The man met Erastus' gaze, and then turned his attention back to the console. His fingers were a blur as they hammered keys and twisted at dials. The signal expanded and resolved, and Erastus began to speak again. 'Maximillian. Do you hear me?'

The machinery wheezed and hissed, before an audible human voice joined Katla's.

'*All has proceeded to plan,*' Maximillian drawled, as though bored. '*My lord was more than right to hold back and relish the battle in the void. They were no challenge at all. Pitiful, really.*'

'Excellent. We have the ships we need, then.'

Erastus breathed a sigh of relief. *It had worked. Against all odds, it had worked.* He almost laughed. He turned back to the – to *his* – communications attendant.

'Get me a signal to Astrid. Once we find out where she is, we can get these ships moving. We can rendezvous with the fleet, and pursue the Norastye.' He shook his head. 'Astrid. Now, if you please.'

'*I am afraid you will not find it quite so easy,*' another voice hissed over the channel. A man's voice, wheezing, though not frail. There was a curdled strength in it. The man at the station grew pale, shrinking back from the console. He knew this voice. He feared it. '*Let us speak, you and I. Let us speak of your little savage, and what might be done with absent pets. Before the end.*'

'I have come under the auspices of a Warrant of Trade, bearing the authority of–'

'*I'm afraid… I just don't care.*' The whispering voice broke into a dry, strained laugh. '*You are merely another usurper. The latest in a long line. Nikolai Vaskin shall not be found wanting, nor taken for a fool.*'

'Nikolai Vaskin?' Erastus asked. 'Should I know who that is?'

The attendant held a hand over the broadcast unit, and his fingers moved to hold the signal. Erastus raised an eyebrow as the man began to speak.

'Forgive me, lord. He is this station's master.'

'And is he…' Erastus paused, waving a hand in the air with a sigh of frustration. 'Is he a reasonable man?'

The man grimaced. 'No, lord. Not in the slightest. The years, they have not been kind. He ruled well, once. As the station failed, as our profits shrank, he grew paranoid. Cruel. Restrictions followed, more control. He pays lip service to Imperial piety, but all he truly cares for is himself.'

'What is your name?'

'Soren, my liege.'

'"Lord" will suffice,' Erastus said, holding back a scowl at the overwrought formality. Soren nodded, smiling gently. 'Put me back through to him,' Erastus said.

Soren readjusted the console's settings, and the voice crackled back into life.

'Do you hear me, usurper? Or do you wallow in your own ignorance? The smallness of outside minds, as I have ever said.'

'I hear you, Nikolai. You said you have someone who belongs to me? I assume you mean Astrid.'

'Is that her name? I had not thought to ask her. It hardly matters. She is not long for this world. Trespassers must be punished. Traitors, looters and privateers... They all meet the gallows.'

'Void justice,' Erastus laughed. 'Is that what you think you are fit to dole out? The rope is an old conceit.'

'But an honest one. There is a purity in justice, and in judgement.'

Erastus shook his head. 'You remind me of my father.'

'Idle flattery will get you nowhere,' the voice said. It paused to wheeze, and the signal thrummed with the hydraulics of bellows. *'I am not so easily wooed to the plight of those who would rob and insult me.'*

'You misunderstand me, Nikolai. I can assure you it was not a compliment.' Erastus' hand had tightened into a fist, rapping against the console. 'I want my warrior returned to me,' he said, and then paused. 'Along with any others of my company whom you have taken hostage.' He gestured to the weapons station, and the officer there began the rites that would channel vital energy into the ship's gunnery systems. 'Refuse me, and I shall hole your station through. Each and every one of you who calls Noatun home shall die.'

'*You are a liar, little lord.*'

'I have been that in my years, many times,' Erastus said. 'I am not lying now.' He gestured again, and the ship's weapons went live. The station would undoubtedly be able to detect it by now. 'You have my warning.'

'*We shall speak more of this, trust me.*' The man's breathy laughter resurfaced again. The hollow joy of a machine, regurgitated like the empty repetitions of a servitor. '*Before your pet is hung by the neck until I am satisfied that she is dead.*'

'Hold.' Katla's voice cut across the channels. '*I am Katla Helvintr. I too bear a Warrant of Trade. Astrid is my daughter, my blood, the continuation of my line. I would not see her die a prisoner's death. Hers is to be a death-in-glory, to draw the eye of the Allfather Himself.*'

'*You ought to have trained your whelp better, then. I am a reasonable man. You will vacate my station and my ships, you shall recompense me in trade goods, materiel… And since yours is the sin of transgression, I shall take whichever of those pretty ships belongs to you. Pay this tithe and I may be moved to return her to you.*'

With that, the channel fell silent.

Chapter Twenty-Seven

Voices of Our Better Nature

'I will get her back,' Katla snarled across the comms-channel. Erastus gritted his teeth.

'Of course you will. We will get her back. You have my oath on that.'

'I will tear this place apart, piece by piece, until they give her back. I will gut it, like vermin. I will tear their master from his throne, and cast him into the void. So help me, by the Allfather and all the spirits of blood and ice and vengeance–'

'If I might interject?' Another voice oozed its way from the broadcast speakers, before it bubbled into sardonic laughter. Gunther Radrexxus spoke. *'Maximillian, most beloved of servants, was kind enough to extend his access privileges to me. I speak to you from fleet-side, as you might imagine. I am terribly saddened to hear of your loss, Katla, and a loss it is.'*

'Speak plainly, worm,' she snarled. *'My daughter languishes in the gaol of fools and malcontents. I do not have the time for your idiot, drug-addled prattle.'*

Gunther laughed again, and Erastus could imagine the slow indulgent shake of his head. *'Very well then. Jarl Helvintr, Lord Lamertine. As much as it pains me to even suggest it… We should take what we have accomplished, and we should retreat. We should not give in to the demands of low-born filth, nor answer to their threats.'* He paused, weighing the effects of his words. *'We must leave her. For the mission. For the primarch. For the Imperium.'*

'What?' The flat anger of her pronouncement was chilling. Even those not involved felt the winter cold creep across the transmission, and shuddered.

'I think what Lord Radrexxus means to say is–' Erastus tried to say, but her furious tirade was already pouring forth. An unending burst of invective directed at Gunther, his house, and all who sailed with him in his 'decrepit, run-down, gaudy ships crewed by idiots, malcontents and addicts in their master's very image.' He was sure he could sense, if not hear, the smile which must be plastered upon Gunther's face. He had to act.

'We will not leave her,' Erastus said. 'She was pledged to me, and swore an oath of service. That cuts both ways. We have a duty to our allies.'

'I am surprised to hear you say that.' Katla's voice was faint. Either the communication was waning, or she was genuinely surprised. Erastus was not sure which was more likely.

'As am I!' Gunther's voice was clear, dripping with bemusement. *'You told us that speed was of the essence. If we do not take these ships, redeploy and then leave… Then our foe will be beyond us, perhaps forever. We shall languish in failure, begging for scraps from the hand of Absalom – and that iron-shod bastard shall show no favour or mercy.'*

'You're right, yes.' Erastus closed his eyes, rocking back on his heels. He rested one hand upon the hilt of Bloodsong. He was not sure which neck he imagined bringing it across. The rush of oil that might mark Absalom's end, or the perfumed burst of blood that would surely accompany Gunther's. 'But I won't abandon her. The Helvintrs gave me their word, and I will keep mine to them.'

'*Then what do you suggest?*' Gunther rasped. '*There is only so long that you can hold a gun at a man's head before he will try and grasp it.*'

Erastus paced the bridge, fingers tapping against the pommel of his sword. He ran his free hand through his short, dark hair. He smiled.

'I'm going to break her out.'

There was darkness, and pain. Astrid awoke slowly, as the agony saturated her. She had been beaten, bludgeoned. She could feel the crusting of dried blood on her skin, and the patterns of bruises blossoming within her flesh. She coughed, felt the tight dryness of her throat, and winced as she tried to move.

Her wrists were bound with thick, heavy chains. She could taste iron, and felt the thick flakes of rust cutting into her. She was not blinded, or gagged. Slowly the light returned. Her swollen eyes cracked open, stinging in the light. The passive illumination of the chamber changed as she stirred, and suddenly it was a harsh spotlight directed at her. She could see the walls now – plain grey metal, unadorned. A cell, to bind her and break her spirit.

'Who...?' she slurred. She spat a bloody gobbet to the floor and tried to move. She swung in the air, suspended by her bound wrists. 'Who is there? Who dares?'

'*Dares?*' a voice said from the shadows around her island of fitful light.

She looked around, like a prey animal seeking its predator. Machinery clanked, venting steam and oil. Plates realigned into the rough form of a human face, rendered abstract and cyclopean like a tribal idol. Diffuse red light seeped from the approximation of eyes. The mouth began to move, mocking the words broadcast from its iron-hewn lips. The voice was human-normal, pitifully reedy and weak compared to the avatar which delivered them.

'It is you who dares. Who transgresses! Who invades!'

Sirens blared with sympathetic rage, and the internal lights of the machine pulsed and thrummed. Its movements were those of a puppet. Mechanisms locked and juddered, ancient and palsied. The speech caught and slurred, robbing it of gravitas and threat. She almost laughed, but held herself in check.

Do not be a fool in the lair of the beast, my daughter, her mother had always told her. *Be strong, and bold, and resolute. But do not be a fool – instead, you must ever be a fighter. You must be strong.*

'You speak through the station?'

'*I am the station,*' it declared bluntly. '*I am master here. I speak with the authority of Noatun Station. I command the Ghrent System. I decide what is legal, what is allowed. You have transgressed. Erred. Sinned.*'

'I am protected under my mother's Warrant of Trade,' she said defiantly. 'Nothing done in the name of the Throne can be a crime. It is our right, to take as we please. To recruit as necessary. Everything you have is available to us if it helps us to fulfil our oaths.'

The construct chortled, the sound like the grinding of scrap metal laced over the projected laughter, as the plates scraped against each other.

'*You think yourself wise, and protected. I know different. You are a fraud, and an implement.*'

'I am–'

'*Be silent!*' it brayed. The light behind its eyes flared crimson, and the voice hitched with a tortured whine. *'I have command here! I have control! I am Nikolai Vaskin, and you will respect me!'*

Astrid let the breath hiss through her swollen lips, strained through blood-flecked teeth. She nodded, and her body swayed in its bonds. 'Very well. Though there are things you should know.'

'Such as?'

'I should tell you,' she said, swinging herself idly as she spoke, 'that I am of value.'

'Is that right?'

Astrid could feel the air shift as the voice was broadcast at her. The weight of its scrutiny lay heavy upon her. Under its eyes the chains felt tighter, and she felt pinned like a specimen under glass.

'You may think you have use, worth, yes...'

It trailed off, and the attention passed. She allowed herself to breathe again. She was sweating, and had to blink droplets of it from her eyes. It made them sting anew.

'But I shall be the judge of your worth and utility,' it said.

She laughed bitterly. Defiantly. 'Then I shall submit myself to your judgement. You have conquered, and deserve the chance to revel in your success. After that there shall be the time of retribution. Of fangs at bared throats. Wolves remember. They remember leniency and mercy, as they remember weakness.'

'You are in no position to speak to me of weakness!' the voice hissed. *'My men shall make you understand, and when you do – then we shall talk again.'* The clanking, clattering thing of artifice fell silent, and the light dimmed with it.

Astrid was alone.

Chapter Twenty-Eight

The Weight of Decisions

'The mission was, all things considered, a resounding success.' Erastus poured a generous amount of wine into the goblet, swirled it lightly under his nose, and then sipped it thoughtfully. The bouquet was rich, spiced, and it warmed the tongue quite admirably. He savoured it, before replacing it on the lacquered surface of the table. 'The crew were adequate, though the next time a more ostentatious ship wouldn't go amiss. Appearance matters, after all.'

'You were given what was required.' Davos leant forward, resting his chin on his hands as he watched Erastus' indulgence. 'You know I do not approve of your…' He waved a hand in the air as he sought the word.

'My?'

'Indulgences.' Davos scoffed at the very mention of the word. 'You are a son of a noble lineage. Our mastery of voidcraft hearkens all the way back to the clans of Jupiter. Your ancestors knew service at the very birth of the Imperium, and that is where our legend was forged.'

'Yes, yes,' Erastus sighed. 'In fire and blood and fury. At the point of a sword and the end of a gunsight. You've told me a thousand times.'

'Because you do not listen!' Davos snapped. 'Silks and airs, as though you were a common merchant!'

'It is a Warrant of Trade, after all.'

'Do not be smart with me, boy.' Davos glowered at his son as he rose from behind the desk. There was fire in him; the burning vitality of a man who had waged war his entire life. Who had stood in judgement over civilisations. 'The worlds I send you to might be charmed by you, my son, but I am beyond such things.'

'You do not have to remind me, Father.'

'Oh, but I do.' The old man laughed, brushing his hands down the front of his crisp blue uniform. 'You have done well, I will give you that, but you must understand one thing. There will come many days when all your pretty words cannot save you. You will stand before them, and they shall count for nothing.' He shook his head slowly and placed a hand upon Erastus' shoulder. The affection of it seemed strange, alien. A gesture atrophied through lack of use, and lack of care.

'What would you have me do then?' Erastus asked. He tried to keep his manner steady, but he knew his voice was as plaintive as his eyes. He had done much, sacrificed much, for even the smallest of gestures of favour. Evelyne was gone, elsewhere. She was burning the frontier to make the old man smile. He hoped she was well. That she was, in her way, happy.

'I would have you hone every part of you,' Davos said. 'You are a man of the name and lineage Lamertine. You are my son, such as you are. When you are ready, I am sure you will rise to the task. You must be as much a blade as you are a man of confidence.' He paused, weighing his own words. 'In your own way, you must be a finely balanced weapon.'

'In my own way,' Erastus whispered aloud. He gazed at the tactical inloads from station and ship, the slowly clarifying details of their situation resolving from the chaos of the hololith. He traced his finger through the air, dipping it towards areas of interest. Their bulwarks along the outer station – each ship shielded and with weapons ready. The slow advance of the three flagships, no longer in fear of the station's guns. Even now, the *Paradox* was making ready to occupy the first docking berth they had taken. He had muted Gunther's idle jabber, but expected him presently.

Slowly, rivers of transit were opening up between the fleet and the occupied portions of the station. Untroubled by enemy fire, shuttle craft and landers moved between the stationary ships and the advancing ones. Wounded and dead being carried back home, supplies and ammunition being moved. Even the clearing of cargo from their prizes. The glacial pace of their piracy was becoming a smoothly efficient torrent.

Behind it though, he could feel the building storm pressure of Katla's rage. He had arranged for her to attend him at the nearest opportunity, and once Gunther was aboard then they could plan in earnest.

In my own way. The thought refused to die. He had attempted, and achieved, so much by aping his father and sister. Doing what they would have done in the situation. Erastus swept his hand through the hololith in impotent rage, taking little satisfaction as the image spasmed and reshaped. He cursed under his breath.

'I won't abandon her,' he said. Even admitting it to himself strengthened his resolve. The ship's strategium was empty – lit only by the flickering light of the tactical display. He paced around it, looking it over again and again as though new details would rise from the morass of signals. 'Whatever else happens, I will not abandon her.'

'That is good to hear,' said a voice from behind him. He turned in time to see Katla stalk into the chamber. Her void-suit was gone, replaced by the understated resplendence of her hunting leathers. Knotwork and runecraft adorned the surfaces, in a mad scrawl of ancient honour marks. Her spear was slung across her back, gold shimmering in the low light of the projection. 'A fine ship, well taken. I commend you.'

'That means a lot coming from you,' he answered with a smile. 'Glad to see you made it here without incident.'

'I would have liked to have seen them try, just to reassure me that one of them had the stomach to attempt a shot.'

'They're not all that reserved,' Erastus said. 'Vaskin holds your daughter by the throat. A knife ready to gut her with. We push too far, too hard, too fast… It all ends in blood.'

'And we burn them for their presumption,' she snarled.

'You look ready for war already, Jarl Helvintr.' He nodded to her changed apparel and weaponry, before patting his own plasma pistol. 'Are you going to war?'

'A limited engagement, perhaps.' She leant forward and scrutinised the hololith with her hunter's eyes, which sparkled with its refracted light. She was tracing the pathways through the ships and station, as easily as a beast picked its path through the snowbound forests. 'He will not let her go, you know this.'

'I do.'

'Then it will be up to us. Me, a band of my finest men. Reave them, set her free, and then out into the sea of stars.'

Erastus scoffed. 'You really think it will be that easy?'

'How could it not be? They're broken. At bay. All advantages are ours.'

'You should know better than anyone, Katla, that a cornered beast is the most dangerous.'

'Look here,' she sighed, gesturing to the scrolling text on the hololithic display. They slid through the air with languid ease as his eyes followed them: diagrammatic summaries, historical annotations, productivity charters. The station's life and soul were laid bare, broken down to figures and tallies. In the end, the Imperium reduced all things to numbers. It did not matter whether it was lifetimes, or simply lives.

'What am I looking at?' he asked, squinting as he struggled to absorb the flow of information.

'This station, for all its bluster, has mercantile roots. Even now, its priorities are trade. Illicit trade, perhaps. Black market dealings and low-tier privateering, but ultimately it lives and dies on its commerce. We have stemmed the tide for now. We hold the blade at their veins, but they have little bite. Enough to scare off raiders and chase away the weakest of offensives, but not to stand against a determined and well-equipped foe.'

'Like us.'

'Exactly like us,' she laughed. 'And with that advantage in mind, I will storm their halls. I will take back what is mine, and I shall spit in the eyes of any who would dare to oppose me. There is nothing more to be said.'

'No?' a voice asked from the door.

Katla and Erastus both turned to see Gunther standing in the doorway. His gaudy coat shimmered in the light from the corridor, rendered gem-like as he stepped into the hololith's glow. 'I would hate to think that we were not of a single mind on this matter.'

'Lord Radrexxus,' Erastus said calmly as he inclined his head. Katla simply glared. Her rage at his suggestion had clearly not abated. Erastus moved himself to stand between the two of them, anticipating violence. 'You did well, distracting their guns and eroding their defences. We would not have survived without your intervention and oversight.'

Gunther snorted. 'Of course you wouldn't have.' He reached up and slipped off his monocle, polishing it idly against his cuff. He looked up, scarcely taking in Katla's simmering rage. 'I do hope you aren't going to hold so small a thing against me, Katla.' He yawned indulgently, and then replaced the monocle – blinking repeatedly, as though testing its worth. 'I merely suggested our best course of action, given the circumstances.'

'The coward's way. The choice of the weak-willed, the infirm.'

'Perhaps you would see it that way, yes,' Gunther said. 'Mine is not the way of the ice and the spear, but it is no less effective. I have taken the blade to as many men as you have, in the service of the Warrant. We've all killed worlds, and cultures, in our time. Whether the swift death from our orbital guns, or the slow grind of Imperial progress. How many times have we pushed the faces of leaders into the ashes of their culture, and known true victory?'

'Many times. We all have,' Katla said.

'Indeed we have!' Gunther said as he drew his own blade with a flourish. It stopped, just shy of Katla's neck. She did not flinch, instead inching closer to the glittering edge. Her eyes were as hard and defiant as iron. 'And we have lost souls along the way, consigned them to the void. Paid its price. We have done all of this in the name of Terra, and in the name of profit.'

'Not her.' Katla shook her head. Her skin touched the blade, and she held Gunther's gaze. He laughed, and drew the blade back. She spat to the ground. 'My daughter is not a price to be paid, nor a token on the board to be given up on a whim. She is the future of my dynasty. She is my heart.'

Erastus was aware of the close confines of the chamber, and the tightness of the air. The walls were beaded with condensation, crawling down the riveted walls and the thick bundles of cabling that fed the room's machinery.

'Enough,' he said. Both of their heads snapped round to look at him, catching him between the scrutiny of the wolf and the serpent.

Gunther smiled broadly, and then nodded. 'As you say, Lord Lamertine. As you say. What would you have me do in your next audacious little plan?'

'I thought it would be obvious, Gunther,' Erastus said, as his smile died. 'You're the distraction.'

Katla laughed, but it stopped in her throat as Erastus' gaze found her.

'And you shall go with him.'

'What? I will not sit idly by while–'

'You will do as I say,' Erastus snapped. 'You cannot be trusted in your current state. You are rash, and that puts everything we have here at risk.' He watched the fury flare in her eyes, and raised a hand to stop her. 'I will go. A handful of picked men. You will plead your case at Gunther's side. Throw yourself at the man's mercy, promise him worlds and all the things within them.

'And I shall tear out his heart.'

Chapter Twenty-Nine

In the Company of Kings

The barricades around the ships had formed slowly, accreting like coral. Layer laid down upon layer, as the station's defenders rushed to fashion new bulwarks of scrap and skill. They brought their weapons emplacements into being piecemeal, stretched out across the access causeways and maintenance gantries. Tech-adepts reluctantly stood amidst showers of sparks as they annealed together the defences, muttering prayers as they did so.

Their utterances died beneath the sudden sound of fanfare.

The doors of the ship slid open, and a pair of figures strode forth. The first was gaudy in his advance. His coat billowed about him, and he smiled pleasantly enough. He raised his hands, twisting them this way and that to show that they were definitely empty.

Empty, save of course for the threat of the ship's guns.

'The mine-clans of Jaskan IV, who are rather gracious if limited hosts, displayed their empty hands not only as a sign of truce…' He brought his palms together with a clap, and chuckled. 'But also to demonstrate that they brought no tools, no begging bowls. They came as equals, that they might come with no expectations.'

He bowed melodramatically.

'I am Gunther Radrexxus, rogue trader and avowed representative of Erastus Lamertine. I would have words with your commander.'

The second figure was silent, in her drab grey and brown. She merely glared at those who had come to greet her, watching as the assortment of soldiers parted slowly and let them pass, cowed by fear more than any promise of their erstwhile lord.

Those who sailed the void knew that ships were untidy creatures. Studies in contradictions. Each vessel was a discrete unit, a known value sanctified by generations of standard template construct patterns and Imperial architecture. Yet every ship had secrets. To know the class and layout of a ship was only the beginning, and once peeled away there was always something that could surprise you.

Erastus and Zofia had donned bulky, nondescript void-suits. Neither displayed rank or signs of favour. They were stripped down and simply dressed, and any reflective surfaces had been smeared with dust and oil – further deadening their outline. They were reduced to ghosts, phantom leavings from battles long past. Survivors desperate for succour, soldiers eager for home. They passed through narrow maintenance passages, ducking under low arches of iron as they skirted the ship's edges.

Erastus' breathing was loud in his ears. The faceplate of the suit was fogging with condensation as they progressed. The sheer exertion of it, so soon after the pitched chaos of the battle, made him stop to catch his breath.

'Keep up,' said Zofia through their vox-channel, her voice immediately in his ear. 'It won't be much further.'

He nodded, as they pressed themselves against the wall and edged past humming cogitator units. Heaving atmosphere processors spluttered and coughed, while pipes gurgled and sloshed around them. Fully active, the ship was like a living thing. Erastus was uncomfortably aware of the sensation of absolute immersion, like the ancient shanties that spoke of void-sailors caught in the gullet of stellar beasts – there to live out punishments for sins against the God-Emperor and the capricious whims of fate.

He suppressed a shiver, even in the heavy, hot confines of the suit, and continued their meandering path. Armsmen had control of the ship, and were defending the bridge. Discipline officers and overseers were holding the crew in check. The soft ripples of takeover, tectonic aftershocks through the chain of command, were spreading throughout the ship. Erastus trusted his men to hold things together in his absence. He was certain that Katla would have put able hands at the helm of her prize, too. It must have hurt, though, when in more promising times the agent of her trust would have been Astrid.

'We will get her back,' he sent across the vox to Katla, knowing she would be entering the beast's lair soon enough. He expected no answer from her, but continued nonetheless. 'You have my word.'

Zofia paused before an external door, and simply rapped it with her sword's blade. For a moment it seemed as though she was testing the metal. She lowered the weapon and reached out, tapping at the access panel.

'The codes are good?' he asked.

She shrugged non-committally, just as the door's systems chimed. A lumen flickered green, and the hatch cracked open with a hiss of stabilising air pressure. They both hurried in, and Zofia closed and sealed the door behind them.

The airlock corridor was squat, grey and drab. Utterly utilitarian. The low light cast by the overhead lumes was a sickly, sodium yellow. Erastus' breathing hitched again in his helm, and he steadied himself against the wall.

'You're sure this will work?'

'Mostly,' she replied distractedly. She was toying with another control unit, flicking switches and inputting access codes with well-practised ease. The lighting changed, becoming a penetrating scarlet, as the first alarms sounded. The air rushed from the chamber, and vacuum embraced them once again.

'Once we're out, we'll move along the ship's exterior to the tertiary docking apparatus. From there we can get access to the upper station, and this lordling's eyrie. He'll be keeping her nearby, I'm sure.'

'And you don't think they'll expect this?'

Zofia laughed dryly. 'No. I shouldn't think so. They'd have to consider us crawling along the hull of a ship, making the leap to the station, getting through their defences and breaking her free.' She flashed him a grin through the clear plex-glass of her faceplate. 'Besides,' she continued, 'if it comes to it, we can always burst their little station. An end to schemes. Pick over the bones of what remains.'

'At ruinous cost. Why do I find the idea of that isn't in the least bit reassuring?'

'Throne knows, Erastus,' she sighed. 'I certainly like the thought.'

The door opened, and the void chill was everywhere. Suddenly the suit did not feel all-encompassing and reassuring. It was a thin veneer of safety and security, ready to be torn away at a moment's notice. Slowly, deliberately, they forced themselves forward. Each step was heavy with the effort, the considered movements that minimised the loss of contact between the magnetised boots and the ship's hull.

Death dwelt in those moments. Watchful, waiting, hungry; like a beast hidden below ice, a swimmer in the black ocean of eternity.

The hull was a pitted and inconstant thing, veering from mountainous spurs of antennae and sensor vanes to shadowed recesses in the plating. Though not a ship of the line, not a juggernaut such as any of the flagships, it had still seen its share of service. Mottled scars ran across the metal where old wounds had been patched and tended to. It reminded Erastus of the forge worlds he had visited in his youth, when his father's sometimes reckless adventurism had driven them to resupply and repair.

Noatun stretched out above them, encompassing the world that was the ship. Black against the dark of the void, studded with lights like its own lesser constellations. He gazed up at the station, and his hands clenched and unclenched. His breathing was erratic, and he suppressed the urge to close his eyes. To block out the looming edifice, the sheer weight of the challenge.

This is not beyond you.

The thought cut through the confusion, the fear, and the frantic beating of his own heart. He pushed on. Each step was arduous, every movement a challenge. There was no other choice, though, than to range forth over the plains of battered, beaten metal.

There was still far to go, before victory.

They passed through the station's corridors like conquerors and kings. Gunther strode ahead, with no sense of fear or shame. Katla was more measured. She had to be. Every moment wasted was another which brought her daughter closer to death at the hands of a lesser man, a lord who did not understand the import of what they did, nor the methods which had been necessary to support it.

Should we have waited? Idled? Tried to explain? Was Gunther's piratical mania truly the only course available to us?

She shook her head. She did not know. To question the skeins of fate, already teased out into the galaxy, was as good as to question the Allfather's will. There was a purpose in every action. In triumph, as in calamity. She had served at the spear's bloody point, and she had stood back to order men to their deaths. On both sides of the line, she had proven herself worthy of command. To lead was to judge the moment, and to act accordingly.

They walked beneath ancient swaying banners and faded tapestries, each speaking of battles centuries past, when Noatun had been a hub of commerce and a cog in the support networks which had cast Imperial crusades out into the galaxy. Neglected, matted with dust, they were forgotten relics of grander times. None of the staff or soldiery looked up at them. Only the newcomers paid any attention. Those who lived and died beneath their own history were inured to it.

She could not have imagined such disregard about the *Queen*, where the sense of lineage was etched into the ship's iron bones, and carried in the hearts of its crew. It bore a soul that this place lacked. Time and neglect had stolen the grandeur, hope and ambition from the station. The withered parasite left in its stead knew only hunger. It had never bettered itself, as the dynasties had, nor had it allowed itself to grow and thrive as the Cradle had. It remained static; too atrophied to seize the future, or to survive the tides of blood that now swept the galaxy.

They will not last, these children, these echoes, she thought with a sigh, as she passed into the sanctum of the enemy.

Here the faded glory was more pronounced. The seat of command turned sickbed. Katla's nose wrinkled at the rot-sweet stench of illness. None of the others gave it any notice; even Gunther was unmoved – though she attributed that more to the excesses delivered to his senses and body over his long years of near-constant inebriation. Nothing fazed the man. He strode through the world with his borrowed swagger, and hid the tired lines of one who had indulged every vice – and found it wanting.

Pale faces stared down at her from behind their stations, lit by the lambency of screens. They were drawn, malnourished. It hurt to look at them, and a sympathetic pang resonated through her. Human empathy, such as it was, calling to its like.

What do they think when they look at me? When they see the beast worn plainly upon my skin? They do not know of Fenris. Or perhaps they do, but would they pair me with that cradle of wolves?

'Speak.'

The voice echoed, resounded. It danced from the walls of the cylindrical chamber, and the various staff cowered deeper into their alcoves. Only the servitors remained unaffected, staring ahead and processing with the simple burbling acquiescence of the lobotomised.

'State your case,' the voice said again. 'Plead your case. Throw yourself before my mercy, as a lord demands. Who takes responsibility for the whelp I find foisted upon me?'

Katla's jaw tightened. She ground her teeth, bit back her retort, and instead ensured her hands were locked at her sides. She had no weapons, but it took all her restraint to stop herself from striding forth and tearing the pretender from his throne. He thought he knew power, but he was a child pretending at rule. A shadow cast upon the wall.

'I am Katla,' she said. 'Jarl of the Helvintrs. Queen of the Hunt. Captain of the *Wyrmslayer Queen*. You hold my daughter.'

'Ah, so she is yours? I did not think she resembled the dandy, nor the king who you both seem to serve.'

'Where is she?'

The central platform pivoted, and the aged man leant forward on his web of supports and cables. His laboured breathing hitched, and his chest shook. It took Katla a moment to realise that he was laughing. Laughing at them. At her.

'She is... quite safe. She awaits her execution, should you decide against my most generous offer.'

'The one where you want everything?' Katla snorted. 'Our spoils, my ship, and all we have sought to claim? You have denied us our due. Spurned the bearers of the Warrants of Trade. What is your claim and authority against ours? Against the laws of the Imperium itself?'

'To claim against law and reason. At ruinous cost to both of us. How many lie dead? Tell me that. Walk the lines and count the bodies, measure the blood that dries upon our decking. Tell me then, that this was worthwhile. That it was justified.'

'We carry authority second only to the Emperor Himself.' Gunther smirked as he spoke. His chest was pushed out in a way he must have thought made him seem grandiose. His hands were a blur of motion, his gestures bleeding together as he cajoled. 'We are rogue traders, who bear His sanction and seal. Just as we bear the missive of His returned son.'

'More lies,' Nikolai hissed. 'To you and your kind, it is as simple as breathing. Perhaps you do not know the last time that the truth passed your lips.'

'We speak with truth,' Katla snarled. She slammed her fist against a nearby console, and the adept at the station flinched back. 'I will not be called a liar by a broken man, yoked to the mast of his holding.'

'What my esteemed friend is trying to say, I am sure,' Gunther said indulgently as he bowed, 'is that a master who does not range out into his domain often forgets what it is to be a sailor upon the void.' He smiled his serpent's smile, all pretence and posing. He drew all eyes to him, like a theatrical player upon the stage. His every glance, movement and word were calculated to focus attention. It was no wonder that Erastus had cast him in this role.

He was the distraction, and she was the heart's plea. Together, they had been directed into the lair of the enemy. Holding his gaze.

Perhaps, she thought, *there is hope for the boy king yet.*

'I will take what is owed,' Nikolai said, his voice riven through with the hiss of the machines which kept him breathing. He hunched forward, wincing in pain, sucking his breath in through his teeth as he glared down at them. 'I will have my recompense, or I will have her head. And you will join her on the scaffold, if you are not careful.'

'My lord, my friend,' Gunther cajoled. 'Let us be civil, no? We have much to offer you, if you have a mind to listen.'

The ship's edge was like the sudden drop of a cliff. Sheer, uncompromising, the slab-sided sheets of metal fell away to empty, open void. Erastus looked down, then up at the looming vastness of Noatun. It hung, predatory and oppressive. Involuntarily he took a step back, and almost bumped into Zofia. She cursed under her breath, reducing the vox to an angry crackle.

'This is how we die,' he whispered to himself. He did not broadcast it. Simply allowed it to fill the silence of his helmet, to eclipse his own ragged breathing and the thunder of his heartbeat.

'Ready?' Zofia asked. Her voice did not waver, her breathing was steady. She seemed calm, focused. She gazed up at the station the way climbers regarded a mountain. Merely another obstacle to be overcome.

He did not, could not, share her enthusiasm. He moved to shake his head, but found he could not move it. He drew another halting breath, and nodded.

Together they advanced in heavy lockstep, forcing themselves into as much of a run as they were able. They hurled themselves off the edge of the ship, and the station reared up ahead of them. Reality spun, perspective altered. They were flailing through the abyss, with the superstructure ahead of them.

He tried to control his breathing, to keep himself focused and oriented. It felt as though everything was slipping away from him. There was no ground beneath him, nothing for him to cling on to. The universe had become the echo of his mind, a broken reflection. Every moment since the Rift had opened had been the fall; his father's death... That had been the moment he had hurled himself into the void, and lost all surety.

Erastus slammed against the station's exterior, limbs slapping against the metallic hull. He gasped, feeling his fingers scrape across the plates, scrabbling at nothing. Then there was the thud of contact, and his gauntleted hands snagged around the grating of a gantry. His muscles strained, and he pulled himself up. He was sweating in his suit, red faced and panting. Zofia was already scrambling up to her feet, dusting herself down before she turned and grabbed Erastus by the wrist. She heaved him properly up, and slapped him on the shoulder.

'Now,' she said with a laugh, shaking her head. 'That wasn't so bad, was it?'

She hung alone, in the darkness of her cell, suspended by her wrists. Waiting. Watching. She had already memorised the comings and goings of the guards, marking the inconstant flow of time by the sounds of their arrival. Low chatter drifted through the gaps in the door, carried in the slivers of light that shone through. She grinned in the shadows, tongue lapping the blood from her teeth.

They had not been kind hosts, but that was nothing new. She had suffered at the hands of attackers and interrogators a hundred times before. One did not serve at the leisure of a warrior queen without growing intimate with violence and threat. Every part of her had to become a weapon, in such circumstances. The galaxy did not look kindly upon weakness.

'Sharpen every part of you,' she whispered through split lips. She knotted her hands together, fingers kneading at the meat of her right palm. She winced, teeth drawing together as she pulled at it. She could feel the length of metal embedded within the skin. A countermeasure, as sure as any defensive emplacement upon a ship. As true as the blades a warrior might hide about their person. Every tool, every advantage, was a weapon. A hidden blade. A subtle knife. In the correct hands, such a thing could change the course of a war. Or a life.

Blood beaded in her hand as she forced the barb out of her skin, and into her palm. She closed her eyes, and began to work it against the lock set into her bonds.

She still had a long way to go.

CHAPTER THIRTY

RISE AND DESCENT

Zofia made her way into the station with slow, determined motions, Erastus ahead of her. Code-scramblers and systems-baffles were deployed to trick the fickle machine-spirits of the doors. Their acquiescence was bought, bribed and otherwise deceived. Even within the re-pressurised passageways of Noatun they kept their helms on, the better to hide their identities. The dirt obscuring their maker's marks and sigils would suffice for now, but only so long as the enemy did not draw too near.

They did not speak. They moved in utter silence, stopping only to consult the maps that flickered down the faceplates of their helms. Eyes tracing along the glowing patterns of lines and symbols resolving into the station's upper echelons.

They had supposed that their foe would keep Astrid close. A prize, or a pet. Zofia glanced around as they walked the corridors, free from the debris and detritus of battle that had so stained their way to the ships. These passageways were different. Cleaner. They spoke of the grandeur that had faded elsewhere throughout the station. Another corridor branched off to their left, the doors panelled with crystalflex, revealing a more sizeable airlock platform, capable of moving out into the open void.

Within, set up with cruel care, there was a gallows. It was new, repurposed or moved from elsewhere in the facility, but its function was clear. Once deployed, the platform would display the hanging dead to the vacuum of space, and to any who might dock and dare to consider crossing Noatun's errant master.

'I think we're on the right track,' Erastus sent over the vox.

'Throne but he was serious,' Zofia breathed. Her eyes caught on every sharp edge of it, and the length of cable that hung and swayed. Waiting. Hungry. It exuded menace. Perhaps that was the point of it. The threat more than the actuality. How many had hung beyond those doors, their bones clattering against the hull in cautionary rattle? 'A gallows. Slow and cruel. No way for a warrior to die.'

'Keep moving,' Erastus sent tersely.

She was aware, very suddenly, of how the dynamic had shifted. Where before she had led, the sight of the pending execution seemed to have rallied his focus. His hand moved to his weapons, ready to act at the slightest provocation.

With what lay between them and their prize, Zofia did not think it would be long in coming.

They pressed themselves against a wall as voices echoed from the next corridor along. The moments drew out, broken only by their breathing, by the thud of boots against metal and the inane chatter of voices.

When the guards crossed into the corridor, that was when Erastus and Zofia struck.

Erastus wheeled suddenly out of the shadows, and his blade came up almost instantly. A throat opened, red and rushing with spilled blood. Zofia struck next, her slashing motion coming a second after his lead. The two men stammered, spluttered, but gloved hands quickly covered their mouths as they lowered them to the floor. It was a gesture that struck Erastus as being... gentle, despite the ruin unleashed upon them.

They pushed on, with a sense of quiet purpose. Somehow, knowing that the absence of the guards would be noticed and that their bodies might be found gave Erastus new impetus. He advanced steadily, eye drifting to the map's pattern before him. Following its glowing lines to their inevitable conclusion. The corridors were no longer the broad thoroughfares for moving men and materiel. They were intimate, the walls close.

He could smell the acrid stench of burning electricals, even through the helmet's filters. The station was sick. Palsied by battle, but also ill to its core. He reached up, and pulled the helm off his head. He clamped it to his belt and ran a hand through his short hair, feeling it slick with sweat. Zofia shot him a disapproving look.

'There's no harm,' he said. 'I know the way from here. So do you.'

Zofia reached up and pulled off her own helmet. There was a hiss of venting air, and she shook her hair out. She remained poised, ready to strike – like a serpent in the low grass.

'We're close?' Zofia asked.

'We are,' Erastus said with a nod. 'Let's hope that our friends are drawing their eye enough.'

'And what is it you think you can offer me that I do not already possess?' Nikolai grumbled. The man, such as he was, had leant forward from his throne again. The cables had dug deep into his flesh, leaving dark lines of pressure in his pale skin. His gurgling breathing rose and fell, and his eyes darted from Katla to Gunther and back again. There was a manic, febrile energy in his limited movements. 'I am lord of Noatun, blessed with the station's grace. I…' He trailed off, before he shook himself. 'I want for nothing.'

'Everyone wants for something,' Gunther replied. 'This place…' He gestured around the chamber. 'It has seen better days, has it not?'

Katla was aware that the margins of the room were swiftly filling with guards. The light caught on their tarnished green plate, and glittered on the polished surfaces of their lasweapons. If Gunther noticed them then he gave no sign. He stepped forward, his coat flourishing as he scrutinised their enemy.

'You wish for riches? We have trinkets and baubles aplenty.' Gunther raised one hand and prised a ruby-encrusted ring from his finger, tossing it before the assembled figures. 'You want to walk your station again, or go out into the wildness of these stellar nights? We have practitioners of medicine who could restore sight to the blind!' He threw back his head and laughed, brayed. Spittle flew from his lips in his manic frenzy. He seemed, in that moment, bestial. Not a man, but a thing aping one. An animal, cloaked in human skin.

He is our friend and our ally, or so he claims, but I have never hated him more. The thought blazed in her mind, shocking her with its intensity. He had stood against her, argued that they should leave Astrid to her fate. What he did now was to serve himself. To regain whatever favour had slipped through his fingers between him and Erastus. He did not serve their king. Perhaps he did not even serve the Emperor. Not when there was the will and whim of Radrexxus to consider.

'Enough,' she said.

All attention shifted to her. Gunther turned, looking as though he had been struck. As though she had robbed him. She brushed past him, glaring up at the totemic form of Noatun's master.

'You wish to bargain. I can understand that. You want to bleed us? Perhaps that too is understandable. You have lost much. We have taken much from you.' Katla sighed. Her hands balled into fists, and she struggled to keep them steady at her side. 'But Astrid is my daughter. Even your heart must understand a parent's love for their child.'

Nikolai scoffed, but said nothing. His silence was all the sign she needed to continue.

'I have been His spear in dark places. I hunted the beasts that others fear to face down.' She gestured to the ruin of her face and body, the horror obscured by ink and brand. The tattoo was dark in the low light, against the paleness of her skin. 'For my kin, I would lay down my life. I would kill for her, aye.' She raised her fists, a pale echo of past triumphs and struggles. 'And I would die for her.'

Nikolai's laughter was cold, and his words yet colder. 'You may yet get your chance to do just that.'

Escaping her bonds had been easy. It was not the first time she had been bound, and far from the only time she had been forced to escape from such captivity.

Astrid gripped the chains, suspending herself in the air even as her movements sent motes of dust spinning. She swayed gently, feeling the rough, rust-caked metal in her hands. She slipped down the length of the chains, till her feet touched the ground with the faintest whisper of contact. She rocked on her heels, becoming familiar with the decking once more.

Even this far removed, she was still a child of Fenris. You did not fight unless you had solid ground beneath your feet. The ice could betray you, and soft land might slip beneath the waves again. As a denizen of the void, she had learned further lessons. Ship and station were as treacherous as the seas.

She surveyed her surroundings, assessing the battlefield as it unfolded before her.

The machinery by which her captor had communicated had fallen silent, the simulacrum of a face idling. Its plates were sharp suggestions in the low light, dripping with kindled menace. She moved past it cautiously, unsure which mechanisms of surveillance were still active. Pressing herself against the wall, she leant her head to the door, and listened. The soft breathing of the guards could be heard, alongside the occasional bursts of muted conversation. Even they were taking no chances in being caught by their masters, in being found idle at their posts. She could hear it in their terse asides. In the way they shifted with subtle agitation. She smiled in the darkness, and drew back towards where she had been hanging.

Astrid braced herself and then leapt into the air, driving her weight down onto the floor with a crash. She heard a curse from beyond the door, and the guards scrambling to open the cell. She was already in motion, hurling herself towards the wall beside the door, even as it swung open and the barrel of a lasgun swept up, round, and into the chamber.

Her hands snapped out and grabbed the gun, yanking it from the man's poorly disciplined grip. She spun the weapon around, and slammed the stock of it into the exposed lower half of his face, relishing the crack of bone and the spatter of blood. She bared her teeth in a frail grin, and brought the gun around again – barrel trained on the second guard.

He hesitated. He actually faltered before her, his aim going low and wide as he fumbled. She wondered if he had ever had a weapon pointed at him before, or if it was merely the thought of failure. Of losing his friend and comrade. Of being made an example of, by whichever cruel arithmetic animated this place. Often the price of failure could seem far worse than the predations of the enemy.

'Back,' she growled, and the man obeyed. He stepped back,

his gait unsteady, and she paced forward eagerly. She moved around him, gesturing for him to take her place at the door to the cell. He shook his head, the bulbous lenses of the goggles bobbing in imitation of an insect. She scowled, and cracked him in the side of the head, watching him tumble to the floor alongside his friend. She dipped low, checked them quickly for supplies and ammunition. She took some charge-packs, and a short blade, and then sealed the chamber behind her.

'There must be a way out of here,' she breathed.

She checked the gun she had taken. A full charge. There were, at least, some graces left to her. She looked at the sword from one of her victims, and let a smile colour her features once more.

'With this, I will find a way, or carve one.'

They rounded another corner to the sounds of gunfire and screams.

Instantly they brought their weapons up, the blue glow of Erastus' pistol a sudden light in the shadows. Men were screaming, and they could hear the sound of armour against decking as they stumbled and fell, or were cut down. A panicked guard almost barrelled into them, babbling incoherently. His gauntleted hands clawed at them as he tried to push past.

'Save me, please, Throne save me from the beast!' he wailed and whimpered.

There was a rush of air, the sound of a swooping attack, and the man's eyes went wide behind the lenses. Blood trickled from his mouth, and he pitched forward onto the decking. A short blade protruded from his spine. It had been thrown, end over end, to bury itself in the man's back.

Zofia and Erastus looked at each other, and then up to see the perpetrator standing, watching them. Her hand lay nonchalantly on her hip. Her breathing was laboured, and for all her pretence it was clear that her battles had been pitched. She forced a smile.

'You came, then.'

'Of course we came!' Erastus exclaimed. 'We just expected–' He paused, considering what to say next.

'That I would need rescuing?'

'Something like that,' he said with a shrug. 'You're hurt?' he asked, noting her bruised and contused face. She simply smiled again, showing blood-slicked teeth.

'Nothing serious. They tried, Throne love them, but they were not the most practised of interrogators. I have had worse in the lower decks, carousing with the crew.' She winced slightly, as though putting those words to the test. 'You have a plan to get us out of here?'

Erastus laughed. 'Of course we have a plan.' He looked to Zofia, and she smiled. 'It is, though, a little more melodramatic than you might be used to.'

CHAPTER THIRTY-ONE

PARTING GIFTS

The council was not going well.

Neither the heartfelt pleas that Katla could muster, which seemed insincere when uttered by the imposing warrior, nor Gunther's bribes and extortions seemed to find any purchase. Nikolai Vaskin remained unmovable and stone-hearted. He glared down at them with a thinly veiled contempt that spoke more to his hatred of any and all outsiders, than it did to the liberties that had been taken against him.

'There will be no dialogue,' he growled. 'There is nothing you have to offer me, save that which I have demanded as righteous tribute. If you wish to make your gutter offers, then you can make them from your own ships – those still capable of movement. Go, grovel to your primarch. Let him drink in your failure, and know that you have been bested by the lord of Noatun.'

'You are no lord,' Katla said simply.

The guards raised their weapons, as the circle of men closed around her. Any one of them could deliver the killing blow. She stared at the enthroned man, and she laughed.

'We will not be held at your mercy, and we will not fail in our duty.' Her features creased, the tattooed skull grinning in sympathetic triumph. 'We will thrive. Out beyond your influence. In the shadows of the void and the light of distant stars. We will fight and bleed and die, but we will do it with a smile on our lips and a song in our heart. We will not die as ailing beasts. We will struggle until the end, because that is the way of the Imperium.'

'Is that supposed to scare me?' Nikolai asked. He was more drawn and cadaverous than ever. The low lumens of the command chamber pulsed with his breathing, peaking with his wrath. The soldiers held their aim steady, ready for his word. The hammer, poised to fall.

The word never came. If he spoke the order, it was drowned out by gunfire. So near, and yet at a remove. The soldiers looked up and around, armour clattering as their movements became panicked. The clicks of vox-communication joined the whispers of the soldiers as they sought any sign of clarity as to what was happening.

A body fell from above, holed through with smoking las-burns. It impacted with a wet, meaty crunch onto the platform beside Nikolai. He turned, glacially slow, and gawped down at the ruin of a man at his side.

Then something else was falling, with far more purpose. Three figures dropped from the aperture above. The guards were already in motion, barking orders as they trained their guns at the command platform. One of the figures was already on their feet, pressing the glowing barrel of a plasma pistol against Nikolai's sweat-sheeted temple.

Erastus smiled, even as Zofia and Astrid brought their own

weapons up. They could not hope to kill all the guards, but they didn't have to. The message was clear. *One step closer, and your master's head is gone.*

'I think,' Erastus whispered to the lord of Noatun Station, 'that it's time we revisited our negotiations.'

'Kill him,' Nikolai Vaskin mewled pitiably. Threat had never come this close. Even the wounds and illnesses and ravages of time had been suspended, pushed back as he gained ever-closer unity with the station. There were Mechanicus adepts who would have killed for his exalted state, and he should know – he had seen many of them nailed to cogs beyond the hull for their rank presumption.

That this interloper, this boy, should come so close. That he would dare...

'Kill them all!'

'Ah...' The boy – Erastus – raised his free hand. 'I wouldn't do that if I were you. Not unless you would like to see Lord Vaskin here reduced to dust and ashes.'

The gun-line trained at him wavered, a few of the barrels dipping. Confusion and fear crossed the crew's faces.

'That's better.' Erastus smiled. 'Now we're making progress, aren't we, Nikolai?'

'What do you want?' Nikolai asked. He felt like a shrunken, broken shadow of himself.

'I want my liberty. I want that extended to all who sail with me. One way or the other, we are leaving here. The only real difference is whether or not you live beyond our passing.'

Silence greeted the rogue trader's pronouncement. Nikolai's eyes darted madly, seeking a way out. He was reduced to a cornered beast, desperate for any avenue of escape. Even now he was looking for advantage, opportunity, a way to chew through the new bonds closing around him. The cables and tethers which bound him to the station were very tight, so very tight, the chrysalis of his station reduced to a shell – a prison. Everything loomed in about him. Claustrophobically so. Restraints clung to his pallid flesh. All who looked upon him, friend or foe, could see the sudden weight upon him – and the brittle strength that came with desperation.

'No,' he breathed. 'Never.'

'I thought you might say that,' Erastus said with a shake of his head. The man raised his hand to his ear, and spoke a single word. 'Now.'

The *Indomitable Soul* and the *Wyrmslayer Queen* both still prowled the void, close to where the *Lustful Paradox* had docked. Their course had been a standard predatory pattern, slowly circling in about it like hunting sharks. They had waited to see if ships burst from the station in attack vectors, or made to run for the system's edge.

Nothing had come. They almost seemed disappointed, sullen, as they prowled closer and closer, before winding back out again. Now they rallied at their king's command. The guns of both vessels were trained and directed at the station's core.

They fired.

Light and fury split the void as the lance batteries committed themselves. The station's void shields flared, star-bright and burning. Capacitors exploded somewhere within, as the shields failed. Smoke filled the suddenly shaking interior of Noatun as the generators gave out. The combined, focused fire scorched the exterior hull of the station, and reduced the gallows to dripping molten slag. Confusion reigned. Even the command core was trembling, the low beat of machine agony as the entire structure convulsed.

As one, the three captains of the Davamir Compact reached into their armour or the folds of coats, and found the relevant switches. The technology was old, rarefied. To have one was a miracle, but each of them had their own. They were symbols of rank, but utterly functional.

The teleport beacons engaged, with no void shields to interfere.

Astrid and Zofia stepped away from Nikolai, and into the corona of light which had begun to halo Erastus. Gunther and Katla were transfixed by their own nimbus of warp-light. There was a sickly flash as reality shuddered, became elastic, and ceased to be corporeal. The reeking, roiling madness of the warp bubbled into being for one terrible moment, and then fell away. The intruders were gone. The prisoner was gone.

And with the shaking of decking, and the thunder of massed ship engines, Nikolai soon realised that the ships he had sought to protect would also be gone. Escaped, stolen away into the stars beyond the station.

Silence fell, harsh and angry and heavy, as Noatun counted its losses.

Days passed, but the pain remained. Noatun's stolen property was not miraculously returned. The wounds and slights lingered, felt by every last soul still aboard the station. Sasha walked the docks, still under the pall of silence. She no longer felt like a vital part of the apparatus. She, and so many others, had been knocked out of joint. She still served the mockery-throne, still stood at the master's side, but nothing was as it had been. Everything felt subdued. The few crews who still haunted the docks didn't laugh or cajole, merely walked the empty expanses in slack-jawed surprise. They gawped, lost for words in the midst of calamity. Robbed, in more ways than they could count.

She was no longer certain that she had a place, at the heart of things. The first purges had followed their master's incandescent anger. The first shots had been levelled against the guards who had failed, even before any shots followed the enemy out into the expanse of space.

Sasha winced as she thought of it. She was walking without direction, listless, caught in the wake of the work crews the way feeder fish trailed behind mega-predators. Or how carrion birds circled a dying animal. Her time on true-worlds had been infrequent. All she knew of ecosystems came from educational scripts and the odd pict-book. She had never known a life beyond the station.

A cry went up, drawing her attention. She watched one of the work crews become suddenly animated as they dragged a hulking container from under some rubble. It was sturdy, and had survived the impact with barely a scratch. It looked like a standard Munitorum macro-supply crate, though as she drew closer she could see that it was marked with various sigils of identification that she did not recognise.

'This is one of theirs,' she breathed. *Perhaps there is something to be salvaged from this after all.*

The surface of the crate was stamped with official notations, bearing a purple serpent and a crown of tarnished, writhing gold. Beyond that it was etched, almost scrimshawed, with whorling patterns of intricate design which flowed from the crown and serpent. They had been etched with a craftsman's care, and with no shortage of love, she realised. Her fingers were tracing along it, even as one of the crew forced a crowbar into the gap at the crate's sealed edge.

'Wait,' she tried to say, but they were already working to open it. There was a hiss of escaping air, and the entire thing bucked with their efforts. Something dislodged from the top of it, practically tumbling into her lap. She looked down at it.

It was a data-slate. Displayed upon its surface was a single, simple pronouncement.

For the future.

She blinked, placed it to one side, and then looked back as the seal broke and the hatch juddered open. Pale, milky light drifted from within and for a moment they were all rendered ghostly. Ephemeral. There was a click, and the light died.

It seemed to her almost like... She shuddered at the thought. Like a stasis field, disengaging. Plenty of goods required those sorts of precautions, though. Rare breeds of livestock, perishable victuals, pristine ingredients caught at the very moment of ripeness. There could be spoils in there that would make them rich, or feed them for a dozen work cycles.

The hope died in her throat as the shadows within unfurled. Uncoiled. The thing in the darkness reached out with massive, too-large limbs. Clawed hands took hold of the edges of the crate, and the metal buckled as it heaved itself forward into the light.

Sasha did not even have the chance to scream, as the future descended upon her, with all its horrific promise.

ACT III

THE SERPENT AND ITS VENOM

We have ever been swords.

We carried that lesson from the moons of Jupiter, and the cradle of Sol. Out into the untamed stars. Though our duties have changed, as the galaxy has changed, our hearts have remained the same. We were lords militant. We were warriors.

How many worlds, indeed how many cultures, owe all that they are to us? To a hand extended, bearing a blade?

The stories tell us that our forebears walked in the shadows of demigods and followed in the footsteps of crusade. That was our crucible, and it is carried in the blood of every man and woman who bears the Warrant.

Trade, mercantile concerns, the hunt for relics or for void-shaped flesh – I understand these wants. These needs. These vocations.

But I will say until my last breath, that at the heart of every rogue trader, there is a fighter waiting to be set loose.

– Excerpted from the memoirs of Lord Davos Lamertine,
Lord Militant Principal of the Lamertine Dynasty

Chapter Thirty-Two

LOST TO THE STORM

The journey had been smooth, beyond the knot of enmity that Ghrent had become. That was, perhaps, worse than any ravage of storm or Rift, or any predation that might befall them. Erastus had long since ceased to walk the observation decks of his ship, and instead remained within a sanctum which was still not truly his own. His father's fingerprint was all over it. Drummed into the dark, imposing sablewood, worn into the subtle gilding around the edges of the desk, and the high cabinets crowded with relics. His father's death mask regarded him from one high perch, eyeing him with corpse-curdled disdain.

Even here, now, halfway across the galaxy, I cannot escape from the scrutiny of the dead.

Endymica waited. There was a reckoning there, he knew, and yet he hungered for it. To see Absalom's dreams cast down and honour restored. He would bring the Technologist before him in chains and strip all rights from his name. Cast him from the Compact before the blade ever touched his neck. When his dreams were ashes, only then would death be allowed to claim him.

Death…

The thought danced across his mind again and he reached out, plucking up the prize that lay before him. He rolled the missive between his fingers and the desk, moving it idly as he examined its casing. It was not the sacred Edict, preserved in a stasis vault until it was needed. It was the garbled message he had found in his father's quarters upon the Cradle. It seemed so long ago, when they had merely been in preparation. When legacy and loss had been the defining concerns.

Now he kept coming back to this message. This moment, caught in time.

'Why did you have it? Why not simply dispose of it? If it were worth nothing. If it contained nothing?'

There was no answer. No echo of his father, no shade in arms to announce calamity or bring clarity. Erastus chuckled to himself, shaking his head as he stood. He turned the message case over and over again in his hands, weighing it.

'Still looking for answers?' asked a voice from the doorway. He turned, and raised an eyebrow. Astrid stood, leaning against the door frame. She nodded to the message. 'You live too much amongst the past, grubbing for meaning in memories. Your father is not there. He walks where you walk, and acts as you act.'

'I'm not sure he would appreciate the sentiment.'

She laughed. 'Ghosts rarely do.'

Erastus was not sure why she had stayed after the flight from Noatun. It was simple convenience that had brought her here in the shared fire of the teleportation. They had clattered to the ground, the three of them, smoking in the aftermath of their translation. The rune-marked floor had been thick with hoar frost and aglow with crawling witch-light. His breath had caught in his throat at the sudden chill purity of the air. The familiar tang of a proper ship of the line.

Of the *Indomitable Soul.*

There had been ample opportunity for her to return to the *Queen,* but she had ignored every chance. Some mission, he imagined, from her mother. Katla, for all her warrior's guile, was not a subtle creature. The hunt was rarely ever so, and when it was, it was a trap. A misdirection.

'I don't believe in ghosts,' he said finally. Unconvincingly.

'All lives leave echoes. And if not echoes, then ripples.' Her smile died. 'If the dead have no way to trouble the living, then how is it that Evelyne can wound you? Dead now, and a segmentum away besides.'

'That's different.' He thought again of the message. The mere fact of its existence was like a promise; a wrinkle in the universe's skin. *Are you still out there, somewhere, Ev? Is that what I'm really looking for?*

'Is it?' Astrid asked. 'Evelyne is dead. Your father is dead. One was taken from you by circumstance, and the other by spite. Both are wounds in your world. Both haunt you.'

'And those are my daemons to face, and to conquer.' He held his tongue. He would not voice his thoughts. Not now. Not yet. Not until he had something in his hands that resembled surety. He would not drown in dreams and fancies as his father had before the end.

Astrid laughed at that. So simple and delicate a sound from her warrior's bearing. 'Is that what you think will happen, Erastus?' She shook her head, and her braids struck her leather armour. 'You are not your sister, but you share her fate. You are lost in the storm. It merely scars your soul, rather than the heavens.'

'I...' He paused, trailing off. He put the missive down, and moved around the desk to face her. 'I know it hasn't been easy. I've done the best I can, in his absence, and without her guidance. This dynasty, the entire Compact, would be in better hands if they were still here. But they're not.' He let out a long sigh, and looked down at his hands. 'They're not.'

'Do you know why I'm still here, Erastus?' Astrid asked.

He looked back up at her, suddenly uncertain. He shook his head.

'I am here because you did me a kindness. You put you and yours at risk, that I might live. That carries weight, for a daughter of Fenris.'

'I did what was expected of me.'

'Yes, and you did it well. My mother will not tell you so, but she is impressed. I am impressed. Perhaps, in his cold and vacant heart, even the Lord Radrexxus is impressed. When we bear down upon the Norastye, maybe in his last moments Absalom will be impressed. Moments like your rescue attempt – those are where you find your way. When the storm fades.'

His fingers closed around the message again, seeking solace if not understanding.

'I know what I have to do, Astrid. Thank you.'

Erastus walked the spinal transitways that threaded through the backbone of the ship, drawing ever closer to the choral chamber nestled along its length. The corridor was lined with fluttering curtains of fine white silk, stirring in the artificial breeze of the oxygen-recyc processors. Golden patterns adorned the walls, etched with the light of distant constellations.

He paused before silver doors, and knocked gently. Even here, on his own ship, it was befitting to show deference. A robed servant opened the door and ushered Erastus inside, into the opulence of the choir chambers. Intricate filigreed glasswork ringed the chamber, affording it a scientific styling, its minimalist décor clashing with the more baroque opulence that existed elsewhere in the ship. It was designed to be a place of contemplation, evoking a soothing state of meditative trance. The original architects had evidently focused more on the wellbeing of the occupants, rather than any rough statement of intent.

Astropaths hobbled amongst the cultivated silicate, caught in the refracted light of the chamber. At the centre sat Haran, wizened and pale, his hollow sockets seemingly sightless. His senses, though, were things beyond mortal sight. The air crackled with invisible potency, and Erastus felt the hairs on the nape of his neck prickle and peak. The venerable astropath's scrutiny swept over him, and he felt as though he were observed from afar. As though the others who Haran had communed with shared in his sight.

'You have come, my lord. Forgive us for our laxity in not attending you upon your inauguration. We have been deep in communion, divining the messages intended for the notables of the Compact.'

'I understand, of course,' Erastus said. 'My father knew the value of your order.' He reached into his coat and produced the missive. 'He trusted in you, as he trusted in this.'

'Ah,' Haran said. His empty gaze had drifted to it, sensing its empyreal resonance. 'Of course. He placed such hope in it. Such faith.'

'Faith?' Erastus laughed. 'Of all the things you might attribute to him, that is perhaps the strangest.'

'Your father, in all the years I had the honour of serving him, proved himself to be a man of singular vision.' Haran paused. 'The coming of the Rift, though… it changed him.' The old man turned to regard Erastus. The pale parchment of his skin crinkled, and his tongue lapped at his thin lips as he weighed his next utterance. 'The loss of your sister changed him.'

'I know,' Erastus said. With Evelyne gone, something had broken within his father. As though he had never prepared for this eventuality, or countenanced its existence. All that had been left had been the second-hand learning he passed to Erastus. The artfully tailored dreams cut apart and stitched back together, desperately altered. Now, simply an ill-fitting costume Erastus had been forced into.

'But part of him refused to accept it.' Haran chewed his lip, wringing his hands. The astropathic choir's leader seemed to be dogged by other worries, as though deeper concerns lurked in waiting. 'He had us scry the heavens and sift through every dying dream. We cast our messages to the void with all the power and symbols of authority that his name could muster. We had all but given up hope, when this message was received. Such as it is.'

'It is a message, then?'

'We dwelt upon it for a long time, my lord. We considered it might be a mortis cry, of some world or ship or station, but it was more than that. There was direction to it. Purpose. This cry sought us out.'

'From where?' He was aware that every muscle in his body had tensed. He knew. He knew the answer before Haran ever voiced it.

'From beyond the Rift, lord. From out of the storms.'

'He thought it was her, didn't he?' Erastus shook his head. 'He thought Evelyne was alive. That the *Untempered Wrath* was still out there.'

'He did. He bade us turn our talents towards re-establishing contact, and if possible to translating whatever sense we could garner from the message.'

'And did you succeed? Have you made any progress during our transit?'

'Inconclusive.' The word fell like a hammer blow. 'We sought clarity, but there was nothing to be found. We cannot commune with our sister choir who sailed with her. No messages have reached us, and we cannot untangle anything further from the last communion. Forgive me, my lord.'

'There is nothing to forgive. You gave your lord hope, even if it was a fool's dream.'

The old man nodded, staring at nothing. 'It is our place to serve, at the whim and leisure of the lords of the Compact.' He held out one frail hand, and it trembled in the air.

'Are you well?' Erastus asked hesitantly.

'There is...' Haran trailed off. His features twisted in something that might have been pain, and his fingers kneaded at the pale blue fabric of his robes. 'As we draw closer to the Rift, I thought that it would overwhelm us. The choir was girded, prepared for the inevitable psychic assaults. But they have not come. There is silence, and the death of thought.' A shudder passed through him. 'There are whispers in the silence, Lord Lamertine. They claw at the mind. We cannot place them. They are shadow, and mist. Wind, beyond thought.'

'Keep me posted.' Erastus rose. His hand had drifted to the hilt of his sword. He turned to leave. 'We will speak of this again.'

'As you say, lord.' Haran's eyeless sight stared through Erastus. He could feel the old man's scrutiny, even as it burned into his back. 'I pray, lord, that you lead us safely to our end.'

Erastus did not respond as he walked from the room, and out into the chill of his ship.

Chapter Thirty-Three

'Come and see,' the voice breathed. 'Oh please, you must come and see.'

And he followed it, into the dark in the innards of the ship. Crewman Abraham Miklos moved through the unfamiliar corridors, following someone he barely knew, on the promise that something transcendent lay ahead. Passing beneath arches carved in imitation of rearing beasts, tracing his fingers along the intricate knotwork, he could well believe that wonders lay here.

To be stranded on another ship was common enough in fleet actions. He had been part of a work detail assigned to the *Wyrmslayer Queen* during the exodus from Ghrent. He, along with a mix of Radrexxus crew, had been lost in the shuffle. They had volunteered their services where they could, and had settled into the work routines of the new ship, until such time as they were out of the warp, and normality could be restored.

The Helvintr crews had a way about them that Miklos liked; a swagger to everything they did, modelled on their leader. He had seen her from afar, and had been impressed with what he saw. She had a much more straightforward manner than the new Lord Lamertine. For all her hunter's roughness, she knew war. She had carried men through it with more than just dumb luck and hope. He wasn't sure Erastus, the *wastrel*, could measure up to it.

The air was getting colder, shaking him from his thoughts. The cowled and cloaked woman ducked beneath a pipe, and disappeared behind a corner. He broke into a jog, chasing after her. He found himself laughing, even as he almost tripped over a loop of cabling.

'Come and see...' Her voice drifted through the condensing mist. 'We're almost there, come and see.' He couldn't actually see her any more, only hear the faint echo of her voice. Why was he still following? Playing this game?

And was it a game? A strange sort of flirtation played out by the Fenrisians? His head swam with sweet wine and strong ale. Against his better judgement, he forged on.

He had met her in one of the refectory halls here, or what passed for them – raucous, barely sanctioned drinking dens more at home in a low-hive commercia than a ship at war. They took joy in their kills, they revelled in it. This was the spoils of that undertaking and mindset, he realised.

How much wider would our reach be if the Old Man had thought like these glorious savages?

The girl had been the same, though he hadn't quite caught her name. She had a relentlessness to her. A predator's confidence. An irresistible grace. Enough to draw him here, down into the cold and the dark.

'Hello?' he called, as he stepped out of the passageways and into a larger chamber. It seemed old, older than the surrounding ship. Marked with a patina of disuse that was only just fading thanks to recent occupation. It had been some sort of storage tank, once. He could not tell if it had held water or waste, time had erased the scents of its past. Now there was the faint reek of incense, and the tang of human sweat.

She stood in the centre of it, and turned to face him. Her skin was Fenris pale, marked with winding black and blue tattoos. She smiled, utterly without warmth. It was a hollow smile. A dead joy at odds with the culture he had observed and admired.

'What is it?' Miklos asked. 'What is it you have to show me?'

The shadows at the edges of the chamber moved, and figures stepped forward from the darkness. They were dressed as she was, in rough-spun robes. The coarse fabric contrasted with the artful masks they work. Silver and bronze and gold, the masks were smooth and shaped into the flowing visages of serpents.

'Do you see?' she asked. Her hands spread, and the figures came closer – forming a rough semicircle of strange, stilted movements. 'I wanted you to see, as I saw.' There were marks on the walls, he realised. Gouges in the metal. Environmental pressures perhaps, but it seemed more primal than that. As though carved by the claws of some great...

His eyes widened. His mouth fell open and he could feel his heart racing, his breathing pounding in his chest. He was suddenly aware of vast scrutiny upon him; not simply from the encroaching figures, but from something older. Something stronger. He looked up, past the impassive masks, beyond the marks in the worn metal.

He saw. He beheld, even if he did not understand. The thing, the impossible thing, that moved down the sheer wall of the chamber. It looked up, and as its gaze met his, he realised that he was lost. He could not even bring himself to scream.

'I... see...' he whispered hoarsely, as it took him in its grasp, and illumination seized him in a rush of blood and pain.

* * *

'Is it ready, I wonder?' Gunther mused to himself, kneeling before the altar. It was a stylised representation of the Emperor in His capacity as Binder-of-the-Void, bracing the heavens upon His broad shoulders. Gold and amethyst veined the marble of its construction, and he marvelled at the craftsmanship. He had commissioned it himself, an affectation that had startled him. He preened momentarily, fussing with his rich silks and perfectly poised wig. Habit, more than anything else.

Here, alone within his sanctum, he was able to cast aside the petty disguises and forced revelries. Here, he could be himself. He could embrace who he was always intended to be. Who life, and his family, had shaped him to be.

'The blood is all,' he whispered. There was comfort in the mantra. It had long since saturated his life. Passed from parent to child, from captain to crew. All who served were bonded. By oath. By blood. By faith. 'In blood are we sanctified, and in faith do we serve.' He looked up again at the statue. It showed Him as a scholar and as a warrior. He held up the very heavens, yes, but He also held a sword and extended a scroll. He was everything, to all men.

He was perfect. A loving father. A guiding light.

Light…

He closed his eyes as he thought of it, and reached over for the communications panel mounted upon a nearby column. There was a snap of static, and then the echo of drawn-out breathing.

'Euryale, my sweet,' Gunther crooned. 'Do you see the lights of home? Can you hear the song of sanctity, playing out across the stars?'

'I hear, my lord. The song is stronger now than ever before.' Euryale's voice drifted through the vox in a distracted hiss. She was not entirely focused, her mind cast to watching the warp. Seeing the world beyond the veil, the roiling tides beyond the ship.

The storm could not touch her or slow her. *The song sings us to our home, and our return. How long has it been since last we graced Endymica? We danced within the void, and the planet sang us away.'*

'Too long, my sweet. Far too long.' He sighed as he stood, shaking out his fine silks. 'Oh it was a wonder, wasn't it? It burned so very beautifully. We swept through the system, and they rose up to greet us. Arms wide.' His eyes were distant, lost in the glow of memory. 'The things we taught each other. And we returned, again and again. We graced them with our gifts and they filled our hulls with plenty. Flesh and faith. Things the others could never understand. But soon, soon enough, they shall. When we return.'

'When we return–'

'When we return again, it shall be in glory,' Gunther said with a sigh. 'We shall lay the groundwork of our triumph, and no one shall stop us. Not the metal men and their plots, not the savages nor the boy king.'

He laughed, a cold and bitter sound. There was no joy in it. The walls glimmered with their superficial gilding, the marble sparkled as though freshly polished. Yet it was all, fundamentally, empty. For all the trappings of a fane, it had no soul.

'Our ascension draws ever nearer.'

Chapter Thirty-Four

It was a place of whispers, and the chill of a distant world.

Katla was always surprised when she braved the sanctum. She did not come here unless it was utterly necessary. The weight of the place pressed in at her, and made her scars ache. She bit back the rising bile in her throat, and forged on into the low light of braziers. Furs hung from the walls, and covered the doorways. Katla pushed past one, and gazed down at the sitting figure of the gothi.

Bodil was old; she had been old when she served Katla's father. Before her, Katla felt like a child again, a little girl left in the darkness with the witch.

'You have come to have me read your wyrd, is that not so?' Bodil asked, baring her ruined smile. 'It has been some time, my queen, since you have walked the path of destiny.'

'It has,' Katla agreed. She sat, lowering herself to the floor so that she was eye to eye with the old woman. Something was burning nearby, flooding the chamber with the harsh notes of woodsmoke and herbs.

'Are you afraid, my queen?'

'I am not. Nor am I a queen.'

Bodil laughed and shook her head. 'Oh, you are a queen. You have always been a queen. It does not matter that you do not sit on the Compact's throne. Rulers come and go. They rise and fall. Yet it is your wyrd. It is what you were shaped for. Rule, the hunt, and the glorious end in His service.'

'Is that to be my fate?' Katla's scars burned with phantom pain as she asked the question. Bodil had been there, so long ago now, when those scars had been earned. She had watched the healers and wound-shapers as they remade her. They had shaped her scars into the visage of the wolf. Into the echo of her soul, bound by ink and brand.

'You know your fate. We have teased it out a hundred times before. You come not to know your fate, but to ask, "Is this when my fate will find me?" Do you not?'

Katla laughed, and leant forward. Others would often quail from her gaze, seek to flee the predator's scrutiny. Bodil had no such fear. She was beyond it. In her, all fears were met and tested and bound with ritual.

'That is it exactly. You told me, before–'

'I told you that the wyrm would hunt you as you have hunted it. That it would find you, and drag you down into the darkness. That it would not slay you, but that you would yearn to be slain. That the hand of a loved one, a trusted blade, would end your life. You will die, my queen, but you will die pure. Untroubled by the corruption of the abyss, and by the poisons of serpents. Death will be a gift, when the time comes.'

'I have never thought of it as a gift,' Katla said distantly. She closed her eyes, collected herself. 'When my father met his end, it was as he had always wished it to be. A weapon in his hand, the foe before him. He died fighting. Perhaps that is all we have ever wanted. Maybe that is all that we deserve.'

'You do not believe that,' the old woman replied. 'You are not a coward, Katla. You are a daughter of the Helvintr. You are the fire that scours, and the ice that binds. Raised up from a world of monsters, to etch your legend upon the very stars.' Bodil picked up a bag, shaking it experimentally. 'Who else can say that, save the Sky Warriors of Russ?'

'I am not afraid,' Katla said.

'I know. Never that.'

'I do not fear death. If anything, I fear failure. I do not want to stand in His sight having done anything less than my best.'

'Your father, Throne preserve him, was much the same.' Her hand jerked up and the bone tiles tumbled from the back, clattering across the floor in a spasm of pattern and chance. 'Hmm...' she murmured, as her long pale fingers traced across the surface of the runes.

'What do you see?'

'The Wolf is ascendant, as is the King-Enthroned-For-War.' Bodil's breathing was steady, her eyes a blur of flickering movements. 'The Serpent waits below, gnawing at the roots of the world. The Serpent is always there, but here it is disguised. Armoured in flesh and iron, it hides its true face until the last moment.'

'And that is when it claims me?'

'That is when it tries, my queen. There is red snow in our future, piled upon black and broken ice. It shakes the bones of the world, and makes the sternest souls bleed. That is your fate, my lady. To stand in the hurricane gale, and to endure it.'

'That is why I was made, Bodil. That is why I was raised up beyond other men. A Warrant is more than simple parchment. It is trust. Generations of trust, shaped and directed, that we might stand here in this moment. That we might be queens and kings.'

'This does not end with you, Katla.'

'I know,' Katla said. She looked sadly at the distant wall, hung with totems and fetishes. She did not know where Astrid was, not exactly, but the sentiment was clear. Wherever her daughter was, she was in Katla's thoughts. 'When the time comes, she will rise. And I trust that you will offer her the same good counsel as I have always received from you.'

Sword met spear, and the hall rang with their clatter.

Erastus bared his teeth, hurling himself into the swing with a savage fury that was worthy of Astrid. She staggered back, barking with laughter. It was not that it was sport, more that there was a furious symmetry to their battle. Each of their warrior souls was inflamed, brought to the surface.

The weapons were simple dulled wood, but they served their purpose. A dozen marks had been battered into their flesh through the training leathers. They were bruised, panting, but unbowed. They struggled on, locked in their frenetic combat. The haft of the spear cracked him in the side of the head, and he flinched back from it. His sword swung round and met her raised guard with a crash of wood on wood.

'You're getting better,' she allowed, with a smile. He went low in answer, around the edges of Astrid's guard. Skirting, probing. Three strikes sought to land, and three were turned away.

'I have to,' he said. His voice was strained, thick with the effort of maintaining the assault. She swung her spear round and he reared back, the dulled blade whistling past his face.

He moved in, along the inside of the spear thrust, and drove the pommel into her sternum. She sprawled to the ground, groaning with sudden pain. Her breathing was harsh as she forced her way back to her feet. She looked at him with a momentary flash of anger, even as he reached out to steady her.

'You all right?' he asked. She waved him off.

'I'm fine,' she said, dusting herself off. 'Fine. You are getting better. You might even acquit yourself well, should it come to open warfare again.'

'They need to know they can rely on me,' he said as he looked at her. 'And so do you.'

'I think I do,' Astrid said. She laid her spear down. 'You have led men into war – provably, now. Not only that but you put your life at risk to ensure that I could be liberated.'

'Not that you needed my help, of course,' Erastus laughed, tossing the training blade to one side.

'It didn't hurt,' she said with a smile. 'Simply know this – I have seen what you are capable of. I trust you. Not because my mother insists that it should be so, but because I have chosen it for myself. My mother thinks of our family as the pack. As the tribe, still on the ice. I think she forgets, sometimes, that we are part of something greater. The Compact is as much our pack, as much our tribe, as the crew of a ship or the lineage of a dynasty. We are all shields, locked in the same line.'

'That's a lot, coming from your family. I know that you don't extend that sort of grace to many not of your blood.'

'Only those who have proven themselves. Who have earned a debt of trust and gratitude. One that lasts the lifetime they have saved.' She laid a hand on his shoulder. 'You are not your father, Erastus. He would never have dared this. He would never have risked this. He would have alienated the Radrexxus, abandoned the Helvintr, and plunged like an ill-forged spear into the heart of the Norastye. Friendless, alone and unsupported. Men like him, they would call that bravery. They would laud it, even as they died. You will not burn, as he would have.' She paused, considering. 'And if you do, then it shall not be alone.'

Before he could respond alarms began to sound. He looked around as the sparse interior of the training circle suddenly flooded with red light. It flashed, strobing in time with the wailing sirens, before a voice cut through the clamour.

'My Lord Lamertine,' Egeria said, 'we are readying for material translation. We are here, my lord. We have made it to Endymica.'

Chapter Thirty-Five

The ships burst from the empyrean in a rush of unlight, as reality shuddered and spasmed and then finally tore open. It was an orderly progression; not the mad tumble of vessels into the real that had blighted Ghrent. There was reason behind it, the culmination of a thousand Imperial prayers for safe passage and sane transit. Crewmen went to their knees, weeping and thankful. It did not matter that they were sworn to the Lamertine Dynasty, thralls of the Helvintrs, or newcomers from the liberated ships of Noatun. Each of them was, in their own way, grateful to have lived.

The Radrexxus ships were quiet, contemplative. There was no revelry or excess, no exultations over the vox. There was only silence. Some thought it an omen, that the most boisterous voices had suddenly turned introspective. It spoke, they claimed, to the gravity of the situation. The long journey through the warp, the betrayal, the battles to see them to their promised end. It had all taken its toll upon the Radrexxus. The mask of

267

bemused, intoxicated indifference had begun to slip – if not to crack entirely.

The ships entered formation, with the Lamertine vessels pushing to the fore and the Helvintr close behind them. The Radrexxus ships were spreading out, forming a sprawling rear-guard. Every weapon was primed, and every shield was raised. They did not know from which quarter their enemy would strike, or if any strike would come.

They would not risk being caught unawares again.

'Auspex returns, my lord,' Kaddas said quietly as he hunched over his station. The din of the command bridge faded as he focused, intent upon the mass of contradictory signals flooding through the console. Lights flickered and danced, birthed and dying in moments. He followed them as best as he was able, but could only watch as the fluctuating readings slipped away from him. 'There are a great many signals. More than the manifests of the Norastye would suggest them capable of.'

'Disposition?' Erastus asked.

'They are spread out, vastly so. It's almost as though...' Kaddas trailed off. Erastus looked at him. He had never seen the man look so affected. His fingers, white-knuckled, clung to the edges of the console.

'As though what?' There were chimes as messages came in from across the fleet, the insistent barks for attention. Erastus ignored them.

'It... it looks like a debris field,' said Kaddas. 'My lord, some great calamity has taken place here.'

Erastus turned and strode from the bridge as quickly as he was able.

Standing on the observation deck was a study in horror.

Erastus was not alone in his shock or his outrage. Many others had been there immediately after translation, when the heavy warding shutters had rolled back to reveal the tranquil void in place of the warp's corroding madness. Relief had quickly turned to horror at what lay before them.

The void was filled with corpses. The macro-scale ruins of murdered ships spun in the cold darkness, orbited by flocks of slowly turning human cadavers. Ship-death was visceral, traumatic in a way that few other things were. To have your entire world upended, ripped open, the very air prised from your lungs. To be unable even to scream, as death took you. Every void-sailor feared it, the darkly intimate shadows of hull breach, reactor failure, boarding torpedo…

That these ships were recognisable was worse, even if they had been the ships of the enemy. The Norastye had proven themselves to be saboteurs, murderers, thieves of glory, but they had not deserved such a fate.

'What in the name of the Throne happened here?' Erastus breathed.

'Victims of their own folly, perhaps?' murmured Astrid. 'Turned upon their own as they turned upon us?'

'Perhaps…' His hand was pressed to the glass, as though he could take the wrecks in hand and stop their death spirals. He had dreamed of these moments. He had imagined what it would be like to hole the Norastye fleet through and send them tumbling into the orbit of a distant star. He had wanted to see the robed fools and would-be cyborgs of that line die and flail in the void. To show that no matter how much of themselves they reshaped, they would ever be prey to human weakness. Even the true Mechanicus could not escape the foibles of the flesh.

Perhaps I do not hate them as much as I thought? Or perhaps it is the idea of someone taking the revenge that is rightly mine?

Erastus shook his head. In the middle of the storm of metal

and bodies, the *Steel Amidst Infirmity* floated – torn open, innards bared to the stellar winds. Its engines had been carved away from the superstructure, and plasma fires burned along its length. He wondered if Absalom was still enthroned. If he had gone down with the ship, like the captains of Old Terra's long-vanished oceans. There was a comfort in that thought. To die, so yoked to duty.

Starlight, faint and yellow, caught on the harsh angles of the broken vessels, but it was the other light that concerned him. The Endymica System bled with Rift-light, with the monstrous anger of the Cicatrix Maledictum. Vast sweeping horns of incarnate spite ringed the system, catching it in the warp's suppurating grasp. It hurt to look at, and he looked away quickly. He let his eyes drift off of it, never letting it gain true purchase. He instead focused again upon the graveyard of the Norastye.

'The weapon patterns are inconsistent. I can't quite identify what caused these wounds,' he said, shaking his head. 'Could be xenos… could be renegades, bearing the touch of the warp. Any weak point in the crossing is a potential vector for attack. The only local power capable of doing this is the fortress-world itself.'

'Then we should proceed carefully,' Astrid said from behind him.

He turned, nodded to her, and then turned his attention back to the ravaged fleet.

'It's hard to believe,' she added.

'It really is.' He found the *Steel Amidst Infirmity* again. It was hard to reconcile; that one of the great flagships of the Compact could succumb to any enemy assault.

He could not imagine his own ship being overrun, or the *Queen* dying to a thousand cuts. Sometimes he forgot about the *Wrath*, and the idea of Evelyne dying by fire and madness. Had it been hard, at the end? Had she suffered? He closed his eyes, fingers braced against the viewport. He closed them into a fist, drumming his knuckles against it.

'It should never have come to this. We were meant to come here together, in unity. In brotherhood.'

'A fine dream,' she said with a smile. 'But such things rarely survive first contact with the enemy. You learn that upon the ice of Fenris. Kin and kind are trustworthy only so long as it serves an interest. The tribes might unite in service of a greater cause, or to fight a singular foe, but it does not always last.'

'The Compact was supposed to be different. Everything my father said about it, made it sound so... romantic. Princes fighting in His name, to advance the very soul of the Imperium.'

Astrid laughed. 'A fine sentiment,' she said. 'A pretty lie to hide ambition. You knew your father, better than most perhaps, and you knew what lay at his heart. What he sought, with every fibre of his being. Service was a part of it, certainly, but there was the hunger for glory. To be remembered. He wished to carve his saga upon the universe's skin.'

'He told me, a long time ago, of the importance of stories. How they were the lifeblood of existence. The universe ran on stories, he would say. The libraries he kept were the envy of many scholarly lords. Archive worlds and knowledge-fanes petitioned him for audiences, and for charity. Did you know that?'

'I did not. Our people disdained written records. The oral tradition is all. Our gothi maintains it – holds all the knowledge of the dynasty, and uses that wisdom to guide our leaders. She advises them directly, and consults the runes to better interpret the wyrd of those who serve.'

They were both, he was suddenly aware, stalling. Unwilling to consider what had come to pass; hiding their unease behind the recitation of family history.

'It sounds...' He shuddered as he gazed out at the competing fires. The natural and the unnatural. 'It sounds almost sorcerous, when you put it like that.'

'Skitja!' She spat on the deck. 'To say such things! It is no more sorcery than the reading of the Tarot!'

He held up his hands. 'I meant no disrespect. Your ways are not my ways, but they are still the ways of a world of the Imperium. We will face this. Together. United. Send word to your mother, and to Radrexxus – see if we can get an answer. We're going to have to move decisively, if we want to survive this.'

There was a peculiar calm upon the bridge of the *Lustful Paradox*, the storm within having long since blown itself out. The music had gone quiet, and the air was not filled with the reek of chemical stimulants. It was still, and tense, primed for action or for sudden movement.

No one moved. They did not look up from their stations, nor cease the clatter of fingers over keys. Hands moved in a blur of motion, completely focused and directed as they took in the information and added it to their comprehension of events. Pale figures glided about the edges of the chamber, pausing every so often to knot their fingers into the hair of an attendant. The questing digits locked tight to their scalps, eliciting soft moans of pain. They convulsed at their stations, collapsing back into their chairs, before the figures moved on, and the cycle repeated itself. Information bled from soul to soul, in a peculiar, cyclical, osmosis.

This, they understood, was necessary. This was the nature of service. The demands of the family Radrexxus. Blood always told, in the end. Blood was what mattered.

At the heart of the silent bridge, Gunther stood. His finery was absent, all ostentation removed as though with a knife. The armour he wore was entirely functional. Angular. Overlapping plates of pale cream and regal purple. His sword was belted at his waist, alongside an ornate pistol.

'Are we ready?' he asked simply.

There was a chorus of affirmations, but they were not the approval he sought. He gestured sharply, his fingers cutting the air as surely as any sump-dagger. Servants shuffled forward, mis-shapen beneath their robes. Some considered them baroque servitors, distasteful affectations. They were neither. They were the worthiest unworthy, and they came to honour him with their touch.

They held bowls, and plunged their hands into them, smear-ing them with bright pigments. Rough fingers drifted across his temples and down his face, trailing whorls of paint along his pale skin. The usual make-up and rouging had been scraped off, and he wore no wig. His scalp gleamed in the bridge's lumens, until the questing digits roamed over it and remade his visage in sanctity.

'Are we ready?' he repeated. The bridge was silent. The paint-streaked servants crept away, slinking back into the shadows. A stutter of vox-static broke the calm, and a voice responded.

'We are ready, my lord. Communion proceeds… I can taste them upon the star-wind. They speak with the voice of kin. The seeds have taken root, the fruit is borne in earnest. They have done this thing, offered it up as sacrifice and sacrament! They are joyous, and they call! They call!'

'Prepare,' Gunther said. He drew his blade, testing its weight. 'Maximillian will be needed in the coming tumult. Send word to him. His services are required once more.'

The fleet eased forward into the field of debris, dislodging the larger pieces from their inconstant orbits. Some were shunted out of the way by the passage of the great vessels, flotsam amidst the sea of stars, while others were annihilated outright as they collided with the active void shields. Flashes of light and energy glittered along the length of the ships, like the bioluminescence of deep ocean predators.

'We do not have to linger on the ice to chase the kraken,' Katla said softly. 'It is there, no matter where we go. We have followed it to the stars, and become predators in our own right, and still there is the beast beyond, and beneath.'

Her father's words. He had always imparted the wisdom of the old world, carried up from the storm-tossed seas of Fenris. Stian had been a fine father, and a better captain. Under his tutelage she had learned much, and been shaped into the woman she was today. She hoped she had imparted as much to Astrid. Her daughter was a ferocious spirit, and a capable warrior. Too trusting, perhaps. Quick to accept the offered hand, without truly suspecting what lay behind it. Intent was everything in the hunt.

'You will learn,' Katla said to herself. 'As we all do.'

She had armed and armoured herself, each plate inscribed with warding marks, sigils of aversion. They would turn aside the strike of a sword or the blow of an axe as surely as they would the touch of sorcery. She stood taller in her armour, bolstered by the strength of ages.

'No word from the inner system, jarl,' one of the serfs called. 'Attempting another sending, but there is yet interference from the wrecks. Beyond that, perhaps they do not wish to listen?'

'Then they are fools!' she spat. 'If they were a loyal world then they would have answered. Either whatever claimed the Norastye has swept down upon them, or they are another nest of traitors as the privateers were!' She shook her head, eyes wild. 'I will not be denied again! Raise them, or ready for war!'

Her gaze drifted across the lie of the murdered ships. The signifiers flickered and danced, even as her mind interpreted and divined. She could be right, of course. It could have been some external threat. Some horror… but the kill-patterns suggested otherwise.

Her hand tightened on the haft of her spear. 'If that is the case then we shall dig whatever foe has done this from their lair, and we shall put them to the torch.'

She tapped the blade of the spear against the side of her throne, before dragging it along its edge. Testing it, as against a whetstone.

'Take us in, carefully.' The tapping of the spear was like the beating of a heart, the rhythm underscoring the threat of coming battle. 'The Norastye were taken unawares. That will not happen to me. No matter what else comes to pass, we shall be ready.'

Gunther closed his eyes and let his mind soar. He remembered Endymica. He remembered every breath of it. Minds called out to minds, and he let his consciousness drift into the sea of will and memory.

It was not a kind world. Even before it had been reshaped to the monumental needs of the Imperium, it had never been kind. Lowlands of dust deserts had given way to snow-wreathed mountains, the cradles of winter storms that wracked the fragile ecosystem with baleful fury.

The hand of man had sheared the mountains down to nubs, and fashioned them into fastnesses – girding the world in iron and rockcrete, pointing the guns ever higher. The stars themselves quaked, so they claimed, beneath their relentless scrutiny. Every resource, every opportunity, had been relentlessly yoked and broken, taken and repurposed by the gluttonous hunger of mankind.

Before ever the Rift had opened, Endymica had been a world transformed.

Time had brought subtler changes to the planet. To the oaths that bound it, and the hand that guided it. Its guns had ceased to be idle, and had instead begun to reap their tally of interlopers and intruders. Some were mere pirates, lesser systems' warlords who thought them easy prey. Later came lost souls, seeking safe harbour; remembering where the high walls had been raised, and where the defences were the most mighty. They died with hope on their lips and despair in their hearts.

They who dwelt within did not care. They no longer pretended to. The time for masks was long since passed. They had killed and preyed for time out of mind, for one master or another, and now the galaxy changed. It turned, and burned, and all was confusion.

As the psychic aftershocks of warp translation shuddered through the system, and the first auspex readings penetrated the fug of debris and radiation which orbed the Mandeville point, so the first transmissions were sent. They passed from fortress to fortress, and garrison force to garrison force. It built within the structure of the world, until it would no longer be contained. It rang out, loud and clear, a single utterance. A word which carried with it such terrible import, lost in its simplicity.

Endymica spoke, and Gunther's lips moved in silent sympathy. It spoke, and the word was: *'Voidfather.'*

CHAPTER THIRTY-SIX

THE FATHER OF SERPENTS

'Voidfather.'

The word cut across the vox, on every frequency open to hear it. It had seemed a whisper at first, indistinct and lost amidst the radiation spikes already marring transmissions in the outer system. Those who heard it thought it was a fragment of garbled signal, a misfired burst of noise, but it resolved. Grew stronger. Began to repeat. It echoed from every speaker and horn able to process it, metastasising from an echo to a shout, a chant, a scream. Every vessel rang with its utterance, and the repetition drummed into the skulls of the crew.

It was coming from Endymica, that much was clear. The world sang with it, resonated, devoted to the broadcast of a single word.

It swamped everything. Erastus hadn't yet been able to contact Katla or Gunther. Instead he could only listen to the maddening repetition.

'What does it mean?' Erastus asked, leaning forward from the command throne. The bridge was primed for combat, bathed in a muted red light. Guards had been stationed around the chamber, more than Zofia and her usual honour guard. Matters had escalated. They had been escalating since the betrayal at Ghrent. The devastation apparent upon the Norastye had crystallised the matter.

'Is it not enough,' he asked again, though none of the crew were foolish enough to answer, 'that we are burdened with rivals and traitors? Without having to endure enemies we do not know and have not seen? To have to chase ghost signals and spectres into what is most likely to be a trap?' He sighed again, his hand resting on his pistol's grip. 'Have we established proper communications with them, or do they keep repeating themselves?'

'Nothing yet, my lord. We have tried to get through to them but there is no answer. They ignore us, or they do not care.'

'Put me through to them, I'll address them myself.'

He strode forward, standing before the throne at the centre of the command dais. Everyone had gone silent, waiting for his orders. Hands had already strayed to weapons, or lingered at the controls of the ship's systems. Everyone was on edge, primed and prepared for violence.

'I am Erastus Lamertine, sworn king of the Davamir Compact. I speak with the authority of the Emperor Himself, and I demand an answer.'

'*Voidfather?*' it said, a questioning, plaintive tone creeping into the broadcast as though it were unsure of what it asked. '*The time is upon us. Communion beckons. We need but the word.*'

'You are not making sense!' Erastus snapped. 'Who are you looking for? What have you done here? I will have answers, or I will dig you from your fortresses, and take them! Am I understood?'

The signal died in a crackle that might have been laughter,

and fell silent. Erastus stared at the speaker for a long moment, and then slammed his fist down against it.

'Your orders, my lord?'

'Ahead full. If they mean to fight us, let us fight. The Norastye may have died easily, but I have no such intentions. We know that much. They coasted into the system, were caught unawares, and betrayed. A fine irony, true enough, but we shall not fall prey to the assaults of cowards. We will burn the traitors from the face of that world, or we shall die gloriously above it. Either way, we do His work. This world must be taken. This passage must be held. We will not shame the primarch. The Edict holds. We go forward. There is no backward step now.'

The air was tense, febrile. Every member of the crew worked feverishly, their labours synchronised in perfect unison. Their breathing was as regular as the whirr of the atmosphere processors, their heartbeats as steady as the reactors of the *Lustful Paradox*.

They were one.

Not in the misguided way that the Mechanicus considered themselves to be united in the machine; they were no interchangeable cogs in the mechanism. They were cells of a vast body, encompassing the ship itself but greater. Broader. A church and creed which had bound them together in blood and sacrifice. They had come together in the wonders of true unity, of absolute devotion.

'The time is upon us,' Gunther breathed. Voices clamoured for his attention – not with the desperate hedonistic need of previous years, but with the ardour of zealots. 'The time has come, at last, for an end to pretence. An end to masks. We shall stand revealed, and we shall be glorious. As is His will! He speaks through us, in every faithful utterance, and lives in every stalwart action. He is there, in every knife blade and gunshot and shell. And if we carry Him in our hearts, then we shall be exalted upon the final days of ruin and ascension!'

He hit a button, and Euryale's channel buzzed to life.

'My sweet, I will need you to make transit to the *Vault*. The children there will need you, in the revelations to come. A mother's loving hand.' He laughed, and then switched to the waiting supplicants of Endymica, without waiting for her response. He knew, in his soul, that she understood. They were connected, as united in purpose as the waiting world he now addressed.

'In the void, there are such beings. Such wondrous beings. Born of the black eternity, shaped by the cosmic tides, evolved for perfection and for purity. The Starborne Sons, timeless children all, call across the firmament – just as you call.'

He grinned, an utterly empty gesture. There was no true joy or warmth there. It was the face of a being who had studied humanity, mocked and aped it for so long that the gesture was as natural as breathing.

Generations of the line Radrexxus long since dead had lived and spawned in their time, so that he could stand here in this moment. Triumphant. Vindicated. He drew his blade, the edge glittering in the soft light of the bridge. It seemed more bone than metal, a thing grown; nurtured and exuded, rather than forged. He turned it appreciatively, feeling the strength bleed from it and into his arm. He felt whole. Complete. Invigorated. The words poured from him accordingly.

'Rise, and know that this is the day of glory! There will be fire and tumult, for there can be nothing else when the faithful are set against the heathen! We shall claw our way from the depths to the pinnacle, and from those heights we shall rain such vengeance upon them. Our hour has been approaching for so long, and now the time comes! We shall ascend! We shall seize the reins of human destiny, and we shall show them the light!' He held up his hand, clenching it into a fist. 'An end, my children! An ending unto masks! Reveal yourselves, and let the light of the stars show your true faces!'

As one the crew tore their masks off and cast them to the ground. The faces that leered out at the world were hideous in their variation. Some were near human, pale and pinched from lack of light, but others were monstrous. Contorted, bestial countenances slavered and snarled, relishing being able to finally look at the world without disguise.

The roared agreement that rushed out from them was fierce in its inhumanity. They clattered their knives against the consoles or drummed them against their armour, as their righteous fury died and they lent their chants to the vox's constant refrain.

'Voidfather! Voidfather! Voidfather!'

She cast the runes again, yet shuddered to see them.

The air was thin in her chambers, cold and weak. She cowered low to the floor, tongue flickering across her teeth as she scrutinised the results. They had not changed. They dared not. She scooped up another tile, and turned it in her withered grasp.

'The mountain promises fire... the world in upheaval, unbridled change. It brings horror... and it brings renewal.' Bodil shook her head. 'All comes undone, all is upheaval. It begins.'

The ship began to shake around her, as the old gothi closed her eyes and destiny unfolded.

Chapter Thirty-Seven

The Fires of Betrayal

The ship was burning. It was dying.

Fire wreathed the *Indomitable Soul*, as the void shields guttered and struggled to fully reignite. The assault had swept down upon them without warning, and still continued. Torpedoes burst against the hull, carving away buttresses – scouring it down to bare adamantine. Sirens howled through the corridors, as the crew hurried to respond. Their movements were sluggish, their reactions dulled. They had been so focused on the threat ahead of them that it never occurred to them that they would be betrayed by their own.

Yet the attack had come from the rearguard, and the Radrexxus ships.

The *Vindication of Terra* and the *Throne's Justice* listed in the storm of fire. Their shields, weaker by far than those of the flag-ship, had quickly been overwhelmed as the Radrexxus fleet's lance batteries found them with eerily coordinated precision. Even as they turned slowly to try and engage, the cruisers were being rent apart under the tide of unleashed energy. Their own return volleys fell short, fired in desperation.

The *Wyrmslayer Queen* dived through the burning void, graceful as a dancer. The *Spear of Ice* and *Shield of Wolves* had fallen in behind her, loyal as hunting dogs. The pack surged through the debris field, weaving around the drifting wrecks, till they could bring their guns to bear against the Radrexxus. Ferocious Wurgen chants rang out over the vox, and tore at the heart of all who heard them. The savage spirit of Fenris was with them, as surely as though they sailed in a longship across the wild sea.

This was their hunting ground, their battlefield. They would not be found wanting.

In the heart of the *Indomitable Soul*, Erastus was already in motion. Klaxons screamed without cease. The emergency lighting was a constant throbbing scarlet, migraine-bright. He blinked back tears as the ship shook again. A console detonated in a rain of sparks, showering its operator with shrapnel. He collapsed, sobbing, to the ground. The guards had tensed, weapons up and panning the chamber. Zofia had already moved to Erastus' side.

'Someone tell me what is going on!' Erastus bellowed.

'Radrexxus assaults on the Helvintr fleet and ours–'

'Relentless fire arcs, plotting to avoid–'

'We're losing the *Forsworn Blade*!'

The binharic scream of ship death echoed across the vox as the prize vessel from Noatun died in the maelstrom of ordnance. He did not have to see it happen to know. Erastus felt the sickness coil in his stomach. The weight of each death was like a physical blow.

I promised them a better future. I promised them safety, prosperity, and now madness makes a liar of me.

And it had to be madness, some sudden fugue of ambition. They had fought beside each other, bled for common cause. That it had all been a pretence for something as petty as ambition was anathema to Erastus' sense of reason. There were tales of what the warp could do to a mind. Fleets doomed by a single flawed translation. Gellerpox could worm its way into a man's soul as easily as a parasite into his guts. The heavens burned with new horrors, and mortal men were caught in the fires – mere chaff for the hunger of the infernal.

He drew his pistol, holding it tightly but keeping it pointed low. Tempers were flaring as tensions mounted, and he could not countenance it going off in error.

'Radrexxus will be tapped into all of our communications, damn him. Get me a secure line of contact with Katla,' he said.

He spared Astrid a glance. Her hands were locked around the haft of her spear, white-knuckled. Her face was creased with rage, lips drawn back around her teeth. She seemed more the beast than ever, more her mother's shadow.

'Turn us about. Send word to the other ships. We must assume defensive patterns, gird ourselves, then we can coordinate our attack.'

The bridge burst into another spasm of frantic activity. Emergency protocols reigned, as befit the dire circumstances. They were well drilled and trained, and under Zofia's stern gaze. Erastus looked up, past her, taking in the walls of the sealed chamber and their etched records of victory. His father's victories, the triumphs of generations past. Where once their gilded words, their promise, might have inspired him, they now seemed nothing more than a cruel joke.

The ship shook again, wracked to its iron bones by the relentless attention of the enemy. He stumbled, bracing himself against the throne. He cursed under his breath. A sudden flicker of movement caught his eye, as a technician moved away from their place at the wall. It was a man, pale and thin, his eyes darting hurriedly around the room. As he moved, his gait became more determined, his face locked into a grimace of certainty. He reached into his robes, and raised his hand.

The gun was black against the deeper shadows of the bridge, and Erastus was already screaming his warning when it went off. Kaddas turned in that moment, caught between his master and the assassin.

Kaddas' head detonated, his body flailing madly before it collapsed at its station. Shouts of alarm and screams of surprise went up around the corpse. Men staggered from their posts, hurling themselves behind pillars or ducking low. The assassin's gun swept round, seeking new targets. His eyes were cold now, resigned to what he had done.

Perhaps betrayal's weight has found him, Erastus thought, lost in the insanity of the moment. *Maybe it has cauterised something behind his eyes, killed a part of his soul.* Erastus swung his weapon round and up in the same breath as the assassin moved to fire.

Erastus was faster. He pulled the trigger with the gun still in motion, and watched the blast of captive fire hurtle across the space of the bridge. The man had no time to react, no hope of reaching cover, as the plasma blast caught him in the midriff. He exploded from the waist, torn apart by competing forces in a shower of viscera and blood ash.

Erastus crossed the space in a moment, striding through the milling, panicking bodies. He stood over the gawping corpse, streaked with its own spattered life; the hollow gaze had already turned glassy. He knelt, took hold of the corpse's throat and turned it. Looking for some sign, some explanation. A mark of corruption, or symbol of fell allegiance. There was nothing, save a small wound. A circular indent in the flesh, a badly healed

puncture. Threads of infection ringed it, slithering tendrils questing into the wider flesh. It hurt to look at it. It resonated with a
wrongness that, even in death, made his skin crawl.

His guards crowded in around him, jostling him and shaking
him from his fixated stare. He looked around as Zofia took him
by the shoulder.

'You're all right?' she asked, and he nodded. 'They must have
seeded him in an earlier work cycle. One of their stimmed-up
killers. Trust the Radrexxus to send amateurs! Amateurs, to kill
a king!' She laughed, all false bluster. Bravado that would have
grated at the best of times now held all the comfort of razor
wire.

'He doesn't have the look of one of them,' Erastus said carefully. 'There is more at play here than we realise. We need to–'

Sirens drowned out his words, and he looked around in
dismay. They only sounded in the event of a boarding action,
but there were no craft yet in play.

The enemy were already within.

They knew the moment was upon them by instinct, a song in
their blood that drove them to their appointed tasks. Gunther
had prepared them well, sowing the fertile soil of the Lamertine and Helvintr fleets while in command of the void assault
upon Noatun. Now they bore fruit, and the children of ruination moved to their tasks.

Some were mere thralls to the power of the cult, reluctant
or unwitting inductees who had known the embrace of the
Starborne Sons. The corruption pumping through their veins
was a veneer of courage, the whispered commandments of
wills grander than their own. They took up makeshift weapons: knives, industrial tools, the occasional lucky acquisition
of a firearm. Others were true warriors of the faith, crusaders

whose lives lived in the shadows had finally brought them to their appointed battleground.

Vast crates of materiel suddenly opened, or burst apart. Stasis fields and augur-baffles disengaged, filling the air with the ozone crackle of archaic machinery. Bio-mimicry systems died, and what had seemed to be containers filled with grox-meat suddenly revealed their living cargoes.

Bullets and las-bolts filled the air as the invaders coiled from their bulwarks. Many of the first victims were mere crew, menial labourers and press-ganged dregs, cut down by precise volleys of fire as the chosen revealed themselves.

Fanged maws yawned wide, screaming in triumph as they advanced through cargo bays and up through the shafts which led deeper into the ship. They boiled like a storm tide through vents and accessways, squeezing bonelessly like vermin through the cracks and hidden ways that threaded the vessel. They lashed out with knives and rough-forged swords, or with the clawed fingers that terminated their arms. Too many arms: some with three, others with four, grasping as they dragged the crew down – whether to be slain, or pulled screaming into the darkness.

They crooned and sang as they fought, simple stunted rhymes as preachers would teach to children. Balms of bastardised faith to keep them focused and honest. When the singing died, it was so that they could echo the system's dire song. They chanted it till their throats ached, and died with it on their lips as the defenders' shots found them. Even as they fell, choking on their ichorous blood, others vaulted over their bodies or trampled them into the decking. Gunfire filled the air, eclipsing their cries for only a fleeting moment.

'Voidfather!' they screamed, on and on. 'For the Voidfather, and the Starborne Sons!'

Chapter Thirty-Eight

Cornered Beasts

She drove her spear through the scrap-iron breastplate of someone who had once been a sworn comrade. Katla watched the light die in the man's eyes, even as he continued to pound his fists against her torso. He clawed at her, as powerless in life as he would soon be in death. Blood aspirated from his parted lips, and his lunatic babble fell silent.

He had been crew. Trusted. Honoured. So many of the deluded fools now surging against her had once been sworn men. She spat, wrenching the blade up and through his sternum. Katla cast the body to the side, stepped over his corpse, and roared her hatred against them.

They cast it back in her face, even as she threw herself forward.

Las-light cut across the bridge, and she spun through it. Her blade was a blur of harsh blue-white fire, hewing through the foe with casual disdain. She lashed out, not caring that they had once been friends and fellows, that they had served with her for years. They had spat on their oaths, to jarl and Emperor both. They were less than men now, less than nothing.

'To break faith with tribe, clan, pack... is to break faith with Him! The Allfather shall cast down the oathbreakers, throw them into the icy pit! Let them drown in their bile!'

She wished Astrid was with her; together they were unstoppable. As it was, though, surrounded by a knot of huscarls, blade to blade with the enemy, it would prove no true challenge. She bared her teeth as her spear split the hissing face of a misshapen mutant thing. She laughed, filled with savage joy.

'There you are! Here is your true face! Wyrmspoor at the heart of glory, the leavings of beasts! You are nothing! I will send you back to your masters in pieces, rendered down to offal! That is the price of trespass in the wolf's lair!'

Her huscarls drummed their blades against their bucklers, advancing in lockstep as they drove the enemy tide back. Things with whipping tendril-filled maws lashed out, spitting acidic venom that hissed against the steel and wood. Axes stove in their heads, shattered their skulls, drove them into the decking to be trampled underfoot.

'*Hjolda!*' she bellowed, and the shield wall held. Impossibly, it held, as the bodies clattered against it and screeched their alien rage. They were the few against multitudes, the true against the treacherous. Imperial heroes had dreamt of stands such as these for as long as there had been an Imperium. There was no better way to fight and die in the service of humanity's dreams.

'Move!' she roared, and the shields parted. Her spear thrust out, tasted flesh and then retracted. *Like a tribesman fishing,* she thought with amusement. *We are hunting the kraken!*

They pushed back against the invading hordes of the enemy, driving them back inch by bloody inch. Ichor slicked the floor, till they were slipping as they moved; almost falling over each other, as though they pushed a beached ship up the shore. The air had the tang of salt and spray to it, impossible beyond the gouting of blood.

'This,' she shouted, 'is the storm! You have all weathered its like! You have known the bite of betrayal, and the pursuit of the foe! You have been abandoned, and you have been hunted! But it is merely the storm!' She laughed, and they chanted her name with every bone-shaking push of the shields and every fall of the axe blade. 'You were raised up from the cradle of storms, the savage mother! You are more than flesh and blood and bone – you are the spirit of fire and ice! Unconquered, unconquerable! How many have tried their blades against the door of that hearth? How many have seen them snap?'

'Fenris!' they cried, alight with savage joy. As though their home had not been invaded, as though the enemy did not pour and scuttle and flow from every aperture – in waves more hideous than those that had come before. They fought, not because they knew that they would win, but for the simple bloody joy of it. Generations of them had left the ice for this promise, or been culled from a hundred other brutal worlds, to serve the line Helvintr.

They did not disappoint. They fought like tribal kings and warlords, no matter what stock had borne them. They hurled themselves against the enemy, over and over, weapons heavy and blood-slicked. They fought for the honour of their jarl and the sanctity of their hall. Some offered prayers, or clung to talismans, and hoped that even here amidst the sea of stars the eye of Russ might find them, and take pleasure in their bold exertions.

'The enemy is weak!' Katla snarled, ducking low to tear a mutant's tendons from beneath them. Their legs gave way, and they screamed piteously, but she was already upon them.

Snapping at their heels, harrying their every step. Forcing them back into the darkness and the shadows that had spawned them. 'Into them! For the Compact! For the Imperium! For Fenris!'

'For Fenris!' they howled as one. Their blades were sheathed quickly, as they drew their sidearms – resting them along the rims of their shields as they opened fire.

The throng of mutant warriors screamed their answer, as they threw themselves into the fire.

The void was stained with flame, with the glittering debris of bleeding ships. Men and materiel vomited into the abyss, torn by the impossible pull of vacuum. Warships did not die easily. It was not a clean thing to murder a star-going vessel, more akin to a protracted genocidal undertaking than the simple cutting of a throat.

To kill a ship was to murder the world it contained.

The Radrexxus ships prowled, inconstant. Some circled towards the wounded fury of the *Indomitable Soul*, eager to taste its end. They rained fire upon its flickering shields, watching torpedoes die in fiery detonations, or the energy of lance fire shunted aside. The shields rippled and blazed, burning as they repelled even the mightiest of assaults. Elsewhere escorts struggled against their shadows, as the ebb and flow of battle turned about them. Turned and turned, pivoting through the outer system. Errant ordnance tore through the corpses of the dead ships, and the Norastye graveyard broke apart like ice. It suffered the indignity in silence, with only ghost auspex returns to mark their passing. The song of the vanished and the lost, played out in the minutiae of combat.

They revelled in it.

Maximillian's senses danced across the broodmind's psychic link, tasting the emotions of his fellows as they went about their duties. War sang from every ship, no matter how ill-fitted. A sacred thing. A holy thing to be savoured.

There was a callous enjoyment in every fluid motion of the Radrexxus fleet, as its sinuous coils encircled the Lamertine ships and chased after the Helvintr contingent. Where the disparate allies were a study in contrasts – the stalwart wall of iron and the hunter's swift evasion – their enemy was of one mind. Their purpose and strategy was unified, winding like something biological. The fluctuations and spasms of a viral clade as it descended.

They had learned long ago to take pride in corruption and subversion. Turning the tools of the oppressor against itself, perverting the institutions and tactics of the Imperium of Man till they were merely more poisoned implements in the arsenal of the faithful.

The assault craft drifted in the void, beneath the fire and fury of the competing fleets, just as they had before the Battle of Noatun. They had waited here, seeded quiescent as dragon's teeth, before blossoming now as their hour came round at last.

The engines engaged with a kick, the tiny craft shuddering as they powered through the crowded near-space of the battle. Point defence snapped out, surrounding them with las-fire and exploding shells. They dived through the fire, shields flaring and hulls burning. Some did not survive the stresses, torn apart under the relentless fire of the Lamertine ships. The rest came on, plunging like a swarm. Melta-rigs and drills flashed in the darkness as they finally kissed against metal, and began their inexorable incision into the body of the ship.

Within, Maximillian waited. His blade lay across his knees, his eyes were closed. The weft and weave of the battle milled around him, and he understood it intrinsically. Instinct guided him, along with the whispered unity of the broodmind.

They had been alone for so long, forsaking the caress of their wider cult. The dynasty had become insular, folded in upon itself. It had grown mighty in its isolation, potent and strange. With the return to familiar shores, they had once again known the call of the wider psychic gestalt. There was strength in his arm that had not been there before; a renewed passion to rend and tear at his enemies. He could feel the guidance of the Voidfather, coloured through with the emotional resonance of the cult's leaders. The Mother of Sight's mind was a beacon, a furious blaze that warmed and shepherded. The Lord of War burned there too, but his mind was a cold flame – the consuming hunger of logistics and combat bled through the psychic link.

It was hard for Maximillian to continue to think in mortal terms. Names died beneath the onslaught of profundity, of titles and dominions. Gunther and Euryale, the Lord of War and the Mother of Sight, primus and magus... What were such things compared to the soul-deep reverence that saturated him now?

He, the favoured blade; the trusted instrument.

'Stand ready, and be prepared to kill,' he whispered. The others within the boarding craft nodded gently, bowing their heads to the sanctus. He-Who-Was-Knife-And-Claw. 'This is not a simple undertaking. A lord of the Compact will be protected. An entire ship of souls willing to give their lives to protect his. It is almost admirable, for the enemy.'

'He is not beyond us,' one of them said from behind their mask. None of the warriors in the pod had names, save Maximillian. None of them required names. 'We will find him, and he will die. It is the will of the Voidfather.'

'And the will is all,' Maximillian echoed. It amazed him, how natural it felt to give up. How complete he felt when he relinquished all control. To give up, to give in, was to be exalted. 'We are one of many,' he said. 'Whether a hundred or a thousand or a million blades cast to the winds, one shall find its mark. That is the nature of the sacred and the chosen. None can stand against us, for in our shadow there are legions.'

There was a sudden chime, and every head turned as one. The diffuse red glow of the meltas faded from the edge of the ship as they retracted. The ramps slammed down, and the interior of the ship presented itself. It was a harsher, purer light than they were used to. Each warrior engaged their multi-lensed goggles and threw themselves forward into the corridors of the enemy demesne.

The way had already been paved in the deaths of multitudes, and they intended to honour those sacrifices.

The ship spasmed and bucked like a living thing, almost throwing Erastus from his feet. He had only just regained command of the bridge and now it felt as though the world was tumbling away to dust beneath his feet. There was no true order, only a momentary imposition.

<THE SANCTITY OF THE VESSEL HAS BEEN VIOLATED,> an artificial voice screamed from the lolling mouths of every servitor. <TRUST IN THE EMPEROR-OMNISSIAH. TAKE UP ARMS IN THE DEFENCE OF THE SHIP. THE SANCTITY—>

'Give me shipwide!' Erastus snapped over the din. He stood over the communications alcove, gun smoking and his sword finally bared. The station's operator thrust the vox-horn towards his master's face.

'This is Lord Lamertine,' he said. He was not sure he had truly embraced the role before now. 'The voice of your king. The ship is under threat and under fire. We are being boarded by agents of the Radrexxus Dynasty. Some amongst our number have taken up arms in their service.' He bit back his own hatred. 'They have paid with their lives. We must consider the Radrexxus, all their gifts and works, as a moral contaminant. Resist them. At every turn, for every inch of ground. Resist. This ship is our home. It is our legacy, and we will not hesitate to defend it until the very last.' He drew his hand through the air, and the signal died – to be replaced again by the relentless thunder of alert and alarm.

Erastus breathed, and looked to Zofia.

'I need you to get something from my quarters, while I meet the boarders. Astrid! With me!'

Chapter Thirty-Nine

They moved along the thoroughfare of the ship's spine, and the enemy followed.

Reports were constantly being routed to Erastus, an incessant buzz in his earpiece as squads fought and held against the enemy. The lower areas of the ship were teeming with the foe, where they were not maliciously propagated ghost signals. The docking bays and cargo holds were lost to hordes of the enemy, wrenched from their grasp by misshapen claw and gun. Calls flooded in of sightings of the enemy, moving in force. Key systems were holding, though. The enginarium, command bridge and gunnery decks were all mounting stern defences.

The ship still moved, and it moved to their design and command.

Erastus turned and unleashed another bolt of searing plasma. It tore through the squad of cultist militia, reducing them to a smear against the iron pillars that braced the corridor. The pillar sagged and buckled under the heat of the onslaught, before it dissipated. Astrid had armed herself with a bolt pistol, and was taking measured, well-judged shots at any interlopers who presented themselves. Every detonation made her bare her teeth in that animal grimace common to her lineage. Like a canid scenting blood.

'I want them off my ship', Erastus growled. 'Once the threat has been dealt with I am going to take the entire fleet and cut the head from the beast. I will burn Gunther from whatever crevice he hides in, and I will see him dead.' The *Soul* shook. He cursed. There was too little time. The ship crawled with the enemy and whatever saboteurs had been seeded within, yet pausing to fight them would cost them dearly in the void war. He trusted in his crew, but knew the tide was swiftly turning against them.

Vengeance is a beautiful dream, if we can live to seize it.

'Fine sentiments, but the truth is that we are outmatched', Astrid said. 'The fleet we could contend with, perhaps. My mother's voidcraft will bring her back into range before long. She leads them a merry dance, where their numbers will not matter. We, though, we are caught in the maelstrom of their making. Upon the open seas you do not fight the storm, nor do you yield to it. You can only weather it.'

'I will not do nothing!' he snapped.

'Then do not! But they have come for you! All their cunning, all their guile, it culminates now! And it is not an assassination, not the spite of man against man. This is the clash of gods and monsters. Of beasts that walk in the skins of men, and turn their craft against them.'

'I had heard rumours of such', he said as he shook his head. And he had. There had always been stories of the corruptive potency of the tyranids, and the things which scuttled ahead of their advance. Xeno-cults such as these were a cancer, pumping poison into the Imperium's veins. He wondered how long it had taken to suborn an organisation such as a rogue trader dynasty. Had it come to them as a prize? A menagerie pet that had broken its cage? Or had it oozed its way into their heart through occult ritual and misdirection? Had they thought they were chasing some grandeur or glory, by prostituting themselves before the abhorrent?

'More than rumours, but then there have always been those of us who would look the monsters in the face and spit in their eyes.' She laughed, and looked away from him. 'Your culture was not steeped in trolls and kraken, Erastus.'

'I'm not sure I have a culture.'

They pushed onwards as he spoke. The ship lurched as it turned in another burst of motion. It was impossible to forget that you were aboard a ship at war. It shook and growled, the decking trembled with the constant pulse of the engines. The guns were firing decks below, but he could still feel every thunderclap as they unleashed. The return volleys died against the shields, or penetrated through them, tearing at the hull. The violation was enough to make the ship buck with machine-agony, and he felt it. He felt it all, rippling through him.

They were linked. Captain and vessel. As bound together as a culture was to the world that had birthed it.

'That is not so,' Astrid said. She reached up and pushed her hair from her eyes. A simple gesture, given the circumstances, but it struck him as somehow poignant. They had both found themselves thrust into an impossible circumstance. 'My mother spoke of your father, and your lineage. This ship, she has a Jovian soul, yes?' She laid a hand on the nearest pillar. 'A good, strong soul. As strong as its sister ship. We are both born of clans, Erastus. Mine simply walked the ice of Fenris, and yours plied the void in the ages before the Allfather.' She gestured down the spinal corridors, littered with ruin and the detritus of bodies. 'You can still build something from this.'

Something exploded further down the corridor, drawing their eye. Astrid placed her hand on his shoulder, bracing him for what was to come.

'You have done all that you can with what has been available to you. It is not your fault that your wyrd is to suffer, and to be betrayed.' She drew back and raised her weapon.

Another raid crew slipped through the wreckage of the door they had just demolished, turning this way and that, sniffing the air as though scenting their presence. When they saw them they let out a scream, a primal shriek of rage and hate that made Erastus wince with its sheer intensity.

Astrid gritted her teeth. 'Now, we fight. Now we show them what it means to fear.'

Immediately the enemy took aim, peppering the walls with stubber rounds as they started to advance up the corridor, ducking behind pillars and firing as they moved. They ran with a scuttling, sinuous pace, an inhuman fluidity that made Erastus' stomach churn. He holstered his pistol, and held Bloodsong with both hands, bracing it as he charged forward. Rounds dinged and skittered off his armour, or sailed just past his head. He could feel the heat in the air as he rushed through the throng and into their midst, vaulting over a fallen beam. He landed hard, swinging as he did. The cultists reared back, baring their fangs as the sword sliced the air before them. The air crackled with the power-field wreathed blade's motion, driving them back.

One swung at him with the butt of its gun, but he caught it with the sword's edge, splitting the weapon in twain with a spatter of molten metal. He brought it down again, through the ruin of the gun and into the wielder's gurning face. It tumbled to the floor, mewling piteously through a veil of blood. He stamped on its sternum for good measure, and turned just in time to parry aside the swipe of a knifeblade.

'Monsters!' he snarled. 'Traitors!'

The thing which had swung at him spat its hatred, twisted mutant features gnarled with the strength of its outrage. Chitinous growths distended its face, forming erratic ridges and protrusions. Ritual scarring had further distorted the hybrid's face, marring it with whirling patterns like the scatter of constellations. Erastus reared back, feeling the next cut score across the plates of his armour. His sword was alive in his hands. Striking, parrying, he moved by sheer momentum of instinct. Muscle memory burned in his every gesture, recalling training with Zofia, with Astrid, and further back; to when he had learned from his father, and from Evelyne.

Lessons of survival gleaned from the living and the dead.

He knocked the thing back with the flat of the blade, cracking it along the length of its chest. It glared at him, drool-spattered jaws agape, and made to lunge forwards before its head exploded with a burst of fyceline stink.

Astrid fired as she advanced, each shot precise. Armour blew away, skulls shattered, and bodies burst with wet, slapping detonations. Erastus threw the headless corpse out of his way, weaving into the fracas. He cleaved arms away in jets of stinking blood, swinging the sabre until his arms ached. He cracked a misshapen alien jaw with the pommel of the blade, and sent it gurgling to the deck.

This was purity. This was what his father had always tried to teach him. The raw, brutal soul of combat. Something that could not truly be taught or imparted, only lived through and experienced.

You never thought that I was ready for such a crucible. The thought made him snarl, throw himself to the next foe, and the next. His bladework became almost rote, the sweeping strikes of a scythe through the harvest. *But I am capable. As capable as ever you were.*

'Where are we going?' Astrid asked at his ear, and he spun to face her. They stood in the midst of the charnel leavings of battle. Blood dripped from the ironwork columns, and ran along the pitted deck. Marble embellishments had been rouged, painted with it. He could feel the poison life of the enemy against his skin, and brushed it away with too much eagerness.

'I have a plan,' Erastus said simply. 'This is the primary transit conduit. From along the ship's spine we can gain access to the primary teleportarium.'

'The teleportarium?' she repeated, blinking. 'Where are we going to go? Where is there to go?'

Erastus smiled, stepping over another bisected corpse as he did so. He gestured with the gleaming blade, down the corridor towards their target. 'I mean to find the beast's heart, and gouge it out. As this all began, so must it end.'

'What do you mean? How must it end?'

Erastus' face locked in a grimace, as though giving voice to the thought pained him.

'With the death of a king.'

The *Wyrmslayer Queen* arced around, and its lance batteries raked the side of a fat, ailing converted merchantman. The ship's shields shone for one glorious moment of defiance and then collapsed, dying a fraction of a second before the ship itself succumbed. Katla laughed as her ship hunted and killed. Even in its depths, fighting alongside her crewmen, she could sense the flow of battle by the shaking of the hull and the scream of the engines. She was the ship's captain and she knew the warlike soul of the great vessel as well as she knew her own daughter. Even so, the bridge's communications were a whisper in her ear.

'For the Compact!' she screamed. 'For the Allfather!'

The ship lurched again. The hunter's strike tore through the engines and crippled the enemy ship. Secondary detonations rippled through its midsection even as the cut continued. The deluge of energy gouged it, gutting it like a fish, before fading as the attacking vessel moved off.

They had sought to pin down the Helvintr, but it was a fool's quarry. The traitors might as well have tried to pin down the storm or the sea.

The *Queen* surged from the debris, as though it carried the fury of the World Sea at its back. Even as the crew fought their staggered battles within, the ship itself coursed through the void with all the fury expected of its kind. The *Spear of Ice* and the *Shield of Wolves* swept by in its wake, adding their own contemptuous broadsides to the dying ship. There was nothing there but spite. Hatred, sharpened to a fine point, driven into the heart of the foe. Their strikes finally killed the wheezing vessel, obliterating it outright as the reactors died in a star-bright detonation.

Their ragged arc carried them round and over the duelling fleets, like the sweep of a god's sword blade. The *Indomitable Soul* lay ahead, beset on all sides by the ravenous maws of the enemy. Boarding pods stained the void like shed blood, flowing from the corrupted enemy towards the flagship. The Helvintr ships sighted them, turning about to bring their weapons to bear – to liberate their kinsmen.

If they broke the deadlock, the crew of the *Queen* knew, then they could force the battle on their terms. The enemy could be beaten back, and if the fleet could be fought and destroyed then the problem of Endymica could be addressed. No weapons had yet fired from the surface or from near-orbit, nor had there been any concerted sortie beyond snatches of auspex that seemed entirely befitting of system's traffic.

Only one problem could be conquered at a time; as the saying went, *The wolves in the mountain can wait, when there are wolves at the gate.*

As they drew nearer communications were restored. The ships could commune as before, and the captains exchanged their terse words. Seeking unity of purpose amidst the tumult and confusion. Even now, pressed as they were – with their backs against the wall – they could still elicit favours, and make demands. Compromises sketched out in the heat of battle, riven by the passions of war.

In such times arrangements could still be reached, though. The web of signals, of priority transmissions and private communications, tightened. Agreements blossomed from the madness, resolving as the *Queen* continued its plunge. Its guns burned, relentless in their firing. Shields and hulls cracked and burned under their power, boarding craft were swatted from the air – reduced to atoms, as though they had never been.

The vengeance, the wrath, of fire and ice drove down upon the enemy ships. The shields caught alight, sheathed and sheened in volcanic fury. It ebbed to an oily smear of iridescent colour, then blazed again, white-hot.

She came for the head of the enemy, and the way to that great trophy lay through the liberation of their fellows.

CHAPTER FORTY

THE COMPROMISE OF WAR

He drove his blade through the throat of an armsman and cast the body down before him. The scent was strong here, so intense that he could taste it in his throat. It was more than the biological reek of a lesser being. It was the psychic stain of its existence. All the living, he had learned, had that miasma clinging to them. The pain of their lives, the confusion and disorder.

It sickened him to think of it. Lives lived without unity, without fraternity, and without hope.

Maximillian tightened his hand on the blade, and raised his needle gun. He fired one round straight through the eye of an advancing sergeant, flooring him. The man spasmed, frothing at the mouth as the poison ravaged his system. The biophaguses had outdone themselves this time. In the generations of innovation and creation, they had worked such wonders. They had raised up the simple art of bio-alchemy into something transcendent.

'He was here,' Maximillian breathed. 'He moves, and he fights.'

He tilted his head in grudging admiration. 'More than was expected of him.'

'We will find him, yes?' said one of the others. He was sniffing the air as well, snuffling. Maximillian frowned. The number stencilled onto his armour was 'Two', and he had come to think of his brood-brother as Secundus. Maximillian was simply the sanctus, the Blade, he had no equal. The others were false peers, echoes of the role that the Voidfather's will had laid down for him. Useful, but ultimately disposable.

These times would pass, he knew. The hunt would ebb, and become something else. His presence upon the ship, within this role, it was all on borrowed time. One day, soon, They would come and the faithful would be exalted from the realm of flesh and matter.

They would serve a greater purpose. A truer faith.

'Things are not proceeding as the nexos inferred from our captives,' Maximillian said. 'The melding of their stratagems has muddied the waters. They were meant to be divided, a hundred times before now.'

'The boy has put trust in them,' Secundus allowed. 'That carries weight amongst the disparate minds. There is nothing more elusive than trust, and so nothing more valuable.'

'That was almost poetic,' Maximillian said with a rare smile. 'Such emotional ebbs should be guarded against.'

'Indeed, honoured Blade.' Secundus bowed his head, and moved off to personally ensure that the wounded became the dead. His sword pivoted down through the chest of one, and the body gasped and fell still.

The battle was not proceeding as had been foreseen. That much was very apparent. They had become too different from what had been planned for, as experience and understanding had bled together. The fleets and their defenders had become hybrid things in their own right. Strange and newborn as much as they were recognisable.

He let his hands ball into fists, and sniffed the air again. There would be resistance, of course, but it was nothing that they could not handle.

All that mattered was the boy king, and ending his pitiable defiance.

'We move on,' Maximillian growled. 'We are close.'

The teleportarium had already been primed at his instruction.

The entire chamber was aglow, runic patterns flowing with lambent light. Everything crackled with a static witch-light charge, corposant dancing along the surfaces like liquid. Tech-adepts laboured to maintain the systems' cohesion in the midst of the attack. Consoles sparked, lumens fluttered. Everything seemed on the verge of criticality, poised to detonate. To culminate.

'Are we ready?' Erastus asked.

One of the adepts bowed its hooded head, stepping back from the controls. It spread its hands, and gestured for Erastus to look at the computations. He walked over, scratching his chin as he attempted to make sense of it.

'The coordinates are correct?'

'The divinations are sacred. The data has been sanctified thricefold. All is as it should be.'

'Excellent,' he said. He looked up at Astrid and then nodded. 'Begin.'

'Erastus, what–' she began to ask, but the tech-priest was already moving. The rite commenced under its iron ministrations, limbs moving in perfect synchronicity to modulate the flow of energy and to triangulate the necessary coordinates. The air was filled with the spritz of sacred oils, as it engaged. Erastus looked across the rising maelstrom of light.

'Thank you, Astrid, for your service. I'm sending you back to the *Queen*.'

'You can't!'

'I can, and I must. I wasn't there, at the end. With him. Whatever enmity there was… I cannot sustain it. I wasn't there when he died, and if this is a final stand then I would not have you divided. Fight well, Helvintr. Goodbye.'

'Erast–'

And she was gone, cast through the ether in a nimbus of fire.

Erastus closed his eyes, and raised his hand to the comm-bead in his ear. 'She should be with you soon, Katla. Good hunting.'

'My lord?' Zofia called as she stepped gingerly through the smouldering chamber, distorted by heat haze as she moved through Astrid's warp wake. 'I have it!' She held up a gilded box, only slightly larger than her palm. 'Quite the fight to get to it. You'd think you would have brought this with you, if it were quite so valuable.'

Erastus tapped his fingers on the top of the console. 'It hadn't occurred to me,' he said softly. He took the box and opened it, looking at the sparkling gold of the brooch. He smirked to himself as he reached up and fastened it upon his armour – near to the throat. He nodded at Zofia, and only then acknowledged her solemn gaze.

'You did it, then?' Zofia asked.

'I had to.'

'I can understand that,' Zofia said carefully. 'Though, I dare say we could have used her.' She looked away from Erastus' withering look. 'Still, you're the captain. Besides, we have some tricks left to us, don't we?'

'We do,' he said. He drew his plasma pistol again. 'Summon the men. We'll head back to the bridge, and we will take this fight to the heart of our enemy. You have my word on that.'

'I'd expect nothing less, my lord.' She drew her own weapon. 'You are a Lamertine after all. No one who took your father's scrip expects to die a quiet death.'

Something detonated nearby, beyond the sealed chamber. The sound of battle roiled about it, echoing through the arteries of the great vessel. Everything remained in flux, poised upon the edge of ruin or retribution. It was the actions of men that would determine what came to pass.

'You may yet have your chance,' he intoned grimly.

The two great loyal ships had drawn even, defying the assaults of the enemy, and now pushed on. Their engines blazed in the same moment, spurring them forwards into the heart of battle once more. The warlike bulwark of the *Soul* kept pace with the ragged spear that was the *Queen*, as their subordinate vessels turned about – burning their own trail in service of their masters.

What the Radrexxus fleet possessed in ships it lacked in true firepower. Most of them had been converted haphazardly, disguising the true intentions of the cult behind merchant's schemes and supply vessels. They had seeded tainted medical supplies from the tribute worlds of Respite, and hidden their most chosen sons within the macro-carnis shipments from slaughter systems like Farastes, spreading the taint in a hundred subtle ways.

From underhand beginnings they had grown, metastasising across the stars. Everything could be utilised, corrupted, turned about and repurposed for the only cause that mattered. Now, with their treachery exposed, their ships were being turned aside. The limited weapons of their fleet could not match the fury of the flagships, and so the nest of defence contracted about the *Lustful Paradox*, congealing in the face of the resurgent enemy.

Not all weapons were things that could be fired. Some could only be directed.

The *Fickle Vault* had seemed like a minor affectation, an afterthought of an addled and distracted mind. Others wondered why Gunther would drag a menagerie ship across the stars at his heels, when the fate of legacy and reputation hung in the balance. It was so beneath note, they thought, that it had not been sabotaged by the Norastye's plots.

But they had tried, the iron men of the Norastye, in their betrayal. They had come with their devices, and they had died screaming in a place they had thought suboptimal in both threat and importance. In such hidden, inconspicuous places, there were more than secrets. In such places, there were monsters.

The *Fickle Vault* had turned and spun amidst the chaos of the fleet action, seemingly forgotten, but now it heeded the broodmind's imperceptible call and dived through the fields of overlapping fire. Lesser ships moved themselves between the *Vault* and the guns of the enemy, sacrificing themselves that it might endure and fulfil its mission. It burned hard, eagerness bleeding into every movement. Its very character seemed to have shifted, from bloodless curiosity, to impassioned devotee.

It drew near, too near, to the *Wyrmslayer Queen*. It was no match for the flagship, not in truth. It was bloated and over-heavy, but it could not compare to a great barque of war such as the *Queen*. When the guns of the flagship began to carve armour from it, like the shattering of continental plates, it continued to stagger forwards. Great glass bubbles of habitat burst upon its surface, raining flora and fauna into the void to freeze and burst instantaneously. None of that mattered. The bulk of the ship was being pared away, cut back to only the essentials, to the core of it. A spur of barbed metal, certain as a blade, thrust towards the enemy's throat. Many of the crew already knew they were going to die, and they relished it. To serve as a sacrifice for future victory, and to burn, that the Star-borne Sons might take notice... There was nothing greater.

Void shields met with a burst of intense light and radiation, a pulse of mutual annihilation that scarred the riven hull of the *Vault* further. Cracks rippled along its prow, even as it finally bit into the body of the *Wyrmslayer Queen*. The front of the vessel crumpled, tons of metal compressed by the sheer force of the impact. It was already shedding multitudes of boarding craft as it died against the side of the ship, a verminous tide flowing off it like lice from a corpse.

The great and noble ship reeled back, struck along its axis. Thrusters burned hard in the dark, struggling to stabilise it as it veered madly. The venting thrust scraped at the void shields of the *Soul*, but came no closer. The vessel's skin rang to the million hammer blows of the invader, docking claws tearing into the hull, drills and meltas buzzing to furious life, air-gates and locks forced by crazed machine-spirits. Things growled and gurgled within their pods, iron simulacra of the usual means of assault. Eyes gleamed in the harsh red light of the interiors, with the malicious hunger of animals.

In a tide of ruin, the enemy came for them.

Chapter Forty-One

The ship had done what was required of it, and she was pleased. Euryale stood on the smoking ruin of the *Fickle Vault*'s bridge, and stared at the smouldering, rune-marked hull of the *Wyrmslayer Queen*, which she had driven the ship into. She could almost taste the arrogance etched into the metal. For so long they had plied the void, presenting themselves as hunters. As heroes. Only those of the sacred blood knew the truth of women and men such as the Helvintr.

They were murderers, all. It made it easy to turn against the Imperium, to barb and poison every borrowed stratagem and tool against them, knowing that they supported such wanton iconoclasm.

'You are monsters,' she breathed. Euryale felt the weight of ages press down upon her. No, more than mere time. The psychic pressure of Endymica was absolute, pulling them into its gravity. It had grown strong, as all the seeds sown by the Lord Radrexxus had sprung to fruition. They were all children of the

Starborne, blessed by the hand of the divine that they might spread love and fecundity across all the galaxy. She had shepherded so many of them into the world, guiding them as surely as she had helped to birth them.

From the lowest of the hybrids, to the most exalted of the Trueborn Sons, she had been there. She had watched them emerge into a world of form and matter, bound to inferior, disappointing flesh. Some were still swaddled in human weakness, but the later generations… It was the face of the gods, writ in mortal clay. When she looked upon them, she could not help but weep.

Such weakness must be beyond us, she cautioned herself with a thought. Her hands gnarled and knit about her staff, and she drew herself up. She was tall, when she did not slouch and shuffle, bearing the long, thin bone structure of one born to the void – common amongst the more peripatetic Navigator houses. House Tarescos was one such house, even before its enlightenment. Nomad. Vagabond. Shrouded House. They had borne so many names and insults down the years, before they realised that they no longer mattered. Only the truth mattered, when gifted the eyes to see it.

Generations had been born to the house in its illumination, shaped by the gifts of the Starborne. She was the culmination, the zenith, and now her mind reached out – a guiding light for the exalted children.

+Into the lair of beasts shall forge the faithful!+ she cast forth into the minds of her followers. Behind her, by the door, two guards let out a breathy hiss of adulation as they hunched forward with her sudden psychic intrusion. Their eyes widened behind the dark lenses of their helmets, and their lips drew back from their teeth in monstrous rapture.

'We are ready, Mother of Sight,' they breathed as one.

Mother of Sight. An old name. Perhaps even if she had not risen to glory as the magus they would have anointed her with it. She cast her warp-sight forth, able to see the rippling movements of her broodkin as they advanced upon the enemy: pods and ships, boarding craft and repurposed tugs. They poured forth like contagion, a wave of infective promise. She turned, looking at the men who guarded her.

'You will get me onto that ship. They will need my guidance, before the end.' She bared her teeth in a smile of triumph. 'We shall deliver revelation upon the heathen, and turn their works against them. The way of the righteous is beset by the unruly and the deluded, but we shall drag them screaming into the light. Even if it burns them.' She paused thoughtfully. 'Even if it kills them.'

The entire world had shifted, unmooring itself. One moment they had been in flight, as true and proud as any spear cast, before reality had crashed down upon them.

This was battle. It was war. They had been braced for the harsh rigours of it, but still this had blindsided them. The ship listed, reeling hard from the assault. Screens were cracked, casting the corridor in a confusion of conflicting light sources. Static buzzed like snow across some, while others were lit green and black. Servitors, wired into their stations – contributing in their esoteric way to air circulation or signals processing – sat slack, idle, dumb and waiting.

Katla pushed herself to her feet, dabbing blood from her forehead with her fingers. In the mad light of the ship's wounding, it seemed black. 'I want a damage report!' she snapped, scooping up her fallen spear and rounding on her huscarls. None of them had a chance to answer. The skirl of sirens was blocked out by the mechanical repetition of a single word.

'*Örlendr! Örlendr! Örlendr! Örlendr!*'

Outsider. Alien. The true enemy was amongst them now. Not the hybrid and the mutant, but the beasts themselves. Katla remembered when she had heard the klaxon before; when the ship had been boarded in ages past. When she had earned her scars at the point of the spear.

She had almost died, then, but her thread had held. It would hold now.

'What is our status?'

'Dead in the void, my jarl!' Eirik called. His face was slicked with blood and ash, already beginning to run into the rivulets of sweat that graced his forehead. He wiped it away with the back of one gloved hand.

'Throne of the Allfather! I want us moving again!'

Gunfire tore through the corridor ahead of them, and the shield wall re-formed with fluid grace. Immediately they began to return fire. Katla spat her hatred, gesturing with her spear even as she drew and braced her volkite. The corridor filled with a sudden rush of crimson energy, the beam carving through the air and reducing the enemy to an ashen smear. The beam's passing had left a scorched trench in the wall, but she ignored it.

Any price, here and now, was acceptable for victory.

'We will fall back to the bridge and coordinate from there. We cannot be abroad with the second wave of vermin crashing down upon us.' She paused, raising her head as though sniffing the air. 'They are here. Now. On our ship. The masters, not the puppets. The beast in truth! The Devourer comes, and we will see it driven back as we have done before! You have all fought too long, too hard, and too far from home to fall here. Now, is where we stand. We hold them here, and we cast them back as we have ever done. Till none remain!'

'Till none remain!' they echoed, clattering weapons against

their shields where they were not already firing. The shield wall drew back, step by step, maintaining their volleys of shot. The air was smoky with the stink of burning flesh and powder.

There was something else, though. She could feel it. It saturated everything, as pervasive as the smoke of war. Coiling and writhing within the guts of the ship. They had been compromised enough already, violated within and without, but this was more. She could hear it, carried in the distant timpani of claws upon metal. It drifted through the corridors, and from the vents, presaging ruin.

I told you that the wyrm would hunt you as you have hunted it. That it would find you, and drag you down into the darkness.

Bodil had warned her, with all the cold comfort of prophecy, and she had ignored it. She had laughed in the face of the beast and the abyss, knowing that it was her duty as jarl and as queen to stand against it. The Imperium depended upon true souls, and truer service. Without that the entire edifice would undoubtedly crumble, the Allfather's will or no.

Katla bit back the thought. She did not fire again, nor show her back to the enemy. The warriors drew closer, their movements fluid. As proud, and as brave, and as strong as any warriors who had plied the ice of Fenris in their youth. They knew that retreat was not surrender, and to take a step backwards was enough to draw the enemy to your spears. She had taught them as much, and life – as ever – had imparted the rest.

The galaxy was vast, and teemed with terrors. These imposters, these monsters cloaked in human skin, were far from the worst of them. They possessed low cunning, the vermin-logic of the betrayer and the saboteur, bred in the shadows because they *knew* their own weakness. Every stratagem and trick they had employed only drove home their own cowardice. They could not hope to defeat the dynasties in open war, and so they had schemed and plotted, and corrupted. Their every act reinforced the brittle strength of their advantage.

Clawed and grubbed from the dirt they wallowed in.

The thought of them made her sick. Teeming through her ship, defiling each sacred space with the taint of their existence. Slaves, offering themselves up on an altar to false gods. They would die with a zealot's mania upon their faces, and think it good and honourable.

'News, my jarl!' Eirik called, snapping her back to the moment. She looked to him, pausing for a moment to lean on her spear and catch her breath.

'Are we operational?'

'The ship ails, jarl, but the iron shipspeakers say that it shall sail once again in true service. The message was not about our progress, jarl. The masters of teleportation speak – your daughter is aboard once more.'

Katla laughed and shook her head. 'The boy is many things, but he does have a habit of keeping his promises. His father, he was never as reliable.'

'The young!' Eirik agreed. 'They have a way of surprising us.'

'That they do.' She smiled grimly. 'He kept his word, though. That counts for much. As much as the enemy try to divide us, we have kept to our oaths. He has held his nerve through all of this. There is something to be said for that.'

Would I have been the same? Had it been me who had ascended, and taken again the throne and the crown? I would have brooked no word against my path, and burned them all from the stars a dozen times over. My blind anger would have ended us before we even got here.

It was hard to admit her failings, or to countenance a different path. All she had, all she trusted in, was the surety of her wyrd. To whatever end it led her.

'To whatever end,' she breathed. Eirik gave her a look, but said nothing. They maintained their dogged pace. Under arches of rune-etched stone and fire-scoured steel they passed, till the dull lumens died away and braziers burned with low, red flames. Smoke filled the air, not with the stench of battle, but with the woodsmoke ache of home.

And we are coming home, Katla thought. *Back to the core of it. The struggle that has defined so much of our lives, and our tumult. We are returning, my daughter, to who we are.*

Moaning whispers flooded around her, and Astrid felt something grab at her – something wet and writhing, corpse-putrid in the liminal space between worlds. She shrank from it, flailing out against the coiling touch of cold and fire, everything and nothing, as the whispering became laughter, became–

The hum of engines, vaster than worlds, as the world became solid again. Astrid panted, scrabbling at the decking. She felt bile rise, heavy and hot in her throat, but she swallowed it down. Cold air assailed her lungs as she drew deep, halting breaths. She could feel frost clawing at her, catching upon her teeth. She thrust her hands forward, and pushed up and onto her feet.

'The bastard,' she snarled. The adepts who had been tottering closer on their iron feet staggered momentarily, as though afraid they would have to flinch away from her wrath. 'When this is over, there will be a reckoning. None set my path, save me!'

'Honoured mistress, wolf-blessed daughter, we have reached communion with your mother – our jarl, may she be anointed in the sight of the Machine-God – and bear her will. You must meet her upon the bridge. The enemy's coils tighten about us.'

'Then I will go,' she growled, 'as is my duty.' Her breathing had settled into a ragged sigh. She knelt and reached for her spear, scooping it up into her grasp. 'There are beasts yet to be slain.'

Chapter Forty-Two

Things moved in the darkness with swift and hungry purpose, clattering over the decking in their pursuit. They had languished too long in the hidden cells and oubliettes of the menagerie ship, sheltered from the prying eyes of guests and observers. Their lesser kin had cared for them, of course – kept them fed on the flesh of those few who would inevitably go missing. Swallowed by the innards of the ship, so they would say. Such a dangerous life, aboard vessels; even pleasure craft such as the *Fickle Vault*.

The exalted inhabitants did not care what came to pass beyond their fief, nor the complaints that such disappearances might cast up. There was only the hunger. Ceaseless, raw and burning. The desire to devour, consume and corrupt all who came into contact with them. Free of their bonds they would tear entire cultures apart, with claw and the potency of their germseed.

It was not bars and chains that had held them in dreadful stasis alone. The minds of their hallowed keepers, the burning animus of the magus and the cold fury of the primus, they had guided them. Bent their urges to the cause of the cult. When they spoke, it was in the mind-whispered echo of the Void-father. Even the exalted Starborne had to respect such power.

Here, aboard the enemy ship, it was cold and strange. The odours of the faithful faded away, to be replaced by the cattle-stink of mortal men and women. They could smell their fear, the hot spice of it in the air. They fought, and they died, and yet that scent never left them.

The smell of prey.

As they skittered down from vents, as they scrambled across the stone and metal of deck floors, they had no desire to convert or to coddle. They came as a storm comes, the surge and the tide. Their eyes were burning embers in the darkness, as they shattered lumens and drove onwards into the shadows. The shadows that were their birthright and their kingdom. The gnarled and broken idols of the cult slid through the arteries of the great iron ship-beast, like a viral phage. To rip the heart from this god of hunters, and cast it to the void's cold and fire.

The darkness dogged their progress like a living thing.

Katla watched the lights die, one by one, snuffed out by the enemy's hand. Only the most zealous of their pursuers still followed, their pale skin inked with flowing text and coiling scarification. Behind them the shadows squirmed with indistinct horrors, sinuous monsters that dragged the wave of shadow along with them. Claws closed around the lumens, crushing their radiance till the only light came from the persistent fire of her troops.

The gunfire tore through the devotees, flooring them with a hail of shot. Each impact, whether against flesh or the corridor walls, cast up another burst of fire. Details clarified where they struck: a coiling of claws and chitinous muscle, fangs glimmering wetly in the flickering light, and eyes watching them with infernal longing. The eyes continued to burn after the firelight died away, tracking their movements. She shivered under that scrutiny, resisting the urge to simply stand and fire until every last one of them was ashes. Her men were the same, teeth gritted as they refused to sell their lives dearly against an enemy which wanted them to be reckless.

'We're almost there,' she husked. Every inch that they fell back was another step closer to the heavy doors of the *Queen*'s bridge. Wrought of adamantine, warded with iron and silver. At their threshold armies had been blunted, and invaders turned back. They loomed, as solid as the mountains. Timeless. Inviolable.

Their backs were almost against the doors as they began to grind open. They filled the rapidly diminishing space with fire, revealing more of the monstrous tide as it crept closer. Bullets and las-bolts burst against the creatures' skin, and they ignored them. They crawled along the floor, the walls, the ceiling, growling as they advanced. They could sense their prey within their reach.

The doors hit their limit with a hydraulic clunk, and the defenders fell back one last time, into the darkness and smoke of the bridge. The fire died away, and they replaced their guns with the gleaming blades of swords, spears and axes. The air was alight with active power fields, and the ozone crackle drove away the smoke and soot in a moment of electric purity. Katla's spear flashed in the darkness, runes burning along the haft and blade.

The wall of blades held, burning in the darkness, as the doors began to ratchet closed again. As the enemy descended.

They fought shoulder to shoulder, turning to guard the other's flank as they advanced through the milling ranks of their own troops and the invaders. They fought their way towards the bridge with a slow and steady determination. Familiar corridors passed by, rendered strange by repeated atrocity. Paths they had travelled previously had been reduced to deathtraps by the twisted ingenuity of the enemy.

All to stop them from reaching the bridge.

Zofia's blade rose and fell in sympathy with Erastus', the weapons complementing each other as the waves of hybrids closed in about them. Some of the mutants had cast away their scrap-hewn blades and their inferior firearms, and lashed out with claws. Others spat venom from acid-scarred lips. Erastus smashed aside another creature with his lit sword blade, watching its face atomise in a cloud of bloody ash.

'Fiercer resistance!' he cried, and Zofia nodded, even as she turned aside another glancing blow. The enemy roiled around them, desperately trying to drag them down and savage them. Shipguard armsmen fired into the xenos, riddling them with bloody holes and burn marks before casting them to the decking. Some drove their boots into the upturned, snarling faces of the enemy. There was no pity for the alien, nor its spawn.

Too many had been lost for them to back down, or to show anything as prosaic as *mercy*. Men had died or been made less than men, and every new wound was all the more galling.

Erastus bit away the bile he could already feel welling in his throat. The battles on Noatun had been brutal, bloody and dirty, but they had lacked this primal struggle. This was a fight they had chosen. This was survival, in the face of the desperate, gnawing persistence of the cultists. They brought whatever weapons they had cobbled together, and even then they cast them aside as the rage took hold.

These things that had once been men, or that were broken

cousins to humanity, hated Erastus and his kind. For their purity, for their unbelief, and for their independence of mind and spirit. He had never felt such hatred from his fellow man, and had rarely got close enough to feel it from humanity's myriad inhuman enemies. It bled from the cultists. Their every step into the ship was a burden upon them, and they loathed that it was tasked to them.

Perhaps, Erastus thought, *they would rather die than continue to live and struggle in a world that despises them?*

The flat of a blade knocked Zofia away, sending her sprawling against a corridor wall. She spun, bringing her sword round to deflect the next blow. Erastus tried to move back towards her, but the melee shifted again. Clawed hands grabbed at him, hurling him further into the sea of bodies. He felt a fist slam into his armoured midriff, succeeding in knocking the wind from him. He sank down to one knee, awaiting a killing blow.

None came.

Erastus looked up. A curious calm had descended. The battle seemed to recede. The cultists milled and flowed around him, intent upon his crew, who yet held, a line of blue and gold, stalwart against the seething purple and grey.

Across the sudden gulf of space and silence, Erastus' eyes found Maximillian.

He was bareheaded, his helmet locked at his hip. His exposed features were blank, drawn and more angular than Erastus remembered. Everything human had bled from him, till this pale, shrunken thing was all that remained. He tilted his head, one way and then the other, taking the measure of his prey.

'So it comes to this, does it?' Erastus asked. 'He cannot even be bothered to do it himself, and so sends his loyal dog to finish it.'

'Nothing quite so…' Maximillian paused, as though the word had been wiped from his vocabulary. Erastus shook his head.

'Petty?'

'Mortal,' Maximillian finished. He advanced, blade up. It looked even more savage now that Erastus found himself on the other side of it. The same way that Maximillian was now on the opposite side of that chosen word, *mortal*.

'You fought at our side,' Erastus said. His blade was kindled, carving a line of fire between himself and his enemy. 'Through the fires together at Noatun. Did that mean nothing? All hollow gestures?'

'It served its purpose.'

Maximillian drove forward, blade weaving. Erastus parried, countered, driving in against his thrusts. The blades met, sparking between their faces. Erastus could feel the heat of it, the seething collision of weapons. Sparks nicked at his skin, evaporating away the sweat that was beading his brow.

'The will of the Voidfather leads to strange places, and all we can do is listen to his song.'

'More madness,' Erastus said, scowling. 'The will of alien gods, whispering in your blood? Spare me. I want nothing to do with it. I'll drive every last one of you from my ship. I will cast your corpses into the furnaces, and I will break your master's ship about his ears. I will rain fire on your toxic nest of a world, and I will hunt every last mongrel of your bloodline across the stars. I will not let a single one of you escape me.'

'This is why you could not be trusted with the gift.' Maximillian's mouth twisted into a sneer, before he pushed forward, staggering Erastus. The Radrexxus assassin ducked and weaved, Erastus' blows failing to find him as he evaded or knocked them aside. His movements carried an ease to them, a sinuous and alien grace. 'You and your kind were too inflexible. Too dogged.'

He struck out again, slashing and stabbing towards Erastus. The king gave ground, but kept his guard up. There was a feral ferocity in his return blows, as he struggled and fought back. Erastus gritted his teeth, slamming their blades together. He turned the hilt, jamming them against one another. Maximillian snarled in frustration.

'That is why you had to be weakened, and gutted before you could pose a threat.'

Erastus' eyes widened. He knew in his heart what the monster's next words would be, before he even spoke them. Even that did not blunt the pain.

'That is why your father had to die. It was an honour to forge ahead, to bear my lord's will into the heart of your fortress. To stand in judgement of the heathen. The unbeliever. The unclean.'

Maximillian punctuated his words with another flurry of strikes, each one aiming to cripple or kill. Erastus responded as quickly as he was able, but the enemy's blade still slipped past him. He grunted in pain as it etched a red line of agony along his flank. Armour parted like water under the blade's stroke.

'It was you?' Erastus panted, voice thick with emotion.

'Oh yes. He was not the fighter he would have had us believe. Your father died weak and alone, knowing only that he was betrayed. And afterwards? A simple thing to play upon your instinctive distrust of the Astraneus. You are, all of you, such base little beings. Kine, cattle, who are forever unworthy of standing as kin. Now it no longer matters. Now he calls us to action! The time is now!'

Erastus pushed back against him. The pain left him, forgotten. His blade came up in a savage arc of fire, and Maximillian fell back. The assassin's eyes were wide with sudden surprise, shock at the fury behind each blow.

Erastus channelled his hate and his resentment into every strike. He remembered the lessons at the hands of his betters: his father, Evelyne, Zofia, Astrid. Every instruction had been for this moment. When he fought it was not in the starched Lamertine style that Maximillian would have expected. He was not an old man, fighting his last. He was young, vital, and he had taken his lessons to heart. Every sweep and thrust of his blade was a hybrid thing in itself. Lamertine discipline melded with Fenrisian instinct. Not a thing that could be taught, but which battle had annealed together. He had been shaped by conflict. Sharpened. Honed.

He hurled himself forward, deflecting Maximillian's stabbing blows. Desperation had bled into the other man's movements, bursts of reactionary lightning. Adrenaline and stranger things boiled in his veins, and he struggled to match the young king's wrath.

Erastus turned the blade aside and lashed out, bringing his fist across Maximillian's face. He left a red scrawl of blood and bruised flesh where the gauntlet had impacted. Maximillian spat crimson-stained saliva to the floor, and his eyes flared with hatred. Both had relinquished control, allowed themselves to glory in the moment, to surrender themselves to battle.

The shaking of the ship altered, the backbeat of their conflict shifting under their feet. The rhythm of battle seemed to shift in turn, and the milling multitudes around them paused momentarily.

All those who sailed aboard fighting ships knew the aches and pains of them. The excesses to which they struggled as they fought, and the ravages the enemy could deliver upon them. Invaders yearned for them, as defenders feared them. All knew how swiftly the circumstances could change.

A ship is a world that can be lost in a heartbeat, if you allow it.

His father's old wisdom ghosted across his thoughts, colouring them crimson with renewed fury. Erastus brought his sword up, driving aside Maximillian's own blade as he gouged into the man's shoulder. The assassin cried out, staggering away from him. Even the blood smelled wrong, the florid scent of it filling the gap between them.

The vox-bead at Erastus' ear went live. Ship systems responded in tandem, filling the fracas with a sudden burst of sound. An impossible sound.

Singing filled the close quarters. A hymnal, carried across the vox by the will of the distant figure it venerated. It rose from a dull bellow to a throaty roar, as though every devotee who carried it in their hearts was being roused to life. They sang because they believed. They loved, with every fibre of their being, and the truest showing of love for Him was hatred of His foes.

'Oh blade of light, that shines through the darkness of the void. That cuts through the bonds of the unclean, and liberates from harm. Oh shield of night, that–'

Erastus shook the intrusion away, and laughed. His features contorted into a grin as he advanced upon Maximillian. Even now, the assassin was looking around in confusion as the hymn carried through the passageways. Stalwart Imperial soldiers rallied, driving back the tide of heathenous vermin with whatever tools came to hand. Erastus watched Zofia drive her fist into the goggled face of a cultist, and then impale him on her sword.

They were fighting on. Driving back the foe with zeal and fury, as surely as the Astraneus were somehow, impossibly, here to fight the Emperor's wars once more.

Did they heed my words? Did they come to their king's aid?

Erastus turned aside the sudden thoughts and bellowed his hate as he pushed forward with his soldiers, back into the melee, swinging his blade for Maximillian's throat in a sweep of fire.

CHAPTER FORTY-THREE

The system's edge burned, reality boiling under the onslaught of so many near-simultaneous warp translations.

They came not in a ragged flood of poorly coordinated ships, but in a grim procession of rank, near funereal in their advance and aspect. Each ship was uniformly black, their hulls etched with gilded script – flowing, spidery words that spoke of the Emperor's wrath incarnate, and the judgement delivered upon the faithless.

They had ever been pilgrims, but now as they returned they were transformed. Reborn, and reconsecrated. Crusaders.

The black fleet swung away from their translation points, still trailing warp-stuff, dancing with witchfire and crackling with unnatural frost. Their engines burned, casting silver light as they powered on into the system. They arced out, like the spreading of wings, bringing light as they forged into the darkness. Dark against dark, black against black, they moved like the shadows of justice. Fire built within the shadow, letting light ripple along the carved oaths. Caught in the flare of distant stars and of imminent war, they remained unbroken.

The Astraneus flagship, the *Remembrance of the Throne*, came at their head, having long since shrugged off its sepulchral trappings. It burned hard for the tumultuous sphere of battle, weaving through burning debris and the cold, dislodged corpses of Norastye wrecks. Flotsam annihilated itself against its shields. They forged on regardless, ablaze with righteous anger.

Fire stained the void anew, as lance volleys and torpedo bursts stabbed out towards the Radrexxus fleet. As surely as it had coiled about its prey, it now dispersed, unwinding to face down the new attackers who beset them. Signals flew between the Radrexxus ships and the inner system, where the brood-mind's psychic attention was now focused upon the Astraneus. Wounded ships peeled away like sacrificial offerings, intent on preserving their master's existence even at the expense of their own lives. They pushed themselves into the fray, their weapons reorientating away from their prone victims and towards the fresh meat that presented itself for slaughter.

The first of the Astraneus kill-fleet powered towards them, and then turned hard – showing their broadsides to the enemy. A sea of fire unfolded before the cultist ships, scoring their hulls with volleys of lance beams and macro-munition shells. They threw themselves into the deluge, fearless, even as the prow of one of the ships melted under the pressure. It folded in on itself, and the vessel listed out of the storm as secondary explosions rippled along its length. It detonated, hewn apart by its own internal combustion, like a warhead attaining criticality.

Lit by the hellfire of the kill, the Astraneus poured onwards. Vengeance rode with them, in every flaming gesture.

Delvetar stood upon the bridge and gazed out at the majesty of holy war. They allowed a smile to cross their pallid features, reaching with one long-fingered hand to take a goblet from an attendant. The water was cool on their lips, and they allowed their tongue to snake out, seeking further moisture.

They had meditated long upon this moment. The Emperor's signs had been sought, by divination and by Tarot. *Had they made the right choice?* And now they returned at the appointed hour. When they were most needed.

And when they had emerged, had there not been a flurry of astropathic missives from the boy king? Was that not the hand of providence, *His* hand, reaching out to steady the course?

The agonies and the ecstasies of a life sworn to the service of a ship. As Arch-Lecter they were sworn to the Creed of the Shrouded Emperor, sacrificing everything before His altar. To serve as His black hand, disciple of His most holy will, was to give up everything. When Delvetar passed on, then the mantle of Arch-Lecter would go to the most worthy of the flock. They would ascend, man or woman, at the expense of all other succession. There was no gain without loss, and so the rank and role would swallow them – consume and define them.

There was only the dynasty. Only the Creed. Beyond it all other concerns were as dust and shadows.

'Scour them from our stars,' they whispered. Their voice was barely a rasp within the bridge, yet the voidborn moved to answer. A chorus of voices confirmed target locks, rhymed off proximity alerts and reports of munition tonnage. Somewhere a priest of the Mechanicus intoned the sacred geometries inherent in void warfare, locking in the equations necessary to fire. Armoured Crusaders, sworn to the Astraneus name, stood around the edge of the bridge, girdling it in iron and silver. Their blades were held ready to strike at a moment's notice.

We must all be so readied, Delvetar thought. *We must be prepared for all the trials He shall lay before us.*

It had been revenge that had first spurred them on to follow the boy king. Exile and the stain of their accusation was an affront that could not be allowed to linger. Better, they had thought, to face them down and bring the case before the crusade armies when they sallied forth. To perhaps even petition the primarch himself.

Delvetar was not of weak stock as the mewling Torvander had been. To stand before the Primarch Reborn would have been a privilege, an honour. The Holy One would have understood, and shriven the dynasty of their unfairly adjudged sins.

'We are not murderers,' Delvetar whispered softly. 'Those who die by our hand are those who He declares must die. We are His shrouded hand, His hidden blade. We do His will, as we walk in His shadow.'

'We walk in His shadow,' the bridge crew chorused softly. The Crusaders rattled their gauntleted fists against their breastplates, and fell silent.

The *Remembrance* began to shake as the first return fire found its mark. The void shields flared, hot and lurid. Swirls and whorls of energy danced before their vison, and Delvetar was reminded of an oil painting they had seen once, long ago. The blues and blacks of the void had seemed deeper within the azure glow of the stasis field, and the stars had seemed to burn that much brighter with their own golden light.

By contrast was the Emperor's great design laid bare, and its beauty made manifest. The darkness and the light were the cornerstones of what was, next to the mad and undulating stuff of unreality.

Delvetar blinked away the flaring of the shields. The greasy oil-smear of it stung their eyes. Cathedral spires glimmered, caught in the light of the enemy's fury. The shields enveloped them in their caustic light, and against the inferno beyond it was the pinion-shine of angelic wings.

'He is with us. In every thought and deed, He endures in us.'

Their faith embraced them in moments such as this. Moments of doubt, and question. It bore the weight of ages, ancient and profound. It had kindled in the earliest days of the Imperium-as-it-became, a dark counterweight to the Cult of the Saviour Emperor. Their forebears had looked out at the galaxy with a weary resignation, knowing that the shadow could not be truly overcome. Only outlasted. They would hurl themselves down into the muck, and the darkness, and they would embrace it as it embraced them. Shrouded. Sanctified.

For the children of the Astraneus there had never been a time before the Creed. It was everything, just as it demanded everything. Now they carried it into the heart of war. The shadow, ablaze.

They surged on, through the fire, and Delvetar sat. 'As He guides us into the tempest, so shall we weather its storms.' The ship shook, buffeted by new agony. They watched through the great gilded viewports, as the enemy ships came at them again. Citadels of spite and heathen joy, ready to be torn down by the hands of the worthy. By the intent of the willing.

'There is a debt to be repaid,' the Arch-Lecter whispered. 'Between the martial sons of Lamertine, and the faithful who walk the path of ashes. Let us prove to him the worth of our lineage.'

The cultists were screaming as they attacked with greater, panicked vigour. Erastus was aware of gears shifting behind Maximillian's eyes, plans reordering themselves to reactionary alien design. The keening screams echoed off the walls, melding with the chaotic sound of the ongoing battle. The ship shook, and behind everything there was the music of battle – scored to the Astraneus hymnal.

Erastus drove his sword through Maximillian's guard, eliciting a hiss of frustration from his opponent. The mask seemed gone entirely from him now, seared away in the rage at being thwarted once again. His movements were jerky, erratic, distracted as the seething consciousness that drove him struggled to adapt to the rapidly changing circumstances.

'My father,' Erastus breathed. 'He was many things, but he did not deserve to die at your hands. To fall to the blade of something so utterly less than a man.'

He cut across Maximillian's chest, and watched him flail out, overcommitting. Erastus carved into his flank, and Maximillian's eyes went wide with pain. He grabbed for the blade impotently, and could only watch as Erastus dragged it back. A rain of fingers hit the decking, and Erastus wasted no time in driving the sword up and through his throat. Maximillian gasped wordlessly, blood filling his mouth, before Erastus kicked him back.

He thrust his bloodied blade to the skies, and the Lamertine's roared oaths drowned out the tumult in a wash of triumph.

The enemy were a wave of chitinous flesh, beating themselves bloody against the sealed doors of the bridge.

Within, the warriors stood ready. Proud, stalwart souls. Ice-marked, and soul-strong. Katla could have asked for no greater honour guard, here at the end of all things. The thrum of battle shifted. She could see the sweep and flow of it beyond the observation windows. It filled her with the determination to fight on. To struggle until death stopped her, and the Underverse dragged her down.

Do His Sky Warriors keep their vigil this far from the frozen seas? Will they know of the valour laid down here? Does the Allfather know what we have given?

The thunder of the enemy stole her thoughts. The doors

buckled and bent, slivers of light shone through the slowly widening gap. She could see claws, digging into the metal, prising it apart like a wight from deepest nightmare. The cold dead of the sea, climbing its way into the hall from which it had been banished.

When the doors finally yawned wide, she was surprised to see a humanoid figure scuttling forward. The woman was shrunken, drowned in robes that were too voluminous for her meagre frame – the better to hide the mutations and deformities that she now wore proudly. Even in as exalted a role as she had been bred for, the genetics of the cult did not mesh well with the esoteric lineage of the Navigator houses.

Euryale smiled without warmth, turning her cold gaze to Katla. If she was aware of the void battle's progress she gave no sign. Instead, she fixed the jarl with her inhuman gaze. Others would have shrunk from such attention, and even those who stood with her seemed to falter. Katla did not. She stepped forward, back straight, head raised.

'Surrender,' the witch crooned. The true-form monsters slunk forward, like tame pets. Crouched low at her side, they were like cathedral gargoyles come to life, tongues lapping the air as they scented their prey.

There was a moment, here, now, where there was a chance. A fulcrum on which events turned. Katla looked at the wizened, twisted features of the witch; pale and curdled with alien heritage. The bile rose in her throat. She could never lower herself to their level, to choose to become less than human – sullied by the taint.

'No.' The word filled the space, as inevitable as a blow.

Her men raised their weapons, firing madly at the ghoulish display of superiority. The purestrains hissed, throwing themselves to the side. Their claws bit into the walls, and they ascended, skirting the edges of the chamber. Bullets and las-bolts followed them, dogging their heels as they moved to out-flank the meagre defence.

Euryale threw up a hand and psychic force rippled invis-ibly, casting aside the shots that threatened her. Cold lambency danced along her staff, whipping the air with lightning as she began to scream. Her jaw yawned, stretching impossibly as witch-light danced in her eyes. She channelled the hateful, impure energies of her inhuman idol. The scratching, chittering horror of the broodmind intruded into the sanctity of the bridge. Wards cracked, or wept sacred metals as the unholy force built.

Katla moved. She hurled herself forward, spear in her hands. It glowed in the low firelight of the bridge, burning brighter than the alien maleficarum that flowed from the witch. A purer light, the echo of the first morning's sun upon the ice. She remem-bered casting that spear as her father's second, in ceremony and in battle during her early years of command. Astrid had since taken up the duty, but the skill had never truly left her.

She cast her spear, a blade of light. A blade of hope, arcing across the confines of the bridge. Euryale saw it, her atten-tion snapping to it too late. Her lip curled in hate, her hands clenched. Fire and static flooded the air, writhing like tendrils as they sought to intercept the blow.

It shattered the bubble of projected force with a thunderclap of dislocated air. Some warriors were knocked off their feet, only able to gaze up impotently from the floor as the spear found its mark. It buried itself in the magus' skull, piercing her third eye with flawless precision. The witch screamed. The forces chan-nelled by her mortal body exploded forth, detonating her skull in a susurrus rush of screeched, alien doggerel and burning biomatter. Power and flesh vomited into the air, staining it with powdered near-human flesh.

Katla whooped, punched the air despite herself. She turned, drew her axes, and beheld the ruin that was becoming of her bridge.

The purestrains were amongst her men. Talons raked at their flesh and armour, gouging them apart with casual, bestial disdain. She snarled, swinging for the crested skull of one, carving a bloody furrow into its chitinous armour. It screeched and flailed for her, but she was already moving, ducking out of reach as someone unloaded a black powder pistol into the side of its head.

'Fear not the beast!' she screamed. 'It walks amongst you in mockery of man, but it is still but the dregs of the sea of stars!'

One of the monsters dropped from the ceiling, landing in front of her and roaring its hatred into her face. She lashed out, hooking one axe under its arm and swinging the other down. The limb atomised at the joint, caught between the competing power fields. It reeled back, and a trio of spears caught it in its chest. It staggered back, screeching and hooting.

In the wake of their matriarch's death, more of the monsters flooded into the chamber. Unleashed, all mortal restraint pared away by the single stroke of a spear. She saw men fall, pinned and devoured by the rush of alien horrors. She watched Eirik, fighting to the last. One of the monsters had impaled him above a console, and still he stabbed at its neck and body with the broken shard of his sword. Claws were already buried in his torso, intestines glistening wetly between them.

She roared her hatred, shoulder-barging the creature. It barely moved, turning to regard her with cold alien understanding. It clenched its claws together, and Eirik screamed in agony, before falling silent.

She raised her blades. This was how she was always meant to be. A line of cold defiance against the enemies of mankind. A champion at the gates. She struck and struck again; no matter where she attacked there was something to hit. The storm of writhing bodies closed in around her, and the clatter of their claws against the decking drowned out the screaming for one terrible moment of constant movement. She buried an axe in the broad chest of one of the genestealers, leaving it buried there as she drew her volkite. The beam cut through the smoke and blood of the bridge, cleaving a burst of superheated air that extended down the corridor, out over the headless corpse of Euryale. At least two of the attackers were cored through, their major organs disappearing in a rush of crimson horror.

Talons closed about her, bearing her to the ground. Her weapons skittered from her hands. The creature that had tackled her stared at her, jaw lolling wide as its tongue snaked and snapped at the air.

Katla spat in its face, screaming her defiance even as the alien's fanged maw descended for her throat.

CHAPTER FORTY-FOUR

DUTY AND DEATH

They advanced through the ship's corridors, drawing survivors and stragglers into their ranks as they went. Men and women flocked to them, streaked in blood and dirt and all the smoke of battle, drawn by the light of their king.

Erastus pulled men to their feet, patted others on the back. He offered quiet words of encouragement, and he gave rousing addresses. When eyes looked to him they did not see the wanton, charismatic youth who had so often been sent from their sight. They saw his father, reborn. A leader they could follow to the end; a man they would happily die with, and for. A man embracing the role that he had never craved, but was always meant for. Their belief almost convinced him. A worthy heir of the Lamertines; not a lesser lord, but an ideal. A symbol, worthy of commitment to bas-relief or glassaic.

He was their king.

The invaders bled from the shadows, their cloaks and robes billowing over rough flak-plate. They died in hails of perfectly coordinated fire, hewn down in their multitudes. They flooded on, like frightened vermin, their nerve utterly broken. Death was preferable to their deluded mania. Many of them tumbled over, eyes wide and staring, throats hoarse from screaming. The newer converts still had their own hair, and had torn it out in chunks, knotted in their fingers. The more vividly corrupted mutants had gouged their bare scalps bloody with their fingertips, like the raking of claws.

The orderly unity that had once defined them had fled, leaving only the dust and ashes of their ambitions.

Erastus slammed his boot into one gawking face, and strode on through the carrion field before the bridge's doors. The enemy had been clawing and prising at the doors, trying to force their way into the command centre of the ship. Similar abortive attempts were being turned back at the enginarium, at the ship's armouries and the gunnery decks.

Lines of defence solidified and held, becoming iron bulwarks around which resistance could gather and anneal. Bit by bit, they were taking back their vessel. Zones of control were spreading, as warriors and crew began to move beyond their established borders – linking up with other stragglers and hunting the mutants through the bowels of the ship. It was hard, bloody work, though none shirked from it. There was a pride in defending their home, and upholding the name of their dynasty. They had remained true where so many had proven false, and they endured where weakness had claimed others.

Erastus strode onto the bridge like a conquering hero, the doors sliding open in response to his affirmative biometrics. The crew were ashen, but mostly unharmed, and gazed at him as he entered. Someone cried out.

'Captain on the bridge! Honour the lord of the Compact, master of our house!'

Scattered applause rose from the bridge stations as the crew welcomed him back. Other more martial officers brought their fists to their breasts, or made the mark of the aquila before him. 'Throne preserve you, for returning to us,' one breathed, his voice reduced to a thin and reedy sob.

Erastus nodded, placed a hand on the man's shoulder, and walked to the command throne. Sitting in it felt as natural to him now as breathing, as comforting as his armour. 'Do we have word on the other vessels?'

'The *Queen* remains idle, my lord. We have reports of massed invasion, and the presence of tyranid bio-forms.'

'Emperor save us,' Erastus swore. 'But… if any can weather that storm it will be Katla and her kin. What of the *Remembrance of the Throne*?' He shook his head in disbelief. 'I had all but given up hope that our missives would find them. Yet here they are.'

'Indeed. The Astraneus have brought their fleet to bear upon Radrexxus. The enemy is rising to meet them. Secondary and ter-tiary threat vectors have moved away from us, and are reorientating to engage with the outermost fleet elements of the Astraneus.' The woman who spoke sat at the station Kaddas had once occupied, focused upon her work. If she knew the man who once manned it had died there, she gave no indication. Duty left no time for doubt. 'The current progress of the Astraneus fleet will bring them round and over the enemy, into our sphere of battle.'

'Where they can serve as a wedge between Gunther and us, and allow us to regroup. Fine work.' Erastus drummed his fingers against the arm of the throne. 'Open ship-to-ship vox with their flagship.'

'Aye, sir!'

When the link was established, it was to a hiss of laughter. Erastus had never seen Delvetar smile, let alone laugh. It was an unwelcome, strangling sound.

'Well met, Arch-Lecter,' Erastus said. 'I did not expect to see you in this battle.'

'And yet the will of the Emperor brought us here. Against all reason and all hope, we have been chosen to stand as His black blade in the darkness. To defend the honour of all from the treachery of the few. To prove that we are not idle murderers or seekers of unearned power. We are servants in the shadow. His servants, now as always. Proven in the blood of the foe.'

The connection dropped away, but Erastus was content. He nodded to his bridge crew.

'I want us moving, and combat ready. We have struggled within for too long, and now we must rejoin the war without. Our enemy thought us weak, our throat bared. He thought his tame assassin would be enough to end me. I am still here, his instrument is not.'

Erastus closed his fingers into a fist and slammed it against the armrest. All eyes were upon him.

'The Radrexxus killed my father. Your former lord and king.' Gasps arose, and angry cries quickly followed them. He ignored them, and pressed on. 'By betrayal, subterfuge and corruption have they sought to tear down our dynasty, and usurp all that we have built. They have crafted a trap, made of lies and spite.'

He let the moment hang; a pall of silence lingered over the bridge, empty save for the rumbling of the vessel as it began to move and fight once more.

'No more,' Erastus declared. 'I swear to you now, if it takes the rest of my life, I shall avenge us upon them all. Not merely this enemy that presents itself here and now, but every wretched bloodline that springs from their tainted wellspring. I will follow every track and trace of Radrexxus, and I will excise their works from the Imperium. This is the moment where we honour our oaths. Ten thousand years of struggle, trade and toil. All for this moment. To stand in the defence of a primarch's will, and to turn back the enemies of man – whether they wear our faces or not.'

He stood, drew Bloodsong again with a flourish, and pointed the blade into the glowing heart of the hololithic representation of battle.

'Take us back into the fight. Bring me the *Paradox.*'

'Not all homecomings will be happy ones,' her mother had said. She knelt in the snow, scooping a handful of it up and examining it with a critical eye. An awareness bled from her mother, a need to be in possession of all the information in any given circumstances. Astrid had been so intent upon her surroundings, amidst the rough grey mountains of the Winter World. Fenris' harsh wind tore at her, and she drew thick lungfuls of the ice-bitten air.

'They won't?' she asked.

Katla laughed, and shook her head. She dusted the snow from her hands and moved forward into the valley before them. A crevice, cut into the mountain rock by the geological pressure of ages. The rocky overhang offered some protection from the gathering gale, and Astrid hurried to follow her. She had been here before, but every time it was overwhelming.

There were few worlds in the galaxy that matched the sullen, storm-wracked splendour of Fenris.

'Of course not,' Katla went on. 'Every time we come here, a part of my soul is left behind.' She paused before a mound of stones, and placed her hand upon it.

To most it would seem ramshackle, an idle confluence of falling rocks. There were signs though. The runes etched into each stone, the necklaces whose cords were trapped beneath – bearing the claws of beasts, and the silver of the Allfather's eagle. It was not a fane. It was a cairn. A grave, to remember one long fallen. Every time she came close to it, Astrid was certain she could smell the ashes of the past, though they had long since passed into memory.

'My father,' Katla said softly. 'When we come to renew our oaths to our savage world, and to tithe what is needful from its grey flesh, I do you the honour of visiting you.' She knelt, and laid her spear before the cairn. 'What you and those before you built, I maintain.'

Astrid knelt beside her mother, head lowered. She did not look to the cairn of her grandfather. Instead, she closed her eyes, and tried not to think of the inevitable.

Her mother gave it voice, regardless.

'Not all homecomings will be sweet, Astrid. There will come a day when you will build my cairn, and speak my memory.'

'I will, Mother. I swear it.'

The memory rose, unbidden, as the ragtag assortment of warriors advanced towards the bridge. The suddenness of the thought surprised her, as though it were not truly her own. Astrid bit it away, swallowed it back much as she had swallowed her fleeting hatred of Erastus.

The king of the Davamir Compact had made her choice for her, yes, but he had given her a gift. A chance to keep her oaths, before the fire consumed them all.

It had not been an easy fight from the teleportarium. Deck by deck, corridor by corridor, they had clawed their way back. Up from the Underverse, and the ghoulish scrabbling of the mutant things. She had hewn apart bulky, muscle-swollen monsters with the faces of men, while her sworn swords stood at her side and unloaded their weapons into the thronging, screaming multitudes.

The screams lingered, long after the throats that bore them had been closed forever.

They came to the doors of the bridge, once so solid. Inviolable.

Warded and etched with all the marks of aversion known to them – they ought to have stood against eternity. Astrid stepped through their ruin alone, avoiding slivers of metal and the cooling bodies of alien monsters.

'Mother?' she asked timidly.

The bridge was quiet. She walked around its outer edge, the ruined precincts left in the aftermath. Astrid's path wound slowly, deliberately, towards the throne at its centre. Braziers were overturned, littering the command dais with ashes. The lack of light cast the central throne in shadow, and obscured the figure who sat slumped in it.

'Mother?' Astrid asked again.

The figure looked round and up, then hooked its hand into a fist and slammed it into their wounded side. Katla lurched forward, out of the patch of shadow, her features knotted with pain.

'There is not much time,' she hissed through gritted teeth. 'I can feel it, slipping away… They wanted me to suffer… I think. For what I did to their… ' She cried out, spasmed in the throne, her hands locking to the arms of it as she struggled to endure. 'Make them pay for this. Make them remember the name Helvintr.' She spat blood, and looked at Astrid. Katla's eyes were wild, unfocused. Tears rimmed them. 'If I die, it will be knowing that victory is near.'

'I–' Astrid hesitated.

'You do not think that you will be able to, but you will. You are my daughter, Astrid. You are a Helvintr. You… are a jarl. You have stood before the bones of our ancestors, and you have been judged worthy. You are my second spear.' She clenched her eyes shut, head lolling from side to side. 'I have never been prouder of you than I am now.'

Astrid knelt, and took up the spear that lay forgotten at her mother's feet. She weighed it, looking at the intricate runic carvings. The gold, silver and cold iron. She traced her thumb along the carved sigil of an eye. She looked at her mother, and stepped closer.

'I love you, *móðir*,' she whispered softly. Astrid leant in, kissing her mother's forehead. The wounded woman – her queen, her jarl and her mother – looked up and nodded.

'And I love you, my daughter.' Katla closed her eyes, prepared for the end. Her breathing stilled, and she fell finally, terribly silent.

Astrid did not look away.

Chapter Forty-Five

The ship moved off with murderous purpose. The ebullient, eager swagger of the *Indomitable Soul* was a direct contrast to the stalled, ponderous grief that shrouded the *Wyrmslayer Queen*, but the Lamertine flagship let its engines burn hard as it pushed itself back towards the battle proper.

The cohesion that had defined the Radrexxus in attack and defence seemed to have fragmented. Ships weaved through the Astraneus fire, void shields blazing and hulls aflame. They responded erratically, unable to focus their attentions. They were distracted children, milling around as though the fight had left them, and all they could muster was petulant flailing – the merest memory of ordered battle.

Only the *Lustful Paradox* maintained any form of integrity. Its shields still held and its guns still fired as it turned apart. It strutted, diving like a monarch of battle through the heart of the void war. It had shrugged off its tattered air of hedonistic disdain, and was instead a barbed weapon at the hands of its captain. Gunther had been an object of derision, yes, but there was a fearful competence that had been plain even in his days of deception. Then he had merely been a serpent in the trappings of a sybarite. Now, he was revealed as a monster playing at being human.

The *Paradox* still moved with its sinuous, effortless fluidity, plunging through the lines of battle. Hunting. Its movements were controlled, lacking the erratic spasm of its fellows.

At its bridge, its captain held control by will alone. Gunther Radrexxus threw his head back against the high back of the command throne, leaving trails of sweat along the intricate etchings. None of it mattered. There was only the moment, only the struggle and the dance of competing intelligences.

The broodmind writhed, wounded. The magus, dear Euryale, was gone. One minute she had burned, stellar-bright, and then she had been snuffed out. Maximillian too... though his command had been lesser. The sanctus was only ever a tool, a specialised implement. An expression of the Voidfather's spite. The weight of the broodmind, the burden of its control, had fallen upon Gunther like a hammer blow. Even now, he could feel the blood dripping from his nose, pounding in his temples.

'Voidfather,' he hissed through clenched teeth. 'Grant me your strength, which endures even in the vacuum of space. Grant me your clarity, which cuts through the confusion of the cattle-mind.' His mind sought that clarity, questing after certainty once more. Thousands of voices clamoured at his senses, slamming down upon them like waves upon the shore. His will was being scoured away, eroded by the oceans of unbound thought.

However did you endure this weight? His thoughts sought Euryale again, unaccustomed to the loss. The effort made him wince. He could feel drool on his chin, streaked with blood as it dribbled sluggishly. He blinked, trying to regain some measure of self.

'Deliver your children, Father! Ease our burden! I would walk through all the fires of conflict for you, I would face down any foe… This weight was not mine to bear, not alone.' He whimpered, despite himself. Even the greatest master of humanity was as nothing before the glory of divinity's own avatar.

He felt the psychic agony abate, and looked up. He wiped his mouth and nose with the back of his hand, smearing his shame into the sleeve.

The biological is merely the conduit for the supernal; from the flesh shall we be delivered when the Starborne raise us up. We shall be exalted.

Catechism bled into his mind, and in its wake he could feel the comforting presence of the Voidfather. He caressed Gunther's brainstem with claws of cold fire, and every nerve caught alight and came alive with the old skill and confidence. He almost laughed, but it caught in his throat, stillborn under the eye of a god.

'I…' He hissed. 'I understand.' There was a flow to his thoughts now, an unspooling web of crude and direct communion. Something had been wrung from it, some subtlety and nuance. All human emotion had ebbed away, replaced by the singular will and drive of their godhead. Now it was the purr of a caged beast, rife with eagerness and pitiless, boundless hunger. It hungered, and it *hated*.

Gunther hunched deeper into the shadows of the throne, and the bridge crew drove themselves deeper into their frenzy. They worked the controls passionately, lips in constant motion as they tried in vain to process the ceaseless rush of alien malevolence. The ship burned hard, driving through the heart of the battle and out again, towards the inner system. An arrow of burning, tarnished perfection, arcing out towards its allies – enough to draw the eyes of the three wounded giants that had set themselves against it.

As the will of the Voidfather clenched around his mind, Gunther smiled. There was glory to be won here, yet, with divine winds at their back.

Erastus had not expected the Radrexxus gambit to be so obvious, so direct. He could only watch, transfixed and horrified, powerless as the events unfolded around them. He had sought communion with Katla to better coordinate their resistance, and had instead found another voice responding.

'My mother...' the voice said through the storm of static, and it took Erastus a moment to recognise it as Astrid's. As she spoke, the strength behind the voice slowly returned – a guttering flame stirred again to its full intensity. 'My mother is gone. The beast cut deep, deeper than we might ever have feared. The flagship is lost... She will not make the journey.'

'Astrid, I'm sorry.' Erastus closed his eyes. The loss of the jarl and her ship was an almost mortal blow.

We are all orphans now. Bereft of parents, and with our allies all but lost.

Everything was madness. The ship shook and screamed. The hololiths blazed like stars, crimson lancing against their meagre signals. The *Lustful Paradox* drove at them, seemingly uncaring for its own well-being. Combined fleet fire chased at it, casting up sheets of flame as its void shields caught alight once more. It barrelled past its own ships, who moved sluggishly out of its way only to wheel about in its wake. The *Paradox* drew the chaff into its orbit, and speared onwards. The *Soul* began to turn, broadsides scouring across the side of the enemy flagship as it hurtled past.

The *Remembrance of the Throne* lumbered after its fleeing prey, a looming shadow propelled upon pillars of silver fire. The Arch-Lecter did not broadcast their intent; instead the vox boomed with warlike orisons and declarations of pious fury for those who had lain with the alien and taken up its foul taint. If they heard Erastus and Astrid's communications, they ignored them. Prow-mounted lances seared the void behind the *Paradox*, scouring some of the faded brass and ragged gold from its rear. The opulence of finer days was being slowly eroded, discarded like the pupal casing that it had been. In their treachery they were revealed, and exalted.

The *Remembrance* rushed on too eagerly, and too rashly. By the time the auspex began to sound, it was already too late.

The *Paradox* flipped, end over end. Retro-boosters fired to stabilise it, straining to contain the monumental shift in the vessel's weight. Behind it, out of the darkness of the inner system, out of the shadows of the vast turning orbs of the planets, they came.

Gunther gritted his teeth till blood stained them. So many new minds burned with his own, singing over and over through the shared psychic bond. He collapsed to his knees, euphoric as he connected with so many other consciousnesses. He felt what they felt, saw what they saw. He was a mote in the eye of the universe, and he surrendered.

Ships drifted and listed, their engines struggling and straining as they pushed themselves beyond means and ability. Men and women froze at their stations, as air and heat bled out of them. They held failing power conduits together until their skin burned and the electricity finally earthed through them into the decking, and they fell dead. The weakest, the most sure of death, fed themselves into the furnaces that sustained their sputtering engines – the better to ensure that their objectives would be met. A crude fanaticism replaced their earlier nuanced zealotry. The mind that drove them on was devoid of sentiment; all it desired was the death of its enemies. All other things were inconsequential, least of all the lives of those who served it. The Voidfather drove them, fuelled them, animated them.

The makeshift flotilla was varied, formed of all the ships that could conceivably have served a fortress-world in ways beyond combat. Repurposed tugs and skiffs surged forward in ragged attack runs, focused upon the Astraneus flagship.

Its guns lit up, reducing the first wave to so much slag and spinning debris. Flaming metal tumbled off into the void or was obliterated against the shields. Still the vessels came on, forcing themselves forward through the suppressing fire cast up by the *Remembrance*. Shrapnel rained down against the hull, and the ships pushed onwards like knives, violating the noble vessel. They swarmed it, stealing all momentum. Explosions rocked it, rippling through its body in cataclysmic waves of devastation. The artful etched script across the hull's exterior was burned away: entire chapters of scripture broke apart as the ship spun, torn by the contradictory forces of the deluge of vessels. Some buried themselves in the ship and pushed, engines struggling as they began to move the vast craft. Others slammed against it and then veered off, committing themselves to ruin.

And behind it all, like the heartbeat of a god, Gunther could feel-hear-sense the great guns of Endymica as they committed themselves at last to renewed slaughter. He felt he could almost taste the detonations of nova-shells and long-range ballistics as they hurtled past the makeshift flotilla. New blades seeking throats. By all the myriad ways of war and betrayal would they render the enemy down, destroy them, and make them weep.

The *Lustful Paradox* dived through the fire, lending its own broadsides to the death spasms of the great ship, in a final spiteful flourish. Shells burst against the leviathan's shields, and lances gouged vast glowing chasms through its hull. The other ship was still fighting, still struggling, but the weight of multitudes drowned it, pulled it under and held it in place. They were killing it by degrees, turning every facet of their lives – even their deaths – into barbed weapons that would destroy the enemy and make them suffer.

The *Paradox* left them behind, ignorant of all save the need to avenge itself. The guiding light of the cult cut and hewed at the minds of its servants, driving each loss into the meat of their brains with bestial potency. The magus, taken from them. Their noble sanctus, cut down. All would be avenged, when the moment came.

When the time came, it would come in fire.

CHAPTER FORTY-SIX

FINAL FLIGHTS

Within the war-sanctum that was the *Indomitable Soul*'s bridge, everything was reduced to an abstraction. The flows of data were collated and formed into hololithic approximations of the battles raging beyond. Erastus had long since learned to parse the information in ways which he could utilise, but to do so in the fullness of war was a thing all its own.

He watched as the crimson tide of the enemy's ramshackle fleet descended to tear the *Remembrance* apart, flooding it like carrion worms devour a corpse. He shook his head, and gestured to the communications officer. Vox-crackle filled the interior of the space, and he spoke swiftly.

'What matters now is that we make each sacrifice matter, Astrid,' he said. 'I have a plan, a way for us to get as many of the fleet assets out. Somewhere they will never be able to follow us. We can regroup, rebuild, and we can strike back against them. Every part of this will carry risk. I need you to trust me.'

'You have my trust,' Astrid said plainly. *'You have my fealty, and*

you have my blade. I will stand with you, until we can drive it through the bastard's throat. We are fighting our way to the hangars. Throne willing we shall make rendezvous with the Shield.*'*

'That will be enough.' Erastus laughed mirthlessly. 'We are sending coordinates, and a course heading. We're going to use an old Jovian trick my father imparted. Pass them down to whatever ships you have left to you. I will gather the Astraneus that remain.'

He cut the feed and another opened, a broad-spectrum transmission to the reeling black vessels of the Astraneus. They were dying, locked in their struggles with the renewed passions of the Radrexxus and forced to watch as their flagship burned and bled into the dark.

'Heed the word of your king,' Erastus said, and then continued, not waiting for a response. 'If your lord is not dead already then they will soon be. It is my priority to get every last strategic resource we still possess out of this system. We endure the fire by forging through it. Listen to my words. If you seek vengeance, if you wish to return upon our enemies in fire and blood, then you must listen to my instructions.'

He signalled, and the transmission began: approach vectors and course orders streamed down the screens, passing through complex Mechanicus cyphers before being cast out across the yawning void between ships.

Erastus turned away from the broadcast stations, and fixed his attention once more upon the hololith. The *Lustful Paradox* was a bullet of crimson light, a blade driven towards their heart. He cursed under his breath.

'Are the Astraneus ships moving to comply?'

'Aye, lord!' an officer called, as they checked the scrolling auspex data. 'They're breaking with the active engagements and adjusting to account for our instructions. The *Shield* is turning about, making ready to burn away from the wreck of the *Wyrmslayer Queen* – I'm not sure many other Helvintr ships are still in the fight.' She paused. 'We still have readings from the *Vindication of Terra*, but I fear we've lost most of our support, including the *Throne's Justice*.'

'And now the *Paradox* comes straight for our throat.' Erastus braced his hands on the armrests of the throne and forced himself up. He stretched, then looked to his crew. 'I'll be at the primary observation deck.' There were gasps of shock, and he raised a hand to calm them. 'All I wish is to look our enemy in the eye, one last time before we're beyond their reach.' He nodded to Zofia. 'With me.'

His honour guard gathered, and Erastus led them out into the still-smoking corridors of his ship.

As much as he appreciated the deeply buried command centre of the *Soul*'s bridge, there was a ghoulish completeness in being able to gaze out at the ravaged void. To see, and to understand, the enemy – concerns of vulnerability be damned – was to fight with the entirety of the heart and soul.

The burning, war-scarred outer system was fascinating in its horrific totality. The gutted remnants of ships, allied and traitor, tumbled through the blackness, riven by their own internal conflicts, blazing with the fires of death and rebellion.

'That all of this should come at the hands of one man,' Erastus breathed. His hand rested upon Bloodsong's hilt, in anticipation of violence; as though merely by holding it, he could turn back the wrath bearing down upon them.

The *Lustful Paradox* moved closer with singular purpose. Its weapons only fired when they had solutions upon the *Soul*. The shields flared up before Erastus' eyes as each savage blow hit them. In places the shields failed, and the hull shook and burned with the enemy's clawing attempts.

He could feel the air growing close, electric. His head pounded momentarily, and he stumbled back. His teeth ached, itching with the building static.

'Back!' he heard Zofia call out, but it was too late.

Reality opened before them, unfolding in a burst of smouldering, screaming unlight. The warp uncoiled in a sickening parody of the biological, like the petals of a flower or the parting of flesh around a wound. Existence suppurated, weeping tears of black flame, before it birthed horror. Desperation, proximity and damage had conspired to leave them open to the intrusion. Teleportation was a risk at the best of times, and now the enemy used it to strike at their heart.

A ragged figure materialised in the maelstrom of toxic light, already moving. Gunther Radrexxus, or a broken parody of the man, landed on the deck, sword already up and swinging. The flat of the blade knocked Zofia flying, and she clattered against the wall of the chamber, her head smashing into the metal. She fell to the ground, unconscious. If any other of his guard yet lived, then they were separated by the burning afterbirth of the teleport translation – or had been atomised in the pulse.

Erastus drew Bloodsong, its power field engaged with a crackle, and blade met blade. He felt the jarring shock of it, amazed at Gunther's rabid strength.

'Still a chance!' the crazed warrior panted. His eyes rolled in his skull, bloodshot and set deep in his too-pale flesh.

All the glamour and pretence of nobility, or even foppery, was gone. Wrenched away. He wore no powder or wig, and his scalp was lined with deep gouges from his own fingers. He swung his blade in sweeping, angry arcs. It was not metal, Erastus realised, but some strange bony material. It sang when his own blade struck it, its unnatural field easily the match for the pure light of his power sword. The flaring of the blade made his skull ache with psychic feedback, the clawing, chittering whisper of the inhuman.

'I will not fail him! I will not fail!' Gunther raved, slamming his blade again and again against Erastus' guard.

'You're mad!' Erastus spat. 'You were never a man at all, just a thing dressed up in our skin. A parasite, waiting to consume the host. And what will you have by the end? A kingdom of ashes!'

'A kingdom!' Gunther laughed. Spittle sprayed from his lips as he mouthed the word, human speech coming less easily to his addled mind and flawed anatomy. 'I will be a king. The Void King! Sitting upon the throne of ages, ready for the coming of the Starborne! Once I take your head, once I topple all other pretenders, then they will honour me.' He grinned emptily.

Erastus winced, stumbling back at the next flurry of blows. He was competent, but Gunther was driven by the hand of his fell gods, the rage and the madness of thousands of shattered minds screaming as one. A savage backhand caught Erastus in the face, knocking him against the glass of the observation deck. Gunther loomed forward, leering at him avariciously. He raised the blade, looking down its length. Erastus could see it clearly now, the biological atrocity of it. Not even the graceful wraithbone of the aeldari; simply a thing grown, excreted. Generated, rather than manufactured.

'The king is dead,' Gunther whispered, almost to himself. His expression hardened. 'Long live the king.' He raised his blade, turning it over in his hands so that the point was aimed at Erastus' throat. He thrust.

The Norastye brooch Erastus wore, the gift, the shield, triggered at his throat. Though it had come from the hands of traitors, they had not dared to defile its mechanisms. In the face of the inhuman Radrexxus, it burned with a baleful purity. Light orbed Erastus, a burst of perfect radiance that enveloped him entirely. Gunther staggered back in the sudden rush of air, the explosion of force. The blade in his hands detonated, shattering at its midpoint. Fragments of the sword were hurled outwards, embedding in the man's face. He snarled, throwing his head back at the pain.

Erastus was already in motion, bringing Bloodsong up and burying it in Gunther's chest. The lord admiral gasped as the blade slid into his armour, piercing him through. He gurgled, and pulled back, yanking with all of his inhuman might. The sword slid from Erastus' grip, and Gunther stood for a moment – transfixed. He laughed again, a ruined and twisted sound. He reached up and triggered something in the lining of his armour.

The teleport homer blinked, crackled, and went live.

'No!' Erastus snapped.

Gunther was wreathed in fire again, falling back into the embrace of the tortured infinite. The blade went with him. Erastus sank to his knees, slamming his fist against the deck.

'You've taken everything from me,' he snarled. 'One day I will return the favour. I will bring my vengeance to the very heart of you.' He spat on the decking, and forced himself back up. He moved quickly over to Zofia. He checked her pulse and cursed under his breath. He reached up and activated the vox-bead in his ear. 'I need a medicae to the observation deck,' he ordered. 'And prepare to execute.'

'*Aye, lord!*' came the response. '*We have word from the jarl.*'

It took Erastus a moment to realise that the comms officer was speaking of Astrid and not Katla. Sadness blossomed in that realisation, before he bit it back and continued to listen.

'*She is aboard the* Shield. *They stand ready.*'

'Then let it be done. By the Emperor's will.'

The *Indomitable Soul* pushed itself near to breaking, uncertain whether it was finding new strength or exhausting what was left to it. It moved through the debris fields with a surety of purpose that evoked earlier, happier days. It had not forgotten that it was a master of the void. It had been forged in the orbit of Jupiter, in an age of wonders, in the light of humanity's birth star. It had been anointed in light, before ever it had forged out into the dark.

Vaster wars and more odious betrayals had failed to lay it low.

It led the loyalist ships in a desperate breakout action, lending its mightier guns to their aid. Cult ships burst apart in single volleys of its cannons, or were reduced to clouds of smouldering metal by coordinated lance strikes. The *Soul* continued on, burning hard enough to fall into line with the smaller and swifter escort ships and then to outpace them entirely.

The numbers had been checked, double-checked, and triple-checked. Mechanicus astro-mechanists had lent their processing power to the task, and consulted extensively with astrocartographs and their own shipwright understanding. It would work, though merely surviving long enough to put it into practice had been nothing short of miraculous.

<The will of the Omnissiah-in-Adamant!> one declared. <We shall know statistical success or we shall experience the apotheosis of matter-energy annihilation!>

The ship began its advance, skirting around the edge of one of the immense gas giants which defined the outer system. Many stellar systems were composed in this way, and each one was a spectacle. The outermost titan of Endymica was a cerulean marble, mottled through with green and vivid ochre. Storm systems vaster than entire worlds broiled and strained within its surface, and the shadow of the *Soul* barely registered upon it. Before such cosmic grandeur, even the most illustrious of men were rendered miniscule. Only the Emperor, who burned with the turning of the universe – who ordered time, and set the very stars in motion – compared to the untrammelled fury of the natural world. In attempting to harness such power to aid the fleet's escape, Erastus risked everything. And yet he felt strangely at ease.

Gravity caught them, and the ship began to shake as it rode the edge of the planet's pull. Erastus surrendered to it, letting it tug at the immensity of the vessel. They were accelerating now, skirting the edges of the gravity well, borrowing from its strength as it buffeted them. Everything was shaking, the engines struggling to compensate to stop them from tumbling into the maelstrom below.

One of the Astraneus ships, a converted prayer-hauler bearing the name *Rudiments of Faith*, misjudged. The planet took it, like an offering to a vast pagan fane. Misaligned for entry, and travelling at far too great a speed, it came apart and detonated in the upper atmosphere, sending contrails of fire across the sculpted marble of creation. The fire faded almost as soon as it was born, torn away by the endless winds of the world.

Everything within the *Soul* was shaking, convulsing with the ship's palsy. The crew had been briefed, and were strapped in where possible. Everything that could be chained in place had been. Systems blew out, lumens flickered erratically, and sirens blared atonally. The ship's machine-spirit brayed, ancient and venerable, suddenly roused to dreadful wrath. Still they pushed on, through the fire and out. The hull and the void shields were glowing, stoked to furious brightness.

The ship sailed on, one last true-cast spear against the coming of night. And then they were propelled up, their progress skirting over the stellar disc of the system. Below, the guns of Endymica fired impotently, clawing futilely to reach them, and the ramshackle fleet could not hope to match them. Even the *Lustful Paradox* had idled. Waiting, watching. They could feel the judgement of vast minds, trailing just behind them – glowing with hunger and malice, like a thing of the deepest winter.

'When we translate,' Erastus said, broadcasting to all the ships which had managed the transit, 'it will be into the teeth of the storm. We were sent to see if the Draedes Gap was fit for the primarch's crossing.' He shook his head. 'I do not think it was ever intended to be this literal.'

Shouts of alarm and fear greeted his words. Egeria wailed over the vox, till he was forced to cut the line. The guards would be there, if matters escalated, but he had every faith that she would do her duty. As they all would.

'Hope is our guide,' he said, and the crew fell silent. 'We have been betrayed, and we have been wounded. Time and again, they have come for us. We have endured. Survived. We have fought, and bled, and lost.' He stood, and his hand reached for the sword that was no longer there. He winced with phantom pain. 'They have an entire planet of the mad and the depraved to throw at us. They will fire their guns and plunge at us with their vessels. We can stand and fight, die in futility, or we can take a chance. Return.'

He looked at them. He took a breath.

'All I will say is that the Emperor walks with us, and we must trust in His judgement. As my father would have trusted, and you would have trusted him.' He waited, held the moment, and then nodded. 'Take us in.'

The warp engines spun up, and the ship seemed utterly at peace. For one glorious moment, it was as though their wounds and their failings counted for nothing. They might have been setting out on a mere diplomatic jaunt, or a harmless trade delegation. Not fighting for their lives, on the edge of hell, with a scrabbling army of the damned at their back.

Then reality opened its skin, and wept with condensed

screams. The infinite and the infernal rushed in at them, and they could only hold their breath as they slid forward and the stormlight of the Rift-torn warp embraced them with the cold tendrils of its longing.

Chapter Forty-Seven

He wanted to scream, but he could not scream. Everything was a single moment, stretched out and pinned out, and set to burning. The ship shook and shuddered and bellowed its machine-rage, and all he could do was watch. Egeria's vox-link was stuck open and she would not stop screaming, screaming, and the percussive banging as she slammed her head against the Navigator's throne. He had not looked at the bridge in so many long minutes, minutes so long they had stretched into hours, metastasised into years. Lifetimes, lived and died in the chrysalis of the bridge – bound only by the fear of what they might have become.

Erastus opened his eyes.

The hololith was dead, replaced by a whorl of tortured, bruised light. He could see, as surely as though he stood at the observation decks and gazed out into the void. He could see the immensity and the absoluteness of the warp, pressing in, before wheeling out. The light was laughing, thick burbling laughter that flowed through the turgid air.

He blinked.

The image had changed. It was the ship, so small a thing. Frail and mortal, and so very small. Things swam in these seas, born of the condensed minutiae of human thought – dredged from the limitless failings of the spirit – and they thought that they could sail a vessel through such tides?

He had realised, or perhaps would realise, that he was adrift in an ocean of madness and revelation, and the very ship he thought his inviolate defender had been nothing more than a holed-through life raft.

Erastus vomited, heaving his guts onto the decking of the bridge. Blood had already flowed there, and less identifiable fluids. He gasped, hunched over the arm of the throne. He could hear the laughter of the daemonic and the weeping of his crew. His eyes slid off the crew, unable to truly see them.

He felt the tendrils of some great animal, as though they already slid through the corridors of the ship. Hewing it apart without firing a shot. It was despair, a pall-beast, feeding on them. He heard its voice, its slithering whisper. If they would only give in…

'The light is gone, the light, the light, the light,' Egeria whispered over and over again.

Erastus reached for his sidearm, not caring that it would not make a difference. Sometimes, to defy was enough.

A howl cut through all that was.

Something swept across the perverted hololith in a flash of bronze and grey. The Shield of Wolves tore through the panorama, thrust like a blade, like a spear through flesh. It cut into the undulating sea of cloying black flesh, the rainbow smear of eternity's blood clinging to it. A voice howled, distorted, over the vox. Astrid's voice. She cursed the warp with all the hateful defiance of Fenris. She implored the God-Emperor of Mankind and all the spirits of her sacred home world to gird them, and bear them across the threshold.

The spell broke. He was himself again. The bridge was crowded with crew, all of them with their eyes downcast. The hololith guttered like a dying brazier, and was still. They had silenced it early, when the nonsense readings had threatened to overwhelm them.

'Forward,' he croaked. 'Keep us moving!'

He reached up and wiped the sweat and blood from his forehead, and prayed. For deliverance. For safe harbour.

For a miracle.

They plunged through the fire and the madness of the Storm of Storms.

The Rift clawed at them with febrile, demented longing. It sought to trap them in puzzles of broken time and twisted knots of memory. They watched friends and family die, a hundred times, and yet still fought on. With Lamertine determination, Helvintr fury, or the cold light of Astraneus prayers. They carved their way out of the darkness, they silenced their own screaming. Ancient sailors had lashed themselves to the wheel and stopped their ears with wax, to keep their course true when unreality clawed at them.

Each ship lashed itself to its duty.

Hundreds died. Madness took them, and the failures of Geller fields. Food curdled, water caught alight and danced its way into nothingness. It became impossible to trust, but the only alternative was to die. And they were not ready to die.

When they limped back into realspace, they were a fragment and a shadow of the might that had crossed into the fire of the Rift. The flagship barely endured, but the lesser ships were all but depleted. All that remained of some were the echoes of astropaths and the tortured repetition of vox-transmissions which would never reach home.

Help us.

Save us.

Betrayers.

Erastus looked at the transcripts, the printouts that sought to enforce logic upon the ravings of the insane, and ordered them burned. He could not look upon them, his mind could not hold them. To dwell on their losses and the realities would be to go mad. He looked at his reflection in a blank, dead screen. Lines etched his skin, worn there by the impossible passage of time. His dark hair had silvered in places.

Whatever the cost. Whatever the sacrifice, they had made it.

'As soon as possible, I want Astrid here,' he stated.

His officer of communications stared for a moment, the man's eyes looking through him, before he shook himself and nodded. As he adjusted the communications feed, the Navigator's sanctum began to whisper again. Like the echo of a nightmare.

'No light, no light, no light.'

They met in his sanctum. Astrid could barely look at him, busying herself with the relics upon the shelves within the chamber. Erastus rose from behind the desk, looking at her.

'I simply wanted to say how sorry I am,' he began. She waved away his concern.

'Don't,' she whispered. 'What has come to pass is our wyrd. It is the hand of fate. It raises some up, and it casts others down. We do not question what has come to pass. We only ask, what comes after?'

'What indeed…' He reached across the desk and scooped up the missive, cradling it like a talisman.

'Your father's dead hope?' she asked, scoffing. She picked up the lithe, golden length of a blade, stabbing idly at the air. 'You truly think that it has any worth, beyond what he gave it?'

'I do,' Erastus said.

She looked at him, weary and confused. 'I do not have time for games, Erastus. We have lost everything. We are lost, ourselves. Our astropaths scream into the dark, and our Navigators see nothing but shadows and fire. We have been led to a fool's end.'

'When our astropaths scream, I imagine that they sound very much like this missive.' His eyes were alight. 'You asked me before if I believed as my father believed. I do. I have to. We have crossed into the very mouth of hell. Into the lost holdings of the Imperium. We are far from home, and we have only our wits, and our will, and our desire for revenge.'

'And you think these things are enough?'

'More than enough.' He held out his hand. 'I believe. I believe in the bonds of the Compact. In the strength of our fellowship. I believe that a new Arch-Lecter will rise, and that together – together we have a chance. All I am asking, is that you stand with me.' He smiled, caught in the golden light of the lumens. 'Will you stand with me?'

Astrid put the blade down. She looked at Erastus' hand. She reached out and took it. There was strength there. Both of them, for the first time in so long, felt strong.

'Where do we begin?'

Epilogue

Victory and Defeat

It had taken time to engineer such a thing as victory from ruin.

The ships had been repaired, till they once again displayed all the pomp and ceremony of the glorious. Their oaths had been re-etched in gold and silver, cut into the waiting hull with the skill of master shipwrights.

When they returned, it was as a triumphal procession. They had coasted back into the crimson light of the home-star with their heads held high. They had docked swiftly, in orderly fashion, and then proceeded into the heart of the great station. The Bladespire rang again with the sounds of occupancy, though none of the seneschals rushed to greet the returning conquerors. The messages and missives that preceded them had been vague and full of woe. No one was eager to face down such calamity.

So it was that the victor strode into the Hall of Equals alone. He waited, dispatching his own picked men to do his will rather than waiting for the indulgence of castellans. The helmeted warrior hurried back into the chamber, a bundle slung under one arm. He knelt, unwrapping it and holding the prize up into the crimson light.

Resting upon its nest of velvet was the Umbral Crown. The dark crystal and metal of it glimmered in the starlight, seeming at once to devour the light and yet shimmering with its radiance. The conqueror knelt, reached down, and took the crown in his trembling, ring-bedecked fingers. Slowly, deliberately, he ascended the dais.

Gunther Radrexxus, the Void King, raised the crown to his head, and took his place upon the throne.

The great vessel was a shadow of its former self. It spun, silent and cold, in the outer system. Frost had settled across its skin, and in its bones, and across every last internal surface. A ship of the dead, ready to slip beneath the water of winter seas and never emerge again – save in sailor's nightmares, crewed by wights.

The old woman picked her way through the skeleton of the great vessel, seemingly without a care to the void-cold that was seeping in. Other survivors clustered together for warmth or desperately sought to restore the machine-spirits of the immense vessel.

'It cannot end like this,' the gothi hissed to herself, breath fogging in the thinning air. 'Not yet.'

She clutched what precious medical supplies she had been able to save or scrounge close to her chest. Others might have sought to steal them, to prise some slim advantage from between her fingers. This was nothing new. Even the sworn swords of Fenris could feel the claws of desperation at their heart. What way back was there from this, when the enemy had wounded them so?

Bodil was beyond such fears. She had read the runes and

chased down fate. She had pinned it in place once before, when her liege had been wounded. Now she would do so again.

She stepped into the winnowed expanse of the bridge, picked her way over the bodies of the slain – valiant and false – before she came to the reclining form of her queen. Behind her all was dead and cold. Beyond the great viewports, the detritus of battle tumbled and spun. Corpses in the void. The dead of perhaps the greatest battle they would ever endure... perhaps.

The old gothi leant close to her queen and readied the salves and unguents. She let her fingers close around one long injector and raised it up, tilting it this way and that as she scrutinised the contents.

'Perhaps,' she whispered. 'Let us pray to all the whims of wyrd and the blessings of the Allfather, that this is enough.' Her old hand trembled as she placed it tight to Katla's still shoulder. She let her fingers tighten as she forced the injector through a breach in the queen's armour. Her fingers brushed cold, bare skin, seeking the right angle.

The needle bit like a drake in an old tale. A serpent rendering its venom. The old woman closed her eyes, her breathing a thready hiss in the vastness of the black and cold. For a long moment nothing happened and Bodil feared she was too late. That all would be for nothing. That they would die here, leaderless and alone.

The body before her twitched. Bodil stepped back, slipping on the icy deck as she did. She crumpled to her knees, grey robes pooling about her.

On the throne, in mimicry of that greater Throne, bound between life and death, between sanity and madness, Katla Helvintr stirred, spasmed.

And began to scream.

ACKNOWLEDGEMENTS

This book was a journey in more ways than one. It began as the first long-form project that I ever worked on, and was lost to the storm of 2020. It is dear to my heart, a labour of love, and something that I am immensely proud of – and yet it could not exist without many others (as is true of most novels).

To Kate and Will, who have been nothing but supportive and enthusiastic about this project and the little cluster of nobility we built together: thank you for taking a chance on this mad odyssey, and especially on Katla.

For my Heroes and Heretics, who were there – as always – to advise, assure, and ultimately to help me keep my head when all seemed lost.

For my wife, Anne-Sophie, and my parents Cathy and Alex: you have been very patient, kind, supportive, and I'm sorry that Jamie beat you with his dedication.

ABOUT THE AUTHOR

Marc Collins is a speculative fiction author living and working in Glasgow, Scotland. He is the writer of the Warhammer Crime novel *Grim Repast*, as well as the short story 'Cold Cases', which featured in the anthology *No Good Men*. For Warhammer 40,000 he has written the novels *Void King*, *Helbrecht: Knight of the Throne* and a number of short stories. When not dreaming of the far future he works in Pathology with the NHS.

YOUR
NEXT READ

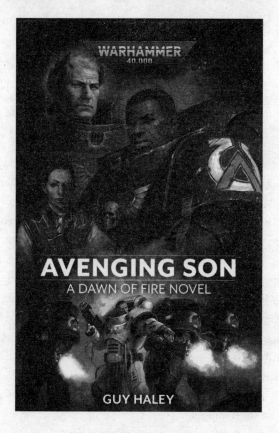

AVENGING SON
by Guy Haley

As the Indomitus Crusade spreads out across the galaxy, one battlefleet must face a dread Slaughter Host of Chaos. Their success or failure may define the very future of the crusade – and the Imperium.

An extract from
Avenging Son
by Guy Haley

'I was there at the Siege of Terra,' Vitrian Messinius would say in his later years.

'I was there…' he would add to himself, his words never meant for ears but his own. 'I was there the day the Imperium died.'

But that was yet to come.

'To the walls! To the walls! The enemy is coming!' Captain Messinius, as he was then, led his Space Marines across the Penitent's Square high up on the Lion's Gate. 'Another attack! Repel them! Send them back to the warp!'

Thousands of red-skinned monsters born of fear and sin scaled the outer ramparts, fury and murder incarnate. The mortals they faced quailed. It took the heart of a Space Marine to stand against them without fear, and the Angels of Death were in short supply.

'Another attack, move, move! To the walls!'

They came in the days after the Avenging Son returned, emerging from nothing, eight legions strong, bringing the bulk of their numbers to bear against the chief entrance to the Imperial Palace. A decapitation strike like no other, and it came perilously close to success.

Messinius' Space Marines ran to the parapet edging the Penitent's Square. On many worlds, the square would have been a plaza fit to adorn the centre of any great city. Not on Terra. On the immensity of the Lion's Gate, it was nothing, one of hundreds of similarly huge spaces. The word 'gate' did not suit the scale of the cityscape. The Lion's Gate's bulk marched up into the sky, step by titanic step, until it rose far higher than the mountains it had supplanted. The gate had been built by the Emperor Himself, they said. Myths detailed the improbable supernatural feats required to raise it. They were lies, all of them, and belittled the true effort needed to build such an edifice. Though the Lion's Gate was made to His design and by His command, the soaring monument had been constructed by mortals, with mortal hands and mortal tools. Messinius wished that had been remembered. For men to build this was far more impressive than any godly act of creation. If men could remember that, he believed, then perhaps they would remember their own strength.

The uncanny may not have built the gate, but it threatened to bring it down. Messinius looked over the rampart lip, down to the lower levels thousands of feet below and the spread of the Anterior Barbican.

Upon the stepped fortifications of the Lion's Gate was armour of every colour and the blood of every loyal primarch. Dozens of regiments stood alongside them. Aircraft filled the sky. Guns boomed from every quarter. In the churning redness on the great roads, processional ways so huge they were akin to prairies cast in rockcrete, were flashes of gold where the Emperor's Custodian Guard battled. The might of the Imperium was gathered there, in the palace where He dwelt.

There seemed moments on that day when it might not be enough.

The outer ramparts were carpeted in red bodies that writhed and heaved, obscuring the great statues adorning the defences and covering over the guns, an invasive cancer consuming reality. The enemy were legion. There were too many foes to defeat by plan and ruse. Only guns, and will, would see the day won, but the defenders were so pitifully few.

Messinius called a wordless halt, clenched fist raised, seeking the best place to deploy his mixed company, veterans all of the Terran Crusade. Gunships and fighters sped overhead, unleashing deadly light and streams of bombs into the packed daemonic masses. There were innumerable cannons crammed onto the gate, and they all fired, rippling the structure with false earthquakes. Soon the many ships and orbital defences of Terra would add their guns, targeting the very world they were meant to guard, but the attack had come so suddenly; as yet they had had no time to react.

The noise was horrendous. Messinius' audio dampers were at maximum and still the roar of ordnance stung his ears. Those humans that survived today would be rendered deaf. But he would have welcomed more guns, and louder still, for all the defensive fury of the assailed palace could not drown out the hideous noise of the daemons – their sighing hisses, a billion serpents strong, and chittering, screaming wails. It was not only heard but sensed within the soul, the realms of spirit and of matter were so intertwined. Messinius' being would be forever stained by it.

Tactical information scrolled down his helmplate, near environs only. He had little strategic overview of the situation. The vox-channels were choked with a hellish screaming that made communication impossible. The noosphere was disrupted by etheric backwash spilling from the immaterial rifts the daemons poured through. Messinius was used to operating on his own. Small-scale, surgical actions were the way of the Adeptus Astartes, but in a battle of this scale, a lack of central coordination would lead inevitably to defeat. This was not like the first Siege, where his kind had fought in Legions.

He called up a company-wide vox-cast and spoke to his warriors. They were not his Chapter-kin, but they would listen. The primarch himself had commanded that they do so.

'Reinforce the mortals,' he said. 'Their morale is wavering. Position yourselves every fifty yards. Cover the whole of the south-facing front. Let them see you.' He directed his warriors by chopping at the air with his left hand. His right, bearing an inactive power fist, hung heavily at his side. 'Assault Squad Antiocles, back forty yards, single firing line. Prepare to engage enemy breakthroughs only on my mark. Devastators, split to demi-squads and take up high ground, sergeant and sub-squad prime's discretion as to positioning and target. Remember our objective, heavy infliction of casualties. We kill as many as we can, we retreat, then hold at the Penitent's Arch until further notice. Command squad, with me.'